W9-ACS-110

4 GUYS
and
TROUBLE

4 GUYS and TROUBLE

MARCUS MAJOR

DUTTON

DUTTON
Published by the Penguin Group
Penguin Putnam Inc., 375 Hudson Street, New York, New York 10014, U.S.A.
Penguin Books Ltd, 27 Wrights Lane, London W8 5TZ, England
Penguin Books Australia Ltd, Ringwood, Victoria, Australia
Penguin Books Canada Ltd, 10 Alcorn Avenue, Toronto, Ontario, Canada M4V 3B2
Penguin Books (N.Z.) Ltd, 182–190 Wairau Road, Auckland 10, New Zealand

Penguin Books Ltd, Registered Offices: Harmondsworth, Middlesex, England

Published by Dutton, a member of Penguin Putnam Inc.

 REGISTERED TRADEMARK—MARCA REGISTRADA

ISBN 0-525-94568-7

Printed in the United States of America
Set in Goudy
Designed by Leonard Telesca

PUBLISHER'S NOTE

For my father,
Ronald L. Major Sr.

Acknowledgments

I would like to thank my friends Victor Sherwood-Saul, Dwayne Carruth, Mike Poindexter, Cecil Parker, and my brothers, Ronald and Ryan, for helping me define true brotherhood.

To my parents, Ronald and Carmen, thanks for your support. Thank you to my great grandmother, Ruth Mitchell, and my grandparents, Carroll and Mimi. To Amir and Tamika (I spelled your name right!) you've been outstanding additions to the family.

Thanks to Kim, Gail and Tonya for your kindness and support. To my cousin Christian, who is no doubt destined to do great things. Thank you to Edwin Garlic Jr. and Sr. and to Danielle Hunt.

My wondrous aunts in Baltimore, Cheryl, Ditra, Crystal, Marie— thank you for being as excited about the books as me. My uncles Steve, Damon and Donald.

My aunts Sandra Faye, Barbara, and uncles Donny, Fred, Mike and Rickey for putting up with me as a far-more-precocious-than-necessary child.

Thank you to my magical editor, Audrey LaFehr, and wordsmith extraordinaire John Paine. Jennifer Jahner for being so patient and helpful every time I call.

To Claudia Menza for your guidance. Thank you to Felicia Polk for all your assistance.

To Sistas With A Vision, thank you.

And lastly, to the authors, I've met in the past year: Eric Jerome Dickey, Sharon Mitchell, E. Lynn Harris, Colin Channer, Carl Weber,

Nina Foxx, Timmothy McCann, Mary Morrison and Tracy Price-Thompson. Everybody has been genuine and kind and helped make this experience very enjoyable. Your advice has been immeasurably helpful.

To the readers, thank you for your support. You can reach me at marcusmajor.com or e-mail me at marcusmajor@aol.com

4 GUYS
and
TROUBLE

Prologue

"I'm so proud of you, baby," Mrs. Truitt said as she hugged Bunches tightly. With both her hands occupied, she was unable to dab at her eyes, and the tears that had been present all afternoon flowed unchecked down her face. Grandmother and granddaughter finally separated and smiled at each other.

Dexter and Mike, who had been watching from a distance to give them some privacy, came over to where they were standing. Dexter reached into the breast pocket of his gray blazer, handed Mrs. Truitt his handkerchief and then reached for Bunches.

Bunches, mindful of her perfectly coiffed hair, flawless makeup, brand-new pumps and immaculate off-white Donna Karan outfit under her graduation gown, reached to give him a safe, ladylike pat-on-the-back hug. Dexter instead snatched her off her feet and twirled her around, sending her cap flying to the ground. Mike picked it up and handed it to Mrs. Truitt.

"Now, there's my girl! Ms. Phi Beta Kappa, I'm so proud of you!"

Bunches giggled at Dexter's exuberance and forgot about her state of high fashion, wrapping her arms snugly around his neck. "Thanks, Dex."

"Yo, man, you're too big to be that rough. You're gonna break the poor girl's back," Mike said. "She wants to go to medical school—not the medical center."

When Dexter finally put her down, she and Mike embraced tenderly. Bunches rested her head on Mike's shoulder while he rubbed her back. "You don't think you're better than us, now that you're an Ivy League graduate, do you?" Mike asked as they let each other go.

"No," Bunches replied. "I *always* thought I was better than y'all." She gave him a kiss on the cheek, leaving a raisin-colored reminder.

"Bunches, you need to stop," her grandmother half scolded, half laughed.

Ibn and Tiffany walked over. They looked dapper as always—Ibn made sure of that. He was wearing a beige linen suit with a powder blue shirt, and Tiffany had on a beautiful tank dress patterned with earthen hues. Ibn planted a kiss on Bunches' cheek. "Phi Beta Kappa, huh?" he mocked. "What, you couldn't make valedictorian? Or at least salutatorian?"

Bunches rolled her eyes.

"Mind you," Tiffany said as she handed the video camera to Ibn, "this is coming from a man who couldn't be bothered with graduating himself." Tiffany and Bunches hugged. "Congratulations, girl."

"Hey, hey. We're not talking about my academic achievements," Ibn said.

"Achievements?" Mike asked, surprised. "What achievements? Most parties attended in a semester?"

Everybody laughed.

"Ib, you have to admit—your scholastic record is a bit spotty." Dexter added.

"What is this?" Ibn complained. "National Pick-on-Ibn Day?"

"Don't pay any attention to them," Mrs. Truitt said. "College isn't for everybody."

"Exactly," he said. "You don't need a piece of paper when you make as much cheddar as I do." Ibn gave Mike and Dexter a playful sneer.

Seeing Ibn reminded Bunches of who was still missing. "Where's Colin and Stacy?" she asked.

"Stacy was a little under the weather and couldn't make it," Tiffany said. "She told me to tell you congratulations."

The three men groaned.

"Be nice, boys," Mrs. Truitt said. "It's not fair to deny someone the benefit of the doubt."

Ibn gave Bunches a wink. "Colin drove to get your graduation gift."

"You guys didn't have to do that," Mrs. Truitt protested. "Believe me, you boys have already done enough for Bunches."

"You sure didn't," Bunches added, not nearly as sincere as her grandmother.

"Oh, please," Ibn said. "You know that if we didn't get you something, we never would have heard the end of it. You just playing that humble role 'cause your grandmother is standing next to you."

They all chuckled again.

"Let's head on over to parking lot eight," Dexter said. "We told Colin we'd meet him there."

Bunches slid one arm inside Dexter's and the other inside Mike's and looked up at both of them. "My, my, I have two handsome escorts."

Dexter cut his eyes at Mike over Bunches' head. "*One* handsome escort, Bunch. Maybe one and a half."

"C'mon, Dex, why do you wanna sell yourself short like that?" Mike responded. "You're not that ugly."

Bunches smiled. She loved all the guys, but she was closest to these two. They had been the ones able to devote the most time to her the last few years because they hadn't had full-time girlfriends.

The group forged their way through the sea of graduates and their families. It was a long hike to the parking lot, made a little longer by Bunches' stopping to hug and congratulate fellow classmates who she recognized.

"Yo, Bunch," Dexter said after yet another one of her stops, "you might want to keep the well-wishing to a minimum. I'm ready to go eat."

"When aren't you ready to go eat?" she replied.

Dexter flexed his massive right bicep, making the fabric of his jacket stretch tightly. "What, do you think this studly body comes about without proper nourishment?"

"He isn't the only one," Mike chimed in. "Save some of this bliss for y'all's class reunion."

Mike took off his jacket and loosened his tie. He glanced at Ibn, who was a couple of steps ahead of him, looking like something fresh off the pages of *Ebony Man* and walking with his usual aristocratic stride. Without even trying, Ibn had a manner and presence that subtly said, "I'm better than you."

Mike couldn't resist. He ran by him, smacking him roughly across the top of his head as he passed. "Take that, Pretty Ricky!"

Ibn started after Mike but stopped after a couple of steps. One, it was too hot to be running around. Second, he needed to check on the state of his hair. "Peasant!" he yelled at Mike.

When Bunches saw the sign for parking lot eight, she was relieved. Her pumps were for aesthetic purposes only, not for hiking. As the group stopped, she scanned the half-full lot. She saw Ibn's black Benz and Dexter's forest green Saab parked side by side, but there was no sign of Colin.

Right when Bunches was about to ask what was up, a cherry red Celica came to a stop in front of them. Tiffany turned the video camera back on.

"Did I say Colin drove to get your gift?" Ibn asked. "What I meant to say was that Colin was *driving* your gift."

Bunches gasped in disbelief.

Colin got out of the car, came around front, and dangled the keys. His green suit was too big, as were most things he wore. Because of his skinny build, Colin didn't wear clothes, clothes wore him.

"Lord have mercy!" Mrs. Truitt said in amazement.

Bunches yelped at the top of her lungs and jumped into Colin's arms, very nearly toppling him onto the hood. "I don't believe this!" she said.

"We can't have you going back and forth to Thomas Jefferson University in that putt-putt Escort of yours," Ibn said.

"Omigod, omigod," Bunches said, still clinging to Colin.

"Get in, girl," said Tiffany, who was videotaping the entire scene. "Let's see how you look in it."

"First, peep the license plate," Dexter said.

She looked down at the front plate: BBYGRL-MD

"We should have got one that said, 'Beneatha,' " Mike said, laughing.

Everybody looked at him puzzled except Bunches, who laughed as she walked to the driver's side door.

"Y'all know," Mike said, looking around hopefully. "Beneatha is the little sister—"

"—from *A Raisin in the Sun*, who wanted to be a doctor. I got it, Michael." Bunches. said.

"Oh," Ibn said, rolling his eyes at Mike's attempt at humor. "C'mon, Bunches, we want to see how you look in it."

Bunches slid behind the steering wheel. She peered at the group through the windshield with the world's widest grin.

"We got it loaded." Ibn said, walking around to the passenger side and getting in. "Let me show you some of the features."

Mrs. Truitt looked at Colin. "How much did you guys pay for this? This is too expensive to be giving her—she can't accept this."

Bunches looked at her grandmother as if she were concerned that Alzheimer's was setting in.

"Mrs. Truitt, it didn't feel like we took a hit at all." Colin said. "We've been planning this for two years."

"Yeah, pooling our money, putting aside some each month," Dexter explained. "The same way we did to buy those rental units we own."

"And the way we did back when we were still in college to get Ibn the start-up money for his business," Mike added. "As a matter of fact, it was originally Trevor's idea for us to combine our resources to give ourselves greater purchasing power."

Mrs. Truitt smiled sadly at the mention of her grandson's name. "I wish he and Bunches' mother were here to see this."

"They are, Mrs. Truitt," Mike said, pointing at his chest. "They're with all of us."

She and Mike embraced.

Tiffany turned off the video camera. "Now I'm hungry, too."

"Yeah, let's get going," Colin added. "Get out, Ibn. I'm riding shotgun with Bunches."

As Colin was making his way around to the driver's side, Ibn whispered to Bunches, "There a little something extra for you in the envelope in the glove compartment, cutie."

Believing Stacy would attend, they had made reservations for eight at a Philadelphia eatery recommended by Bunches. Called Cafe Melange, it specialized in Cajun and soul food. Tiffany and Colin sat on either side of Ibn. Bunches was in between Mike and her grandmother.

Dexter sat next to the empty chair, which was good. He needed the extra space for his two orders of catfish.

They were nearing the end of their meal when Mrs. Truitt broached the topic of the future with her granddaughter. "So, you're okay with me moving back home?"

"Mom-mom, I'm twenty-one years old."

"Does she think that that's supposed to mean something to me?" Mrs. Truitt asked, looking at everyone sitting around the table. She returned her gaze to Bunches. "You're my baby."

"I'm just saying, you've been wanting to move back to Charlotte for years," Bunches said. "That was always the plan after you retired. You have your mother—who needs you—down there. I want you to be happy, too. Trust me, I'll be fine."

Mrs. Truitt looked at the rest of the people seated around the table before stopping at Dexter. "I must admit, I do like the thought of Bunches living in the apartment above you and Mike, where y'all can look out for her. But I am not comfortable," she added, "with you not accepting rent for it."

"Mrs. Truitt, please," Dexter said.

"You could be renting it out to a tenant and making money on it. How about I send you a check every month?"

"Mrs. Truitt, if it would make you feel better, send us whatever you're comfortable writing on a check and stuffing in an envelope every month," Colin said. "Just be prepared to have it sent right back to you."

"The last thing I—we all—promised Trev is that we would look out for his sister," Mike said. "At no point and time did he say, 'And please, take as much money from my grandmother as possible.' "

A chuckle rose from the table.

"So, what's on the itinerary for the rest of the day?" Tiffany asked.

"We're all gonna head back to Ewing to help Bunches and Mrs. Truitt finish packing," Dexter said, stuffing a hunk of cornbread in his mouth.

"Mom-mom, when are the movers coming?" Bunches asked.

"Tomorrow. I rented a U-Haul for your things. I'm pretty much finished with packing what's going to Charlotte with me, I wasn't sure what you wanted to take."

Ibn looked at Tiffany. "Do you have something to do?"

"Later on, but I can stay for a little while," she answered.

"If you have to leave, you can take the car. I'll ride back with Dexter."

She gave him a distrustful look. "Okay."

Bunches caught Dexter hungrily looking back toward the counter, where the desserts were. "What are you doing?" she asked.

"Trying to decide whether or not I want another slice of pecan pie."

"Wow, you're greedy." She laughed as she looked at his dishwasher-clean plates. "That doesn't make any sense."

"Well, since you'll be living right above him now, maybe he can get a home-cooked meal occasionally," Mrs. Truitt said.

Bunches looked at her grandmother incredulously. Now she was certain that Mom-mom's mental faculties had deserted her. "Sure, whenever you wanna make the trip up from North Carolina, the kitchen is yours."

As everybody laughed, Bunches focused on Mike. When he smiled, his dimple was too cute. As he returned her gaze and leaned over to kiss her on the forehead, Bunches had to quell her impulse to tilt her head—so his lips would meet a more agreeable target.

One

Three years later . . .

Ibn turned the key and stepped inside his two-story Yardley model house, situated at the end of a cul-de-sac. Ibn had paid to have it custom built three years ago, and had paid plenty for the land, too, adding thousands to the cost for its exclusive location. He had wanted it built in Evesham, the land of SUVs, nannies and soccer moms, where all the rich white people lived.

He slowly shut the red door behind him and carefully laid his keys on the coffee table so they wouldn't make noise. As he was tiptoeing up the stairs, he caught himself. Why was he acting like a burglar in his own house? Sure, it was late—very late, in fact—but it wasn't like he had been out doing dirt. His boy Dex was going through a rough time and needed his support. What? That's a crime now? And it wasn't like he had to be worried about waking Tiffany up. He knew she would be awake, ready to grill his ass about where he had been.

He went into the darkened bedroom. "Hey, Tiff," he said as he unfastened his black Movado watch and set it on the dresser. There was no response, but he knew she was awake because he felt her gaze burrowing two holes through his back.

The silent treatment is better than an argument, he figured, and left to go take a shower. He undressed, leaving his clothes in a pile, wrapped a towel around his waist and walked into the bathroom. He looked into the mirror and conducted a quick pose-down, finishing by rapidly flexing his pectoral muscles one at a time.

Have I told you lately that you are the man, Ibn Barrington? I haven't? Well, let me apologize for the oversight, but I assumed you already knew.

After finishing his reassuring heart-to-heart chat with his image, he turned on the shower. Before he could get in, he heard the bathroom door open. When he turned around, he was facing Tiffany, who looked rather frumpy with her messed-up hair, half-asleep face and old-lady reading glasses.

"What?"

She didn't answer. She wrapped her arms around his waist and undid his towel, letting it fall to the floor. She knelt down in front of him, resting her knees on the towel.

Ibn was thrilled. His girl was ready to accommodate her man with a little three a.m. fellatio. An early-morning appearance of the "Tiffanator." He did wish she would lose the glasses, though; they were a mood killer. He reached down and attempted to take them off, but she stopped him. Oh well, he thought, guess she wants to see what she's doing. He closed his eyes, spread his legs and leaned back against the wall.

The second she started massaging his member in her hands, he was as erect as a flagpole. He felt her pulling, shifting, sniffing and probing his entire package, but the warm sensation he was expecting never came. One of two things that wouldn't be coming this early morning apparently, because he slowly realized he wasn't being indulged, he was being *inspected.*

He opened his eyes as Tiffany let go of him and stood up.

"Jesus Christ, Tiff." Ibn felt violated.

She gave him a nonchalant look, not the least bit ashamed.

"My underwear's on the bedroom floor if you'd like to check that, too, Agatha Christie," he said sarcastically.

As he stepped into the shower, Ibn was still appalled. Not for the fact that his woman had thought he had been out whoring, but because she didn't think he had the decency to wash his dick off if he had.

Mike opened the front door of the duplex and looked for his newspaper. God forbid the guy throw the paper onto his front stoop, he groused as he walked over to the driveway to pick up his home-delivered copy of the *Philadelphia Inquirer*. On his way back to his door, he gave a moment's thought to repeatedly ringing the doorbell to Bunches' upstairs apartment, but decided against it. She had worked late at the hospital last night and needed her rest.

Mike shut the door behind him and made his way down the hallway, stopping to straighten Dexter's framed poster from the movie *Black Caesar*. Mike looked inside his roommate's bedroom. He saw Dexter kneeling beside his bed, praying so intently that his forehead was glistening. As Mike continued into the kitchen, he found himself chuckling. It seems that Dexter had found religion at the same time he found out he got a woman pregnant. Typical incorrigible Negro. Faced with a little adversity, and his ass goes running to God. Mike could almost picture God folding his arms. "To hell wit that nigga, Saint Peter. He wasn't thinking about Me when he was throwing his dick at women like it was confetti at Mardi Gras."

He was laughing out loud as he sat down at the table with a bowl of cereal, clearing a space for himself by brushing Dexter's midnight snack dishes aside. Dexter walked into the kitchen. "What's so funny?"

"Nothing," Mike said, feeling guilty for making light of his friend's plight. "Just thinking of a joke someone told me."

"Do you have to work today?"

Mike motioned to his sweatpants and New York Yankees T-shirt. "You got me confused with someone else," he said grandly. "District managers don't work weekends."

"That's right, I forgot about your promotion."

"Leave it to you to forget about an extra fifteen K per year and company car."

"You're coming up in the world," Dexter said, really meaning it. He had always felt that Mike was too talented to just be selling men's clothes.

"Yeah, though I do feel silly owning a degree in journalism and working retail."

"Fuck it, get that money."

"You know. Besides, don't you remember we're supposed to be meeting Colin and Ibn in Camden to look at a piece of property?"

"Oh yeah. I forgot."

"I guess you can be forgiven for having your mind on something else."

"*You* know." Dexter took a huge white porcelain serving bowl out of the cupboard and started filling it with cereal. Mike was tempted to make a crack about him not being the one eating for two, but thought better of it.

"When I passed your room today, I noticed you were renewing your acquaintance with the man upstairs."

"What? Oh, yeah," Dexter replied. He put so much milk in the bowl that the heaping mound of cereal brimmed to the top.

"The angels in the central office probably had trouble recognizing your voice. I'm sure you're on the inactive list."

"Look who's talking. When was the last you saw the inside of a church?"

"Just last week. I got a three-piece dark meat, some fried okra and some . . ."

"I said 'church', not Church's, you jackass," Dexter said, laughing.

"Oh," Mike said. "Then you're right, it's been a while." He was glad to see his buddy laughing. Last night when he had found out about Denise's pregnancy, his mood had been anything but jovial. "Though I am going tomorrow with Sharice."

Dexter shook his head and sighed. "You still on that tip?"

"What's wrong with Sharice?" Mike asked, though he knew very well.

"Nothing, nothing at all. I, like most every other man in New Jersey that has had the pleasure of meeting Sharice, find her quite *right* to look at, at least. I'm just surprised to hear that she's going to church. Unless it's to thank God for blessing her with that sweet body of hers."

"Dex," Mike explained patiently, "until Sharice moved back up here from Atlanta, we hadn't seen her in five years. She has changed a lot. You're still judging her by how wild she was in college. She's an elementary school teacher now, more mature—for instance, do you know that she's now a born-again Christian?"

"You don't say?" he replied sarcastically.

Mike decided it was pointless to continue with the conversation. He knew how hard Dexter was on a woman once he had his mind made up about her. Hell, he was almost as bad as Ibn.

"But enough of Sharice's newfound religion. What were *you* asking the Man for?" Mike asked. "You aren't shallow enough to be praying for a male child, are you?"

"Naw, that wasn't it."

Mike knew it was none of his business, but he was intrigued. "For strength to get you through this?"

"Not exactly." Dexter pulled out a tablespoon and started shoveling cereal into his mouth.

"For His will to be done?"

"Not exactly."

Mike pressed on, thinking that maybe Dexter prayed for the same thing he had prayed for last night. "For the health of Denise and the baby?"

"Nope."

"For the relationship with Denise to blossom into a lifelong love affair?"

"Nope," Dexter said in between shovels. He was doing serious damage to his massive pile of cereal.

"For a child that will become a cereal tycoon so that you can get a lifetime supply of free Cap'n Crunch?" Mike asked.

"Not even." Tiring of Mike's questions, Dexter decided to take his food back to his room.

Mike was so curious by now that he didn't even get on Dexter for leaving a trail of cereal on the floor. Before he left, Mike made one last attempt.

"I give up, frat. What were you praying for?"

The reply came from down the hall:

"A miscarriage."

"Serves his ass right."

"What kind of thing is that to say, Stacy?"

"Fuck him. Men like Dexter and Ibn think they can just go around humping anything without consequence, so fuck 'em."

"That's nice language to be using this early in the morning."

"Nice langu—fuck you, too, Colin. You gonna stay out until two in the morning with your silly-ass fraternity brothers and then lecture me about manners?"

Colin rolled over on the almond-colored four-poster bed and looked at Stacy. Though his vision was fuzzy, he could see she was sitting at her vanity looking at him in the mirror.

"I called you. You knew where I was."

"But I don't know what you were doing."

"What's that supposed to mean?"

Stacy got up and walked over to the matching almond dresser to get her brush. When she sat back down, she was no longer looking at Colin in the mirror.

Tired of squinting, he reached for the nightstand and put on his glasses. He couldn't see a lick without them and had worn glasses ever since he could remember.

"Why do you always think I'm doing the worst?"

"Did I say you were cheating?" Stacy snapped.

"You might as well have. It seems all I get from you are accusations . . ."

"What?" Stacy turned around to face him.

". . . and lately it's been getting worse."

"Colin Rogers, are you trying to start a fight?" Stacy was practically on her haunches, ready to leap.

Colin mulled it over. Saturday was his day to relax, and Stacy had ten times the stamina he did when it came to fighting. It would just unfold as it always did, with Stacy first chastising him like he was a child. Then he would say something back, and she would get upset and start crying. He would feel guilty about hurting her feelings and relent. Then she would seize the opening to pitch a fit for hours, hurling epithets as well as various knickknacks at him. He decided he *didn't* want any. He removed his glasses and shut his eyes.

"No, I'm not."

Stacy kept staring at him to make sure he was sufficiently cowed. When she was confident he was, she resumed applying her makeup. After a minute, she decided to throw him a bone. "It's not you I'm questioning, Colin. It's your friends. I know they don't like me."

Colin lay there motionless, silently groaning. She gave him zero credit. What kind of fool did she think he was? To let his boys dictate what woman he was going to be with. Hell, if that were the case, she would have been long gone. "Remember that Tiffany invited us over for dinner tonight."

Stacy exhaled loudly.

"What's the matter with that? I thought you liked Tiffany."

"I don't have anything against Tiffany—other than thinking that she's a fool for putting up with Ibn's cheating. It's just that I forgot. Hell, I'm already supposed to be going shopping with her and the 'princess' this afternoon."

"How do you know she even knows about Ib's womanizing?"

"Well, if she doesn't, then she's an even bigger fool, because every-one else does. Like I said, I'm okay with her. I could go ten lifetimes without looking at Ibn, however."

"It's just one night, Stacy. What was I gonna do, tell her no?"

She busied herself applying eyeliner.

"All right, I'll tell Ibn we can't make it," Colin said wearily, finding his eyeglasses.

"I hate when you do that—did you hear me say I wouldn't go?" she said, irritated. "I just hope I'm not expected to reciprocate by having them over."

Colin adjusted his glasses and looked over at her. She was rubbing her lips together so that her lipstick was spread even. Despite her best efforts, Stacy was not a pretty woman. Colin had never had a pretty woman, partly due to the fact that he lacked the confidence to pursue one. Stacy's features were not soft and delicate, but rather had a dis-tinctive and robust flavor that Colin found attractive. He knew his boys didn't think she was good-looking, but he couldn't care less. In fact, he kind of liked it. It made him feel special that he could see something in her that others couldn't, like she was solely and uniquely his because of it.

Colin's gaze traveled from her face to another part of her anatomy. Bending over in the mirror like that, she was giving him ideas.

"Why don't you come back to bed?" he asked softly.

Stacy straightened up. "I'm already dressed, Colin, and I don't feel like redoing my hair."

Colin knew it was useless to press her if she wasn't in the mood. He took his glasses off again and rolled over, turning his back to her. "Where are you going, anyway?"

"You know full well I'm going car shopping."

An alarm bell went off in his head. "I thought we were gonna do that together."

"I wanna do it by myself. I'll bring you after I made my selection, before I sign anything."

Yeah, Colin thought, right in time to co-sign for some loan with a ridiculously high monthly payment. Unbeknownst to Stacy, he had been doing some research on the cars that he knew interested her. For the past three weeks he had been checking the Internet for customer approval ratings, checking finance rates and going to the same dealerships she was for some test driving and comparative shopping. He had an idea how much he was willing to pay for each model. And since Stacy was returning to college full-time, he would ultimately be footing the bill.

"You gotta get made up just to go car shopping?"

Stacy turned from the mirror and looked at him. "Eyeliner and lipstick is not 'made up.' I'm going out in public. You should want me to look presentable. I represent you."

Colin ignored this. "Are you close to choosing what kind of car you're getting?"

"I've narrowed it down to three: a Benz, a Lexus or a BMW."

Colin rolled toward her and squinted at her like she was crazy. After a couple of seconds of letting the comment hang in the air, she burst out laughing.

"What, I don't deserve the best?"

"What you deserve and what we're able to afford are two different things."

She sat on the edge of the bed and ran her fingernails along his scalp. "Ibn got Tiffany a Lexus."

"Maybe you should get a man that makes Ibn's money."

Stacy stood up and said lazily, "Do you think he has any openings in his harem?"

"That's funny, Stacy. Do you want to audition for a spot?" he asked, annoyed.

"Damn, Colin, I was only kidding. You're so damn sensitive." She picked up her purse and car keys off the dresser. "So, are you doing anything with your Saturday, or will you be lying there all day—ass unwashed."

"I'm gonna meet the fellas later in Camden. We're thinking about buying another row home."

"Oh, another meeting of the distinguished brothers of Phi Slumlord Chi. Be sure to give Daddy Dexter my regards. I'll begin shopping for a Father's Day gift for him," she sneered.

"I'll be sure to do that."

Before she left the room, Stacy paused at the door. "You know, if you loved me, you'd get me that Lexus instead of putting money into another one of those broken-down houses." She walked out.

Colin stared at the doorway. He wondered if she was going to pop her head back in the room to say she was only kidding again. He got his answer when he heard the front door slam.

Bunches rolled over when she heard Mike's front door close, both grateful and disappointed—if that was possible—that his playful ass didn't ring her doorbell. Though she liked seeing him, she was too beat this morning.

She fluffed her pillow and yawned. This had been her first night in her own bed in a week. Her schedule had been so intense that she had been staying at her girlfriend Cherie's apartment in the city rather than commuting back across the bridge drowsy and fatigued. But rest wasn't in the cards for her today. In a couple of hours, she had to get up. She had agreed last week to go shit-shopping and have lunch with Tiffany and Stacy. Then she had to drag her tired ass right back to Philly for a workshop for interns. On top of that, her car was acting up and needed to go to the shop.

She sure would be happy when her workload lightened a bit. Bunches missed spending time with the fellas. Hell, she missed being pampered. The boys had spoiled her rotten, to be sure. She scratched through the purple satin scarf tied around her head. She was badly in need of a perm, not that it mattered much. Her social life teetered between nonexistence and parody.

Cherie had been trying to fix her up with this guy named Quincy, who was interested in her. Bunches had declined, citing her schedule. Besides her studies and work at the hospital, Bunches was a mentor to a little girl named Tiana, whom she adored. She wasn't about to let any man cut into their time together.

She and Mike were mentors to two children from Camden, both of whom had lost their mothers to AIDS. Mike's charge's name was Xavier. Oftentimes, she and Mike would do things with the kids together. Bunches made a mental note to call Tiana when she got up. She wanted to take her to the library and check out some books on horses, which had really captured her fancy of late.

Besides, looking for love wasn't a huge priority for her. Bunches already knew the man who was best suited for her. Yet he still didn't see what was plainly evident—that no one would ever love him like she did. If only he would cross the line from friendship and open the door. She would take care of the rest.

She had forgotten her musing a few hours later. She was sitting on a small sofa waiting for Tiffany to emerge out of the dressing room at Neiman Marcus. It was just the two of them because Stacy had canceled on them.

"You know, Tiff," she called through the shutter door, "I have to admit, I was relieved when you told me Stacy wouldn't be joining us today."

"She's not that bad," Tiffany replied. "You and her are too much alike. That's why you can't get along."

"Look, if you're gonna start insulting me, I'll just head on home," Bunches said. "In what possible ways are me and Stacy alike?"

"Well, you both love Colin, for one."

"I'll grant you that—maybe," Bunches acceded. "Though, in my opinion, the jury is still out on whether she really loves him. What else?"

Tiffany laughed. "Calm down, girl. All I mean is that you both are headstrong, and that you always want your way."

"Humph. I'll thank you to kindly refrain from drawing parallels between me and Ms. Stacy Gant." Bunches said in a purposely haughty voice, which made both of them chuckle.

"I guess soon we're gonna be adding another member to our little shopping circle," Tiffany said. "Do you know Denise?"

"I've met her two or three times," Bunches answered. "I like her. She seems down-to-earth."

"A woman gains a positive endorsement from Bunches Truitt? That's rare," Tiffany teased. "Though it would be nearly impossible for her if she was dating Mike instead of Dex." She emerged from the dressing room. "What do you think?"

Tiffany was wearing a Moschino gabardine dress with a plunging neckline. It was more than a little form-fitting, which was fine and dandy with Tiffany because she had the form to pull it off.

"Wow," was the only response Bunches could muster. Sometimes she forgot how pretty Tiffany was. She self-consciously looked down at her own clothes and touched her nappy hair.

"It is sharp, isn't it?" Tiffany asked, turning in front of the large three-sided mirror. She pulled at the hips of the dress. "I think I'm gonna get it."

Out of Bunches' peripheral vision she saw a white man in his fifties. His wife must be doing some shopping in the department. Yet he was staring at Tiffany like he just knew he was in love.

"Do you want one?" Tiffany asked, looking at Bunches through the mirror.

Bunches walked over and looked at the price tag on the sleeve. "Uh-uh, too rich for my blood."

Tiffany flipped her wrist. "It's my treat. Consider it an early Christmas gift from Ibn."

Bunches chuckled. "You sure are loose with Ibn's money. He doesn't ever complain?"

"A little, but he doesn't really mind. In fact, I think he kind of likes it. It makes him feel like he's doing more than he actually is," Tiffany's face turned more earnest. "He thinks this is what makes me happy."

Bunches studied her face. "Tiff, you okay?"

"Of course, why wouldn't I be?" She said carelessly. "I have a man who's so good-looking that women freeze when he enters a room. He's paid, and buys me anything I want, and owns a big dick and knows how to use it. What more could I possibly want?"

She and Bunches exchanged tight smiles in the mirror. Then she abruptly turned back to what they had been talking about.

"As you know, the one person he likes doing for as much as me is you. So, you should get one, too. If only for Ibn's well-being," she added dryly.

"No, thank you. I'm gonna have to pass on Mr. Barrington's generosity today." Bunches said.

"You sure?"

"Tiff." Bunches stood shoulder-to-shoulder next to Tiffany, facing the mirror. "Look at you and look at me. I don't have the curves, titties or ass to pull that off."

"Nonsense. Get yourself a Wonderbra and call it a day."

"All a Wonderbra does for me is make me wonder why I still don't have any cleavage when I'm wearing one."

Tiffany laughed and put her arm around Bunches' shoulder and squeezed it. "Why don't you try one on, anyway?"

"No, thanks. Not after seeing how it looks on you." Bunches noticed that the man from earlier was still ogling Tiffany. She nodded in his direction. "Apparently, I'm not the only one who appreciates how you look in that dress."

Tiffany finally noticed the man. She gave him a coy Marilyn Monroe over-the-shoulder glance, tossing her hair for effect. She punctuated it by blowing him a wet kiss. "Come here, big boy," she mouthed.

The man's face turned beet red, and he almost knocked over a lingerie display as he ran for the sanctity of his wife.

Tiffany and Bunches fell out.

"You need to stop."

"I like messing with them. Being their forbidden quadroon fantasy." Tiffany walked back into the changing room. Bunches retook her seat on the sofa to wait for her to finish. But quickly she turned toward the door that Tiffany had disappeared behind.

"Hey, wait a minute. What did you mean earlier?" she asked.

"What do you mean?"

"When you said that it would be impossible for me to think highly of a girl that Michael was seeing?"

"Oh, so you did catch that."

"Yeah, I caught it. What did you mean by throwing it?"

"Nothing." Over the slatted door Tiffany looked at Bunches knowingly. "I didn't mean anything."

"Um-hm, yeah, right." Bunches said, managing to conceal her blush behind indignation. "Well, I suggest you buy a bigger-size dress. 'Cause obviously that tight-ass one you have on is cutting off the flow of blood to your brain."

Two

"Can you believe the gall of that girl?" Ibn asked. "Inspecting my dick for the ghosts of ass past."

Mike and Colin laughed at the completion of Ibn's recounting of the previous night's episode with Tiffany. Dexter allowed himself a chuckle, but he was still too preoccupied with his own problems to fully enjoy Ibn's story. The four of them were nearing the end of their lunch at Sam's Bar and Grill in South Camden, where they ate together at least once a week. Earlier, they had decided to pass on the row house, feeling that the asking price was too steep.

"Yo, Mike," Colin said, sitting on Ibn's side like always, "how appropriate is it that he referenced a Charles *Dick*-ens story?"

"You know. Though instead of *A Christmas Carol* he should have used *Oliver Twist*."

"Or *Hard Times*," Colin snickered.

"All right, all right," Ibn said. "that's enough."

"Maybe *A Tale of Two Titties*. It doesn't really fit this instance, but maybe as a title for Ib's lifetime body of work.

"No, I got it, I got it." Colin said with an anticipatory snort. "*David Copafeel.*"

Even Dexter started chortling at that one. Ibn, unable to resist his three friends' infectious giggling, allowed a chuckle to escape.

"I can't believe you have the nerve to be offended," Colin said after the laughter had died down. "As many times as you have cheated on—"

"*Allegedly* cheated," Ibn interjected.

"You're lucky Tiffany lets you leave the house at all. You just better thank God that dicks aren't removable. She'd keep yours under lock and key."

"Who says dicks aren't removable?" Mike asked. "You just better hope that Tiffany doesn't cut your shit off and plead justifiable peniscide."

"And that there aren't any women on the jury." Colin added.

"You know," Mike continued. "Because after they hear of your many skank-filled episodes—"

"*Alleged* episodes," Ibn interrupted.

"Tiffany will walk out free, and you'll be one dick-detached, doin'-time nigga."

"Hard time."

Colin and Mike were laughing when Ibn spoke.

"Yo, Dex, I always say you can measure a man by who his friends are and by who his critics are. Look at my critics here." Ibn motioned across the booth with a grand sweep of his arm. "The president and the CEO of Player Haters Anonymous."

"Yo, frat, you brought it up," Colin said.

"Correction, Colin, Tiffany brought it up." Mike added, "So she could inspect it."

Ibn looked at him. "What do you mean?"

"Ib, you said at first the way Tiffany was acting, before she did her amateur urologist impersonation, she was getting you aroused so much that you thought you were gonna get a blowie."

"Yeah, so?"

"What she was doing was checking to if you *could* get aroused. She was figuring that if you had just come back from skanking it up, you'd be too spent to do so."

The other three men at the booth mulled this over for a minute. Then decided that Mike was right. They were impressed that one of their brethren had that kind of insight.

"Damn, I didn't think of that." Ibn rubbed his chin thoughtfully. "I just thought she was being sadistic."

"Plus, she was probably sniffing around. To see if there was too strong a scent of soap, like you were trying to mask something. Besides, some guys have enough sense to wash their dicks but forget that a female's scent will get into their pubic hairs as well."

"Good point," Ibn acceded.

"Yeah, Mike, you sure do know women," Colin said.

"Especially for someone that doesn't have one," Ibn added.

"Hey, hey, now, I'm working on it."

"Yeah," Dexter said, finally adding to the conversation, "with Sharice Watson."

The explosion was immediate, as Mike could have predicted.

"Oh, Jesus Christ!" Ibn threw his fork down and looked at Mike disgustedly.

"She's back in the area?" Colin asked.

"She moved back up here last month," Mike said lamely, shooting daggers at Dexter.

"I don't know what the fascination is between you suburban boys and loose women," Ibn said, shaking his head. "It's like you guys are intrigued by the ho lifestyle. Back in Newark, we know the role of skanks and keep them in their proper context."

Mike, who was already agitated at Dexter for bringing up Sharice, was getting a little pissed at the way Ibn was speaking of her. "Ib, let's assume everything you've heard about Sharice is true, which is a hell of an assumption to make, but just for argument's sake, let's say it is. Do you think that she can even begin to approach the number of partners you've had?"

"Probably not."

"Then what does that make you?"

Ibn spread his hands out on the table.

"Mike, how many times do I have to tell you, the double standard is alive and well," he replied. "I admit I'm an asshole when it comes to being faithful, but dammit, the men and women of a society can't both be assholes. I mean think about it, *someone* has to be decent, for the sake of the kids."

Colin and Dexter laughed, which provided Ibn incentive to continue.

"And women aren't fucked up enough to act like men anyway. The smart ones know that already. The dumb ones say stupid shit like, 'Why is it that if a man sleeps around with a large number of different people, he's a hero, but if a woman does it, she's a slut?' I'm like ' 'Cause that's the laws of nature, and they're not to be trifled with.' "

Their favorite waitress, Lorraine, a large woman in her mid-forties, came over with the slices of pie that Ibn, Mike and Colin ordered. As she cleared the remainder of their lunch plates, she noticed Dexter had barely touched his food. "What's the matter, chocolate? You ain't hungry?"

"Not really, Lorraine."

"Do you want me to wrap it for you?"

"Yeah, thanks."

"You gotta eat. We gotta keep that sexy body of yours together," she said salaciously, rubbing Dexter's muscular back.

"What, Lorraine? You cheating on me?" Ibn asked with fake alarm.

Lorraine picked up her platter of dishes. "I'm tired of waiting on you, Ibn. As far as I can tell, you're too in love with yourself to have time for anyone else." She playfully winked at him as she walked away.

"Well, she's got you nailed down," Colin said.

"See, Colin, that's where you and Lorraine are wrong. I can always juggle my schedule to make time for some pussy. There's *always* that five minutes." Ibn took a forkful of his slice of pecan pie. "So, anyway, where was I?"

"You were entertaining us with your bullshit theory of male and female roles in society," Mike said.

Ibn scoffed. "Bullshit? Natural law is nothing to be played with, son. As I was saying, some silly women question why it's not acceptable for them to skank it up like men. The really dumb ones are foolish enough to give it that 'old college try,' which, by the way, is where that term derives from, 'cause it is often in college where said hoey activity occurs," he said solemnly, like he was really educating his friends with pearls of wisdom. He took another bite of his pie.

"You need help," Mike said.

Ibn ignored him. "Look at the organs themselves, a penis and a vagina. A tool of insertion and a receptacle. Women don't fuck men, they get *fucked*. A woman is the vessel, a man can simply wipe his dick off."

"And he better do a good job of it before he gets home, in case his girlfriend wants to inspect it," Mike said.

Ibn continued. "So, let's say a woman decides she wants to go against nature and start fucking every man that she's attracted to. Bad move. She's gonna be hated by respectable women who, let's be real, can't stand to be around no ho. She's gonna be disrespected by men, who only want to use her, because no man wants to make another man's slut his lady. She's scorned by black society, which is conservative by nature. But that's okay, because she's getting hers, right? Well, somewhere along the way, maybe after the fifth man—hell, maybe after the twentieth man wipes his dick off on her, whatever—that woman will question just what it is she is doing. Her grandmother's voice will speak to her and tell her that's enough. Her mother's voice will speak to her and tell her to quit it. Her body will tell her, that's enough wear and tear, and to stop. Her socialization, her values, her family and finally her religion all tell her that she is doing some shameful shit. Which is why so many women run off to the church after they skank it up."

Dexter started cackling, and Mike grimaced. He knew what was coming.

"Sharice is a born-again Christian now, isn't she, Mike?" Dexter snorted.

"There you go," Ibn said triumphantly.

"I liked it better when you were brooding," Mike said to Dexter. "Besides, she isn't the only one that's had a sudden religious awakening." He looked at Ibn and Colin. "This guy was praying for a miscarriage this morning."

"Damn," Colin said.

"Are you serious?" Ibn found it humorous. "So scraping isn't an option, huh?"

Dexter shrugged his shoulders. "Denise doesn't believe in abortion, and to be honest, neither do I."

"*Scraping?*" Mike asked. "And just how many uteruses have you had 'scraped,' Mr. Barrington?"

"None," he said earnestly. "I always use a condom."

"Yeah, right. You've probably killed more babies than Pharaoh."

Ibn raised his glass at Mike and took a sip.

"So," Dexter continued, "a miscarriage is the only way I can see my way out of this. Other than that, I'm just . . ." he took a deep breath before he finished, "gonna try to make it work with Denise."

Ibn nearly spat out his soda. "Are you serious?" he asked. "Aren't you being a little hasty?"

"What else can I do?"

"You can support the child without being with Denise."

Dexter fidgeted. "Ib, the thought of my child being raised in a home other than mine . . ."

"Dex, I know it's not ideal, but neither is bringing a child up in a home where the parents aren't happy with each other," Ibn said. "That's much worse."

"That's true," Colin put in. "I know that when I was growing up, I would have preferred my parents split up rather than their constant fighting."

"Maybe we'll be happy." Dexter shrugged.

"Yeah, okay," Ibn said in a disbelieving tone.

"Why you putting the brother down for doing the right thing?" Mike snapped, stretching his hands out with irritation.

"Please, Mike," Ibn replied, "since when is making yourself miserable the right thing?"

"Since when is having children out of wedlock the right thing?"

"Out of wedlock?" Ibn laughed. "Nigga, join us in the twenty-first century."

"So, what does that mean? It's progressive to have bastards?"

"Bastards?" Ibn looked at Colin and Dexter, giving them a "do you believe this guy" look. They stayed neutral, as they usually did when Ibn and Mike went at it. "What, is Sharice beating you over the head with her newfound Bible already?"

Mike grimaced. "Ib, call it what it is. 'Bastard' is any child born out of a marriage. Any adult with an ounce of sense knows that a child is a blessing regardless, but you can't tell me that it doesn't do something psychologically to the child when he sees that his mother and father didn't think enough of each other to get married. It's almost tantamount to saying that his parents were two people who got their freak on and things got out of hand and 'nine months later, here your ass came.' Or, 'I liked your mother well enough to fuck and all, but not to make mine. You were a mistake.' "

"So, getting married to someone you don't love, or hell, even like, is better? It's gonna end up in divorce, anyway, so why bother?" Ibn asked.

"Maybe so, I'll grant you that. But how many relationships built on love fail as well? How many couples start out loving each other and end up wanting to kill each other? What happened? They'll tell you they 'fell out of love.' " Mike looked at Dexter, who dropped his eyes to the tablecloth. "So, just as people fall out of love, they can fall in love, and it doesn't necessarily have to be at first sight. You can know somebody in one fashion and grow to love that person. Whether it's gradual or something that blindsides you, those kind of stories happen to men and women every day. I think having a mutual interest in a child is a good foundation to build on or at the very least a hell of an incentive to see if you and her can be one of those couples."

Ibn sneered. "What are the odds on some fairy-tale shit like that working?"

"Ib, trying to make it work for the sake of a child and failing is a lot better than having the son or daughter thinking they weren't worth the effort. I know it's easy for me to say because I'm not in the position yet, but once I help bring a child into the world, my happiness is no longer the paramount concern. What's best for the child is." Mike paused and looked at each of his friends, not wanting to linger solely on Dexter.

"It seems to me that each year society comes up with more and more creative ways to justify our inability to do the right thing by our children. To excuse our selfishness and slackness and then we wonder what the hell is wrong with 'these bad-ass kids.' It's no mystery to me. The tree is rotten and so is the fruit."

Colin saw Mike's point. "I just read a study where kids raised in a home with their mother and father were significantly less likely to participate in juvenile crime, did much better in school—"

"Nobody is arguing that the two-parent household isn't the ideal," Ibn said, interrupting Colin, "but it isn't always practical."

"Practical for whom?" Mike asked. "See, that's the selfishness I was talking about."

Dexter was tiring of the parenting topic, so he decided to change the subject. "Is Tiffany still pressuring you to get married, Ib?"

"Nah, not lately. She's finally given it a rest." Ibn thought about continuing his debate with Mike, but changed his mind. "By the way, I just got the new analog phones in. You guys can stop by and pick one up when you get a chance."

"How's business?" Colin asked.

Ibn smiled slyly and nodded his head up and down. His way of saying he was making a shitload of money.

"This cat was always the entrepreneur," Colin said. "Remember in college? When everybody else was selling club tapes, he was selling pagers out of his trunk."

Dexter smiled. "Yeah, I remember. Now he's a wireless tycoon."

"I've been waiting for those digital phones to come in," Colin added.

Ibn looked at him. "Yo, frat, tell Stacy not to break it, either. She done went through three phones in the last six months."

Mike and Dexter snickered.

"Stop lying," Colin said defensively. "It was only two."

"Nah, it was *three*. I remember she came in to get one after she lost one in Rancocas Park." He looked at Colin curiously. "What was she doing in the park at night, anyway?"

Colin shrugged his shoulders.

"Well, gentlemen," Mike said, getting up, "I'm gonna take my leave of you now."

"You going to work?" Ibn asked.

"No, I don't have to work weekends anymore. I gotta go into the city and pick up Erika."

"Where's Bunches' car?" Colin asked.

"It's in the shop."

Ibn looked up at Mike, worried. "What's wrong with it? Is it okay to drive?"

"No, dummy. I told you it's in the shop, didn't I?"

"You know what I mean, asshole. Is the problem serious? Is she having trouble with her car."

Mike had known what Ibn meant. The one thing that all four of them could always agree on was their devotion to Erika. They would not tolerate her driving around in an unsafe vehicle. Mike knew that if there was even an inkling that her car wasn't sound, his friends would trip over themselves to get her something else, especially with her commuting back and forth to Philly, often at night. He noticed that all three of his friends were looking at him intently, awaiting his answer.

"No, her Celica is fine. It's just some minor work. Tune up, timing belt and brakes."

"Yeah, Toyotas are reliable," Dexter said. "Remember, that's why we got her one in the first place."

"Yeah, and next year she'll be done with medical school. We should do something for her," Colin said.

"We do. We let her live rent free," Ibn said, laughing. "That girl's been riding for years."

"Where has Bunches been, anyway?" Dexter asked, "I haven't seen her all week."

"She's been staying at a girlfriend's apartment in the city." Mike put some money on the table to cover his part of the bill. "You know, that reminds me of something. Since she *is* about to be a doctor, how about you clowns start calling her by her proper name?"

Ibn scoffed, "She was introduced to me as Bunches, and thus she will forevermore remain Bunches."

Colin laughed. "Why did Trev call her Bunches, again?"

"Don't you remember?" Dexter asked. "He said when she was a baby, everybody was always saying how pretty she was, but to him she just looked like a bunch of rolled-up fat. So he just started calling her Bunches."

The four of them laughed and then grew quiet. Each was thinking about their fraternity brother Trevor, who had died of leukemia at the age of twenty-three. His mother had died in a car accident when Trevor and Bunches were young, and their father had never been a factor, so they were reared by their grandmother. From his hospital bed Trevor had made the four of them promise to take care of his little sister, Bunches, whom he doted on. It was a promise they had kept. Bunches had an IQ that tested through the roof and had received scholarships through college and medical school, so the four of them supplemented her education costs in addition to paying for her housing and car. Between the four of them, she had accumulated an obscene amount of clothes and shoes. They never wanted her to have to worry about holding down a job but to devote herself full-time to her studies.

"The name doesn't exactly fit anymore, does it? With her cute self," Colin said.

"Ya know." Ibn looked at Dexter and Mike. "Are you guys keeping an eye on things? How's the ADS?"

"The ADS is fully operational and ever vigilant," Dexter answered, springing to life and forgetting his woes for the time being. "I don't shirk my duty as the first line of defense. Believe me, I have dates fearing for their lives when they come by to take Bunches out."

Ibn gave him a thumbs-up. "That's good. 'Cause y'all know she doesn't want me to have to come over there."

"ADS?" Colin asked.

"That's what they call their 'Asshole Defense System,'" Mike answered. "We have to let her grow up, fellas. She's not a child."

Dexter rolled his eyes. "Now you see why I have to be so vigilant."

"Seriously. Hell, she's gonna be a doctor."

"Exactly," Ibn replied. "So, you know my screening process for shorty is going to get even stricter. Frauds, playboys and hoods need not apply."

"Be careful now, Ib. If all women had those guidelines, you'd still be a virgin," Mike said, making them all laugh.

"Fuuuck you," Ibn answered.

"All right, fellas, I gotta go." Mike checked his watch. "I'll get with y'all."

"All right, man."

"See ya later."

He waved good-bye to Lorraine on his way out.

"What do you guys have planned for the rest of the day?" Colin asked.

Lorraine came by and put a Styrofoam container full of Dexter's un-

eaten lunch on the table. His mind turned back to his current predicament. "I think I'm gonna stop by Denise's."

"You and Stacy still coming over tonight, right?" Ibn asked Colin.
"Ready for another thumping at spades, like last week?"

Colin nodded.

Ibn turned back to Dexter. "Dex, now that Dudley Do-Wrong is
gone, are you serious about trying to make it work with Denise?" Ibn
asked.

Dexter nodded his head.

"Why you calling my boy Dudley Do-Wrong?" asked Colin.

Ibn fingered his glass. "Hey, y'all know I love Mike, but what can
you say about a man who wants to preach sermons but doesn't have the
common sense to leave the Sharice Watsons of the world to their own
devices, or should I say, 'vices.' That girl has put more dogs to bed than
the Humane Society." He shook his head. "I don't know what is it,
with that guy and his fondness for skanks."

"You've never been one to leave the Sharice Watsons of the world
alone," Colin offered.

"True. But unlike Mike, I know to keep them in their proper context. Hey, hos can be some of the best people on this planet, as long as
you don't catch feelings for them. Then they're deadly."

"Did you ever mess with Sharice?"

"No, our paths never crossed." Ibn looked at the bill and put down
some money, making sure to leave Lorraine a big tip. When he looked
up again he realized that Dexter and Colin were staring at him questioningly. "What? I'm serious. I never did."

Three

Colin looked in on Stacy. She was in the kitchen of the Bethune community center, leading a group of twelve children (all girls because the boys were away on an outing) and two aides in a cooking class. They were baking oatmeal raisin cookies, and Stacy had turned something fun into something educational, because the children were enjoying their activity. The next weekend it was the girls' turn to go, and the boys would be doing the cooking.

The boys who frequented the community center were at a Phillies game, Colin had found out. He was surprised that Stacy hadn't asked him to chaperone the event, especially since two of the boys, Corey and Andre, were "mentees" of his. Actually, it figured. Stacy would rather call him in to help out with the boys when it benefited her, to take them off her hands. Since Stacy rarely worked weekends, Colin rarely "volunteered" on weekends.

Still, Colin saw how excited the girls were. He admired how Stacy did that, made learning fun for the children. She stressed hygiene when talking about the need for clean utensils. She incorporated math when measuring out the ingredients, reading when reading the recipe, even social studies by telling the girls that the guy on the oatmeal canister was a Quaker and how a large community of Quakers lived nearby in Pennsylvania Dutch country. She had a great rapport with the children, especially when she was in a good mood.

He left the kitchen and settled on the couch in the television room. He stretched and yawned, his lack of sleep from the night before finally catching up with him. After he had left the restaurant, he planned on going home and catching a few winks before dinner with Ibn and Tiffany, but Stacy had had other ideas. Though she didn't work weekends, she wanted to stop by to check on a new worker the center had hired and make sure things were running smoothly. Once she got here, she ended up taking control of the whole project.

Colin had to admit, that was one of the things which attracted him to Stacy in the first place; her take-charge assertiveness.

Colin took off his glasses and set them on the coffee table. Then he stretched out on the couch and put his feet up. There. He was now comfortable. Just as he had always been comfortable yielding to Stacy in almost all matters involving their relationship. It had been that way since the beginning, and Stacy was hardly the type to relinquish control willingly.

Not that Colin minded, anyway. Truth be known, he didn't want to rock the boat. Stacy had come along in his life at a time when he really needed someone. Colin hadn't had near the amount of women as his friends. In fact, he had the same amount of sleeping partners in his life that Ibn had in a good week. The way he saw it, in order of fewest women had, it was him; Mike, whose number was fairly low; Dexter, whose number was fairly high; and then Ibn, who was in another stratosphere. Four. That was Colin's number. The first had been his high school sweetheart, Lori, who ended up cheating on him. The second had been a quiet girl named Sandy that he had met his freshman year in college. She did him dirty as well. The third, a girl named Michelle, he hooked up with junior year. It ended quickly, and yes, she also stepped out on him.

Then there was Sherry and Pamela, girls who he had attempted one-night stands with his senior year, mostly because of Ibn's urging. "Attempted" he thought, because both times he had been unable to perform, so he could hardly count them as women he had. His self-worth was shot at that point. He not only couldn't keep a woman happy in a relationship, but apparently he couldn't even get it up for a woman.

But Stacy had come along and changed all that. She transferred to his school her junior year, his last semester. She had spotted Colin on campus and bore in on him like a charging rhino. She had pursued him so relentlessly that she made him feel special. And valued. And needed by someone.

And the sex with Stacy was fantastic, not that he had a whole lot to compare her to.

He knew from the start Stacy was bossy, but he didn't care. In fact, though he knew his friends hated his comfort level of such an arrangement, he liked that Stacy took charge of the course of their relationship. If they did things her way, then she would be less likely to be unhappy and look for somebody else. No, he definitely didn't mind—hell, when had he ever proved that he could make a woman happy when he held the reins? He hadn't. So, if the consequence of having someone in his life was to be badgered a bit more than necessary, it was a trade-off he was willing to make. At least he had someone.

"Get up!"

Colin felt his shoulders being manhandled, and he was shaken out of his slumber. Stacy was hovering above him.

"Don't be embarrassing me like that."

"H-huh?" Colin squinted up at her.

"You heard me. This ain't no flophouse. Come on into the kitchen, and give me a hand."

"Yo, Tiffany, where you been? What are you cooking? You forget we're having company over? Why weren't you answering your celly?"

Tiffany wasn't even in the door yet, and Ibn was already bearing down on her. She closed the door behind her with her foot and lifted her shopping bags to show him where she had been.

Ibn twisted up his face with disgust. "That's great, Tiffany. We'll just eat those Neiman Marcus and Lord and Taylor bags for dinner. Why weren't you answering your phone?"

Because I didn't want to hear your mouth. Duh. "I must've had the ringer turned off," Tiffany said as she made her way through the living room and into the dining room. "Don't worry, I'll have dinner done in plenty of time."

"I was about to call my mother over to cook," Ibn groused as he lay back down on the couch. He picked up the newspaper again to check on his other stocks.

Tiffany set her bags down on the table and looked at him. Hey, I have an idea, how about your ass cooking? "That won't be necessary," she said. "It won't take me long. I already defrosted the chicken."

Ibn muttered something under his breath that Tiffany ignored as she went into the kitchen to wash her hands.

She had found herself doing more and more of that lately. Ignoring Ibn. Or biting her tongue because she didn't have the energy to fight with him. And not because she didn't feel it was necessary to be heard or that she was scared of confrontation, either, but because of a reason far more troubling to her. She found herself not caring because she didn't think it would help matters. Nothing was ever going to change between them, because Ibn didn't think anything needed changing. Except maybe her ass getting home quicker to cook dinner.

Tiffany took the chicken out of the refrigerator and began washing it. She decided she was just going to fry it. She had made a pasta salad to go along with it that morning.

Her indifference was a sea change from what she had felt for him during the first few years of their relationship. They had met when Tiffany was in grad school, during a particularly rough period of her life. Her parents were going through a bitter divorce, and as an only child she felt them pulling her every which way, trying to win her loyalty. She loved her mother, but she was always her daddy's little girl; she was spoiled rotten by her father. So when more money started going to the lawyers than to her, she was in bad financial straits, with credit cards maxed out and student debts piling up. And she was lonely. She was always able to garner attention because of her looks, but it was the wrong kind of attention. She wouldn't allow herself to come cheap to any man.

Ibn was visiting her campus as a traveling member of his fraternity's step team. Their eyes met, and from that moment it was on. Ibn took control of every facet of her life, and Tiffany let him. Ibn became her confidant, her lover, her guide, her provider—her everything. He paid off all Tiffany's debts and put her through grad school. Tiffany was once again a kept woman, with Ibn assuming the role of her father. And Ibn got to have on his arm a woman worthy of being kept, which was of huge importance to him. Tiffany had come to realize that Ibn needed her as much as she needed him, because he needed to show the world what he had gotten for himself: a good girl.

She realized Ibn's insatiable need for the proper appearance. It was almost a sickness with him. His appearance and his woman's had to be immaculate at all times—which is the real reason he never complained when Tiffany spent money shopping. He and his woman had to have the best cars, and they couldn't have a speck of dirt on them. They had to have the best home.

Tiffany dried her hands and looked out the window over the sink and into their huge backyard. No, it was Ibn's backyard, and it was Ibn's house. She had no ring. If Ibn told her to get out tomorrow, what could she do?

Besides, the cost of being Ibn's showpiece was high. For while Ibn had to have a wholesome, pretty woman to present to the public, behind closed doors he believed he could fuck any ragtag piece of something he could. And that made him a hypocrite. What did he think? That decency and respect are necessary only for public perusal?

Tiffany had never caught him cheating red-handed, but there were too many stolen glances, too many muffled giggles, too many hidden innuendos and too much secrecy for Tiffany to believe that Ibn was faithful. Putting her out there like that to be a source of ridicule in the community. For someone so worried about public perception, he sure didn't mind making her look like a fool.

She grabbed a Snapple raspberry tea out of the fridge and sat down. She looked at the mail Ibn had laid out on the kitchen table. One envelope was addressed to her. It was from a company in Maryland. Tiffany had sent her résumé to them a few months back.

She got up, walked over to the counter and put it in her purse. She was surprised Ibn hadn't asked her about it. But then again, he was probably too preoccupied with her not being home to cook to notice anything else.

It hadn't always been like this, Tiffany thought as she looked under the cap of her tea to see if she was an instant winner. No such luck.

One notion she was rapidly abandoning was the thought that Ibn was going to change for her. She had first consoled herself every time she couldn't account for Ibn's whereabouts with the thought that once they got married, all his philandering would stop. But who was she kidding? She would just be promoted from cheated-on girlfriend to cheated-on wife, and that was hardly an elevation. It was a lateral move, at best.

And she was tired of being stagnant.

Bunches smiled when Mike pulled his Altima up to the curb in the Graduate Hospital area of Central Philadelphia. Still wearing her intern clothes, she got up from the bench and slid into his car.

"Whaddup, doc?"

"Hi, thanks for coming to get me."

"No problem." He wheeled his car back into traffic.

"So, Mr. Lovett, how was your week?" She shifted her body so she could face him.

"You want me to recall my entire week for you? You know that's almost impossible for me, Erika. I challenge life with the zest of Hemingway, engage in love with the passion of Casanova and absorb knowledge with the zeal of—"

"Uneventful, huh?"

"Yep. Went to work and came home."

She laughed. "How are the boys doing?"

"That's right, you've been away." He pulled out into traffic. "It's been a momentous time for Dexter. He found out he's gonna be a dad."

She looked at him wide-eyed. "No! You serious?"

"As serious as a fat man at a buffet five minutes before closing."

"Daaamn." She gazed through the windshield. She began sucking her bottom lip, which Mike knew she always did when she was lost in thought. "Denise, right?" she finally asked.

Mike shrugged. "Yeah, the irony is, he was about to cut her loose."

"There's nothing ironic about it," she said quietly.

"What do you mean?"

"Michael, the number-one mistake you guys make is thinking that you are smarter than women. What, you don't think that Denise knew Dex was about to let her go?"

Mike thought about it. Dexter hadn't done much lately to reassure her otherwise. "I don't know. Maybe."

"Maybe?" She turned so she was sitting sideways on the seat. "I know it's a difficult thing for the limited male mind to do, but try to put yourself in Denise's position while I paint you a picture."

"Your sexist insult aside, okay. Proceed."

"She's in her late twenties, childless, wants to have children and has been dating a man for the past, what, eight or nine months, right?"

"Something like that."

"Lately he's become distant, his phone calls more infrequent. When they do speak, they oftentimes end up in an argument. Whereas in the beginning he couldn't get enough of her, now it seems like he could take or leave her. He's losing interest. What can she do? She gave him her body months back, and to be honest, other than sex, their relationship isn't built on much else. Follow so far?"

"I'm with you."

"Every woman knows that if a man doesn't love her, he has no will to stay with her and work through the difficult times. So, Denise starts to panic. Dexter is a quality man, a good catch. Educated, no children, good-paying job—this may be her last best chance. Her biological clock is ticking. What's a girl to do?"

Mike found a meter and parked alongside it. He figured that since they were in the city and the weather was nice, they could walk down South Street and do some window-shopping, which he knew Bunches enjoyed doing. Plus, he wanted to check on his old store.

"So the sex between them has been sporadic at best lately because they haven't been seeing each other much, and when they do, they fight. Denise knows what's coming. Soon, after one of these arguments Dexter is gonna give her the 'since we can't seem to get along, maybe we need to take a break from each other' speech, and it will be for all intents and purposes over. Uhn-uhn, sistah ain't going out like that. So, she has to beat him to the punch."

"Yeah," Mike said thoughtfully. He studied Bunches' drawn face. She looked beat from all her studying.

"She has to catch *him* out there. So she dreams up a situation where they can get together when she knows Dexter won't be expecting to get any. Remember, they probably haven't been getting together on the regular for a while, so she knows he won't be prepared. She seduces him and puts it on him, works him out but *good*. She knew he wouldn't refuse it because of the infrequency of their get-togethers lately, so he hadn't hit it in a while. Besides, he's thinking to himself that this is one last fling, that this stupid-ass girl doesn't know that she's history. She *knows* he's thinking this. Which is why she coordinated their meeting to occur right around the time when she was ovulating."

"Damn." Could she be that devious? Mike wondered.

"Dex is thinking, 'One last time for the road.' Denise is thinking, 'One last time for the road all right, brah, the road to matrimony. I ain't your ho.' "

"But why would she want to marry him? She knows he doesn't love her."

Bunches massaged the back of her neck. "Because he might learn to love her. Besides, even if it doesn't work out, she'll still have the child she wanted and a man that she knows will help her support it. Her body wouldn't have been given in vain. Women get tired of being used, Michael. Dexter is an ass sometimes, but women know when a man is about something. Hell, have you ever noticed that with all the women Ibn has had—"

"*Allegedly* had," Mike said, imitating Ibn.

"—how come none of them have ever turned up pregnant?"

"He says because he always uses a condom."

"Because *they* always make sure there's a condom used. As well as birth control pills, spermicide, sponges, RU-486, Norplant and every other prohibitive measure under the sun," Bunches said, laughing. "They know Ibn is for bed, not for bred. Can you imagine a woman telling Ibn she's pregnant? After calling her a whore and claiming it's not his, he'll then try to pressure her into having an abortion." She looked out the window and saw his old job up the street. "Why did you stop here? You don't work here anymore."

"It's still my responsibility," Mike answered. "I just want to see how's business."

Mike and Bunches walked into the Dapper Male Big and Tall clothing store. Since it was empty of customers, Bunches and Terence were free to exchange their usual greeting.

"Hey, diva." Terence waved.

"Hey, gooor-geous!" Bunches answered salaciously.

Terence sucked in his cheeks, put his hands on his ample hips and posed. "I'm *so* glad you noticed, girlfriend."

Mike saw Jeff, the other employee in the store, roll his eyes at the exchange. Jeff had little tolerance for Terence's "mary-dosiness," as he called it. The fact that Terence was of Irish descent like him appalled him even more. Mike didn't mind in the least. One, because Terence had enough sense to "butch up" when he had to, and second, the female customers loved him. Besides, Terence was excellent at his job. He could sell wool to a shepherd.

"How's business?" Mike asked.

"We had a good day," Terence answered. "The customers have been saying that since the management change," he slowly raised his arms skyward like a blooming rose, "a breath of fresh air has hit the place."

"You're funny," Mike said. Terence now had Mike's old job as store manager. The store television they had to entertain the customers while they shopped was showing a Sixers game. Mike realized that it had to be a tape since it was September, over a month away from the opening of the season.

"*Allan dives for the ball and lands in the front row. What an effort!*" the commentator gushed.

Terence placed his hand to his chest. "My, Mr. Iverson can land on me *anytime* he wants to."

Jeff looked at Terence, shook his head and walked to the rear of the store.

"He is cute, isn't he?" Bunches asked.

"Um-hm," Terence said. If he had noticed Jeff's look, he chose to ignore it, because he was now onto his favorite topic in the world: black men. Though Terence was as white as they came, with his strawberry-blond hair and fair skin, he dated black men almost exclusively. He peppered his reasoning with statements like "Once you had some black joy, you'll never mess with another white boy," and "The only thing a white man can do for me is sell me some insurance." He studied the screen as it was showing a close-up of Iverson. "He's too skinny for me, though. I'd break him in two."

Bunches looked down at Terence's forty-eight-inch waist and was about to say something, but he raised his index finger at her. "Don't go there, girl."

Mike walked over to the register to check the day's receipts.

"So, what's your type?" Bunches asked. Mike and Jeff made eye contact. Jeff had a look on his face that said he didn't like where this conversation was heading. Mike chuckled as he saw Jeff walk into the store's rear office.

"Oh, that's easy," Terence said excitedly. "Mike's friend. That man is *fine*."

Bunches looked over at Mike with her mouth agape in fake horror. He smiled at her reaction. She loved this kind of silliness. Mike gave her a signal to let him handle this.

"Oh, yeah, I forgot you had a thing for Dexter."

"Dex-ter?" Terence curled his upper lip. He thought about it for a second, then his face softened. "Well, Dexter is built like a brick shithouse, I'll give you that. But he's too hard-looking for my taste." He looked at Mike, "You know who I'm talking about, the one with the funny-sounding name. I've only met him once."

Mike looked at Bunches, who seemed about ready to burst.

"Oh. You mean Colin. I don't think Colin is that funny-sounding a name. Do you, Erika?"

Bunches shook her head. If she had tried to speak, she would have lost it.

"Colin?" Terence searched his memory for a Colin. When he found it, he looked at Mike exasperatedly. "Not Colin. He's cute and all, but then you get to the same problem as Iverson—he's too skinny. You know who I'm talking about, the *mean* one." Terrence was working himself into a lather. He looked at Mike, then at Bunches, who had been reduced to staring at the floor to not burst out laughing. "Y'all know who I'm talking about. What is his *name*?"

Terence was frothing at this point, so Mike decided to put him out of his misery. "Oh, you mean Ibn."

"Yes, Lord, Ibn!" Terence exhaled loudly, "*Ibn*." He closed his eyes and repeated it, as if the very name itself gave him an orgasmic release. Though he had trouble remembering the name, he had no problem giving a detailed description. "That wavy jet-black hair, those bushy eyebrows, those full, curly eyelashes and smooth hazelnut complexion . . ." Terence's eyes remained closed as if he had zoned out. He emitted a soft moan.

Bunches and Mike looked at each other in amazement. All this from one meeting?

Terence continued, "Those broad shoulders and muscular arms, that tight upper body which goes down to . . ." Terence stretched his arms out and brought his hands together to make a letter V. "Bam! That *ass*. That sculpted godsend of an ass. Whew!" Terence finally opened his eyes and looked at Mike and Bunches, who were still staring at him.

"What?" he asked.

"No, I'm feeling you," Bunches said. "When I was a kid, I had the most ridiculous crush on Ibn. You couldn't tell me the sun didn't rise when he opened his eyes in the morning."

Mike smiled to himself. He remembered when she was a pudgy twelve-year-old with braces. Bunches would turn to a pile of goo when Ibn walked into the room. In Mike's opinion, she wasn't being completely honest with Terence. Mike thought that Bunches still carried a little torch for Ibn.

"And now?" Terence asked.

"I got to know him. It ruined it for me." She and Mike laughed.

"Lucky you. *You* got to know him. Too bad he's straight. What a waste of a good man." He looked at Mike. "He *is* straight, isn't he?"

"Afraid so." Mike checked his watch. He wanted to see Sharice that evening.

Terence wasn't done yet. "He has an exotic look to him. Is he from here?"

"No, he's not. He's a mixture of black and coolie. He was born in Guyana." Bunches said.

"What's 'coolie'?" Terence asked.

"An Indian, from Asia."

"Oh, you mean like Gandhi?"

"Yep."

Jeff came out of the office to lock the front door of the store.

"Where did you say he was from?" Terence asked.

"Guyana. Guy-an-a," she repeated phonetically.

"Guy-an-a." Terence repeated. "Hmm, ask him if he wants some Guy-and-a-*dick*."

Jeff spun on his heel and went back into the office.

Bunches and Mike left the store smiling.

"What's next, skipper?" Bunches asked as she and Mike climbed back into his car.

Mike remembered how tired Bunches had looked earlier. "Well, if you were up to it, I thought we could do some shopping, but I see you're ti—"

"Up to it?" She bounced in her seat and clapped her hands excitedly. "What you buying me? What you buying me?"

Mike looked over at her and laughed. "What do you need?"

"What do I need, or what do I want, Mr. New-Position-Bump-in-Salary?" she asked as they got back out of the car.

"Either." He fished for quarters in his pocket. Bunches handed him three out of her purse.

"I tell you what, fella. How about I treat you today? What do *you* want?"

Mike wheezed, grabbed his chest and leaned against the parking meter for support.

Bunches folded her arms but couldn't contain her laugh. "Oh, that's cute, Michael."

He held his index finger in the air, signaling that he'd be okay in another minute. He leaned over, resting his palms on his knees and continued breathing loudly.

"Ha-ha," she said sarcastically.

"Erika, what are you trying to do, test your lifesaving skills? My body can't take shocks like that. I ain't a kid anymore."

She stepped forward and hugged him. He kissed her forehead, as he had been doing since she was twelve years old. She felt warm and snuggly inside.

"With all you and the guys do for me, I can't get you something nice?" She slid her arm inside his, and they started walking.

"Oh, don't worry about that. You're gonna pay all of us back with free medical care. I'm sure Ib's keeping a running tally somewhere."

"His vain ass will probably want plastic surgery."

"By the way, do you mind the fellas still calling you Bunches?"

She didn't answer for the next several steps as she mulled it over. "No, I don't," she finally said. "Actually, I kinda like it. It makes me feel like my brother is still with me."

"Oh. Okay, *Bunches*."

"You call me Erika." She smiled at him and he returned it.

"By the way, I couldn't help but notice in our conversation in the car how attuned you were to what Denise and Dex are going through. It's almost like you were there."

"*All* women have been there, Michael."

Mike stopped walking. He wondered what man had gotten through Dexter and Ibn's airtight "asshole defense system" and hurt Bunches. "What man had you out there like that?"

"No one—are you crazy? I was speaking of all women, *except* me. I got too much self-respect for that desperation bullshit," she said, making both of them laugh.

"It's almost unfair to play them. They're *too* easy to beat."

Ibn laughed. "You know." He and Stacy had just finished beating Tiffany and Colin in spades. Ibn and Stacy were natural partners because they were both cutthroat and liked to talk a lot of shit while they played. Colin and Tiffany stubbornly insisted on being teamed up, saying that wanted to exact revenge together for all the ass-whippings they had suffered in the past. So, as usual, they lost and were stuck with cleaning the dinner dishes while Stacy and Ibn drove to the video store for a movie.

"This is a *nice* car, Ibn."

"Thanks."

Stacy ran her fingers over the leather. "I could get used to this real fast. But that tight-ass Colin won't get us one."

Ibn gritted his teeth. The only downside to the couples getting together was having to watch Stacy belittle Colin at every opportunity.

In her eyes, he did nothing right. He didn't chew his food correctly, he couldn't shuffle the cards the right way, he took too long to bid on how many books he could make—and don't let him say something that she disagreed with. Then it would get ugly in there. Though, in Ibn's opinion, it got "ugly in there" the moment Stacy's homely ass came through his front door.

It was hard for him not to intervene on Colin's behalf when Stacy demeaned him. The situation was made all the more pathetic when Colin would try to make a joke out of what she said instead of confronting her. A couple of times Ibn had had all he could stand and was about to say something, but Tiffany would kick him under the table to tell him to mind his own business. He stopped at a red light and looked over at Stacy. She had leaned back the seat like some fucking queen, like she just *knew* she belonged in a car like this. She also had her eyes closed, no doubt contemplating what approach she would use to talk Colin into getting her a Benz.

Ibn seethed. He needed a kick from Tiffany right about now. "These cars are expensive, Stacy."

"Colin's just being stubborn," she answered, not opening her eyes. "What about all that extra money he makes from those rental properties?"

"Stacy, we reinvest most of that money. Eventually we want to buy apartment buildings with twenty to thirty units. I couldn't afford this car if it wasn't for my business."

"We could afford one," she said stubbornly.

We? From what Colin had told him, Stacy's job as a youth counselor didn't pay, which was why she was going back to school to get her master's. Ibn also had the feeling that she and Colin often sent money down to Stacy's family in Virginia. If Ibn lived six lifetimes, he still wouldn't understand what Colin saw in Stacy. Hell, between Colin's love for shrews and Mike's affinity for skanks, Ibn was in constant amazement at his friends' choices in women. Dammit, it was up to him to straighten those cats out. It was his *duty* to do so. Though it would require some tact.

"Stacy, you do realize that we left two very attractive people in that house."

She opened her eyes and looked at him strangely. "What?"

"What I am saying is that Colin and Tiffany are two people that because of their looks are gonna get a lot of attention from the opposite sex. That's just reality, I know that and you know that. There's always one person, be it the man or the woman, in every couple who has more options than the other person. Therefore, since me and you aren't lucky enough to be the beautiful ones of our relationships, we have to be the better people. You know, we have to be the supportive ones. The ones that'll work with our partners to achieve their goals. We have to have the more pleasant personalities and bring that to the table. Otherwise, why would Tiffany and Colin stay with us? They're the prizes, not us. They can simply exercise their options and find someone who would make them happy. Someone who is in their corner and who will work with them, not against them." He pulled into an empty space at the Blockbuster.

Stacy didn't say a word as they walked toward the store. Good, Ibn thought. Gave your ass something to think about, didn't I? On their way in, Ibn nearly bumped into a white man who gave him a strange look.

"Let's go to the drama section," Stacy said.

That figures, Ibn thought. Though maybe it would be more appropriate for Stacy's ugly ass to be in the horror section. They browsed up and down the aisles for a while. Stacy went over to look at the new releases along the wall. Ibn picked up one of the few boxes with black people on it. It looked interesting, a movie called *Cappuccino*. He was about to call Stacy over when the white man who had given him the funny look earlier approached him.

"Excuse me," he said somewhat nervously, "but do you know you could be making twelve hundred dollars a day?"

Ibn eyed him suspiciously. "What do you mean?"

He reached into his pocket and handed Ibn a glossy card.

Ebony Handyman Productions
"We lay pipe, afrocentrically."
**Maker of the world's finest ebony
and interracial adult movies.**

In one corner of the card was a red, black and green flag. In the other corner was a Nefertiti silhouette. The man spoke again.

"You have the look that we are looking for—"

"What!" Ibn glared at him and raised his hand reflexively. This guy was dangerously close to getting some "cappuccino" upside his head.

The man cringed and took a step back. "Sir, I was just offering—" He looked around. People were staring. He lowered his voice, hoping Ibn would do the same. "There's no need to get upset."

"No need to get upset! I'm just trying to go to the video store, and I get accosted by a perv like you. I moved to the suburbs for this shit? What the hell you doing here anyway? There ain't no X-rated section at Blockbuster. Jesus Christ, there are kids in here!"

The man gave up and quickly started to head for the door.

"Clear a path, everybody!" Ibn exclaimed. "Make way for the smut peddler!"

"Your apartment looks nice, Sharice," Mike said as he settled onto the couch.

Sharice gave him a puzzled look, then walked out of the kitchen, over to her stereo and turned it off, for which Mike was grateful. He had heard the Yolanda Adams song "The Battle Is the Lord's" blaring before he got to the door, and Sharice must have had it on repeat mode, because this was the third time it was playing.

"What did you say?" she asked.

"I said your apartment looks nice," he repeated. Actually, it looked like a miniature Christian bookstore. Numerous religious tracts and pamphlets were scattered throughout the living room. On the walls were various framed, sentimental pictures with different Bible verses written on them. Mike had counted four Bibles in his quick scan around the living room. In a narrow bookcase in the corner were books by T. D. Jakes, Benny Hinn and Charles Stanley. He also noticed that all her CDs were gospel. Back when they were in college, Sharice had been a devotee of hip-hop.

"Thank you." She sat down next to him on the couch and smiled. It was the kind of familiar, warm smile shared by old friends getting reacquainted after a long separation. Mike returned it. "I'm glad you stopped by. I was hoping you would call me today."

"Actually, this is my second time in the city today. I was here earlier with Erika."

"Who's Erika?"

"Trevor's little sister. You know, the one everyone calls Bunches."

A curtain of sadness fell over Sharice's face at the mention of Trevor's name. She fell quiet. "That was a sad time," she finally said.

"You're telling me."

"Mike," Sharice looked at him hopefully, "was Trevor saved when he died?"

Mike hesitated before answering. He hadn't expected that question. "I believe so, Sharice. I know he was brought up in the church."

She was relieved to hear that Trevor wasn't eternally damned. She clasped Mike's hand. "Well, I'm glad I could steal you away from Bunches."

It's funny she said that, Mike thought. When he and Erika had gotten home from their shopping excursion, he had called Sharice. When he said he was coming over, Mike thought he had detected a look of disappointment in Erika's face. While he was still on the phone, she had left to go upstairs to her place, barely bothering to wave good-bye on her way out. Mike figured that it was because Erika had been busy at the hospital all week and was looking to hang out with somebody. He was about to call Sharice back to cancel when Dexter walked in. He told Mike that he would see if Bunches wanted to catch a flick with him later.

"So, Sharice, when did you convert?"

She looked at him quizzically. "Do you mean, when did I get saved?"

"No, well, I guess . . ." Mike furrowed his brow. "What I mean is, didn't you used to be Jewish back when we were in school?"

She looked at him like he was crazy. "Michael Lovett, you know full well I was never Jewish."

"I'm confused," he said. "If you weren't a practicing Jew, then why were you always celebrating Passover?"

She was totally lost. "Huh? Passover?"

"Yeah, Passover. Remember? You used to 'pass over' me for this man. Then you would 'pass over' me for that man. Then you would 'pass over' me for the next guy. . . ."

Sharice leaned back on the sofa and laughed, exposing what had to be the whitest teeth that Mike had ever seen. After she was finished she looked at him tenderly. "Mike, you do realize I spent more time with you than any other man on campus."

"I know. We were always together." Mike also remembered Ibn used to ridicule him mercilessly, saying things like, "Mike, why you take that ho everywhere you go? Everybody else just takes her from the couch to the bedroom." Considering all the time Mike spent with Sharice, Ibn and his other friends couldn't understand why he wasn't fucking her. They didn't know that Mike simply enjoyed Sharice's company.

She was thinking the same thing. "So, how come you never tried anything with me? I wasn't your type?"

He looked at her like she was crazy. She laughed. She knew how ridiculous that question was. There were only two kinds of men who didn't want to jump Sharice, dead men and gay men. Check that, maybe just gay men. Because if any *body* could raise the dead, it was Sharice's.

"I really liked you, I'm sure you knew that. In fact, the only thing I remember us arguing about was when I thought you were diminishing yourself, you know, selling yourself short." His pleasant way of saying screwing everything with a dick. "I wanted you to see me differently than the other men in your life. It was kind of difficult, because at the time you weren't trying to hear that. You didn't want to be loved, you just wanted to be . . ." He stopped short.

"I know I was out there, Mike," she said quietly. "The Enemy had such a hold on me that I didn't know what was best for me."

"Who?"

"The Enemy," Sharice answered. She saw the puzzled look on his face. "*Satan*," she said, disbelieving his ignorance. "You are still going to church with me again tomorrow, right?"

"Yeah," he said somewhat sheepishly. Hell, he thought Sharice's "enemy" back then was clothing, because she wore as little of it as possible.

"Good," she said, getting up.

Why? Because there is a lot of work to be done here? Mike wondered how much of the Christian literature had been put out for his
benefit.

"You hungry? The chicken should be about ready."

"Yeah." Mike watched her as she walked to the kitchen. Damn,
Sharice had body for days. Enough body for two sistahs or three white
women. And had the nerve to have a flat stomach. She was a genetic
freak, a "throwback," as Ibn liked to say. In Ibn's way of thinking, this is
how all black women used to look in Africa before they were sullied by
the Europeans.

Mike remembered the first time he saw Sharice. It was his sophomore year, and he and Trevor were walking across campus when they
spotted her. Trev had said, "Damn! They should call that girl IHOP,
because she is *stacked*." Mike smiled at the memory. And judging from
how fine she still was, in the ensuing ten years Sharice hadn't lost a
thing.

She called out from the kitchen, "What parts do you want, Mike?"

"I like dark meat, Sharice."

As he was getting up to join her in the kitchen, one of the pamphlets on the table caught his eye. He picked it up. It was titled "R U
Ready?" and read

If you died tonight, would you be prepared to face God?

Mike felt ashamed. Here he was obsessing on this girl's body while
she was trying to save him from hellfire. He deserved to be jabbed in
the ass with a pitchfork.

"Hi," Denise said, opening the door.

"Hi." Dexter stepped into the living room of her small apartment
and sat down on the couch. Bunches hadn't wanted to do anything but
sleep, so he had given Denise a call. He looked around her apartment.
It seemed different from before. No longer was this the living space of a
girl he was fucking; this was now the apartment of his child's mother. It
was small and her furnishings were sparse, but Dexter had never seen a
time that it wasn't clean. And it usually smelled great, because Denise

was an excellent cook and always had some delicious new concoction for Dexter to sample.

"I'm on the phone, I'll be done in a minute."

"Okay."

Dexter studied her intently as she walked back toward the bedroom. This was the first time he had seen her with the knowledge that his seed was growing inside her. He had expected to somehow see her differently, like . . . like . . . well, he couldn't say exactly, but he was hoping for maybe a soft, angelic glow on her face or something. Something. Anything that would jump-start his heart and replace the apathy that he currently had in it for her.

He then noticed on the coffee table a home pregnancy kit. He knew that Denise had left it in such a prominent place on purpose to let him know she wasn't bullshitting him. Upon closer inspection, he could see that the test was clearly positive. It pissed him off. He could imagine Denise carefully putting it there after she found out he was coming over, taking a couple of steps back and admiring her handiwork, like it was art or something. Look at it, sitting there like a fucking trophy. He wouldn't be surprised if the next time he came over it was mounted on the wall. Though maybe it would be more appropriate if it was his head on the wall. He heard Denise giggling from the bedroom, and he felt the bile in him rise to his throat. What the *fuck* had this bitch got him into?

No, he said to himself, you're not gonna do that. He got up and walked over to the window. The mother of your child is not a bitch. One thing's for goddamn sure, you are not gonna be one of *those* men. Do you hear me, Dexter Holmes? That ain't gonna happen. You are not gonna pour all your negativity on her and have it affect your baby's health. Regardless of whether or not she did this intentionally, you should've known better to let some *bitch* trip you up. See, right there, is what I'm talking about. Cut that name-calling shit out and be a man about it.

"Sorry about that."

Dexter hadn't heard Denise come back in the room. She was wearing a long T-shirt, gray shorts, and white cotton anklets. "That's okay. How do you feel?"

"Fine," she said. She put away the pregnancy kit hurriedly, as if she had no idea how it got out there in the first place.

"Who were you talking to on the phone?"

"Marla." Denise smiled. "She made me laugh when she told me about some of the weird cravings she got when she was pregnant with her kids."

So her fat-ass, big-mouth, no-man-of-her-own friend Marla knew? That meant everybody in the state would know by next week. Well, Denise definitely had made up her mind to keep it. There was no point in having the conversation where they could discuss "their options."

"How far along are you?"

"Five weeks." She stood looking at him, expressionless. Dexter knew she was waiting for him to give her some idea how he felt about the situation so she could react accordingly.

"Sit down, Denise."

She sat on the other end of the couch. As she turned to face him, Dexter saw the wariness on her face. "I had an idea and I want to run it by you first, to see if it was okay." She seemed poised to react negatively, as if she expected some bullshit to come out of his mouth. "I want to start looking for a house for us to live."

Denise exhaled, quickly turned her face away and said, "Okay." She got up and walked hurriedly to the kitchen. "Do you want something to drink?"

"Yeah, please."

"Iced tea okay?"

"Yeah."

Dexter supposed he should've felt good about the poorly concealed smile on Denise's face, but he didn't. When he had seen it, a numbing chill had run through his bones.

Four

"Damn, the craziest things happen to you," Mike said. Ibn had just told Mike and Dexter about his brush with the porn business at Block-buster. Colin was in the kitchen getting something to eat. They were all at Dexter and Mike's house getting ready to watch the Monday night football game between the Jaguars and the Titans.

"That was a ballsy-ass white man to ask you some shit like that," Dexter said.

"Yeah, he's just lucky that there were kids in there," Ibn grumbled. "I wanted to slap his sorry ass up. Approaching me with that bullshit. Porno? Hell, y'all know me, I look down on legitimate actors."

"Why?" Colin asked, carrying a tray of buffalo wings and blue cheese dressing and some plates into the living room.

"You know I frown on all that shit. The entertainment business. Models, dancers, actors, or anybody else that has to shake their ass or use their body to make a living. It's like saying you're some fucking dummy who has to use your body because you have nothing to offer upstairs."

Mike spread his arms wide along the back of the couch. "That en-counter in the video store wasn't the only offer you had from a white man this weekend because of your looks," he said.

"What are you talking about?" Ibn asked, sucking the meat off a chicken wing.

"Terence thinks you're a studmuffin."

Dexter and Colin started snickering.

"Who the hell is Terence?" Ibn asked. When he saw that they were too busy laughing to answer him, he racked his brain. Where had he heard that name before? Suddenly, it came to him. He looked at Mike. "Are you talking about that *antiman* you work with?"

"The one and only."

"Lemme tell you something. You tell that fat, faggot motherfucka that the only part of my body he's gonna find in his ass is my foot, if he doesn't keep my name out his mouth."

Mike shrugged off this threat. "Take it easy, Ib. Besides, it's not your *name* he wants in his mouth."

"Fu-uck you."

"Yeah, Ib, have a heart," Colin added. "Why dash the man's dreams?"

"And fuck you, too."

There was a knock at the front. "Are you decent?" a voice called out.

"Come in, Bunches," Dexter said.

She walked in and, seeing Ibn, scrunched her nose. "Uh-oh, wrong question. Decency is probably the last thing that's going on if you're here."

"Did I miss a memo or something? Is this National Fuck-with-Ibn Day?" he asked.

Bunches laughed and walked over to him. She'd had the day off and had taken full advantage of it. She had gotten her hair and nails done and was wearing a brand-new outfit: black Guess jeans and a purple acrylic-cotton blend fitted shirt with a square neckline, Enzio boots and a black belt. She wrapped her arms around his neck and gave him a kiss on the cheek. "Are they picking on you again?"

"You know that, Bunch. These cats don't appreciate me," Ibn said. "How you been, cutie?"

Bunches sat on the arm of the chair and started playing with his hair. "Fine."

"You look good, Bunches. Those jeans almost make your skinny self look like you got a butt," Colin said.

"Yo, sport, you talking? You'd have to eat every wing on that tray just to be called malnourished."

"She smells good, too," Ibn added.

"Oh, Ib, you're such a charmer, you are." She pinched his cheek.

"You going out tonight, Erika?" Mike asked.

"Um-hm," she answered, without bothering to look at him.

"On a date?" he asked.

"Something like that. I just came down to borrow some eyedrops for my contacts." She looked at Dexter. "Do you have any?"

Dexter had a mouthful of food, and he had to swallow before answering. "Look on the dresser in my bedroom," he replied.

Ibn looked at Colin, and they both nodded knowingly. Colin had been stirring ever since he heard the word "date."

"Bunches, can I borrow that movie you showed us a while back?" he asked innocently.

"Which one? *Sankofa?*"

"Yeah, that's it."

She had no idea what he was up to, and she pointed toward the door. "It's upstairs in the living room. I'll bring it down when I go get my coat."

"Don't bother. I'll get it." He jetted out of there, and they heard him bound up the stairs.

Bunches went down the hall.

"Yeah, Colin has been dying to see that movie again, Bunch," Ibn said loud enough for her to hear.

The Jaguars kicked off, and the Titans ran the ball back to the thirty-two-yard line. Bunches came back into the room. She looked into a wall mirror and started putting in the eyedrops. While she was making sure her eyeliner was still okay, she and Mike made eye contact in the mirror.

"So, where are you going?" he asked.

"Just out," she replied casually.

Colin came back into the house and waved the tape at Bunches. "Thanks."

"No problem. Just don't let Stacy break it," she said, and winked at him. She sauntered over to where they all were sitting and started massaging Dexter's shoulders, lightly scratching with her fingernails. "Who's playing?"

"The Titans and the Jaguars. Air McNair is about to open up on these boys," Dexter answered.

"See, that's why I'm Mr. Football and you're not," Ibn snorted. "If you had half a brain, you would know that—"

He was interrupted by the faint sound of a doorbell. Someone was ringing Bunches' place.

Bunches abruptly took her hands off Dexter's shaved bald head and stepped back in horror. She had been so preoccupied that she had failed to see how the situation foretold of disaster. All four of the guys were together, and she had a man coming over. She attempted to make a dash for the door but was beaten to it by Ibn.

"My man," Ibn called out the door, cordially flashing a wide grin. "Bunches—I mean, Erika—is over here. Come meet the family." All the while he used his body to shield Bunches away from the door.

A tall light-skinned man with horn-rimmed glasses stepped into the apartment. He smiled when he saw Bunches. "Hi, Erika."

"Hi, Quincy." Her face was uneasy. She was anxious to get going. "Why don't we head on upstairs? I'll get my coat and we'll go." She made a move in that direction, but Quincy was forestalled by Ibn, who put an arm around his shoulder and began to lead him over to the couch.

"Bunches, it's not like you to be so rude. Why don't you go upstairs and get your coat while I introduce Quincy around?" He pretended not to see her fuming. "Come meet the boys, Q. This here is Dexter Holmes."

"Pleasure to meet you, Dexter." He extended his hand.

Dexter ignored it and gave him a quick, suspicious nod.

"This here is Colin Rogers,"

"How ya doing, Colin." Colin did shake his hand but didn't say anything. He just stared intently at Quincy, as if he were trying to read his mind. Quincy looked away, clearly uncomfortable.

"And the gentleman over there is Mike Lovett."

Mike waved at him. "Nice meeting you, Quincy."

"The pleasure's mine." Quincy waved back and relaxed a little. At least one of them was normal.

"And I'm Ibn Barrington. Have a seat, Q. You like football, don't you?"

"We don't have time for that," Bunches said.

"Are you still here?" Ibn asked. "You could have been upstairs and back by now. I was about to get the brother something to drink."

Bunches weighed her options. Suddenly, asking Quincy to come to her house wasn't such a good idea, despite her ulterior motive for doing so. She rarely had dates pick her up at the house because of Dexter's hassling them. He alone was bad enough, but with Ibn's fool self here, too, who knew what they were capable of?

But, if she acted too much of a fool and started cursing the guys out, Quincy would think she was nuts, and she wouldn't blame him. Who needed that kind of drama on a first date? Besides, the fellas weren't crazy enough to really do anything to him, and wouldn't have the chance anyway. She would grab her keys and they'd be gone.

She walked over to where Quincy was sitting. "I'll be *right* back."

"Take your time. Q's in good hands," Ibn called out from the kitchen.

Bunches left, and they heard her running up the stairs. Colin went to the door and locked it behind her. He strolled over and looked out the window. "Is that your car out there, Quincy?"

"The black one? Yeah, it's a Mazda 626."

"With the Pennsylvania plates, number JHY 219?"

"Um, yeah," he said warily.

"JHY 219," Colin said as he walked to the couch and sat down next to Quincy. "JHY 219," he repeated softly. He fixed Quincy with an engrossed stare.

"So, Q, are you in a fraternity?" Ibn asked from the kitchen.

"Yes, I am," he said proudly. "I'm an Alpha."

A sound of disgust came from Dexter. "That figures," he muttered.

Quincy was still wondering what to make of Dexter's reaction when Ibn walked out of the kitchen carrying two beers. "What's your last name, Q? Where you from?" Ibn gave one to Dexter, who opened it and began drinking. He then sat on the other side of Quincy.

"Carson," Quincy replied. He shifted his body away from Colin, who was making him uncomfortable with his staring. "I'm from Malvern."

"Carson from Malvern? Do you have a brother, Q?" Ibn asked.

"Well, uh, yes."

"What's his name?" Ibn asked.

"Samuel."

"Sammy Carson from Malvern, Pa." Ibn thoughtfully rubbed his chin. Then a look of recognition lit up his face. "I know that nigga!" he said, happily slapping Quincy on the knee.

"Um, I don't think so," Quincy replied. "He's only twelve years old."

"Trust me, I *know* that nigga," Ibn said. Mike muffled a laugh. He was the only one out of Quincy's line of sight, and he had been amusing himself listening to Bunches frantically walk around upstairs trying to find her keys. She was doing so in vain, because Colin had taken them when he went upstairs to get the movie.

"What do you do, Q?" Ibn asked.

"I'm a law student at U. of Penn."

That drew another sound of disgust from Dexter. "Just what the world needs, another goddamned ambulance chaser."

Ibn pushed the other beer in front of Quincy. "Have a drink, Q."

Mike knew the brother was done for now. If he took the drink, all hell would break loose with his first sip. ("What, nigga! You drinking and driving! With *our* Bunches! Get the fuck out of here!") And if he said no, then he'd just better be careful how he said it.

"No, thank you, Ibn . . ." Quincy said.

Leave it at that, kid. Leave it at that, Mike thought.

". . . I don't drink," Quincy added smugly.

Dexter scowled at him. "He didn't *ax* ya if ya drank, muthafucka."

Quincy looked at him, bewildered. "Excuse me?"

"I'se said," Dexter stood up menacingly. "He didn't *ax* you if ya drank, mutha-*fucka*," he repeated, tilting his head from side to side to emphasize each syllable. Quincy looked at Colin, who was still staring at him like a mental patient, for help. He then turned to Ibn, who all of a sudden was very interested in the football game.

"I just meant—"

"I'se knows what ya meant, *nigga*. Jus' cuz I didn't get book learnin' at some Ivy League school don't mean I'm stupid, muthafucka!" Dexter took a step toward him with his fists clenched by his sides. Ibn sprang to life, standing between Dexter and Quincy, who was scared as hell sitting on the couch.

"Take it easy, Dex. Q didn't mean anything by it," Ibn said.

"Naw, fuck that! This boozhee Negro tryin' to play me. What, jus' cuz I'se like an occasional *dra-ank*, it makes me sum kinda aka-holic?"

Mike almost lost it at this point. Normally he would have come to the poor brother's defense by now, but he was enjoying Dexter's performance too much tonight.

"Naw, that's not what you meant, is it, Q?" Ibn looked at Quincy pleadingly, as if to say, "You best save yourself."

"No, brother, I—I meant no offense."

"See, Dex. It was just a misunderstanding." Ibn said.

Hardly placated, Dexter mumbled something and sat back down. The sound of Bunches coming down the steps meant it was time to put this to an end.

Ibn sat down next to Quincy, whose forehead was glistening with sweat. "Please understand, Q, that you are looking at four men to whom the single most precious thing in the world to them is Bunches—Erika, as you call her."

They heard the doorknob jiggle. "Unlock the door," Bunches cried, exasperated.

"So I'm not gonna apologize if we get worked up, because no matter what happens between you two, you'll never love her like we do."

"Oh, this is just our first date," Quincy said nervously.

"Open the door!" Bunches shouted.

"Understood. I'm just saying that if your intentions aren't to come correct, I would hope you would have the intelligence to make this y'all's *last* date." Ibn, Dexter and Colin stared at Quincy until he nodded.

"I understand," he said quietly.

"Good," Ibn said, slapping Quincy's knee again.

"Michael! Open this goddamned door!" Bunches yelled at the top of her lungs.

Ibn walked over and opened the door. "Oh, Bunch, were you out there long? I guess we couldn't hear you over the game."

She pushed him out of the way and saw Quincy had become a sweating, disheveled mess. She looked at Ibn, Colin and Dexter disgustedly, then searched the room until she found Mike, upon whom she fixed her most pissed-off glare.

"You'll have to excuse these fools, Quincy. I assure you they're harmless."

Ibn gave Quincy a look of caution over Bunches' shoulder, as if to say, "You can believe that if you want to, son."

"Some people are caught in a state of perpetual arrested adolescence," she added, continuing to glower at Mike. He averted his eyes to the TV. Bunches grabbed Quincy's hand. "Let's go."

Ibn, Dexter and Colin followed them to the door. "Have a good time," Ibn said, and slapped Quincy so hard on the shoulder his knees buckled. Then he leaned in close to Quincy's ear. "Just remember what we talked about," he whispered.

"You say something?" Bunches snapped at Ibn.

Ibn held his hands up. "I just said have a good time."

Bunches stormed out the door, dragging Quincy in tow. Ibn, Dexter and Colin came out on the lawn to see them off.

"When will you be back?" Dexter asked.

"When I get back!" Bunches answered angrily. She and Quincy got into his car.

"JHY 219, JHY 219," Colin intoned like it was a mantra. Bunches looked at him like he was a fucking weirdo.

Quincy and Bunches took off. Once the car was around the corner, the three of them nearly fell down on the lawn laughing. They made their way back into the house.

"Did you guys like my use of broken English and the way I slurred my words?" Dexter asked. "It's a new wrinkle I've been working on."

"I noticed that," Colin answered, "Kudos are in order, Dex. A brilliant piece of improvisation." He and Ibn applauded. Mike joined them.

"Thank you, thank you," Dexter said, bowing.

"Yo, what if Denise has a daughter?" Colin asked. "Imagine how hard we're gonna be on the fellas that take her out."

They all fell abruptly silent. His statement had instantly sucked the joy out of the room.

"Sorry, Dex," Colin said. "I didn't mean to remind you."

"That's okay, frat." Dexter grimaced as he sat down on the couch. "The situation remains there whether it's spoken or not."

Ibn looked at Mike suspiciously. "How come you stayed so quiet when we were messing with that dude? Usually you try to rein us in."

Dexter and Colin looked at Mike. Like Ibn, they were waiting for an explanation.

Mike shrugged his shoulders. "To hell wit' that cat, I'se didn't like the looks of that boozhee Negro nohow."

They laughed. Mike joined them in front of the TV and grabbed a buffalo wing.

"Colin, when you put Erika's keys back, don't put them in such an obvious place this time. We don't want her to think she's going crazy," Mike said.

"Put them in my bedroom on my dresser. She went in there," Dexter added.

As they turned their attention back to the game, Ibn spotted a look of discomfort on Mike's face. "What's with you?"

"These wings are too spicy," Mike answered, wrapping his bones into a napkin.

"Man, you're soft," Ibn sneered. "I'm about to put some hot sauce on mine."

Mike stared at the carpet. Ibn was right about him being too soft, but the queasiness he was currently feeling had nothing to do with the wings and everything to do with a feeling he felt guilty for even having.

Five

Lunchtime was rapidly approaching at 1500 Market Street, fourth floor, where Colin and Dexter worked as marketing analysts for Penn-Del Investment. Colin hung up the phone and took off his glasses and leaned back in his chair. He thought he felt a migraine coming on. He had been on the phone most of the morning with a consultant from Herf Industries, trying to convince him of the merits of his firm's mutual funds. Sandwiched around that, his mother had called—twice—to saddle him with the bothersome minutiae of her life.

Colin didn't understand why she felt it was proper to call him on his job with trivial nonsense. But how could he tell the woman who brought him into the world, who was ultrasensitive and getting up there in age, that she was a pain in the butt? No, Colin decided, he didn't need that drama. No one could spread guilt and despair over a perceived dis like his mother. Well, except maybe Stacy.

Even as a child, any minor, unintentional slight Colin had committed toward his mother was blown up like it was an affront against God and country. He remembered one incident when he was fifteen years old. Colin and a classmate, Gloria, were studying at the Bergen County library for a project they were working on for history class. When his mother came to pick them up, Colin made the mistake of opening the car door for his classmate and not his mother.

Mrs. Rogers was quiet all the way to Gloria's house, but as soon as they dropped her off, she chewed Colin a new asshole all the way home. *"You a sorry-ass sumthin'! How dare you open the door for that little bitch and not your mother!"*

"Hi, Colin."

He stopped strolling through the brier patch of his past and put his glasses back on. Stephanie was leaning over his cubicle looking at him.

"Hey, Stephanie. You feeling better?"

She smiled. "Yes, I am. So you noticed that I was out yesterday?"

"Of course, why wouldn't I?"

"Humph," she muttered playfully. She came into his cubicle, reached over and brushed a piece of lint off his shoulder. "You look nice."

"Thanks, so do you," he replied.

In fact, Colin noticed, she looked very nice. He liked the way she was wearing her hair—twisted tightly at the roots with auburn highlights on the ends. She had on a black suit with wide-legged slacks. The jacket lapel was open to the top of her cleavage, with a soft white, wide-collared rayon shirt, laying over top. Beyond just the clothes, Stephanie was an attractive woman, and she had a wonderful smile that made her even prettier.

"Thank you," she said. "You like the boots?" She lifted her boot onto the arm of his chair and raised her pant leg.

Colin noticed the boot, plus her sculpted calf. "Very nice."

Stephanie smiled and set her foot back on the floor. She rested her arm on the top of his cubicle, not wanting to leave. "So, how was your weekend?"

Colin shrugged. "It was okay, I guess. I didn't do much, just a little car shopping."

"You getting rid of your Accord?"

"No, I love that car. I was shopping for something for my lady."

"Oh," Stephanie said softly, and straightened up. They were joined by Dexter, who'd overheard them talking.

"Hey, Steph."

"Hi."

Dexter looked at Colin. "Ibn's downstairs waiting. You ready to go to lunch?"

"Yeah," Colin said, rising out of his chair. "Can we bring you any-thing back?" he asked Stephanie.

"No, thank you. I have some work to do. I'll see you guys when you get back," she said over her shoulder as she walked away.

Dexter shook his head as he and Colin made their way to the eleva-tor. "You can bring her back something, all right, but it ain't food."

Colin dismissed him, "Aw, man . . ."

"Aw, man—nothing. You're not blind. You know she has a thing for you."

Colin scrunched his face up. "I don't know that."

"Oh, you don't? Then why do you always have to bring up Stacy when you're talking to Stephanie? Like she wants to hear *that* shit."

"Well, if you are right, then it's good to let her know that I'm not available."

"But Steph is *cute*, Colin," Dex said as he pressed the button for the lobby.

"Regardless, I have Stacy."

Dexter nearly bit a hole through his tongue as the elevator doors opened.

Bunches was taking advantage of the warm weather and studying at Rittenhouse Park. She and her stack of textbooks were sitting on steps that led down to a fountain. The park was bustling with activity. Vari-ous groups of people were tossing Frisbees, eating lunches, chatting and reading books. Suddenly she felt uneasy, as if eyes were on her. She looked up, expecting to see some bum scoping her out—and instead saw three bums.

Colin, Ibn and Dexter were standing about fifty feet away eyeing her cautiously. Colin was waving a white handkerchief in the air, and Dexter had his hands clasped together as if he was praying. What caught her eye, however, was what Ibn was holding aloft. It was a Pat's cheesesteak, and she was hungry. She suppressed a smile and buried her head in her book, turning away from them.

"Come on, Bunches, forgive us," Dexter said as they approached.

She looked around as if she'd heard something but couldn't figure out where it was coming from.

"Yeah, you know we don't know how to act," Colin added. "You know it's only because we care about you." He sat down next to Bunches and put his arm around her. She looked at him so icily he quickly removed it.

"Daaaamn," he said.

"Bunch, don't be like that," Ibn said.

"Don't be like what?" she asked testily. "Don't be pissed off that I can't bring a date home without you clowns terrorizing him?"

"Yo, we thought you wanted us to check him out," Ibn said. "We figured that was the reason you were taking so long to come back downstairs."

"Don't be ridiculous. I couldn't find my keys."

"Yeah," Dex added, "you left them on my dresser."

"So you see, it was all a misunderstanding," Ibn said.

"Ibn, I'm serious. Y'all's nonsense is getting real tired. It ain't cute anymore. I'm twenty-four years old."

"I know, I know."

"Do you? Do you? Do you?" She pointedly asked each member of the trio.

All of them shook their heads resignedly, and Bunches softened a bit. Truth be known, she enjoyed the attention the guys lavished on her.

"And you, thinking you can seduce me with food. Like I'm still a child."

Ibn smiled. "Yeah, you were much easier to deal with in your 'Munch-a-Bunch' days. Where is that chubby little girl I remember?"

"She grew up," Bunches answered. "But she still likes cheesesteaks, so gimme that." They laughed as she snatched the cheesesteak out of Ibn's hand.

"Just the way you like it, with Cheez Whiz and fried onions," Colin said. He reached into the bag they had brought along. "We also got you a Frank's vanilla cream soda and peanut butter Tastykake for dessert."

Bunches' mouth was full, so she gave them a thumbs-up as way of acknowledgment, which made them laugh again.

"How did you guys know I was going to be out here?" she said, wiping her mouth.

"Mike told us you like to come here in between classes."

"Oh," she said. Mike knew her schedule. He used to join her when he could, but since he'd got his promotion, he hadn't had time. At least she thought it was because of the promotion. "Speaking of Michael, who is this girl Sharice?"

Ibn scoffed at the mention of her name. "And on that note . . ." He stood up.

"What?" Bunches asked.

"It's just that Mike is being Mike, as usual," Dexter said. "Making his usual bad choices in women."

Ibn tugged at his belt, agitated. "Naw, Dex, this time really takes the cake. Do you know how many niggas I know that done did Sharice in the butt or told me how good she was at licking their balls?"

"Ibn, please, I'm trying to eat here."

"Sorry, Bunch. It's just that Mike gets me so mad with this. What is his fascination with whores?"

"Ib, you heard Mike," Colin said, feeling compelled to stick up for Mike since he wasn't there to defend himself, and also, because he was sure that Ibn raked him over the coals about Stacy when he was out of earshot. "Maybe, she is different now, being saved and all. People do change. You're judging her from years back."

Ibn snapped his head back in disgust. "Colin, going to church don't mean jack to me. Some of the freakiest women I know sit in somebody's church every Sunday. Searching for redemption. Maybe Sharice has changed. *Maybe*, I'll give you that. But it's highly unlikely 'cause I know what kind of freak she was."

"You sound like you know from firsthand experience," Bunches said as she bit into her cheesesteak.

"Naw," Ibn said, backpedaling. "I just listened to the stories. The exploits of Sharice and her tireless pussy are legendary, you know, tall tales on a par with Davy Crockett or Paul Bunyan." He smiled mischievously. "Except she didn't do her best work with a strong blue ox, but with long black cocks."

"Damn, Ib," Colin said.

"I know y'all thinking I'm being an asshole—"

"Yep, and a hypocrite as well," Bunches interrupted.

"—but I know how her mind works. She knows Mike is a good guy. If she gets with him, it's instant credibility for her, which is what she needs now that she is back in the area where she did most of her dirt. Why didn't she hook up with him years ago?"

"She could've grown up," Colin offered.

"Frat, let's say she is coming correct, has done a one-eighty as far as her feelings toward Mike and no longer has the desire to screw brothers left and right. All highly unlikely, I still say, but just for argument's sake, let's assume her religious awakening is genuine, and she's not perpetrating a fraud. Do you think all those men that she done skanked it up with are gonna buy her transformation? She can barely step out of the house without bumping into one of her old tricks. What, they gonna respect her now? They still gonna try to fuck her. What is she gonna say, 'I'm saved'? They gonna be like 'Good, because I *saved* some dick for you. On your knees, be-yotch.' "

"Who cares what they say?" Bunches countered. "If she says it ain't happening anymore, it ain't happening anymore."

Ibn unbuttoned the cuffs of his shirt and began rolling them up. "Okay. Then what would that mean for Mike? He has to spend the rest of his life fighting niggas 'cause they disrespecting his woman? He'd have to move her hoey ass to Alaska just to get some peace." Ibn threw his arms out. "Why my boy gotta be cold? And Jesus Christ, what if they have kids?" He shuddered at the thought.

"You mean, it's serious?" Bunches asked, alarmed. More alarm than she intended.

Ibn took note of her apprehension. "Not yet, but I have a feeling it might get to be. He's always liked her. Always made her out to be something more than what she was. What he has always failed to realize is that once you get past the titties and the ass with Sharice, there's not a whole hell of a lot else."

"Well, even if you are right, what can you do? He's a grown man." Bunches said, annoyed. "If he wants to be a fool for some woman, then he's gonna be a fool."

"To hell with that, Bunch. What does brotherhood and friendship mean, then? If a person has a weakness in an area, then his boys should look out for him."

"What's Mike's weakness?" Colin asked.

"Y'all know what," Ibn said casually. "Love-of-hoe-itis. Y'all know that song when Snoop Dogg says 'We don't love dem hoes'? Mike should be forced to listen to that until it sinks in."

Dexter, Colin and Ibn laughed. Bunches stared at her soda bottle, lost in thought.

"And I am not a hypocrite, young lady," Ibn said. "I admit I'm an asshole."

"An admission absolves you from culpability, then? I was just wondering if your theory of boys protecting each other from that which will do them harm applies to you."

"Of course it does."

"Then Colin, Dexter and Michael had better figure out a way to protect you from yourself because you're your own worst enemy."

Ibn joined in the laughter even though it was at his expense. "I thought I told you before, that dry wit of yours is unbecoming." He checked his watch. "I've gotta head back across the bridge. I'm expecting a shipment at the Voorhees store."

"So? You're the boss. What's your hurry?" Bunches asked.

"I wanna check to make sure everything's cool."

She looked at him shrewdly. "Um-hm. I noticed you've taken *off* your tie. You're probably not heading anywhere except to do some dirt. To get a little afternoon delight."

Ibn's look of chagrin was more than ample proof that she was on to something.

"Ibn, why do you have to be such a dog?" she asked, irritated. "Why can't you just be happy with the woman that you have?"

Ibn made a point of never discussing his philandering around Bunches, feeling it would compromise her relationship with Tiffany, though he had no doubt where her loyalty ultimately lay.

"Bunches, you don't know what it's like to be me. It's hard. Women throw themselves at me on a daily basis. Add that to the fact that I have a sex drive from hell and . . ." Ibn shrugged his shoulders, "difficulties are bound to come up."

"And panties are bound to come down," Dexter added. Colin and he snickered.

Ibn studied Bunches' face. She wasn't finding any of this amusing. "Maybe there is something wrong with me. After you graduate med school, maybe you can help me diagnose and treat it."

"I can do that now. The diagnosis is immaturity, and the treatment is growing the hell up. It amazes me how a man can have a quality woman in front of him and still want to chase other tail," Bunches said, really talking about more than just Ibn and Tiffany. "And you got the *nerve* to talk about Sharice's whoring."

"Do I have to explain to you the difference between men and women again?" Ibn asked.

"Spare me the 'double standard' speech," she said, extending her palm stop-like toward him. "I want my lunch to stay down."

"There's that troubling sarcasm of yours again," Ibn said.

"Keep it up, Ibn. You're gonna lose Tiffany."

Ibn gave her a superior smile. "Please, Bunches. I keep Tiffany well-dressed *and* well-tressed, well-heeled *and* well-wheeled, well-fed *and* well-bed. She's well-jeweled and dammit, well-ruled. Trust me, she ain't going nowhere." Dexter and Colin laughed.

"You can rhyme all you want, Jesse. I still say the one piece of jewelry that is most important to Tiffany is the one you refuse to give to her."

Dexter stood up and tucked in his shirt. "Didn't you say that Tiffany has stopped pressuring you about marriage?"

"Yeah, she has," he said triumphantly. "She's finally given it a rest."

Bunches was about to eat one of her Tastykakes but stopped in midair and looked at Ibn. "And you think that's a good thing?"

Ibn looked incredulously at Dexter and Colin. He had stretched out on the steps with his arms folded behind his head, soaking in the sunshine. "You *damn* right that's a good thing," he said finally. "You guys ready to go?"

"Yeah," Dexter said.

"I'm gonna stay a little longer," said Colin. "We're only a couple of blocks away from the office. I'll walk back."

"Penn-Del Investment doesn't want you back by a certain time?" Bunches asked.

"No, they don't care as long as the work gets done." Colin cracked his knuckles. "As long as I'm back by three. There is a group of seventh-graders coming from P.S. 23 that I'm meeting with today."

"Yeah?" Ibn asked. "What for?"

"They're doing a mock stock market at their school," Colin said. "I just take them around the building and explain the different jobs to them."

"Oh." Ibn looked down at Bunches and flashed her a wide grin. It was the same skirt-raising smile he had used a million times. "I'll see you later, cutie."

"Un-hm. Thanks for the meal and good luck whoremongering," she said wickedly.

"Just for you, I decided not to. I'm really gonna head back to Jersey."

"Don't do it for me, Ibn. Do it for yourself."

"I'll see you back at the house, Bunch."

"Okay, Dexter."

"All right, Colin."

"Later, Ib."

Dexter and Ibn had started to walk away before Dexter turned around. "Colin, what time should I tell Stephanie to expect you back? You know she's gonna ask me."

"Ha-ha."

Ibn and Dexter waved one last time and disappeared.

"Who's Stephanie?"

Colin sat down next to Bunches. "A woman that me and Dex work with. Dex thinks she has a thing for me."

Bunches looked at him suspiciously. "Oh? And what do you think?"

Colin shrugged his shoulders. "I don't."

Bunches studied his face. "Geesh, Colin, how can you see out of those things?" She took off his glasses and started wiping the smudges away with a handkerchief. She looked through them. "Daa-amn, you *are* blind."

Colin squinted at her, blinking rapidly, "You know," he blurted out, "I'm thinking about getting one of those C-class Benzes."

She handed his glasses back to him. "Yeah? Life must be treating you well."

"I'm doing okay. Besides, they start in the low thirties, they're pretty reasonable."

All of this seemed very mysterious. "You trading in your car?"

"No, but we need to get something else. Stacy's car is about done."

"So in a way, you'll be getting two new cars."

"What do you mean?"

"If you get a Benz, Stacy will start letting you drive your Accord again."

Colin clucked his tongue. "Ib's right about that sarcasm of yours, Bunch." He picked up her last peanut butter cake and bit into it. "So, what do you think?"

"You already know what I think."

"No, I don't."

"Yes, you do."

"Well, humor me again."

"I think you have a lot more to offer a woman than a fancy car. And any woman that doesn't know that isn't a woman you need to be with."

Colin chewed slowly. Sometimes Bunches' bluntness aggravated him, but he knew she would tell him what she really thought, which is why he'd wanted to ask her.

"What makes you think Stacy has anything to do with it?"

Bunches narrowed her eyes at him.

"All right," he relented, "she might have something to do with it, but we do need a car. And what's a little extra a month if you're getting something you like? I mean, if I don't live a little now while I'm young . . ."

"Colin."

"After children come, then there'll be a whole new set of priorities. . . ."

"*Colin,*" Bunches repeated. She reached over and grabbed his hand. "You know that if there's one woman on this planet you don't have to justify anything to, it's me. I'm just saying, ideally a couple's happiness should come in working toward and reaching the same goals. But if it doesn't, then you should make yourself happy before you worry about making someone else happy."

Colin thought that over. He brought her hand up to his lips and kissed it. "When did you become so wise?"

"Wise nothing, I just can't stand Stacy. And I'm sure the feeling's mutual."

"No," Colin said defensively, "Stacy likes you." It was a blatant lie and he knew it.

Stacy especially resented that Colin helped support Bunches monetarily. (*"Who does that bitch think she is that she can't work? Royalty? Some fucking African princess of some country I don't know about? Tell me, so I can curtsy next time I see the bitch."*) And then there were all those conversations centered around her belief that either he was already fucking Bunches, or hoping to. Colin remembered those arguments vividly because Bunches was the one thing he didn't let Stacy get her way on, which only aroused her suspicions more.

"Colin, I know I'm still in school," Bunches said levelly, "but I get there by car, not by short yellow bus."

Ibn fished along the dashboard for the ticket to give the parking attendant.

"Did you mean what you said back there?"

Ibn paid the fee and drove through the gate. "Yeah, I changed my mind. I think I really am gonna head back to the store." He looked at Dexter as he pulled up to a red light. "Did *you* mean what you said back there?"

"About what?"

"About letting Bunches grow up. Not interfering so much."

"Actually, Ib, I never said that. I just acknowledged that I interfered."

They both laughed as the light turned green. Ibn had to get into the left lane, pulling ahead of a horse-drawn carriage slowly plodding along in their way.

"So, this Stephanie really likes Colin, huh?"

"Ib, the girl is starry-eyed around him, bumping into furniture and shit. And cute—ten times better looking than Stacy, twenty times better if you want to include personality. She does the same thing as me and Colin, though she hasn't been there as long. I figure she's making at least forty-five, maybe fifty grand. But he won't even give her a chance."

"Because of *Stacy*."

They both shook their heads. No words needed to be said on that particular subject.

As they pulled up in front of Dexter's office building, Ibn double-parked and put on his flashers.

"All right man, I'll catch you later," Dexter said as he got out of the car.

"All right."

Dexter turned around and leaned in the window. "Do you think maybe we should, you know, ease up on getting so involved in Bunches' love life?"

Once again there was a momentary silence between them. They already knew what the other was thinking.

"Oh, *hell* no," they said in unison.

Six

Ibn drove through the main entrance of the Hamilton Mall and headed to the Strawbridge & Clothier side of the sprawling complex. Tiffany had called him at his store asking him to meet her here at six-thirty. When he asked her why, she wouldn't say and hung up. His repeated attempts to call her back on her cellular had gone unanswered.

He drove up and down the rows of cars, looking for Tiffany's Lexus. And he was getting agitated. Just as he was about to make another pass through, he saw the car in a far corner of the lot, parked off by itself.

As he headed in its direction, she turned her car on and came to meet him halfway. The two luxury cars slowly approached each other, his black Benz and her pearl Lexus, like two cautious boxers.

When their cars were alongside each other, Ibn heard club music pulsating from Tiffany's car. He recognized the song "Follow Me."

"What's going on, Tiff?" he asked, a little irritated. He didn't like playing games, and he didn't like that she had been sitting by herself in a Lexus in an isolated part of the parking lot. That shit wasn't safe. When she didn't answer, he was about to start basing, but was stopped in his tracks when she lowered her window all the way. Her pretty, expressive face was cloaked in a sad smile. Her spirited, animated eyes that danced whenever she was excited or happy were dull with melancholy.

"Come on," she said, and started to pull off. Ibn did a K turn and followed her.

As they drove wherever the hell they were going, Ibn noticed Tiffany repeatedly glancing at him in her rearview mirror. Whenever they stopped for a red light, she would look at him the whole time they were waiting for it to change. It was almost as if she expected to look back one of these times and find him gone. Which wasn't too far from the truth, Ibn thought, because this shit was getting tiresome.

Each turn they made took them deeper and deeper into the boonies. Soon, they were on an isolated stretch of asphalt with only a few, well-spread-out houses to break up the monotony of densely packed forestry. This girl better have a hell of a reason for taking my ass out in the middle of the Jersey Pinelands, Ibn muttered to himself. When he saw Tiffany's right-turn signal blink again, he hesitated before he followed. She was turning down a dirt road, and he'd just had the Benz washed earlier that afternoon. Now he was truly pissed.

After going several hundred yards down the road Tiffany stopped abruptly in a clearing. Ibn had to slam on his breaks. Damn, he almost hit her car.

Tiffany turned off her engine and turned on her interior light. Puzzled, Ibn watched her as she stood up. It appeared that she was sliding her skirt off. Hey now, this is starting to get interesting. She stole a few furtive glances as if she was making sure no one was watching. Keep going, baby, Ibn thought, it's just you, me and the bears. Dusk had fallen, so he turned on his headlights to help her out as well as to enhance his own viewing. Tiffany looked in the rearview mirror and gave him a sly grin. She knew he was a voyeur at heart.

She sat back down in the driver's seat and kept her eyes on him through the mirror. As she slowly unbuttoned her blouse, Ibn turned off his radio and unzipped his pants. He could hear the sound of club music emanating from Tiffany's car. Ibn lifted the tilt steering wheel to give him more room to maneuver and deal with "the matter at hand."

By the time Tiffany slid her bra straps off, revealing her slender shoulders, Ibn was in full masturbatory stroke. When her window came down and a naked arm motioned for him to join her, he was ready. He turned off his car and headlights.

With his penis swinging in the wind, Ibn stalked toward his lady. He went around to the front passenger-side door. He opened it just in time to see Tiffany's splendid ass shimmying toward the backseat. Valiantly, he tried to stop it by palming a cheek in each of his hands and slurping his tongue along it. His heroic efforts were in vain, as Tiffany continued on to the backseat, selfishly taking her behind with her.

Ibn opened the rear door. Tiffany's nude body was now laid out on the backseat with her legs spread open. Her right leg was on the rear window ledge next to a speaker that was pulsating with the throbbing bass line of "Get Deep." She started pumping her hips to the beat of the music, which she did so well it made him salivate. She then slid her hands down to her inner thighs to give Ibn a better look at what was awaiting him.

"Come get deep inside me, baby."

Ibn quickly undid his belt and slid his pants and boxers to his ankles, where they rested on top of his shoes. As he climbed into the car and on top of her, his hip brushed against her pussy. She was already wet. A good thing, because Ibn wasn't interested in any foreplay and, for once, neither was Tiffany, who was already begging him to fuck her.

Ibn wrapped one arm underneath her and gripped the edge of the seat with his right hand for balance. His feet dangled outside the car. He slid his penis inside her and his tongue into her receptive mouth. Ibn was glad they brought two cars because he planned to drill Tiffany through the seat, floor and undercarriage of this one.

He was also relieved that they were in the middle of nowhere because Tiffany was making a lot of noise, as if she was trying to make herself heard over the Jungle Brothers song, "I'll House You," which was now blaring through the speakers.

Ibn took a break from his thrusting to brush the hair out of Tiffany's face, where her perspiration had matted it.

"I love you, Ibn."

He sucked her chin and redoubled his efforts. Tiffany moaned and tugged at the back of his shirt, which was becoming drenched with his sweat.

"You're not done with me yet?" she asked him in his ear.

"Not even."

As "Always There" played, Ibn got off Tiffany and turned her over.

Climbing out of the car, he stood up and wiped the sweat out of his eyes with his sleeve. He looked skyward. Damn, it was almost dark. Ibn reached back in the car and grabbed Tiffany by the hips. He raised her up, so that she was bent over with her left knee resting on the seat. He took a second to enjoy the visual of her ass poking out of the car and decided to tease her. He reached between her thighs and slowly traced the back of his hand from her navel to the small of her back. Then he lightly touched her eager clitoris with the tip of his penis. Tiffany arched her back and groaned in anticipation. Ibn firmly grabbed her by the hips and went back to pumping.

A breeze stirred up and blew against Ibn's bare ass. Mary J. Blige was singing, "Let No Man Put Asunder" accompanied by Tiffany's various yelps and moans. Though he was unable to see her face, Tiffany's growling noises excited him to the point where he finally succumbed and ejaculated.

He ducked his head back in the car and turned Tiffany on her stomach across the backseat. He lay on top of her. Both were exhausted and were still for a couple of minutes.

"Yo, Tiff."

"Yeah, babe?"

"Thanks for driving."

They shared a chuckle and decided to get dressed. Ibn stood outside and fixed his pants and adjusted his sweat-soaked shirt. He had a shirt identical to it in his trunk but didn't get it, because he would then have to explain his reason for having it to Tiffany. He was glad that he had not visited one of his tricks. He would have been a little spent before this encounter with Tiffany, and this had been some of the best sex he had had with her in a long time.

"Damn, Ibn, I feel like I need to ice down. You trying to kill me?" Tiffany asked.

"I aim to please."

"And you always had good aim, didn't you?"

Ibn laughed.

"Come here, babe," she said.

Ibn sighed. Tiffany liked to be held after sex, but he hoped that she wasn't expecting to cuddle with him out here in the middle of West Bumblefuck. He got into the front passenger seat.

Tiffany crawled on top of him and eased the seat back as far as it would go and rested her head on his chest. Ibn shut the door and turned off the interior light, worried about draining the battery. He opened the panel to the moonroof.

"It's been a long time, hasn't it?" she asked.

"What do you mean?"

"Since we did *this*."

Ibn looked down at her. "What are you talking about? I had you on the patio, night before last."

Tiffany looked at his face to gauge whether he was serious. When she realized he was, she wildly burrowed her head into his chest and dug her nails into his arms like she was in pain.

"Damn, Tiff! What's the matter with you?" Ibn asked.

She pushed herself off him and left the car barefoot. Ibn followed her.

"What the hell is your problem?"

Tiffany stopped and turned around. Even in the darkness he recognized the look on her face. It was the same sadness he had seen earlier in the parking lot, but this time it was accompanied by tears.

"Ibn, look around you. Don't you remember this place? This is the first place we ever made love."

Ibn looked around. "Oh, yeah," he said. They were only about ten miles from the college Tiffany had attended.

She sucked her teeth and shook her head like she was disgusted at the sight of him. She got into Ibn's Benz and turned on the ignition.

"Tiffany, come on. Wait."

She wheeled the car around toward the dirt road.

"Wait!" Ibn yelled. "I'm not sure if I know how to get back!"

Ibn watched as the taillights of the Benz disappeared.

Seven

"What's wrong with a place like this?"

"Nothing. I just don't want to live in a duplex."

Dexter leaned back on the couch. The look of obstinacy on Denise's face was pissing him off, and he was struggling to keep his anger from rising to the surface. He chose his next words carefully, saying what he felt, but diplomatically.

"Denise, after the baby is born, I'm sure you're not gonna want to rush right back to work . . ." (*Not that you make any real money at your bullshit job, anyway*) ". . . and we're going to incur a lot of new expenses . . ." (*Like getting your non-driving ass a car*) ". . . which would make getting around for you and the child easier . . ." (*'Cause if you think you're lugging my child around on buses and subways, you're crazy*) ". . . If we buy an affordable duplex . . ." (*Which is at least three steps up from the tiny apartment in North Philly your complaining ass is currently living in*) ". . . we could live in a quality area . . ." (*My child ain't being raised in the hood, that's for goddamn sure*) ". . . and rent the other half of it out to help pay the mortgage. What's wrong with us getting a little help? . . ." (*C'mon, woman, work with me, damn.*)

Denise looked at him, indifferent to his logic. "I want us to have our own house."

Dexter marched into the kitchen to check on the catfish he was frying. He breaded another piece and steeped it in the hot oil. He had learned long ago that you can't reason with an irrational female. If a woman decides that she isn't going to listen to common sense, then you might as well save your breath. He hated to see the way women could get their minds made up that they were right about something—no matter how specious their rationale was—and *fuck* what anybody else told them different. Normally, he would cut a lady loose the first time he saw this trait in her.

But Denise wasn't going anywhere. Which she knew, which is why she could afford to be stubborn. Truth is, she held all the cards. If she was adamant about what type of house she wanted to live in, what could Dexter do? Say no? Buy what he wanted to and gamble that she would eventually relent? He ruled that out as too risky. She might call his bluff and decide that she'd just stay in North Philly. Being raised in Newark, he wanted to keep his child from living in the inner city at all costs. He went to the refrigerator and bent over, looking for margarine for the rice he was making. He heard Denise join him in the kitchen.

"Dexter?"

"Yeah?"

"My friend Marla lives in a duplex, and she was telling me how much she regrets signing the lease. How she wishes she had more than a wall to separate her and her children from the noisy family and bad-behind kids that live next to her."

So now Marla had more influence than he did on where he was going to live? He could imagine her and Denise's conversation. ("Girl, make that man get you your own house. He's got the money.")

"Denise, we would own the place. We would choose who we rented the upstairs to."

"I just think an upstairs-downstairs would be better for us to have, for our kids."

Dexter nearly fell face-first into a big bowl of potato salad. Did she just say *kids*, as in more than one? He composed himself before speaking, but still looked in the refrigerator instead of facing Denise.

"They make duplexes where you can have an upstairs."

"I know." She hesitated. "It's just that I want a single-family home with our own yard. I've either lived up under or next to people my entire life."

Now they were getting to the real reason. And what?—it was now his responsibility to provide her relief? What was he, her one-way ticket out of the 'hood? Dexter wished it had been that easy for him.

The refrigerator felt too cold, and Dexter fiddled with the temperature-control knob. He thought about the first time he and Denise had met, at Club Exodus. He still remembered how good her ass had looked in those tight brown leather pants. He hadn't been able to take his eyes off it the entire night. He just had to have it, so he pursued it, and got it. And now look at where it had landed him. But hell, Dexter sighed, he was hardly the first brotha brought down by a black woman's rump. He bet that the great ancient civilizations of Africa were brought down over something to do with a fine sistah's ass.

And once he had hit it, Denise's pussy was far too good for him to just make her a one-night-done-right encounter. Besides, he kinda liked Denise, just not near enough to wanna spend the rest of his life with her.

He closed the refrigerator and turned around to face her. She looked very anxious, and he frowned. Regardless of what happened between them, they were always going to have to deal with each other because of the child. Growing in this woman's belly was his seed, his own small piece of immortality. That alone meant that he should treat her with respect. And while he certainly didn't love Denise, he did understand her. Most of all, Dexter wanted to make that look on her face go away.

"Okay, Denise, I'll see what I can do." He leaned over and gave her a kiss. This action startled her, but she seemed to enjoy it. At the very least, the anxiety left her face. For the next eight months, he wanted Denise to have as stress-free a life as possible. If he had to curse her out or show his ass, it would wait until after the baby was born.

She left the kitchen, probably to preserve "the moment" that they had just shared. Dexter eyed her as she walked out. Denise had a tight package, that's for sure. Later that evening maybe they could practice being a married couple and fulfill some conjugal duties.

"Where's Mike?" Denise asked from the living room.

"I don't know. He's probably over at Sharice's."

"Who's Sharice?"

"Some girl he's into."

Denise's eyebrows lifted. "Really? Since when? I mean, has he known her long?"

"They've known each other forever, but she's only recently moved back into the area." He walked into the living room and handed her a plate of food. "Why do you care?"

"Thank you—I don't. It's just that Marla has been asking you for months to hook her up with Mike, and now it might be too late."

Dexter chuckled to himself and walked back in the kitchen. Marla was a bossy, ignorant, loud two-hundred-pound woman with two children and zero prospects. He was supposed to set her up with his boy? What, Mike wasn't supposed to want better? Dexter thought as he fixed himself a plate. How come women never ask what they are bringing to the table, what it is exactly *they* have to offer a man?

In bed that night, Dexter did get a taste of what life with Denise might offer. She, too, was interested in practicing being a married couple. She spurned his advances. "I have a headache," she said, "and you smell like fish."

"Stacy," Colin said as the waitress walked away to tend to yet another request, "she's doing the best she can."

"Like hell. She acts like she don't want to work, like she's doing me a favor."

Colin could hardly blame the waitress for having an attitude. Stacy hadn't given the poor girl a moment's peace since they sat down. She complained about their seats, the silverware not being clean, the room being too chilly. And that was before the waitress had made the mistake of giving Colin too warm a smile. Then it was on. Stacy made a special request, then sent the food back when it arrived. She repeatedly stopped the waitress, asking for more napkins, refills, ground pepper and anything else she could think of. At one point the waitress, whose name was Gail, gave Colin a look that made him cringe with embarrassment. He recognized the look, for he had seen it many times. It was a combination of a "you deal with this bitch?" and "why aren't you saying something before I have to hurt this girl and lose my job?"

Colin sympathized with Gail, but he refused to intercede on her behalf. He had already convinced Stacy not to call the manager over to

complain about her performance. If he said anything else in her defense, Stacy would interpret it the wrong way and accuse him of wanting to fuck Gail and unleash all her fury on him. Hell, Colin thought,
better Gail for one hour than me all night.

"See, that's why I wanted to go to Le Bec Fin," Stacy said.

"Le Bec Fin is too—"

"Expensive." Stacy finished for him. "I know, I know, you don't
have to tell me."

Gail walked over to the table with the mints Stacy had requested.
"Will there be anything else?" she asked, trying her damnedest to keep
the exasperation out of her voice.

Stacy took a sip of her coffee to make Gail wait for her answer.
Colin fidgeted during the awkward pause. Stacy then flipped her wrist
toward her disdainfully and said, "Just the check."

"You didn't let me finish, Stacy. I was gonna say that we should
watch our money now since we . . ." Colin hesitated, "are about to buy
a Benz."

Stacy jumped up and came over to sit on Colin's lap. As she was
hugging and kissing him fervently, Gail brought their check over
and set it on the table. Before she walked away, Colin and she made
eye contact over Stacy's shoulder. She gave him a halfhearted smile.
When Stacy released him and went back to her chair, she noticed the
little leather folder on the table.

"When did that bitch put the check on the table?" She looked
around, searching the room for Gail.

"While you were hugging me. I guess she didn't want to interrupt,"
Colin said. Damn, so her mind was already back on the waitress? Her
celebration over getting the Benz certainly hadn't lasted long. It was
almost as if she knew in advance she was going to get the car.

Later, as they were walking through the parking lot, Colin patted
his pockets frantically. "I left my credit card in the check folder."

Stacy sighed exasperatedly. "Colin, you are so careless."

He handed her the keys. "Here, you go bring the car around. I'll be
right back." He briskly headed back to the restaurant before Stacy
could answer.

Once inside, he sought out Gail. Stacy had made sure Colin had left her a minuscule, insulting tip when he paid the bill. He apologized for Stacy giving her such a hard time and handed her a twenty.

Gail looked at him and smiled. "Did you propose tonight?" she asked him.

"Oh, you mean the display—no, she was just excited." Colin answered.

Gail hesitated before deciding to say, "You know, when I saw you coming back in here, I was kinda hoping it was to ask me for my phone number. You're a handsome guy."

Colin looked down and away, trying in vain to conceal his blushing. "No, um, it was just to apologize, but thank you for the compliment."

"You're welcome."

Stacy was wheeling the car around to the front entrance of the restaurant. As Colin got into the car, he was still smiling.

"Did you get your card back?" Stacy asked as she pulled off.

"Huh? Oh, yeah."

"What's the goofy grin for?" Stacy asked.

"A brotha can't be happy?"

"Not if a sistah don't know why." She eyed him suspiciously. "You didn't give that bitch any more money, did you?"

"Which *bitch* are you referring to?" Colin asked, still feeling his oats because of Gail's interest in him.

"I'm referring to that—" Stacy then picked up on his innuendo and glared at him. "Fuck you, Colin. You gonna find out what kind of bitch I can be."

Colin sighed. "As if I don't already know," he wanted to say but didn't dare. He didn't want to walk home.

Eight

"Yes, Mrs. Rogers," Ibn said, sitting on the sofa, talking on the phone. "Yep, he just ate some of my mother's cooking—two plates of it, in fact."

Colin looked at Dexter and shook his head. Dexter just shrugged and continued flipping through Ibn's copy of *Vibe* magazine.

"Mmm-hmm, definitely, I agree with you wholeheartedly," Ibn continued. "He shouldn't put all his eggs in one basket . . . Right . . . right . . . He should *definitely* date other women."

"Here we go," Colin muttered.

"You and me both, Mrs. Rogers, you and me both." Ibn looked at Colin and shook his head dejectedly. "I don't know what he sees in that girl, either."

Dexter laughed, while Colin gave Ibn the finger.

"I'm gonna work on him at this end, don't you worry about that," Ibn said, "I'm looking out for him, don't you worry 'bout that." Ibn chuckled and broke out in a wide grin. "You're right, he sure is lucky to have a friend like me."

Colin made a motion like he was going to gag.

"Oh, yes—I'm definitely coming up for Thanksgiving, but I'm sure I'll see you before then . . . Okay, I'll give everyone your love. . . . Ha-ha, yeah, except her . . . Okay, good night."

Ibn closed Colin's phone and flipped it back to him.

"Thanks for running interference," Colin said. "She was wearing me out."

"No problem," Ibn said, taking off his shoes. "I like talking to your mom, especially when she starts riffing on Stacy. That shit is funny."

"Yeah, it's downright hilarious," Colin said as he put his phone back into his pocket.

"Why don't you just tell her what the deal is, Colin?" Dexter asked. "That you're not a child and you're tired of her constant badgering. That she needs to respect you as a man."

Ibn spoke up before Colin could answer: "Who are you talking about Dex? Mrs. Rogers or Stacy?"

Ibn collapsed on the couch next to Dexter, both of them howling.

"You niggas look like two magpies—a regular fucking Heckle and Jeckle giggling over there," Colin said, throwing a couch pillow at them. "Why don't you just finish the story you were telling us before my mom called?"

"Yeah, Ib," Dexter said, exhausted from laughing. "So, Tiffany took you out into the woods, huh? Why the woods?"

Ibn decided not to tell them about the significance the wooded area held to Tiffany. "I dunno, probably some idea she read in a magazine. Boys, I fucked the shit out of her. If there was any animals watching, I showed them the *proper* way to hit it from the back."

"Daaaamn," Colin said. "Tiffany seems so mild-mannered."

"Don't let that prim and proper act fool you. My baby can get downright porno when need be."

"Where is Tiff, anyway?" Colin asked.

Ibn flinched with annoyance. "She went to her mother's in Maryland."

"Again? Didn't she just go down there last week?"

"Um-hm." Ibn relaxed his shoulders, rotating them around. "She's probably dealing with her needy, worrisome mother. She must be going through another one of her self-inflicted crises. She's been a pain in the ass ever since her husband left her, which I can hardly blame him for doing. But Tiffany wouldn't tell me, though, because she knows I can't stand her."

"Her mother can't be as bad as mine," Colin said wistfully.

"She can miss work like that?" Dexter asked. The doorbell rang.

"Apparently so." Ibn got up and walked over to answer his door. "Especially when she knows her man will handle all the bills."

Bunches stepped in. She had come straight from work and was still wearing her hospital garb. Ibn turned and looked at Dexter and Colin. "Did anybody order a skinny girl?"

Bunches ignored him, smiling at Colin instead. "I noticed that there is a brand-spanking-new Mercedes out front. You wouldn't know anything about that, would you?"

Colin smiled back at her. "You like it?"

"Oh, no, it's repulsive, a monstrosity—of course, I like it!"

"Well, you'd better take a picture, Bunch, because this will probably be the last time you see it once Stacy gets a hold of it," Dexter said.

"Ha-ha," Colin replied.

"Ya know," Ibn added. "I'm just surprised he got out of the dealership with the C-280. I'm sure Stacy was pushing his ass toward the E-class models."

Bunches felt bad for Colin. Even in his moment of triumph he still had to hear his friends' shit about Stacy. To cheer him up, she said, "Let's go for a drive, Colin."

"Hold on," Ibn said, "We need a woman's opinion to settle what we were talking about before you got here."

"What? About you and Tiffany communing with nature, filming your episode of *Open Blouse on the Prairie?*" Colin asked.

Bunches raised her hands. "Spare me, please," she said.

"Prairie? I told you it was in the woods. Not that, anyway. What we were talking about before that."

"Oh, Lord." Colin rolled his eyes.

"Oh, no frat, don't ask for God now. You were feeling strong ten minutes ago," Ibn said. He looked at Bunches. "Here's the simplest question in the world. Would you please tell these misguided brothers which one of us is the best looking?"

Bunches looked at the three of them, amazed. "I can't believe y'all. . . ."

"I know it's preposterous," Ibn said, shrugging his shoulders, "but can you believe these cats wanted to argue?"

"What's *preposterous* is that three grown men would debate it,"

Bunches said, cutting him off. She looked at each of them. Colin was still wearing the charcoal suit he had worn to work, sans the jacket. Dexter had evidently gone home and changed because he was wearing a blue and white FUBU sweat suit. Ibn was impeccable as always, wearing a tight cream muscle shirt and brown slacks with razor-sharp pleats. "Is this how you guys amuse yourselves? What's the matter, did your PlayStation break or something?"

"Oh, please, Bunches," Dexter scoffed. "Women do it, too, except they do it behind each other's backs. Or—and this one really gets me—they ask their man to knock them."

"Yeah," Ibn agreed. "I done lost count of how many different times Tiffany has asked me, 'Do you think she's prettier than me?' " he said in a deliberately whiny voice.

"Exactly," Dexter added.

"Really?" Colin asked. "Stacy never asks me that."

"That's because she already knows the answer," Ibn replied.

Dexter and Bunches stifled laughs. Colin took longer to realize what Ibn had said.

"Fuck you, man," Colin said to him.

"I'm just playing," Ibn said, trying to look sincere, but not near pulling it off. "You know I think Stacy's positively peachy."

"Yeah, right."

"So anyway," Ibn said, turning back to Bunches. "If you don't mind."

She sat down in a chair and crossed her legs. She rolled her tongue around her mouth while she thoughtfully studied each of them again.

"Oh, please, it shouldn't take you this long—"

Bunches shushed Ibn with a wave of her hand. "I can make a case for each of you because of your varied attributes and qualities," she finally said.

"Yeah, right," Ibn said derisively, "you just don't wanna hurt these boys' feelings."

"No, I'm serious," she said. "Take Colin, for instance. He's got a swimmer's build, which a lot of women go for. He has elegant, noble features, a sexy smile, and I don't know whether you guys have noticed, but he has some real nice eyes underneath those Coke bottles he insists on wearing."

"It's not by choice, Bunch," Colin protested. "You know contacts irritate my eyes."

"Two words for you: laser surgery." Bunches said, shooting her index fingers at him.

"Two words for you: permanent injury," he replied.

"Swimmer's build?" Ibn asked incredulously. "Is that some kind of secret code for 'bony'? Tell him to take off his shirt and show that bird chest of his. You'll think the swallows have returned from Capistrano."

"Lean and mean, son, lean and mean," Colin said.

"Colin, please. I ain't even trying to call a male a man unless he weighs at least two hundred pounds," Dexter put in. "As far as I'm concerned, you're just a little boy."

"Which brings us to you." Bunches turned her attention to Dexter. "Six feet two inches and two hundred and thirty-five pounds of chocolate thunder."

"There it is," Dexter said. He took off his sweatshirt to show the T-shirt underneath. He then struck a sexy pose by putting his palms behind his head, which made his biceps swell.

"Very impressive," she said. "And the shaved head is very appealing to a large number of sisters."

"That's right. Brothers like me have made a comeback. We have been down since the early 1900s, when our hero and icon, the most honorable Jack Johnson, all praise be upon him, was in his heyday."

"What do you mean, 'brothers like you'?" Bunches asked.

"You know, Tyson, Tyrese, Taye Diggs . . ."

"Dexter," Bunches scoffed, "you don't look as good as those guys."

"Ouch!" Ibn roared. "Reality rears its ugly head!" He looked at Dexter. "No pun intended, Dex."

"Yeah, Dex, I'd rather be a little boy than an ugly man," Colin added.

Bunches stood up. "Whoa, whoa, Dexter's far from ugly. He's just gruffer than those pretty boys he was naming," Bunches said.

"And Bunches, you gotta remember I'm just as cut up and defined as those niggas, but a whole lot bigger. I'm a *man*, goddammit," he said.

"There is such a thing as too much of a good thing, though, Dex. You muscled-up brothers always seem to be injuring something. The last thing a sistah wanna deal with when she trying to get her freak on is one of you weightlifting jokers pulling your hamstring in bed."

Ibn, Colin and even Dexter had to chuckle at that, but Ibn stopped abruptly and looked at Bunches. "Wait a minute. What do you know about 'getting your freak on,' young lady?"

She ignored his comment and faced him. "Which brings us to you. The one and only Ibn Barrington."

Ibn stretched his arms wide so that she could get an unimpaired look at his splendor. "There'll never be another, baby," he said.

"I'm not gonna bother listing your physical attributes—"

"Because there are so many, right?" he asked.

"No, because I just don't think I can be as eloquent as Terence. You know, with his fine use of terms like 'hazelnut complexion' and whatnot." Bunches grinned.

"Ouch. Reality makes a comeback," Dexter mocked.

"How dare that *antiman* speak my name," Ibn muttered.

"So, anyway, much like Dexter, too much of a good thing can become a negative," Bunches continued.

"Meaning?" Ibn asked.

"Meaning, some would argue that you're too good-looking. What woman wants to compete with her man as to who the pretty one of the relationship is? I betcha if I go upstairs, I'll find you and Tiffany have matching vanities."

"Now you're just being silly," he said as he loaded NBA 2001 into the PlayStation.

"I probably am. Yours is probably twice the size of hers."

Everybody got a chuckle out of that.

"So, I guess I win by default, then," Colin said, picking up the other controller to play against Ibn.

"What, because I'm *too* muscular? What kind of bullshit reasoning is that?" Dexter asked as he headed to the kitchen.

"I believe the young lady said 'gruff' as well," Colin chimed in.

"Bunch, tell these two fools that they are vying for second place anyway," Ibn said. "Just do me a favor and do it gently, I don't want their hurt feelings spilling all over my carpet."

"Why do I have to choose?" Bunches protested. "I love the three of you equally."

"Uh-uh, you're not getting off the hook that easily. Bunches, just tell them, they'll get over it. Trust me." He and Colin paused their video game to await her decision. Dexter came out of the kitchen holding a bag of potato chips.

Bunches looked at each of them again. "Okay, but only because you're pointing a gun to my head. I'm gonna have to say the all-around, most attractive one of you is . . ."

Ibn stood up to give his acceptance speech, using the controller as a microphone.

". . . Michael."

"Oh, Jesus Christ!" Ibn sneered.

"If you wanna make jokes," Dexter chimed in, "then you need to audition for *Comicview*."

"C'mon, Ib, let's play the game," Colin added with fake indignation. "Such nonsense doesn't deserve a response."

Bunches chuckled at their reaction. "What did Jack Nicholson once say? 'You can't handle the truth.' " She pointed her finger at them.

"We can handle the truth," Dexter said, sitting on the couch next to Colin. "Just don't ask us to accept the absurd."

"Yeah, the only reason you're choosing Mike is because he ain't here," Ibn added.

"I don't know what you two are talking about. Michael is *cute*. He has a warm smile, bedroom eyes and a sex appeal that y'all wouldn't know anything about."

"Apparently we're not the only ones that don't, because that nigga spends a lot of time alone," Dexter chortled.

"Dexter," Bunches replied with a patient, almost condescending quality to her voice. "Michael could have just as many women as you and your trollop-chasing brother-in-arms, there," she said, motioning at Ibn. "He just chooses not to."

"That does it," Ibn said, putting down the controller. "Bunch, I want you to take a week or two off, go sit on a beach somewhere and relax. Obviously, you been under too much stress. I'm serious, just send me the bill, sweetheart, and go wherever you want to go. Just get well. 'Cause if you say some more outlandish shit like that, we're gonna have to have you committed."

"Where is he, anyway?" Bunches asked, getting to the point she had been curious about all along.

Colin checked his watch. "I don't know. But we're supposed to be playing poker tonight."

Bunches walked over to the coffee table to pick up her purse.

"I thought you were here to see me," Ibn asked with insincere hurt in his voice.

She leaned over and gave him a kiss on the cheek, "I always wanna see you, daddy." Bunches stood back up and gave him a slow wink.

"Now, *that's* what I wanna hear."

What she wanted to hear was Mike's voice. Or better yet, to see him. Bunches pulled her cell phone out of her purse and dialed Mike's number.

Mike and Sharice were sitting at her kitchen table, struggling mightily with the *Philadelphia Inquirer*'s crossword puzzle. When his cell phone rang, he walked into the living room to get the phone out of his jacket pocket. "Hello?"

"Hello, Michael."

"Hey, Erika. What's up?"

"Something's gotta be up? I can't just be calling."

Mike smiled. "You misunderstood. It was a greeting, not a request for justification."

"*All right,* then. I'm just calling to see if you remember that we're taking Xavier and Tiana out this Saturday."

Mike furrowed his brow. "Erika, do you honestly think I'd forget the children?"

"I don't know. You might. You've obviously been preoccupied the last couple of weeks."

"Look who's talking. You're the one who disappears for a whole week at a time."

"I was studying for my big anatomy test."

Mike looked back in the kitchen. Sharice was bending over to take something out of the oven. Me, too, he thought. Sharice was wearing yellow shorts and a WWJD T-shirt. She wasn't trying to be sexy, she just was. He turned away and walked toward Sharice's balcony door. "By the way, do you know a three-letter word for 'exaggerated sense of self-importance'? This crossword puzzle is kicking my ass."

"Hmm, yes, I do. I-b-n." They both laughed.

(*"Is that fool coming or what?"*)

Mike heard Ibn's voice in the background. "Where are you?" he asked.

"At Ib's. The boys are waiting for you. Some male-bonding ritual thing."

"Oh, yeah," Mike said, "I forgot we were playing poker tonight."

"You forgot? See, I told you you've been preoccupied."

(*"He forgot? Is he still sniffing around that skank Sharice?"*)

"Tell Ibn to shut the hell up."

Instead, Bunches held up the phone so that he could hear the room's comments clearly.

(*"Why is he always at her place? How come he never brings her around?"*)

(*"He knows better than to bring her hoey ass around me."*)

(*"Mike's hanging around probably hoping that she'll revert to old form and let him tap it because he never hit it before."*)

That last comment burned Mike. He recognized that it had come from Dexter. He heard Bunches put the phone back to her ear.

"Tell Dexter to go tend to his bastard-to-be," Mike snarled.

"I'm not gonna say that," Bunches said.

Mike thought it over. She was right, that was a cruel thing to say. "Yeah, you're right. Don't tell him I said that."

Bunches was silent for several beats. "Is it 'ego,' Michael?"

He turned around to make sure he was out of Sharice's earshot before speaking again. "Damn, don't start in with your bullshit, too. No, it is not my ego, Erika," he said in an angry whisper. "I just happen to enjoy her company. What, is that a fucking crime now?"

There was a pause before Bunches answered. "I meant the crossword puzzle answer, Michael. The three-letter word," she said quietly.

"Oh," Mike said sheepishly. "Erika, I—"

He cringed when he heard the dead air. He closed the phone and put it back in his jacket and walked back to the kitchen table, where Sharice was sitting with a look of discomfort.

"Mike, can you do me a favor and please refrain from cursing around me?" she said.

Mike gulped. He thought he had been whispering. "Huh?" he asked.

"When you were on the phone, you said 'ass' and 'hell,' and I think I heard a 'bastard,' too!"

"Oh," he said, relieved that she hadn't heard the tail end of his conversation with Erika. He said lightly, "Those words are in the Bible, Sharice."

"Yes, but I don't believe you were using them in that context."

He could tell by the righteous indignation etched on her face that this wasn't a subject to kid around with her on. "Okay, Sharice. I'll try not to."

She smiled at him. "Thank you."

"You're welcome." He thought of what he had heard Colin ask when he was on the phone with Erika. (*How come he never brings her around?*) Mike could imagine what kind of fool Ibn would cut if Sharice told him that his foul language offended her.

"What children are you not forgetting?" Sharice asked.

Mike wrote the word "ego" in the appropriate tiles. "Huh?"

"On the phone, I heard you talk about not forgetting the children."

"Oh. Me and Erika are mentors to two children from Camden. Hers is named Tiana, and she lives in a group home. Mine is named Xavier, he lives with his grandmother. We've been doing it for almost three years now."

"Yeah? That's admirable."

"It was Erika's idea," Mike said, "though I must admit, I do enjoy spending time with them."

"Them? So you usually see them together?"

"Well, if I stop by to talk to Xavier, I'll usually go alone. But most times when we go places, me and Erika like to take them out together."

"Oh?" Sharice said, looking at Mike over her coffee mug. "How often do these field trips happen?"

"Every couple of weeks or so." The subject was old to him, and he focused back on the puzzle.

"What about your friends? Are they mentors, too?"

"Well, Colin's girlfriend, Stacy, works with troubled youths. So Colin often stops by her job. He's taken an active interest himself in a couple of those children. As far as Ibn and Dexter, I don't know why Erika hasn't asked them."

"Because she's a clever girl, that's why." Sharice took a sip of her coffee.

Mike looked up. "Do you have a thesaurus?"

"Look on that bookcase."

When Mike got back to the table, he looked at Sharice. "What do you mean, 'clever girl'?"

She smiled. "It's just that if I wanted to guarantee some quality time with a quality man, I couldn't think of a better way to do it. Even if you wanted to back out on her, she knows you won't let down the kids."

"You're being silly," he said, dismissing the idea. "Erika lives in the same house as me. We see each other all the time."

Sharice was not letting up, though. "But she probably only sees you in passing because of your schedules, right? And didn't I hear her complaining about you not being available to her when you were on the phone?"

At that, Mike looked up at her. "Were you eavesdropping, nosy?"

"I was overhearing," Sharice laughed.

"Well, I won't deny that out of the four of us, I'm probably the closest to Erika, but not in the manner that you're implying."

"And what manner was that?" Sharice leaned forward and asked sweetly, "Are you gonna sit there and tell me that it never occurred to *you* to ask Dexter or Ibn to become a mentor?"

"Huh?" Mike shrugged his shoulders. "I don't know—what are you saying?"

"That she might not be the only one who wants to guarantee some quality time together. Maybe you haven't asked your friends because *you* don't want to share her." Sharice looked mischievously at him over her mug.

Mike waved at her. "You need to switch to decaf. Or maybe stop reading so many of those fairy tales to your class."

"Okay, okay. No need to get defensive." Sharice gave him a disbelieving mocking look.

Mike laughed. "Oh, okay, I see how this works now. If I say nothing, then my silence is an admission of guilt. If I deny it, then you read my defensiveness as incriminating."

"Who, me? I don't know what you're talking about." Sharice said, her face full wide-eyed innocence.

Mike decided to turn the tables on her. "Why are you asking, anyway? You jealous?"

Sharice traced her forefinger along the rim of her mug. "Why would I be jealous? I get to be with children every day."

"That's cute, Sharice."

She wrinkled her nose at him. "I thought so."

"Hey, she called from Ibn's house. Maybe she goes for Ibn, like every other woman on the planet," Mike said, returning his attention to the crossword puzzle.

"Unh," Sharice rolled her eyes. "I hope that's not the case. But I'll say a prayer for the girl tonight, just to be certain."

Bunches sat silently, slouched down in a chair, watching Ibn and Colin's boxing match on PlayStation. She was trying to keep the scowl that her phone conversation with Mike had caused off her face.

"I'll talk to you guys later," Dexter said, standing in the foyer.

"All right, Dex," Colin and Ibn said in unison.

Dexter noticed Bunches' foul mood. "You okay, Bunch?"

Colin and Ibn glanced over at her. Bunches nodded without looking at any of them. They focused back on their match.

Dexter slid his sweatshirt back over his head. "You coming home with me?"

"No, I'll be home in a little while," she said tensely.

"Why the long face, Bunch?" Colin asked, his thumbs rapidly smacking against the controller.

Bunches noticed Dexter staring at her contemplatively, like he was deciding whether or not to say something.

"Ooh, that had to hurt!" Ibn said as he landed an uppercut on Colin's boxer, sending him sprawling. While the ref was counting, Ibn turned his attention to Bunches. "You hungry?"

She didn't like the attention—especially Dexter's puzzled look—she was eliciting and decided to snap out of her funk. "Nothing," she said, sitting up. "I was just thinking about this patient I met today." She saw that Dexter was still looking at her. "I'll be home in a little while," she repeated.

Dexter accepted it this time. "Okay, bye," he said, and left.

"Sweetheart, why don't you go eat something?" Ibn said. "You really are looking thin lately."

She was hungry. "You got anything good?"

Ibn smiled wryly as he reset the game so he and Colin could play again. "Did I neglect to mention my mother stopped by this afternoon and made her favorite child his favorite dishes?"

Bunches practically leapt out of her chair. "Negro, you trying to hold out on me? Why didn't you tell me Mrs. Barrington cooked?"

Ibn laughed. "I'm telling you now."

Bunches was already on her way to the kitchen. "You're supposed to tell me that when I hit the door, not waste my time asking me to judge some bullshit beauty contest."

"Bullshit?" Ibn asked incredulously. "I'm a specimen, darling."

Bunches lifted the different pots on the stove. The aroma made her mouth water. "Mmm, now this is what I'm talking about," she called out from the kitchen.

"You know my mom can throw down," Ibn replied. "Eat up. Put some meat on your bones."

"Speaking of which," Bunches said, "Colin, you know your scrawny self needs to be in here getting you a plate, too."

"First of all, I'm wiry, not scrawny—and secondly, I already ate."

Wiry? Is *that* what they call bony now? Bunches thought as she washed her hands. "Ibn, where's my girl?"

"Tiff? She went to see her mother—again," Ibn said.

"If you don't like it," Bunches said, grabbing a plate out of the cabinet, "then give her a reason to stay home."

"What?" Ibn paused the game. "A reason to—look how I got this girl living. She lives like a queen."

Bunches decided not to respond, not feeling like getting into it with him. She knew Ibn's attitude was that he believed that his money could make up for all his other shortcomings. Besides, she thought as she looked at the clock on the microwave, her favorite show was coming on. That would help take her mind off her conversation with Mike. This staying over at Sharice's all the time was getting on her nerves.

She came out of the kitchen with a plate of jerk chicken, yellow rice and red beans, sipping a glass of iced tea. She joined Colin and Ibn in the living room and set her plate on a TV tray. She let out a sigh of resignation, which was ignored by the men. She wanted to watch Animal Planet, but they were still immersed in playing their stupid video game.

"Down goes Frazier! Down goes Frazier!" Ibn cried. He tossed the controller onto the sofa, stood up and raised his arms victoriously.

"Aw, man," Colin said dejectedly. It had been the umpteenth beating in a row that Colin had suffered at Ibn's hands.

"Damn, son," Ibn said with mock disgust, "don't you get tired of these ass-whippings?" He jabbed a finger in Colin's face. "Where's your pride, boy? Huh? Did you put it out with the trash?"

Bunches had had enough. She wished that Colin would win occasionally. She grew tired of watching him be Ibn's personal whipping boy. A role that, as far as she was concerned, Colin was far too comfortable with.

Damn, she thought. Who lost to the same person every time? And who wouldn't get tired of it?

"It's just a stupid game, Ibn. Furthermore, Colin shows far more class in defeat than you do in winning."

Ibn shrugged. "That's irrelevant. Besides, you show me a good loser and I'll show you a *loser*."

Bunches bit into a piece of chicken. She was ready to say something else to Ibn when Colin spoke up.

"Hey, Ib knows boxing—what can I do?"

"That's right," Ibn gloated. "I might not know molecular physics, but I do know the fine art of whipping a nigga's ass." He nonchalantly jabbed a thumb at Colin. "Mainly this nigga's ass."

"Man, be quiet," Colin said, "let's play again."

"Must you?" Bunches asked, taking a sip of iced tea. "I wanna watch the *Crocodile Hunter*."

Ibn looked at her askance. "The what?"

"You heard me. Turn to Animal Planet."

"You mean that crazy nut who fucks with those crocodiles and snakes?" Colin asked.

"Yep." Bunches said. "Turn to it."

Ibn hadn't had quite enough of Colin's ass yet. "Can't you watch it in the bedroom?"

Bunches rolled her eyes. She was making an exaggerated, agitated effort of rising when Ibn finally relented.

"Okay, okay, I'll put it on." He walked over to the TV grumbling under his breath.

"Thank you," Bunches said sweetly.

The reason for the vehemence of her insistence was twofold. She really did want to watch Steve and Terry's adventures with the reptile world, but she also didn't think she could stomach the sight of Colin being Ibn's exclusive punching bag any longer. Not if she wanted her jerk chicken to stay down.

Nine

Dexter, Stephanie and Colin were eating lunch at a Caribbean restaurant on South Street when Dexter's phone rang.

"The food here is delicious," Stephanie said. She was wearing a magenta blouse and a long black skirt. "How did you guys find this place?"

"We have a buddy who's Guyanese," Colin answered. "He's been coming here forever. He says the food here is almost as good as his grandmother's back home."

"By the way, I heard you call Dexter 'frat' earlier. Is college where you guys met?"

"Um-hm," Colin said as he swallowed a forkful of curry goat.

"My little brother is in a fraternity, too. He's an Iota."

"I'm sorry," Colin said with fake sympathy. "He must be a great disappointment to your family."

Stephanie laughed. "Everybody thinks their fraternity is the best."

"True," Colin answered. "Fortunately for me, mine is."

"Well, he assured me that his is, so there." Stephanie said with mock indignation. She and Colin laughed.

"All right, then. Bye." Dexter closed his flip phone.

"Denise, right?" Colin asked.

"Who else?" Dexter asked. He picked his fork back up but wasn't as interested in his curry chicken as he had been before the call.

"Is Denise your girlfriend?" Stephanie asked.

Dexter looked up from his plate at Stephanie. He had never been asked to define his relationship with Denise before. "Yes." He looked at Colin. "I'm gonna knock off a little early today to take her to the hospital."

"Is she okay?" Stephanie asked.

"Yeah, it's just a routine checkup. She's pregnant."

"Congratulations!"

Dexter smiled weakly. "Thanks." He put his fork down for good and stood up, reaching for his wallet.

"Don't worry about it, Dex, I got it."

"All right, then," Dexter said, taking a final sip of his iced tea. "I'll see you guys back at the office."

"Okay."

"Bye." Dexter numbly walked out of the restaurant.

Stephanie's eyes followed Dexter out the door. "Was I wrong to congratulate him? He doesn't seem too excited."

"It wasn't a planned thing," Colin said. He smiled tightly. "But I have a feeling he'll be happy once the child is born."

"As will you. Right, Uncle Colin?"

He chewed slowly as he mulled that over. "Yeah, I am looking forward to having a little whippersnapper running around."

"So, how come you don't have any of your own yet?" Stephanie asked as she jabbed at her plantain.

Colin's eyes dropped to his food. Stacy always put Colin off whenever he talked about marriage and children, saying that she wanted to finish graduate school first. "Because my girlfriend hasn't decided whether or not she wants to be fruitful yet," he said. "She says working with the troubled youths on her job is the best form of birth control one could have."

Stephanie put down her fork and shook her head at him. "That's a shame, because I think you'd make a fantastic father."

Colin smiled at her. "Thanks. I'm not sure you're right, but thanks anyway."

"Well, *I'm* sure," Stephanie said. "I see the way you interact with the kids when one of the classes comes to tour our building. You have a real gift for it. Why do you think the company made you its liaison to the Philadelphia public schools?"

"Because I'm the only one who wanted to do it?"

"No, because you're the only one who *could* do it," she said emphatically. "These kids that your girlfriend works with, were they the ones in the lobby the other day when we we're leaving the building?"

"A couple of them, Corey and Andre," Colin said, taking a sip of iced tea. "Sometimes they give Stacy a hard time, so I take them to give her a break. I told them to meet me because I wanted to take them somewhere."

"Where did you go?"

"To the African American Historical Museum on Arch Street. They had a new exhibit I wanted them to see."

Stephanie looked at him in amazement. "Two teenage boys meet you, after sitting in school all day, to go to see a museum exhibit just because you asked them to, and you don't think you have a gift? I mean, I can see a Sixers game, professional wrestling or something like that, but to go to a museum? I don't know many children who would be willing to go along with that."

Colin never thought of it that way. Lord knows, Stacy used him enough on her job. He often thought he put in as much time as she did. Yet Stephanie stirred a chord in him, and he decided to tell her how he felt about those needy kids.

"It's been my experience that children just want somebody to listen to them. To take an active interest in them. To be a voluntary participant in their lives. Not because of coercion, some court-mandated community-service–type thing, like those hypocritical professional athletes who plea-bargain a drug charge down to giving a couple of speeches and then they don't want anything to do with the children when they're done." Colin looked at Stephanie to make sure she was really interested. She was, so he kept talking. "And kids are perceptive, they won't want anything to do with you if they sense you're only there for the paycheck. When I'm talking to one of the kids, they have my undivided attention, and they sense that. I remember what they tell me, not like that fake one-ear-and-out-the-other concern so many adults who work with children have perfected. Children can sniff out a bullshitter in a second. Especially these children, who have been given the back of the hand by society and exposed to the backsides of more adults than most. They know I'm with them because I want to be, not because I'm one of these fraudulent poverty pimps who would be out of a job if it wasn't for the very misery they are supposed to help put an end to."

Colin realized he was being too preachy and ended his soliloquy. He was sitting here sermonizing like he was Mike. He was about to apologize to Stephanie for rambling on when he noticed her eyes had a starry gaze. Embarrassed, he immediately went back to concentrating on his food. It was a gaze that was familiar to him, though not too often from personal experience. But he had seen Ibn elicit it often enough to at least recognize it.

Dexter and Denise were sitting in the small waiting room of Dr. William Harris, the same obstetrician, Dexter was informed, who had delivered Marla's children. Inside the waiting room was another expectant couple and their son, a toddler, who was scurrying around the room. The TV hanging in the far corner was turned to channel seven, showing an episode of *Divorce Court*.

"Payton, come over here," the mother said.

Payton, a capricious mix of blond hair, hazel eyes, and stubborn nature, ignored her and continued to explore the leaves of the potted plant. His father finally rose out of his chair and retrieved his son.

Denise and the other woman exchanged smiles.

"Is this your first?" she asked Denise.

And only, Dexter thought.

"Yes," Denise replied, "this is our first."

Dexter, who was leaning in his chair with his legs crossed and his eyes closed, raised an eyebrow at that. Apparently, Denise really was under the notion that they were going to have 'children' together.

"Well, you're gonna love Dr. Harris," the woman went on to say, "he's terrific. He delivered Payton."

"I hear he's very good," Denise replied. "He comes highly recommended to us."

By the all-knowing, all-seeing Marla, Dexter thought. Therefore, he had to be the best. Why Denise listened to Marla so much was beyond his grasp. He rolled his neck and yawned.

Five minutes of relative silence had passed—interrupted only by the occasional "Payton, stop. Be a good boy"—when Dexter felt a nudge in his side. Assuming it was accidental, he ignored it and leaned the other way to give Denise more room. He then received a sharper jab in his kidney and opened his eyes and looked at Denise.

"What?" he asked, irritated.

At his tone of voice, she cringed with a combination of anger and embarrassment. She quickly glanced over at the other couple to see if they had noticed. She was sure they had and were pretending not to.

"Wouldn't you like to read this article?" Denise asked, putting a magazine in his lap.

Dexter looked down at a copy of *Parents*. It was turned to an article titled, "What to Do If Your Child Won't Stop Crying."

"No, I wouldn't." Dexter put the magazine on the other side of him, shifted, and resumed his catnap.

Another elbow soon followed. Now Dexter was agitated.

"What is it now?" he said, louder this time.

Denise glared at him, using her eyes to motion across the room. Dexter followed them.

While he had been napping, another young couple had walked in. They were sitting quietly near the TV reading a copy of *Parents* together. Payton's dad was also immersed in an article in the magazine, while his wife entertained Payton.

Dexter turned back to Denise and gave her a look of utter indifference, turned his body even more away from her and shut his eyes again.

Denise let out a snort of disgust.

You can snort all you want, Dexter thought. Grunt, whinny or bark, too, he didn't care, but she wasn't going to get him to play the "everything is rosy" game. He simply wasn't that good an actor. Hell, even Samuel Jackson wouldn't be able to play that role convincingly.

Tiffany sat down on the couch and dabbed at her eyes. She had just finished packing her car and was startled at how quickly she had been able to do it. Nothing in the house was hers, except clothes and jewelry, and most of them had come courtesy of Ibn. She really was just another accessory of Ibn's, no more important than his Benz or his Rolex.

She picked up the letter off the coffee table. She had written it earlier that morning, as soon as Ibn had left to "check on some pledgees." Check on some pledgees, my ass, Tiffany thought. That man must really think I'm stupid. No, what he most likely thinks is that I'm gonna sit idly by and let him do whatever he wants, anyway, so his lies don't have to be sophisticated. And Tiffany couldn't blame him for his arrogance. Not when she had put up with too much, for too long, already.

She finished reading the letter and set it back down on the table. It contained everything she wanted to say. She put a porcelain elephant paperweight on it so it would stay in place.

The finality of her undertaking pressed down on her shoulders, trying to keep her on the couch. She knew this time was different than the half-dozen, halfhearted, half-assed attempts she had made to leave Ibn before. A picture of her and Ibn hugging at Disney World stood on the fireplace. Hell, before, she had made sure she packed pictures of her and Ibn together so that she would get nostalgic as soon as she missed him and begin to weaken. How was that serious?

This time it was well planned. She already had a job lined up in Baltimore. She even had potential replacements for Ibn lined up—one particularly nice prospect she had met last time she was at home—though she wasn't ready for that, just yet.

She stood up and looked around. No, this time was it. She simply couldn't afford to give Ibn any more of her soul. Or her time. Though her biological clock was still just a faint tick, it was simply getting too late in the day for that. She picked up her purse and put on her sunglasses.

Tiffany walked through Ibn's foyer and shut the door to Ibn's house.

Ten

Mike and Dexter were sitting at the kitchen table talking about the foul fortunes of the Phillies when the phone rang. Mike got up to answer it so Dexter could finish his Cap'n Crunch gorging.

"Michael, can you bring some lotion up here?" Bunches asked, "I'm all out."

"Those stairs go both ways," Mike replied.

"C'mon, Mike, I just got out of the shower. I don't want to catch cold."

"Just got out of the shower?" Mike asked, checking his watch. "We're supposed to be leaving now."

"And you're really helping matters now, aren't you?" Bunches asked.

"All right, all right, I'll be right up." Mike noticed that Dexter stopped his spoon in midair before putting it in his mouth. He set the phone back on the counter.

"Bunches needs some lotion, I'll be right back," Mike said as he left the kitchen. He went into the bedroom, grabbed his bottle of Jergens, and headed for the front door. Dexter didn't say a word, but Mike felt his eyes on him as he walked through the living room and out of the apartment.

Mike found Bunches' door cracked, so he walked in. The place had the smell of soap and the steaminess of a freshly taken hot shower. He called out, "I'm gonna leave the lotion here on the table."

Bunches came out of the bedroom wearing only a lavender bath towel wrapped around her. She still had her shower cap on. "Michael, don't leave yet, I want to talk to you."

Their eyes met briefly when she grabbed the lotion. "Thanks, have a seat," she said, and turned away to walk back into the bedroom.

Stupefied, Mike sat down on the couch. His eyes mapped a course from her heels up to her thighs, and finally rested on her tight little behind bouncing underneath the towel.

"You know that I'm in the process of talking to different hospitals, deciding where's the best place to do my residency next year, right?" Bunches asked from the bedroom.

Mike wondered if he was making too much of her nearly nude appearance, whether he was misreading the situation.

"Well, I've been thinking about Tiana," Bunches continued. "I've been thinking that once I'm settled in, that maybe I could look into adopting her."

Maybe it was nothing, Mike thought, not listening. After all, she needed the lotion before she could get dressed.

"But I've also been thinking that maybe the quickest way to get her out of the group home would be for me to become a foster parent, then put in for her adoption later."

But she could've easily told him to leave the lotion on the table and leave, which is what he thought she wanted him to do and why she had opened the door for him in the first place. Mike wondered why she just didn't do that.

"Of course, it will be difficult for me to find the time in my schedule to take those classes required to become a foster parent," Bunches added.

And why did she feel comfortable enough to be around him half naked? Mike wondered whether this was a compliment or an insult.

"What I also was thinking is that I do want to get married someday. Do you think it'll be a problem for my future husband? Am I asking too much of a man to accept me and my—by then—teenage daughter?"

Most of all, Mike wondered what to make of his erection. He looked down. His penis was pressed so tightly against his jeans he could see its outline along his thigh.

"Michael?"

He snapped out of it. "Huh?"

"I'm talking to you."

Mike tried to remember the question Bunches had asked him. "Yeah, well—I think adoption is a noble act."

"What? Michael, come in here where I can hear you."

As Mike stood up, he noticed that his hard-on was very noticeable. He untucked his T-shirt and tried to hide the bulge by letting it hang over his belt. Though it was only covered partially, he figured it would subside momentarily.

Mike walked gingerly into her room. Bunches was facing her closet with her back to him, nude from the waist up. She had jeans on and her hair was still loosely tied in the scarf she had worn under her shower cap.

Mike immediately sat on her bed. Bunches undid the scarf, and thick black spiral curls fell along her shoulders and neck. They were a perfect contrast to her smooth, nut-brown skin. Mike's eyes traced along the graceful lines of her collarbone, shoulder blades and back.

And his erection was sticking around.

"So, do you think a man would have a problem with me and Tiana being a package deal?" Bunches asked, still keeping her back to Mike. She fastened her bra in the front and then slid it around and put her breasts into the cups.

"Erika, any man that is not gonna accept you because of Tiana isn't a man you need to deal with," Mike said. "Only a fool wouldn't realize what a catch you are." Right about now, Mike meant that shit.

Bunches slid a Hilfiger T-shirt on and turned around. "I'm glad to hear you say that." She hesitated, then added. "I needed the confidence boost."

She walked over and reached down on the floor near where Mike's legs were and grabbed her Nikes. Mike rose quickly to hide his aroused state, but he wasn't sure whether or not Bunches had seen it. He kept his back to her, pretending to look at a keepsake on her dresser as she sat on the bed and began lacing up her sneakers. There was an awkward silence. Well, awkward to Mike. He couldn't tell if Bunches noticed it or not.

"So," Mike said, leaving the room. "I'll be downstairs waiting."

He had made it all the way to her front door before Bunches spoke. "Yep, Michael, you've done wonders for my confidence."

"In December, the WWF is coming to the CoreStates Center," Xavier said. "That's where I want to go."

"Ugh." Bunches rolled her eyes.

"All right, I'll see what I can do," Mike said. His embarrassment of earlier was forgotten. "All I ask is that you hold up your end of the bargain. You know what that is, right?"

"I know, I know. Behave myself in school."

Mike stopped at a red light and looked in the rearview mirror. Xavier was a skinny light-skinned kid with thick, heavy eyelids that always made him look half asleep. He was wearing an oversize Phat Farm baseball jersey and baggy jeans. "Xavier, when I stop by that school, please don't have me standing in there being embarrassed. When I talk to your teachers, the first thing out of their mouths *better* be that you've been acting like you got some sense. Your behavior should be on point regardless of whether you're an A student or a D student. I mean that. But I'm wasting my breath here, because you already know how to act, right? I know I'm not gonna see any red N's on your report card. Am I?"

"No," he said softly.

"Honor roll *would* be nice," Mike continued.

Xavier groaned.

"But more important is that you try your hardest. If you give it your best effort, you'll make progress, because you're a bright kid. I know you don't like math—I didn't either when I was in school—but that just means we have to work harder at it because it doesn't come easy to us. Like never missing a homework assignment, right?"

"Right."

The light turned green, and Mike pulled off. "You have my new cell phone number, right? Whenever you have a big math test, I want to know so I can stop by and we can study together. Okay?"

Bunches turned and looked at Xavier's forlorn expression. She could tell that the thought of "Taskmaster Michael" hovering over him, cracking the whip on the eve of a math test wasn't an appealing prospect.

"Don't worry, X-man, you'll be fine. I'll see if I can come, too. We'll get through it together." She gave him a wink.

Mike saw Xavier cheesing so ridiculously in the mirror that he had to smother a laugh. He knew that the boy had a huge crush on Erika.

"I *always* make honor roll," Tiana said, not liking all the attention being focused on Xavier. She was an adorable bronze-colored little girl with long, thick lashes and braids, which she was currently wearing back and tied up in a pink-and-white scrunchee.

"Uh-uhn, T, you're on what is called the principal's list," Mike said. "That's straight A's."

"Oh, yeah," she smiled broadly. "Principal's list."

"I'm very proud of you, sweetheart." Mike smiled at Tiana, whom he thought was just about the cutest thing on God's green earth. She returned his smile with one that spoke volumes. It had the self-assurance of a little girl who knew she had a grown man wrapped around her finger.

Xavier muttered under his breath.

Bunches, who was not so quick to succumb to Tiana's charms, whirled on her. "Just don't let me hear about you being *grown*, sitting in anybody's classroom trying to tell an adult how to do her job anymore. You don't give teachers 'word for word.' You stay in a child's place. Do we understand each other, little girl?"

Tiana recoiled under Bunches' stern glare. "Yes," she said timidly.

Mike saw by Xavier's smug expression that he liked hearing Tiana being chastised. Damn, he thought, Erika doesn't forget anything. Tiana had had one incident with a substitute teacher a few months back, and Erika still brought it up. It's not as if she had let Tiana off easy when it happened. Whenever Erika was disappointed in a person, she had a way that would make them feel lower than snake piss. The only person that hated letting her down more than Mike was probably Tiana. When that whole incident had happened, Tiana had been an utter mess until Erika let her back in her good graces. Besides, Mike couldn't see why Erika hadn't realized that the substitute teacher was entirely to blame, anyway. She had to be. Because as far as Mike was concerned, Tiana could do no wrong.

Mike pulled into the parking lot of the Franklin Institute. When they got out of the car, Tiana and Xavier bolted on ahead of them, chattering excitedly as they headed to the entrance.

"You know, next year after I graduate, I'm gonna see about getting Tiana into a private school. She's not being challenged enough where she is now."

"But she's being challenged enough by you. Why are you so hard on her?" Mike asked. Any trace of what had happened in her bedroom earlier was gone. Erika was focused on the children.

"Me? You're a fine one to talk." She replied. "I was about to ask you the same thing with Xavier."

"I have to," Mike said as they walked along. "Look what I'm up against as far as other influences in his life. His heroes are rappers, wrestlers and athletes. Most rappers nowadays are so devoid of talent or have gotten so lazy with their writing that they aren't rapping about shit. Then I'm up against wrestlers on TV with their lewd gestures and foul language—"

"So, are you really gonna take him to see wrestling?" Bunches asked.

Mike looked ahead to make sure the kids were out of earshot. "Don't tell him anything, Erika, but I already got the tickets." Last week when Mike was at the box office buying tickets for the Living Proof gospel tour, which he wanted to surprise Sharice with, he had picked them up.

Bunches looked at him in disbelief.

"What? I wanna see The Rock, too. That's my boy." Mike laughed.

"Some role model you are."

"The way I see it, since he watches it on TV, anyway, I can at least take him to see it live so I can point out that it's fake and explain that it's just entertainment."

Inside, they took advantage of everything the Institute had to offer. Tiana loved the 3-D movie showing in the Omniverse Theater titled *The Serengeti*. It made it seem as if they were in the middle of the Serengeti encountering all sorts of wildlife. Xavier got a big kick out of the dinosaur display.

Bunches and Mike were sitting on a bench together when they heard Tiana giggle loudly. She was walking through the human heart exhibit with Xavier. She made eye contact with Bunches, who returned her smile.

"You're still gonna have it easier than me, Michael," she said, turning to him. "I have to worry about the same things as you, but you won't have to worry about boys, or even worse, grown-ass nasty men, trying to get into Xavier's pants."

"True."

"You got to stay on little girls, especially smart ones like Tiana. They can be so manipulative. Soon she's gonna want to start looking at boys, and she's gonna command a lot of attention because of her looks. I don't want her to cheat herself by losing focus. She already knows how cute she is, but I'm trying to teach her that it's not enough to be pretty and skate by on your looks. You need to be smart, too."

"A twenty-first-century superwoman."

"You got it."

Erika was studying Tiana intently, and Mike smiled. The look on her face said that if Tiana was going to sell herself short, it would be over her dead body.

Mike rubbed her back. "I can't think of a better example for her to have."

"Example? I don't know what you're talking about. I was a fat girl, remember? I didn't have any boys knocking my door down."

"Well, you got some now." Mike said. "Like Quincy."

"True, but most of the times it's when they're trying to escape, after Dexter has scared them to death."

Later that evening, Bunches and Mike were driving home from the video store, where they had stopped after dropping the kids off.

"You know, Michael, it's getting harder and harder for me to leave Tiana in that group home," she said.

She didn't have to tell him, he had noticed. The scenes were getting progressively more and more heart-wrenching. Whenever one of their days together was winding down, Tiana would start to get upset. Bunches would have to switch places with Xavier and sit in the backseat and hold her. By the time they got back to the house that Tiana shared with seven other children, she would be crying. She would cling to Bunches, asking three or four times at least about the next time she would see her and would finally only be consoled a little when Bunches promised to call her before her bedtime. Mike would have to turn away, and he really admired how Bunches kept it together.

"Yeah, at least Xavier goes home to a grandmother," Mike said. "I know Mrs. Johnson and the other workers at the home do the best they can with the children, but it's not a family."

After picking up some Chinese, they went home. When they got to their doors, Bunches handed Mike his carton of sesame chicken so she could look in her purse for her house key.

"You're going upstairs? I thought we were gonna watch the movie together," Mike said.

Bunches looked at him, feigning shock. "You're not going back out? I assumed you were gonna go see, um, what's her name?"

He hadn't missed the edge in her humor. "Sharice."

"Yeah, Sharice. Is she giving you a whole day *and* night off?" Bunches asked.

"She's went with her church on some retreat." It was always something church-related with Sharice, Mike thought. It seemed like the church got 10 percent of her income and 90 percent of her time.

"Oh. I figured it had to be *something*," she said as they walked into the house.

Mike ignored her. Instead he went into his bedroom to check his messages. There was one from Ibn:

"Yo, nigga, why aren't you answering your celly? . . . "

Mike looked on his bed, where his cell phone sat folded. He had forgotten to bring it with him.

". . . You probably don't even have it on you. I don't even know why I bothered getting you one. The whole idea is for people to be able to reach you when you're out, frat. Anyway, listen, if you see my home number on your caller ID, don't pick up the phone. It'll be Tiffany calling to check up on me 'cause I told her that I was with you. That me and you went up north to check out some pledgees at your brother's college. Remember, don't pick up the phone if you see my number. . . . Yo, man, I'm hooking up with Hope and Racquel's freaky asses in Burlington—"

Mike stopped the machine. He had gotten the gist of it. He didn't need the details.

"What a jerk. That shit is pathetic."

Mike turned around to find Bunches standing there. He hadn't heard her enter the room.

"How often do you lie for Ibn?" she asked.

Mike's face turned red. He tried to act nonchalant. "First of all, why are you sneaking up on a brother?"

"I'm not sneaking. I came in here to ask you if you want half my shrimp fried rice for half your sesame chicken."

"Yeah."

"Now answer my original question."

Mike looked away, uncomfortably. He picked up his cell phone and set it on his dresser. "I'm not lying, Erika. I'm just not answering the phone."

"Oh, okay. So the next time you see Tiffany and she asks you about your little road trip to Seton Hall, what will you say?"

"*Then* I'll lie." Mike said, trying to be funny. He could tell by her reaction that his attempt had missed its mark. She went back in the living room.

When Mike joined her a couple of minutes later, she had already put the movie on. He picked up the plate she had made for him and joined her on the couch. He looked over at her. Bunches was chewing silently with her eyes fixed on the television. He decided to test the waters.

"What's the name of this movie, again?"

"*My Favorite Year*." She took a bite of her egg roll.

"It looks old. Is that Peter O'Toole?"

"Yes, and it is an old movie. My mother was a big Peter O'Toole fan. She took me and Trevor to see this movie when we were kids. It was one of our favorites."

"Oh." Mike looked over at her. It wasn't often that she mentioned her mother. Mrs. Truitt had died in an automobile accident when Bunches was nine and Trevor was fourteen. Their father had never been a factor in their lives, so the siblings had learned to rely on each other and had been extremely close.

They were five minutes into the movie when Dexter walked into the house.

"What are you doing here?" he asked.

Mike looked at him like he was crazy. "What do you mean, why can't she be here?"

"I'm not talking about Bunches, jackass. I mean you. I was getting ready to sublet your room to pick up some extra cash."

Bunches laughed.

"There's ten thousand comedians out of work, and you want to be one." Mike said sarcastically.

"Hey, Bunch," Dexter said as he headed for his bedroom.

"Hi, Dexter." She looked over at Mike. "I've even noticed that sometimes your car is missing early in the morning when I leave for class."

"Your powers of perception are daunting, m'lady," he replied, mimicking O'Toole's British accent.

Mike felt her stare still on him and looked over at her. She wanted an explanation.

"Sometimes, if it gets too late, I'll crash on Sharice's couch. We're not doing anything—she's a born-again Christian, you know. Very into her faith . . ." Mike stopped short. Why was he explaining himself? "Not that it is any of your beeswax," he said lightly.

"So, why are you telling me?" She turned her attention back to the screen.

"I just didn't want to compromise Sharice's virtue."

"It's a bit late for that," Dexter said as he came into the living room. He picked up the plate of egg rolls and sat down in a chair, resting the plate on his lap. "That particular battle was lost long ago, my friend."

"Help yourself, Dexter," Bunches said snidely.

"Don't mind if I do," he said, already midway through his first one. "What are you guys watching?"

"My Favorite Year," Bunches replied. "I'm trying to broaden your boy's horizons, expose him to a little culture. You know, give him a little class."

"Yeah?" Dexter laughed. "How far into it are you? I could use a little class, too."

"You said a mouthful, which is quite a feat considering how you are inhaling those egg rolls," Mike said. "But it's a bit late for that. That battle was lost long ago, my friend," he added in as derisive a manner as possible.

Dexter looked at him, then looked at Bunches, and burst out laughing. "You see how he defends Sharice, Bunches?"

"I've noticed," she said, not as amused.

"He's ready to turn on me over some girl he ain't seen in years. Me! His boy, his ace boon coon. His diaper buddy, his—"

"Can I watch the movie, please?" Mike asked.

The three of them were still as they watched the movie. Then Mike noticed Dexter starting to get a little fidgety.

It was during a powerful, poignant scene. O'Toole's character, Alan Swann, was being chastised for not being a bigger part of his daughter's life. He hadn't even seen her in over a year. Upon finding this out, one of the other characters in the scene told him, "Shame on you." After a dramatic pause, Swann soberly agreed. "You're right, Belle. Shame on me, indeed," he said.

Spurred on by his shame, he finally did go visit his daughter, but was too cowardly to get out of the car and speak to her.

"See, that's what I can't have," Dexter said quietly. "A child of mine not knowing her father. That's why I'm getting me and Denise a spot together."

Bunches looked at him. While Mike had already known of Dexter's intentions, this was the first she had heard about it. "Yeah?"

He nodded.

"Dexter, you wouldn't be like this guy," she said. "He isn't involved with his daughter at all. It's an extreme case."

"Still. I want my child to live with me. You miss out on too much with that weekend dad shit."

After the movie, Dexter stepped out. He was in such a hurry that he didn't bother telling Mike and Bunches where he was going. Mike figured he knew. While he was washing the dishes, Bunches went into the bedroom to talk to Tiana on the phone.

"Tiana told me to tell you good night," Bunches said afterward as she walked into the kitchen.

"So how is my angel face doing?" Mike asked.

"She's fine." Just then she caught sight of the mound of dishes. "Whoa, where did all these other ones come from?"

"They've been sitting here since this morning, courtesy of my housekeepingly challenged, dishwashing-impaired roommate."

Bunches picked up a towel and started drying the dishes. She let out a soft chuckle.

"What?"

"I was just thinking how easy Tiana would have it if you were her father."

"What do you mean?"

"Michael, she has you wrapped around her ten-year-old finger. You would let her get away with murder."

"No, I wouldn't."

Bunches stopped drying and stared at him skeptically.

"Grand larceny, assault, and arson, maybe. But I would definitely put my foot down with murder, dammit."

Bunches laughed.

"But I wouldn't have to worry about disciplining Tiana anyway," Mike said.

"Why not?"

Now it was his turn to look incredulous. "Erika, don't you know that little girl can do no wrong in my eyes?"

Bunches smiled. "Yeah, but she knows that, too. And that's where you might have problems. You'd create a little diva, with attitude to spare."

"Maybe, but is that the worst thing? It's better than having a daughter with low self-esteem. Those are the ones quicker to fall for, and tolerate, bullshit from men."

Bunches was pleased that Mike thought that way. "True. Speaking of bullshitting men, Johnny Handsome called while I was on the phone."

"Who, Ib?"

"Who else?"

"What did he want?" Mike asked.

"He's on his way home and wanted to make sure that you hadn't spoken to Tiffany, that you guys still had your lies coordinated."

Mike knew Bunches was disappointed in his playing a part in Ibn's deception. She held him to a higher standard than the other guys. "Erika, why are you acting surprised? You know that Ibn cheats on Tiffany."

"Yeah, but what I didn't know is that you were his enabler."

"So, what did you tell him?"

"I told him Tiffany was probably sitting in their living room waiting to put a cap in his ass. That you had talked to her earlier before you got the message and that she was plenty pissed off."

"You didn't." Mike said. He looked over at her to see if she was telling the truth. Her face was blank as she continued drying the dishes.

"I did let him worry for a little while, but I eventually told him the truth," she finally said. "It's something about Ibn. Even when he's in the wrong, I can't stand to see him suffer. I guess I love him too much."

"Enabler number two." Mike took the stopper out the sink.

"Nah, you're his boy. It's your place to say something."

"I get on Ibn all the time." Mike said while he dried his hands. "He doesn't listen to me. You know full well that Ibn is gonna do what Ibn wants to do." He picked up the plates and started putting them in the cupboard. "So what did you say to him?"

"I told him he should be ashamed of himself," Bunches said as she hopped up on the counter to sit. "Skulking around with other women when he already has a good one at home."

"What did he say to that?"

Bunches paused and looked at Mike earnestly before answering. "He said, 'You're right, Bunch. Shame on me, indeed,' " she said with a perfectly executed British accent.

Later that evening, Bunches and Mike were watching Jean-Luc Picard restore civility throughout the universe when there was a knock at the door. Mike opened it and Ibn came barreling in, waving a piece of paper.

"Read this shit!" He thrust the paper at Mike. He then noticed Bunches sitting on the couch. "Hey, Bunch," he said.

"Hey, Fibbin'," she said.

Ibn didn't respond to her needle. He was too busy·studying Mike's face as he read the letter.

Mike finished and let out a deep breath. "Wow," he said.

"Yeah, do you believe the audacity of that bitch?"

"What happened?" Bunches asked.

Mike looked at Ibn. "Sure, let her read it. I'm sure she could use a laugh, too."

Bunches took the letter from Mike and began reading.

Ibn scratched the back of his neck with agitation. "I'm so tired of her bullshit. That girl has been riding for years, and she still finds shit to bitch about. I put her through grad school. I paid off her student loans—nothing is enough for her. Think about it. How many twenty-eight-year-old women do you know that drive a Lexus, live in the kind of crib she does, has the wardrobe she has, all provided by her man, mind you—she doesn't pay for jackshit—and still complain as much as Tiffany does?"

"Ibn, I'm finding it kind of hard to sympathize with you. You're a se-rial cheater," Bunches said.

"True, I admit I'm an asshole when it comes to other pussy. If she said something about that, at least it would be a legitimate beef. She doesn't even mention that in the letter, though. Does she?"

Bunches scanned it again.

"That's because while she may suspect, she doesn't know. I never get caught."

"What is she referring to here about 'reaching an epiphany' on a drive back from the woods?" Bunches asked.

"I was about to ask the same thing," Mike said.

Ibn scowled. "First of all, what the fuck is an 'epiphany'? That's what I want to know," he asked. "That silly-ass girl can't even break up with a person right."

"It's like when something is exposed to a person and all of a sudden everything is made clear. A revelation," Bunches answered.

"Humph." Ibn sneered. "Well, last week she took me out to a spot in the woods and we had sex." He hesitated before he continued. "She got her panties in a bunch because I didn't remember that it was the first spot where we had did it."

"Did it?" Mike asked, "You mean, made love?"

"Yeah," he said.

"Oh, Ibn," Bunches said, her voice thick with disappointment.

Ibn winced and shifted from foot to foot. "Bunches, that was five years ago. I have sexed Tiffany in parks, on beaches, in caves, everywhere. Why was I supposed to remember that one?"

"Because it was important to your lady, that's why. Ibn, a woman's first time with a man she loves is special." Bunches momentarily turned her attention away from Ibn. "Don't you agree, Michael?"

He shrugged his shoulders. "I wouldn't know, Erika. I've never been a woman."

"Thanks a lot." Bunches gave him a twisted smirk before turning her focus back to Ibn.

"Is all her stuff gone?" she asked.

"Yeah, her closet is empty. You *know* she wasn't gonna leave her clothes."

Ibn is so silly, she thought. "Where do you think she is?"

"She probably went to her mother's. That's where she always goes when she calls herself breaking up with me." Ibn looked at the TV distractedly. "I don't see how y'all watch this *Star Trek* bullshit."

Mike ignored that comment. "So, what are you gonna do?"

"I'm gonna enjoy my freedom, at least for as long as it lasts," Ibn said. He nodded his head rapidly, clasped his fingers and stretched his arms. "She'll be back. I just wish I knew she was pulling one of her stunts today, I would've stayed with those hookas I was with earlier. You best believe they didn't wanna let 'Ibsky Doodles' go." Ibn checked his watch. "But hell, the night *is* still young."

"What makes you so sure she'll be back?" Bunches asked.

"Baby doll, she always comes back. Tell her, frat."

Mike nodded his head. "That much is true. But I don't ever remember her writing any letters like this one." He took the paper back from Bunches and perused it again. "This 'lack of growth . . . unfulfilled needs . . . don't see a future for us' thing sounds kinda serious, Ib."

"Please, Mike." Ibn snatched the paper from Mike and balled it up. "Don't tell me you're falling for her bullshit. Just last month she's in my ear nagging me about wanting to have children, and now she doesn't want anything to do with me? All this is, is a power play to get me to marry her."

"So, why don't you?" Bunches asked.

" 'Cause I ain't ready for that. And I ain't being buffaloed into it by Tiffany or anybody else."

"Well, then, it sounds like it's a standoff," she said. "One of you is either gonna have to relent, or it's over."

"Yeah," Ibn said as he walked into the kitchen to throw away the paper. "But when she comes back this time, we're gonna get some things straight." He checked his watch again. "In the meantime, I'm gonna enjoy myself. I'm thinking about hitting a club tonight. You guys down?"

Bunches was amazed. This was extreme, even for Ibn. "Your lady moves out on you, and you're going out?"

"Of course." Ibn shrugged indifferently. "Tiffany would like me to sit home and stress over her. I don't know when that girl is gonna learn that shit just doesn't work with me. If she wants to play Ms. Inaccessible-with-the-Pussy, then I'll go find somebody else. Believe me, there are plenty who want Tiffany's spot in my bed."

This was the side to him she couldn't understand. "Damn, Ib."

"I'm just being real, Bunch. So, you guys down?"

"Nah, man, I'll pass," Mike said.

"While you're in ho-procuring mode? No, thank you," Bunches said.

Ibn shrugged. "You're probably right. You two would only slow me down. Y'all stay here and act like some broken-down Huxtables, then." Ibn looked back at the screen and sneered. "Watching *Star Trek*, no less." He headed to the front door. "Where's Dex?"

"I don't know. He left out of here a little while ago."

"Well, I have to go home, shower and change clothes." Ibn opened the door and stepped outside. He spread his arms and inhaled deeply. "Y'all smell that?"

Bunches walked up behind him. "Don't tell me, 'fresh pussy,' right?"

Ibn gave her a double-take and feigned shock. "Damn, Bunch, I was gonna say, 'opportunity.' Why do you have to be so crude?" He leaned over and gave her a peck on the cheek. "See y'all."

She closed the door behind him and turned to Mike. "Do you think he believes his own bullshit?"

"Good question." Mike pondered it for a minute. "I'd have to say yes. It might be ludicrous, but it's not false."

"So, how long you giving him this time, Heathcliff?" She sat next to him on the couch.

"Who?"

"If we're the Huxtables, you're Heathcliff, right?"

Mike laughed. "Oh, I didn't know what that fool was talking about."

"So, what's your over-under betting line?" Bunches asked.

"You mean before he's begging me to go down to Maryland to convince Tiffany to come back to him?"

"Yeah."

"Well, Clair, I say about three weeks."

"You're crazy. He won't last that long."

"I got a twenty that says he will."

"You're on." They shook hands to seal their wager and resumed their TV viewing.

"Uh-oh, it looks like Jean-Luc is gonna disobey the Prime Directive. Starfleet is gonna kick his bald ass," Mike said.

"By the way, if I win the bet, put my twenty dollars toward getting Xavier those new sneakers he wants. His birthday is coming up."

"Thanks, but I already got it covered." Mike looked at Bunches. "I'm more interested in how I'm gonna get my money if you lose. You have been known to welsh on a bet or two."

"Who, me?" she asked innocently.

"You see anybody else sitting here?"

"Well, then make me pay it. Add it to my rent."

They both got a big laugh out of that one. Then, without thinking, Mike leaned over and kissed her on her forehead like he had done a thousand times before. But it felt different today. Sensual.

Bunches smiled at him. Mike wondered if it had felt different to her, too. If it had, though, she wasn't tipping her hand. Bunches took one of the end pillows and placed it on his lap, where she rested her head.

She had done this a thousand times before as well. But Mike questioned if her intention this time went beyond mere comfort. Maybe Bunches had seen his arousal earlier in her apartment and wanted to see it again.

"So, I can't move now?" he said, playing it cool.

"Why?" She looked up at him. "You got somewhere else you gotta be?"

Mike shook his head. Truth be known, he felt mighty comfortable, too. "I like your hair like that, Erika."

She turned back toward the TV. "Yeah?"

"The way the curls frame your face. It's very attractive."

"Um-hm."

Mike leaned down and planted another soft kiss on her temple. He had to fight down the urge to aim lower down.

"You'd better stop kissing on me all the time, Michael," Bunches said without turning from the TV. "People might get the wrong idea."

"Ibn is always hugging and kissing on you," he said, unfurling one of her curls. It snapped back into place when he let it go.

"Your point?"

"My point is that you never worry about people getting the wrong idea when he does it."

"You're not Ibn."

"Oh, so that's how it is."

"Yep. Ib's a man's man. A man of action, who takes what he wants. I like that. I don't go for the namby-pamby, touchy-feely kind."

Though he was certain that Bunches was kidding, Mike was a little stung. "Well, I suggest you hurry up and get over there to your 'man's man' before some other skank fills that vacancy in his bed."

Bunches chuckled. "Oh, I got your *skank*, buddy . . ."

"Yeah, the same place I got your *namby-pamby*," Mike answered, making them both laugh.

"It wouldn't be the *wrong* idea with Ibn, anyway." Bunches yawned casually. "I've been hitting 'Ibsky Doodles' off on the regular, at least once a week, for a while now."

Bunches heard Mike gasp for air. "Erika, you aren't serious, are you?"

"No." She sighed softly. "Truth is, Ibn hasn't bedded me in years." Just then a fight broke out on the bridge of the *Enterprise.* "Yeah, Jean-Luc, handle your business, son!" Bunches yelled at the screen.

She felt Mike's stare along her cheek, which she ignored for about ten seconds before deciding to let him off the hook. Partly because she didn't want him to stress, but mainly because he had stopped playing with her hair, which she had been enjoying. She pinched him on his thigh.

"Calm down, Lovett. I'm only having a little fun with you."

Slowly, Mike's heartbeat started to return to its normal rate. "Why do you insist on scaring me like that?" he asked.

"What, am I too loud? I'm sorry."

"That's funny, Erika. Now there are ten thousand *and one* comedians out of work," he said. He brushed his fingers through her curls. "You know what I'm talking about. Damn, I'm still trying to shake the thought of you and Ibn out of my consciousness."

Bunches turned her head and looked up at him, pausing for a couple of beats before she finally spoke. "Now, see there, Michael, I didn't even know you cared."

Eleven

"I didn't expect to see you back here tonight," Denise said as she opened the door.

"I wanted to talk to you." Dexter took her hand in his and led her over to the couch. She looked at him uneasily.

"I was just watching some movie with Mike and Bunches, and it got me thinking—"

"What movie?" Denise asked. She nervously checked her watch.

"I don't remember the name of it—it's not important. Anyway, Denise, I want to tell you something." She seemed jumpy, but Dexter ignored it, not wanting to lose his train of thought. "Regardless of how we reached the point we're at, we're here. You're the vessel for an amazing occurrence—what I mean is, that growing inside of you is our child. You and I are bonded for life as only two people who bring a child into the world can be. I have no doubt you're gonna be an excellent mother, and I'm gonna try and be the best father possible—"

"I know you will, Dexter." She smiled tensely.

He squeezed her hand before he continued. He figured her anxiety was due to his rudeness at the doctor's office. "I want you to know that the reason I want us to live together is because I—" Dexter fidgeted. "I'm committed to giving us the best possible chance to make it as a family, long-term."

Denise reached over and hugged Dexter tightly. When she released him, he saw that her face was truly relaxed and happy.

"Dexter, listen. I want you to have Thanksgiving dinner with my family."

She wasn't wasting any time, Dexter thought. He guessed she wanted to strike while the iron was hot. "I don't know, Denise. I usually go up to Maplewood and spend Thanksgiving with my mother and stepfather."

"That's why I'm giving you so much notice." She still clung to him. "Please, Dexter, I want you to meet my family."

"I'll see what I can do," he said. She gave him a long kiss, which Dexter interpreted as one of gratitude and relief.

"You smell good. What's that perfume?"

"Jean-Paul Gaultier." She finally released him.

Dexter then noticed she looked good as well. "You going somewhere?" he asked.

There was a knock at the door. The expression on Denise's face transformed from euphoria to concern. "Yeah." She got up to answer the door. "I wish you had called before you came over."

Marla and a young, skinny dark-skinned brother Dexter didn't recognize walked in.

"Hey, girl—hi, Dexter," Marla said with surprise in her voice. She looked at Denise. The man with her looked at Dexter, too.

"Hi, Marla."

"Dexter, this is Kwame," Denise said as she closed the door behind him.

Dexter and Kwame nodded at each other. Damn, Dexter thought as he looked at Kwame's slender build. Marla's big ass must wear him out in the sack. Guess opposites do attract.

"Are you coming with us, Dexter?" Marla looked at Dexter's jeans and sneakers.

Us? Dexter thought. "No. I just stopped by."

"Without calling first," Denise added as she sat in a chair.

Dexter's look turned harder. "I gotta call first, now?"

She folded her arms. "I would appreciate it. Then maybe I wouldn't have made plans."

That's fair, Dexter thought. He had put her in an awkward position. Now she was gonna have to cancel on Marla and her boyfriend, who had taken the time to come by and pick her up. Marla walked over and sat next to Dexter on the couch.

"So, Dexter," she crossed her legs to the best of her ability, "when are you gonna introduce me to your cute roommate?"

Dexter looked at her questioningly and then over at Kwame. Marla shook her head.

"I'll see what I can do," Dexter said. He looked back at Kwame, who was still standing near the door, trying his damnedest to look tough. If he wasn't Marla's man, then who the fuck was he here for? And why was Denise waiting to tell them that she couldn't go out tonight?

"So, you ready?" Marla asked. Denise didn't respond. She was avoiding eye contact with everybody in the room. " 'Cause you know women get in free at Club Nubia only until ten."

Denise had a perplexed look on her face, like she was deciding her next move. She finally looked at Dexter.

"You're welcome to stay here if you'd like," she said.

Dexter was stunned. Club Nubia? Why was her *pregnant* self going to shake her ass at a club, anyway? With a roomful of men trying to freak her on the dance floor. Like this skinny nigga standing by the door, maybe. Club Nubia? A smoke-filled club—wait a second, don't even tell him that she was gonna be *drinking*. With little Dexter IV incubating inside her?

Dexter gave a second's thought to telling Denise where she could stick her invitation, but he summoned every ounce of self-control he had to keep his cool. This was made even harder by the fact that he caught sight of a quick smirk on Kwame's face.

"No," Dexter said, getting up, "I'm gonna head back over to Jersey."

As soon as the words were out of his mouth, Kwame stepped aside to give him an unobstructed path to the door.

Denise looked totally flustered, trying to figure out what she should do. From Dexter's point of view it was too late now, anyway. "Dexter, can I see you in the bedroom?"

"Nah," he said as he headed to the door. "I don't want you to be late. I've wasted enough of your time."

*   *   *

"I wanna go see a movie tomorrow," Stacy said. She and Colin were dressed for bed. The lamp was still on because Stacy was doing a crossword puzzle.

"What's out?" Colin asked.

"I don't know. That new Denzel movie."

"What's it about?" he asked.

"I don't know," Stacy replied. "I just hope it's nothing like that *Bone Collector*. I wanna see something lighter."

Colin smiled at the mention of that title. A couple of days ago, he and Ibn had been in a video store and had come upon *The Bone Collector*. Ibn had held the box in the air and said, "Look, frat, the Sharice Watson life story."

"What's so funny?" Stacy asked.

"Nothing," Colin answered. He took her hand in his. "I agree. Let's go see something romantic."

Stacy laughed harshly. "Colin, you wouldn't know romance if it crawled into this bed and bit you in the ass."

"What? I'm always ready. You're the one that never wants to anymore."

Stacy sighed. "See, that's what I'm talking about. You don't know the difference between fucking and romance."

"Oh, I see, and you're the authority. When was the last time you surprised me by doing something romantic?"

"I've given up."

"You must be getting me mixed up with somebody else, because I don't remember you ever exerting much effort. It's seems to me, I'm always the one reaching out to you." Colin let go of her hand.

Stacy reclaimed it. "I'm just saying that we can both make more of an effort."

The phone rang.

"Who in the hell is calling this time of night?" Stacy asked as she reached over and picked it up. Colin had no idea. Even his mother had enough sense not to call this late.

"Hello? Yeah, hold on," Stacy said unpleasantly. She handed the receiver to Colin over her shoulder.

"Hello?"

"Yo, frat, Tiffany catted out again."

"Yeah?" Colin asked.

"Yeah," Ibn replied, his voice light and airy like it was a joke to him. "I'm not *meeting her needs*."

Colin chuckled. Ibn's impersonation of Tiffany's voice was pretty good. "Well, you seem to be taking it well," Colin said. Stacy rolled over and gave him a hostile look.

"She'll be back," Ibn said. "Well, I just wanted you to hear it from the horse's mouth, before Stacy's nosy self heard it on the street."

Colin ignored his dig at Stacy. From the warbling background noises he could tell Ibn was in his car. "You headed home now?"

"Naw, I'm going to that trick Racquel's house," Ibn replied. "I'll get with you."

"All right, man, I'll talk to you later." Colin ended his conversation and handed the receiver to Stacy, who put it on its base on her nightstand.

"So, Tiffany left Ibn again?" she asked.

"Yeah."

"Good," Stacy said gleefully, putting the puzzle aside, "that girl finally wised up."

"Don't start celebrating too soon. You know that she always comes back." Colin draped his arm over Stacy's waist and started kissing her shoulder.

"So, what's Ibn gonna do now?"

"Hmm?" Colin was too preoccupied with what he was doing to answer. He moved his mouth to her neck and his hand to her breast. Stacy shrugged her shoulders in irritation to get him to stop.

"What?" Colin asked.

"I don't feel like it."

"See, that's what I mean," Colin said. "You never feel like it anymore."

"See, *that's what I mean*," Stacy said nastily. "You don't know the difference."

He groaned and dropped his head onto his pillow.

"Besides, it's not the truth," she said. "We had sex three nights ago."

"What?" he answered testily. "So that's my quota for the week or something? When did it become such a chore for you?" He had felt that Stacy had just been going through the motions for a while now. And it worried him.

"Don't get an attitude, Colin, I just don't need it as often as you do."

The phone rang again. "Must be your boy, Lone Wolf again." Stacy rolled away and reached back over to answer it.

"Hello? Yeah, hold on." She held the receiver in between her thumb and index finger like it was a soiled diaper and handed the phone to Colin, "Speaking of chores, your mother is on the phone."

Colin looked at the clock and sighed. It was after eleven o'clock. His mother apparently felt any time was a good time. "Hi, Mom."

"What did that child call me?"

Colin rolled away from Stacy. Damn, here we go. "Nothing."

"I ain't stupid, boy. What did she call me?"

Damn, Colin thought, why did Stacy have to get her agitated? Like she wasn't enough to deal with already. "She didn't say anything."

Stacy let out an evil snicker.

"Listen, Colin, if you're gonna sit there and let that low-rent hussy talk that way about your mother, then—that's a sin, that's what it is. You can go to any bar in America and find another Stacy, but you only have one mother."

Colin hugged the receiver tightly to his ear. Stacy would go off if she heard that. "I know," he said, "—that I only have one mom," he quickly added. He didn't want his mother to think he agreed with the first part of her statement.

"Do you?" she asked, her voice rising. "I wouldn't know. You make it seem as if I'm a burden."

Colin closed his eyes and grimaced. She was really getting worked up. He was about to get out of bed and go into the living room so he could console her in private, but Stacy climbed on top of him, effectively pinning him to the bed. He motioned for her to get off, but her only acknowledgment was a wicked smile.

"You're not a burden to me, Mom."

Stacy rolled her eyes and whispered, "Stop lying." She then started kissing Colin's chest.

"Then why don't you come visit me more often? You know your old mother hasn't been feeling well lately. . . ."

Colin tuned his mother out. She could've been speaking Chinese for the amount of attention that he was paying her because Stacy had moved down his body to his belly button and was licking it.

". . . I just hope it isn't because of that trifling thing you call a girl-friend. You let her run you. I don't know why you can't find a decent woman that . . ."

Stacy was now kissing his inner thighs. Colin desperately wanted to get off the phone so he could give Stacy his undivided attention.

"Um-hmm, Mom, listen, I'm gonna have to call you back in the morning."

"Why? What's going on?"

"I'm in the middle of something." Colin moaned, partly because his mother was getting on his nerves but mainly because of what Stacy was doing to him.

"What?"

Colin saw Stacy looking up at him while hungrily rubbing her cheek along his penis. "I gotta go. I'll call you back tomorrow, okay?"

"Fine, Colin, if you can't spare a couple of minutes for your mother, maybe you shouldn't even bother calling me back. Don't do me any fa-vors," she said. "I know you'd rather not be bothered with me at all."

"Please, Mom," Colin said, "you know that's not true."

Suddenly, Stacy sucked her teeth and threw Colin's dick aside like it was yesterday's newspaper. She pushed herself off the mattress and stood up.

"Sometimes, Colin, I just don't know. If I didn't call, would I ever hear from you?"

He closed his eyes in pain. That question was like a fucking Zen rid-dle. They would never know the answer to that because she never gave Colin the chance to call first.

When he opened his eyes, he saw Stacy putting on her robe. He didn't have the time to soothe his mother's fragile psyche right now. "Yes, you would. As a matter of fact, I'll call you back in an hour to prove it. Okay?"

Stacy gave him a look of utter disgust.

She hesitated. "All right—"

"Bye." Colin clicked the phone off before his mother could say anything else.

Stacy was tying her robe tightly closed. "Why do you put up with her worrisome ass?"

"Take it easy, Stacy. You know how temperamental she is. She's going through the change of life."

"Oh? What change is that? From being an entire person to just an asshole of one?"

"Yo, Stacy, that's my mother you're talking about."

"Whatever." She headed for the door.

"Where you going?" he asked.

"To the kitchen, I'm hungry."

"I got something for you to snack on." He grabbed his still erect penis and used it to motion for her to come back.

"I don't want that." She folded her arms across her chest, studying Colin. "I'm going to make an omelet. You want one?"

"But this here is cholesterol free."

She turned and left the bedroom.

"What?" he called out. "I can't believe you're just gonna leave me here pointing north like I'm some kind of weather vane."

"Ask your mama to do it. If you can get off her nipple long enough."

Twelve

When Mike awoke that morning, he lay in bed for an hour trying to collect his thoughts. He was more than a little troubled by what had transpired between he and Bunches the night before. Nothing happened, of course—he wouldn't allow that—but the undeniable fact was that he felt like he wanted something to happen.

Mike threw the covers back and sat on the edge of his bed. This is crazy. Sharice was the woman in his life. Maybe he was just using Bunches because Sharice wasn't available to him last night.

Yeah, Mike convinced himself, that was it. It was Sharice that he wanted and he was just projecting feelings on Bunches that were meant for Sharice. Sharice was the woman he wanted.

Mike stood up and walked toward the bathroom. As a matter of fact, he decided, he was going to pick up a gift for Sharice from Sears today.

Mike and Brandon, the groundskeeper for Sharice's apartment complex, struggled, but finally managed to get the TV through her front door and onto the stand.

Sharice thanked Brandon for his assistance and closed the door behind him. She turned and faced Mike with a big smile on her face. "You're something else. It's not my birthday."

"I don't need a holiday to do something for someone I care about, Sharice."

She wrapped her arms around him and gave him a kiss on the lips.

Mike returned it with one of his own. Recently, she had taken to kissing him and cuddling with him, though they never took it past that stage. He knew that because of her religion, she was practicing celibacy. While he did respect and admire her decision, it was still difficult for him because he was so attracted to her.

"Don't give me too much credit. My motives were partly selfish. I spend a lot of time over here, and that thirteen-inch black-and-white relic you have was getting on my nerves."

Sharice looked at it and laughed. "Poor thing. It used to be color. It still comes in and out occasionally. I would've gotten around to buying another one eventually."

"Yeah, well, I got tired of being held hostage by your fickle TV."

Sharice let go of him and walked over to her new TV and stand, which had come with the TV free. Mike liked the mauve-colored dress she had on. It looked good against her skin tone. "You know I don't watch a lot of television, anyway. It's hard to find anything that isn't full of sex and profanity."

"You like that Pax channel. You got me *Touched by an Angel* to death."

"Hey, that's a quality show." She ran her hands along the top of the TV. "How big is this thing? It's huge."

"Thirty-one inches." He and Dexter had a twenty-seven inch one at their place, and he'd wanted to top it. Mike started flipping through the instruction manual.

Sharice studied him for a moment, then went over to the couch and sat down. "Mike, I want to thank you again for taking me to that gospel concert last night."

"You're welcome. Wow, Sharice, this thing has a lot of features."

"So, what did you think of it?"

"The concert? I enjoyed the music. I especially liked Dawkins and Dawkins."

Sharice shifted her weight on the couch. "I know you enjoyed the music, I'm asking you what do you think—or rather, what do you feel?"

He looked warily at her. "What do you mean?"

"Did you feel the Spirit move you?"

"Oh," he said, feeling at a loss. Whatever he had felt last night, it paled in comparison to what Sharice and most of the other people around him were apparently feeling. While he was enjoying the music, clapping and tapping his foot a little, other people were shouting, speaking in tongues, and working themselves into a frenzy.

"I don't know, Sharice. I never thought I was attuned enough into how God works to know when He is specifically moving me. I mean, how would a person know?"

"You *know*," she said adamantly. "He moves different people in different ways. Me, I get the flushed cheeks and a tingling all over my body, like goose bumps."

"What you just described," he said lightly, "I get that when I watch a great individual athletic performance, or from a R. Kelly ballad."

"Oh, no, it's different!" Sharice said firmly. "Once you develop a better relationship with God, you'll know the difference."

Mike knew he was treading on treacherous ground, so he tried to choose his next words carefully. "Sharice, there's a reason I'm a little cautious. When I was a child, I would sit in church every Sunday—my mom saw to that—and I would notice things. Like every week almost like clockwork, how the same three or four women would get 'happy.' I noticed how the women competed as far as dress, and the snide remarks that would be made if somebody wasn't up to snuff. My uncle was a deacon, and on Saturday nights he, the reverend, and a couple of the church elders would all gather at his house to watch porn movies. Eight hours later they'd be the most pious, righteous brothers you'd ever want to meet." Mike shook his head at the memory. "I was supposed to believe these men when they were telling me the proper path to the kingdom of God? Where does the Good Book say, 'Thou shall watch Vanessa del Rio gang-bang videos incessantly?' Show me, I must have missed that."

When Mike saw the look on Sharice's face, he knew he had not been careful enough.

She recoiled at his flippancy. "First of all, Christians aren't perfect, we're just forgiven. For you to condemn an entire religion based on the actions of a few people in one congregation—"

"I've been to a lot of churches, Sharice—"

"—is silly. Just *silly*. If that's your attitude, then why do you go to church with me every Sunday?"

Damn, Mike thought. He knew this was a no-win conversation. "To support you."

She threw her head back and cackled harshly. "Me? You should be there for *you*. My soul is taken care of. If you don't want to go, then don't go."

"I'm a very spiritual person, Sharice. I'm just not a big believer in organized religion."

"Everybody who doesn't go to church uses that weak justification."

"Where does it say a person has to sit in a church in order to be a good Christian?"

" 'Not forsaking the assembling of ourselves together'—Hebrews 10:25. It's not a chore for us, Mike. Christians feel at home in church."

Mike decided against his better judgment to press on. They had to talk about this sometime. "Sharice, please, you can't tell me everybody sitting in that church is there because they want to be there. Now, *that's* silly. Most of the people are there either because of fear, because of habit or because of a sense of obligation. You trying to tell me that on most people's one day off, they wouldn't rather sleep in and chill out instead of getting dressed up to go sit in somebody's church?"

Sharice's eyes were ablaze. "Yes!" She pounded her fist against her knee for emphasis. "Believe it or not, some people look forward all week *to* Sunday. When we can meet together in the Lord's house and praise Him, and thank Him for the blessings he's given us during the week."

Mike wasn't in the mood to back down. "Sharice, you're not naive. You see the way those men in that church ogle you. They wanna 'meet together' with you, all right. For a little one-on-one counseling in the parsonage, maybe. Exorcising *all* kinds of demons."

Sharice gasped but then quickly recovered. She pointed her finger toward the door. "Get out."

"What?"

"Leave my house," she said coolly.

"If that's what you want."

As Mike got into his car, he muttered to himself. At least she didn't say, "Get thee hence." He looked in the rearview mirror. When was he going to learn to just shut up sometimes? Hell, he had almost finished programming the TV. He had wanted to watch the Penn State football game in thirty-one-inch surround-sound comfort.

Mike decided to stop by Ibn's Voorhees store on the way home. One of his employees, Nate, told him Ibn was in his office in the back. He knocked on the door.

"Come in."

"What up, man?"

"Hey, Mike. What brings you by here?"

Mike settled in a chair and looked around. Ibn's office was immaculate. The two hanging plants were green and healthy looking. Along the wood-paneled walls were dust-free shelves on which sat pictures, fraternity paraphernalia, and trophies from Little League teams that Ibn's store had sponsored. The most impressive item in the room was the mahogany desk. On it Tiffany's picture was displayed prominently.

"What, I can't stop by and see my boy? I'm trying to learn some secrets from the wireless communication tycoon."

Ibn gave him one of his classic smirks. "Yeah, right. You have no interest in my business. What really happened? Did the Holy Roller put you out?"

Mike's uneasy laugh gave Ibn his answer.

"I figured it was just a matter of time." Ibn went back to looking over the invoices on his desk.

"What do ya mean?"

"Mike, from what you've been telling me, this is a whole different Sharice than the one we knew before. Right?"

"Yeah. Well, it's the same person, of course, but you know she's different because of her faith."

Ibn reached into his desk to take out another pen, but still didn't look up. "Do you think it's a change for the better?"

"Of course. You know that. She was letting guys stick and dick her at random before."

"No question it's better for her. I'm asking, is it better for you?"

Mike mulled that over. He needed some clarification before answering. "What do you mean, Ib?"

Ibn finally looked up at him. "Mike, I'm asking, do you want what is best for Sharice?"

"Of course," Mike said emphatically. "You of all people should know that, as much as you get on me about my relationship with her." He hesitated before adding, "I think you know how I feel about her."

Ibn accepted Mike's declaration without skipping a beat. "Loving somebody and being good for somebody are two different things. For instance, Tiffany knows I love her. Right now she's questioning whether loving me back is in her best interest."

That was a mature viewpoint for Ibn to be taking, Mike thought. Tiffany had been gone for over a week, and he seemed to be handling it very well. It looked like Erika was soon going to owe him twenty dollars.

"So, what have you been doing in her absence? Turning your house into Sin City?"

"Oh, no," Ibn said, faking alarm at the thought. "Are you crazy? I don't like bringing hoes to my crib. I have neighbors, Mike. I'm an upstanding member of the community."

"Yeah, right." Mike thought about asking Ibn why he questioned his motives with Sharice, but decided not to. "So, you staying here all day?"

"No," Ibn said. "I'm gonna come back later on this evening, though. Right now I'm about to head over to Camden for a haircut." He looked up at Mike's head. "I suggest you join me, Eddie Munster."

When Mike and Ibn stepped into Amir's barbershop, Amir was sitting in a barber's chair. He looked at Mike and Ibn with a pained expression on his face.

"Yo, Willie," Amir said, "we need to give serious consideration to relocating to another area. There's too much riffraff around here. I'm taking a beating on my property values."

Willie and the customer he was cutting both laughed.

Ibn turned to Mike. "How come every time we come in here, this Q-dog gotta talk shit to us?"

Mike shrugged his shoulders. "He can't help it, frat. It's obvious that the boy lacks culture."

"Culture?" Amir interrupted. "Lemme tell y'all something. One Omega man has more culture in his purple and gold pinkie than you clowns have in your whole fraudulent fraternity."

"And class," Ibn added, shaking his head at Amir. "A dreadful lack of class."

"Good call, Ib. But then again, should one really expect class from a man who belongs to an organization where they woof at each other?"

"You're right, Mike. How silly will they look when they're seventy years old, still making dog sounds to each other?"

"Yo, fellas," Amir said. "Y'all made a mistake. Admit it, renounce your shit and get down with the purple and gold. Or, live with it. But, please don't hate." Amir's face turned serious. "It lessens you."

They all laughed.

"Nigga, just get out of that chair and cut my shit," Ibn said.

Amir playfully punched Ibn as he got up. "So, what's up with you, Mike?" Amir asked as he put the smock around Ibn.

"Same old." Mike shrugged his shoulders from the chair he was sitting in. He picked up a copy of *Upscale* magazine and started flipping through it.

"You still working at that spot in South Philly?" Amir asked.

"No. I still work for the same company, though."

"I need to stop by there and pick up a suit. Is that sweetboy still working there?" Amir asked.

"Who, Terence?" Ibn and Mike made eye contact. Ibn gave him a look that said, "Don't start."

"I don't know his name," Amir said. "All I know is that he has too much sugar in his shoes."

"Yeah, he's still works there," Mike said, looking back at the magazine.

"You want your usual cut, Ib?" Amir turned on his clippers.

"Of course. Why mess with perfection?"

Amir scoffed. "That's what I ask," he said, "whenever you try to guard me on the basketball court. 'Why is this fool trying to mess with perfection?'" Amir started on Ibn's hair. "Though now that I think about it, I guess you finally did learn, because I haven't seen you at the courts in a while."

Ibn waved his hand beneath the smock. "Amir, please. I haven't been at the courts in a while because I got *tired* of seeing that look of disappointment on your face when I schooled your ass. Damned tired of it." Ibn grimaced like he was in pain. "I was starting to feel guilty, especially when I would embarrass you in front of your daughters." He sighed deeply. "That look of despair on their faces would be so tragic it would haunt me. The final straw was when one of them handed me a note written in crayon that said, 'Please, Mr. Mean Man, stop embarrassing our daddy. He can't play a lick, but he's *our* hero.' " Ibn sniffled. "That shit was downright poignant."

Everybody in the shop laughed. Amir waited for it to subside before he came back at Ibn.

"What? The only thing you were *tired* of was my balls across your face when I dunked on you. When we play, it's like I'm building a new restaurant called Dunkin' My-nuts."

Mike had to put the magazine down on that one, he was laughing so hard.

A clean-cut, chubby boy of about fourteen walked into the shop. He was wearing an oversize FUBU jersey, baggy khakis and a pair of Lugz boots.

"Hey, Courtney," Willie said. He leaned his customer back and started applying shaving cream to his face. "How ya doing?"

Courtney half waved to him. He put fifty cents in the honor box and grabbed a bag of barbecued corn chips before sitting down.

"What's this, Courtney?" Amir asked, mimicking Courtney's lackadaisical wave. "Mr. Gordon spoke to you."

"Hi, Mr. Gordon," Courtney said as he settled in the chair next to Mike. "I'm fine, thank you."

"That's better," Amir said. "You know your mother raised you better than that."

Mike and Ibn saw Courtney roll his eyes—after he made sure Amir's back was turned.

"Actually, Amir," Mike said, returning to the earlier topic, "I am thinking about a career change. I think I wanna do something where I work with kids."

Ibn looked at him from his chair. "Yeah?"

Mike nodded. Lately he had come to realize how much he enjoyed the time he spent with Tiana and Xavier. How rewarding it was to see their eyes open to the new thoughts, experiences and ideas that Erika and he gave them. And how he had learned so much from them as well.

"Well, if you decide to become a teacher," Amir said, "you can have my brother's old job."

"Hey, that reminds me," Mike said, "where is Myles? I haven't seen him in a while."

"He moved down to Maryland with his lady."

Ibn sprang to life. "Oh, yeah, we seen her with him." He looked at Mike. "Remember, a while back at the mall?"

"Oh, yeah." Mike let out a sigh of appreciation. "I think I would move out of state for her, too."

"Ya know," Ibn added.

Amir laughed. "But you know something, to be so good-looking, she's a real sweetheart. She's good people."

Ibn closed his eyes as if he was recalling the woman's image in his mind. "I remember that she had an accent. Where's she from?"

Mike looked at Ibn. If he had any sense, he'd better be concerned about *his* woman in Maryland, not Amir's brother's.

"She's Cuban." Amir turned around and picked up a different set of clippers.

"It's rare that you'd find a black woman from this country who is that pretty who doesn't come with a serious attitude," Willie said.

"Un-hm, that's what I hate that about them!" Courtney said, licking his by now orange fingertips. "That's why I only mess with white girls."

The man in Willie's chair rose as if he had been shot and stared at Courtney. Willie's knees buckled, and he had a look on his face that went far beyond mere pain. Ibn's mouth fell open in horror. Even Mike reflexively leaned in his chair away from the kid, just in case lightning struck him down.

Amir turned off his clippers and looked at Courtney. "What you have just said is so problematic, on so many levels, I almost don't know where to begin. My first thought is to snatch your stocky ass up by your neck, drag you out into the street and run over you with my truck, but instead, since you're just a baby, I'm gonna try to educate you." Amir turned his clippers back on. "First of all, let's me and you take a journey to the birthplace of civilization and meet the mother of creation. . . ."

For the next ten minutes, while he cut Ibn's hair, Amir went on an eloquent discourse, stating the many wonders, beauties and mysteries of black women. He spoke with such persuasiveness and reverence that Mike almost wanted to run out of the shop, drop to the ground at the sight of the next sister he saw and hug her knees. By the time Amir was done, even Ibn damn near had a tear in his eye.

". . . so keep that in mind, next time you 'messing' with one of your white girls," Amir said, wrapping up his speech. "Okay?"

"Yeah," Courtney said quietly.

"Now, I'm gonna spare your mother the pain of telling her what you said. 'Cause, dammit, she deserves better than that." Amir shook his head and sighed. "Fellas, I don't know what's gonna become of our people when we got young bucks saying the most outlandish nonsense."

"Courtney, at your age you shouldn't be worried about *messing* with anything except your books, anyway," Willie added.

"Yeah," Amir agreed, looking back at Courtney, who had made his way back to the honor box to get a giant Slim Jim. As he bent over, his oversize pants sagged off his hips. "Boy! Pull up your pants! Why don't you get one of those white girls you're so fond of to buy your chunky ass a belt?"

When Mike pulled up in front of his house, he looked for Bunches' car. He hadn't seen much of her all week, and it concerned him. He wondered if she too was uncomfortable with their interaction last Saturday. And if so, how? Mike felt they needed to talk but wasn't exactly looking forward to the prospect because he was afraid of what might come out of such a conversation. His newfound attraction to Bunches was troubling enough, but if she in any way reciprocated, then it could become downright complicated.

He walked into the house and checked his phone. Mike saw that there was a message from Sharice. Mike wondered if she had called to unload on him or whether the phone call was conciliatory in nature. He called her back.

"Hello?"

"Hey, Sharice."

"Hi." Her voice turned softer when she recognized it was Mike. "What are you doing?"

He decided to throw her a bone. "Penance, for upsetting you earlier."

Sharice chuckled lightly. "Oh?"

"Yeah. I'm sorry for stepping over the line, Sharice."

"Apology accepted. Though I didn't react the way I should have."

"Oh?" Mike was genuinely surprised. The old Sharice had never been eager to accept culpability. As far as he could tell, this new and improved Sharice was even more reluctant to do so. He hadn't expected her to feel one ounce of remorse for kicking him out, especially since in her mind, she had done so in defense of her beliefs.

"Yeah. I prayed on it after you left. I realize the Enemy is going to attack me from all directions and try to get me to doubt my faith. I have to realize that these tests are coming and that I have to be strong to withstand them . . ."

Oh, Mike thought. He had never thought of himself as a conduit for Ol' Slewfoot. Is that what he was now? The Devil's mouthpiece?

". . . so I prayed that God will touch your heart, as he has mine."

Mike couldn't think of anything to say, so he said nothing. After a short pause, Sharice continued.

"Whatever man I end up with, the one thing I'm going to insist on is that he's saved," she said. "I just can't see trying to make a relationship work where I'm the only one committed to Christ."

"That would be like my parents," Mike said. "Week after week, my mom would dress me and my brothers for church while my dad lay around in his drawers waiting for football to come on."

"See, I can't have that. It would never work."

"That sounds reasonable," Mike said, wondering if all this was being said for his benefit. He decided to find out. "You mean your man would have to be a Christian, too, right?"

"Not just that, Mike. Me and my man would have to be equally yoked. His commitment has to be as strong as mine. He has to turn his life over to Christ, too."

Mike thought that over for a second. "But you wouldn't want him to take such a step just to please you, would you?"

"Oh, no," she said adamantly. "That wouldn't be a real commitment, so it wouldn't last. He should do it because he wants to. What I can do is tell him about the many glories of Christ, and what He has done for me."

He knew she had always been aware that he enjoyed her company, but that had been the old Sharice. This new, pious Sharice was taking some getting used to.

"So, what do you think about that?" she asked.

"I think that's more than reasonable, Sharice. I'm sure you'll find what you're looking for."

Mike felt her smile through the phone.

"So, are you coming back over here, or what?"

"Do you want me to?"

"Yes," she said quietly, then added, "I *need* you."

"You do?"

"Yeah. I don't know how to program this TV. You know I ain't even trying to miss my *Touched by an Angel*."

Thirteen

Dexter walked out of his room and sat on the sofa next to Mike. The phone in his room was still ringing.

"Why don't you answer your phone?" Mike asked.

"I checked the caller ID. It's just Denise."

"Why are you avoiding her?"

Dexter had decided not to tell his boys about Denise's taste for the nightlife, which he felt didn't reflect too kindly on her character. She was still going to be the mother of his child, and he didn't want his friends to think less of her, which he did, because in his mind, only the silliest of bitches would go to a club while they were pregnant.

"We had a disagreement last weekend," Dexter said.

"So, now you're being unavailable to her? That'll show her!" Mike mocked. "What if she needs you for something important?"

Dexter picked up the remote and shrugged. "If it was something important, she would say so in her message. And it's more than just 'showing her.' I need some time to cool off before I deal with her. And at the same time, hopefully she'll get her priorities straight as to who and what is important."

"Let me guess. You should be priority number one, right?"

"That's right. She pissed me off the other night. Really fucked with my head. Dammit, if I'm gonna be losing sleep—"

"Then she's gonna be staring at her ceiling, too."

"Damn right."

"I hear you."

"It'll be a week tomorrow. I'll start talking to her again," Dexter said. "By the way, she has a friend who is interested in you."

"Yeah? How does she know me?"

"She's seen you in passing." Dexter grinned mischievously, "So, you want me to hook it up for you? Maybe we could double-date, or something."

"What's that stupid look for?" Mike asked.

"What stupid look?" Dexter tried to straighten his face out.

"What's this girl like, man?"

Dexter stroked his goatee, which he had been growing out the past week. He tilted his head back while doing this to appear thoughtful, but also to avoid eye contact with Mike. "She's got a lot of personality, which I know you like. She's very down-to-earth, no pretense about her. Always on point. She's funny, self-sufficient—"

Mike laughed. "Dexter, who do you think you're talking to? I know you're spouting euphemisms. 'Lot of personality' means *loud*. 'No pretense about her' means *ignorant*. 'Always on point'—that's a new one. I'm not sure, but it probably means *street*."

Dexter laughed.

"And I noticed you haven't said anything about what she looks like," Mike continued.

"Is that important?" Dexter asked.

"It must be. Usually the first thing out of your mouth when describing a woman is the physical."

Dexter ran his tongue along the inside of his cheek. "Well, let's just say she's altitude challenged."

"What does that mean?" Mike asked. "She's short?"

"Not really." Dexter busied himself clicking the channels on the TV and looked at Mike out of the corner of his eye. "She's just a little underheight for someone of her poundage." He tried to sneak this by Mike by saying it rapidly.

"Oh. So, she's a little chubby?"

Dexter winced.

"More than a little chubby?" Mike asked.

"Let's just say she's had a long and rocky love affair with food."

They both cracked up. There was a single familiar knock on the door.

"Come in, Bunches," Dexter called out.

"What's so funny?" she asked, coming in and taking the chair next to Dexter. She avoided looking at Mike.

"Mike. He doesn't want to double-date with me and Denise."

Bunches finally looked at him, but only after she was sure she could keep the anxiety off her face. "Why? This Sharice chick got your nose that open?" She studied his face while awaiting the answer.

"No," Mike said, though that was a major part of it. "Dexter's not being totally forthcoming with you."

"Huh?"

"He means that I'm not telling you—" He held his hands out in front of his stomach with his palms facing in and puffed his cheeks out. "—the *whole* story."

"Oh." Bunches said, looking at the TV, doing a good job of appearing indifferent.

"This guy." Mike jabbed a thumb in Dexter's direction. "And he's supposed to be my boy."

Bunches turned back toward Mike. "I didn't know you minded girls with a little chuckle on them."

"I'm afraid that Marla goes way beyond a little chuckle," Dexter said. "Though you can't tell her she ain't he finest thing on two feet— flat as they may be."

Mike looked over at Bunches and saw she was casually watching TV. He was glad to see things were back to normal.

Ibn picked up his phone, hesitated, then put it back down and looked at it. He breathed deeply and picked it up again, this time forcing himself to dial the number.

"Hello?"

Damn, Ibn thought. He decided not to hang up this time. "Hello. May I speak with Tiffany?"

"She ain't here," a harsh voice replied.

"Can you tell her I called, Mrs. Robinson?"

"I can, but I won't. And I'd appreciate it if you wouldn't call my house anymore."

Ibn sighed. "What's your problem?"

"My problem is you. You don't know how to treat my daughter right, and I'm glad she's finally figured that out."

Ibn gripped the phone tightly. "Oh, so you're Ms. Concerned Mother now? Please. While you and her father were going through y'all's situation, who do you think took care of her? Who had to stay up at night holding her in his arms while she cried because you both were heaping all y'all's bullshit on her, with y'all's selfish, supposed-to-be-the-parents asses. Who paid her way through grad school, fed her, made sure she had a place to live, and clothes on her back? Who paid off her student loans so she could start her career free of debt? Student loans she had to take out because y'all's preoccupied asses forgot you had a daughter in college. Too busy being vindictive with each other and making your lawyers rich to tend to your daughter's educational expenses."

Mrs. Robinson answered in her nasal, Southern twang. "Negro, please. You had a live-in girlfriend. You did what you were supposed to do."

"What!" Ibn took the receiver from his ear and glared at it, disbelieving what he had just heard.

"You heard me. You had a live-in girlfriend available to you. You were supposed to do that, and more."

"What kind of bullshit is that? I didn't know you thought of your daughter as a commodity. She didn't come with a price chart. So, tell me, in your opinion, what is the going rate on a blow job? A week's worth of food and a new outfit?"

"Listen to me, you foul motherfucker. Don't be calling my house anymore—"

"Actually, I didn't call to talk to you, anyway."

"Tiffany can do much better than you. Like the young man she's out with right now, for instance. He's a definite step up from your sorry ass. I know you cheat on my daughter, dipping your nasty West Indian dick in every piece of pussy you can."

"Oh, so that's what this is about? You still preoccupied with my dick?"

"What?"

"You heard me. I see how you look at me. You're just mad that I'm fucking your daughter instead of you."

She wheezed.

Ibn had gone too far but was too far gone to care. "That's right, I peeped your game a long time ago. You're trying to compete with your daughter. Wanting her youth, beauty, and everything else that she has, thinking that your man wouldn't have left you if you still looked like Tiffany. And if you can't have what she has, then you want her to be as miserable as you. But guess what? I don't care how much you're begging for it, I ain't gonna fuck you. You hear me, old lady? *I ain't gonna fuck you!*"

She hung up.

Well, Ibn thought, that didn't go as well as I would've liked.

When Mike was certain that his phone was really ringing and that he wasn't having a nightmare, he reached over and picked it up. "Hello," he said groggily.

"Yo, man. I can't sleep."

"Huh?"

"I said, I can't sleep."

Mike fell back against his pillow. This asshole. "So, since you can't sleep, none of us can? It's—" Mike looked at his digital clock, "Damn, Ib, it's two-thirty."

"I know what time it is. Yo, man, I got the Robinson girl on my mind."

This nigga. "So, why are you calling me instead of her?"

"I tried to call down there. Her mother always answers the phone."

"So?"

Ibn hesitated. "Me and her had words."

Mike propped himself up onto his elbows. "That's good, Ib. Way to get back in Tiff's good graces."

"That ho bitch started it."

Mike yawned. "Whatever, man. Are you done unburdening your soul yet?"

"C'mon, Mike, persevere with me. You supposed to be my boy."

The only light in Mike's room was the red numbers from his clock.

His forest green venetian blinds kept out any moonlight. He liked his room dark. "I'm trying, Ib, but two-thirty is two-thirty. I gotta go to work tomorrow."

There was a pause at the other end.

"I want you to go to Maryland for me."

"Dammit, Ib, I ain't going down—"

"Yo man, you got to do this for me, this one time—"

"One time?" Mike asked incredulously.

"One *last* time. Mike, Tiffany listens to you. You know she thinks higher of you than she does of me."

"And for good reason. I'm not the one cursing out her mom."

"C'mon, man, look out for a brother. I'll name my firstborn after you."

Mike closed his eyes. At this point he just wanted to get off the phone. Besides, he had known this request was coming. "All right, I'll see what I can do."

"Thanks, frat. I appreciate it."

"Yeah, yeah. I'll talk to you later."

"Wait. So, when you gonna go down there?" Ibn asked.

Jackass. Mike clicked the phone off and rolled over. Damn, it had only been a little over two weeks. He owed Erika twenty dollars.

Fourteen

"Dexter, couldn't you have handled it more maturely?"

Dexter looked up at Denise as he stretched out on her couch. He had finally decided to return one of her calls that morning. "What do you mean?"

"Instead of giving me the cold shoulder, don't you think we should have talked about it?"

Dexter shrugged. "I wanted to talk that night."

"Which we could've done if you had told me you were coming over. Instead of just showing up unannounced. I could've been anywhere."

Denise was genuinely confused by Dexter. One minute he gave off long-term hints; the next he acted like he couldn't be bothered with her.

"I took a chance on you being home, and you were."

"But I was on my way *out*," Denise snapped. "Besides, I told you, you were welcome to stay here. If you wanted to talk, you would've."

Dexter looked back at her. She was standing over him with her arms across her chest, scowling at him. Who the hell did she think she was yelling at? But then again, she knew exactly who she was yelling at. Dexter could disappear all he wanted, because that extra heartbeat in her belly assured that he wasn't really going anywhere.

"Denise, what the hell were you doing going to a club anyway?"

She seemed ready for that question. "I wasn't trying to meet anybody, Dexter. Kwame got a promotion at work. We were just taking him out to celebrate."

"What I mean is that you're pregnant."

"No, really?"

"Yes, really. You shouldn't be going to a club."

Denise flipped her wrist at him and headed for the kitchen. "You're being silly, I'm not even showing yet."

Dexter shot up off the couch. What kind of ghetto mentality was he dealing with here? Before he could respond, she finished her thought:

"I know one thing. I'll be glad when we move in together. So you can't pull any more of your disappearing acts."

Damn, Dexter thought, Ibn might have been right. He might have been a little hasty in making that offer.

"I was thinking I'd like to live in Bucks County. We should go to a couple of open houses that I've . . ."

Dexter shut his eyes tightly and tuned her out. Who wouldn't want to live in Bucks County? Did she know how much a house there would cost? Evidently, she didn't, or she wouldn't be saying such outrageous bullshit. This all had to be a bad dream. It just had to be. When he opened his eyes he would wake up and tell Mike all about this nightmare. All he needed was a pinch.

He got a poke instead.

"Dexter"—she jabbed a finger into his shoulder—"were you listening to me?"

Denise had come out of the kitchen. She had some food dangling on the end of a fork under Dexter's nose.

"Uh, yeah. I heard you."

"Try this," she said.

Dexter looked at it suspiciously. "What is it?"

"Just try it."

He half opened his mouth and then turned away. "You aren't feeding me any swine, are you?" That was something else they needed to talk about. He wanted her to stop eating pig.

She sighed. "I know you don't eat any pork. Will you just eat it?"

He finally relented. As he was chewing, she smiled knowingly.

Dexter swallowed. "Damn, Denise. That is banging! What is it?"

She laughed. "A new chicken dish I'm trying."

"Well, lemme tell you something, you're succeeding." That was at least one thing that he had to look forward to. Denise was an excellent cook. Dexter swallowed and hungrily looked toward the kitchen for more.

"Who told you to grow that goatee?" she asked.

"Nobody."

"It looks good."

"Thanks."

She put the fork down and pushed Dexter onto his back and lay down on top of him. She held him tightly.

"I thought you were mad at me," Dexter said.

"I am," Denise purred. "But I missed you."

Mike and Sharice were snuggled on her couch watching an episode of *Highway to Heaven*. During times when they were cuddling like this Mike figured that either Sharice had been born with the use of only four of her five senses or was the best actress in the world, because she seemed oblivious to the erections that their close contact would bring about, including the one that was currently rubbing up against her thigh.

"Do you have any plans for Thanksgiving?" he asked.

"No, I don't."

"Then why don't you spend Thanksgiving with me at my parents' house?"

There was a pause before Sharice spoke. "I don't know, Mike."

"C'mon, Sharice. What are you gonna do, put a turkey potpie in the oven? You know it's a sin to spend Thanksgiving alone. It says so right in the Good Book."

That made her smile. "Oh, yeah? Where does it say that?"

"Um, you know, Third Corinthians, chapter two, addendum 1A. 'Thou shall never pass up a home-cooked meal.' Declining a Thanksgiving dinner is an abomination, so sayeth the Lord."

Sharice laughed. "You know full well that's not in there."

Mike was enjoying her playfulness. "Well, if it isn't, it should be," he continued. "As a matter of fact, that might be one of the missing books. It's probably written in the Dead Sea Scrolls."

"Besides, I wouldn't be alone," Sharice said. "You'd be sitting right next to me with your potpie, right?" She raised her head to look at him and gave him a squeeze.

"Sharice, you know how fond I am of you, but if you think I'm gonna incur the wrath of my mom by skipping out on Thanksgiving, then you got another think coming. My mother ain't above going upside my head."

Sharice chuckled and laid her head back on Mike's chest.

"So, what do you say?" he asked.

"Who all is gonna be there?"

"My parents, my brother, Erika, my grandmother, some of my aunts and uncles, a couple of cousins."

"That's it?"

"Yeah." Mike had a feeling he knew why she was reluctant. "It's just family."

"Erika isn't family."

Bingo. "She might as well be. My parents treat her like their daughter. But she'll be the only one there not part of my family, unless my brother brings someone with him from school." Mike hesitated before adding, "Ib, Dex and Colin go to their parents' for Thanksgiving."

"Why did you feel the need to tell me that?" she asked, keeping her eyes on the TV.

"Just to let you know that you wouldn't be seeing them," Mike said cautiously.

He felt her body tense up. "Why would I care if I saw them?"

Mike wanted to choose his next words carefully. One, he wanted to be diplomatic as possible and spare her feelings. Second, Sharice felt good as hell rubbed up next to him, so he didn't want to piss her off and get shown the door again.

"I was concerned that you were thinking that they might see you as you were, instead of as you are. Not letting you evolve."

"Oh." Mike felt her body relax, but she still didn't look at him. "And you don't see me that way?" she asked, her voice barely above a whisper.

"Sharice, I've always seen you as you should be. I'm just glad that now you share my high opinion of you." He planted two tender kisses along her hairline.

Sharice whimpered softly and buried her head into his chest. Overcome, she began tugging at his shirt. Not knowing what to say to console her, Mike rubbed her back. When she finally lifted her head, Mike tried to kiss her, but Sharice slid down his body and parted her legs so that his penis was between her thighs. She started gyrating slowly, rubbing their crotches together through their clothes. When she started unbuckling his belt, Mike spoke.

"Sharice, I—"

"Shh." She finally looked up at him as she moved her index finger to her lips. "Shh," she repeated. When she was confident that Mike wasn't going to talk, she went back to the task at hand and unzipped his pants.

When their eyes had met, Mike noticed that playfulness in Sharice's face of a couple of minutes earlier was gone. He worried whether this was a good or bad omen. Yet when the sensation caused by Sharice's lips around his penis hit him, he no longer cared.

Dexter pulled Denise off the couch and onto the floor, making sure he brought her down on top of him gently. While she licked his lips, Denise rubbed his temples with her thumbs and stroked his scalp. Dexter moaned appreciatively and Denise smiled. She knew his bald head was his weak spot. She straddled him, grabbed his ears and plunged her tongue into his mouth. Dexter strained his neck trying to inhale her and ran his hands up her back. She stopped kissing him and sat up and slid her sweatshirt off her head.

"Wow," he said softly.

Denise smiled. "They're getting bigger, aren't they?"

He sat up and urged her onto her back. Dexter lay down beside her. He started kissing the area around her nipple while sliding his hand between her thighs and began massaging her over her sweats.

Denise gripped the back of Dexter's head and began licking the top of it. Dexter opened his mouth as wide as he could and took in one of her breasts. While using the suction from his lips to hold it in place, he ever so lightly brushed her nipple with his tongue.

Denise convulsed, let go of Dexter's head and jerked back onto the carpet. As Dexter untied her pants and slowly ran two fingers toward her wetness, she moaned softly and spread her legs wider. Her hands fell limply by her sides.

Dexter teased her with his fingers, touching everything except what she wanted him to before finally relenting. He also moved off her breast and started licking his way down her belly.

"Wait, before you go," she panted, pointing at the dry breast, "don't forget the other one."

Mike scooped Sharice in his arms and carried her into the bedroom, his pants falling down along the way. He laid her down on the bed.

Mike sat on the edge and reached for his wallet to take out a condom. Sharice clutched his free hand and started hungrily sucking on his fingers. After procuring the condom he turned to face her.

He was startled by the look on her face. She looked like a wild woman. Sharice let go of his hand and quickly slid off her jeans. She rolled onto her stomach and propped herself up on her elbows. She looked over her shoulder and wiggled her ass at him seductively. "It's all yours."

Mike admired it as he put on his condom. It was so breathtaking, it almost seemed a shame to defile it. However, he figured, a man's gotta do what a man's gotta do.

Denise was begging him to "put the real thing in," so Dexter took his fingers out of her. He sat up in between her legs and began poking her in the thigh with his penis.

"Put it in, Dexter, put it in," she pleaded.

He traced it along her pubic area, but wouldn't put it in.

"Put it in! Put it in!" she exhorted.

Dexter smiled and finally slid inside her. He looked down at her stomach.

Cover your ears, Dexter IV. Daddy is about to do his impersonation of a jackhammer.

Sharice and Mike were in rhythmic lockstep as he rode her from behind, and she was making one hell of a ruckus.

"It's all yours, Mike . . . It's . . . all . . . yours!" she yelped in between grunts.

Mike needed to be closer to her. He laid her flat on her stomach and moved on top of her. He placed his palms on the back of her hands, locked his fingers into hers and resumed pumping her.

"Pfffft," Sharice sucked in her saliva as he reentered her. She turned her face toward him best as she could, "Why are you doing this to me . . . huh? . . . why are you doing this to me?"

"Sharice, I've wanted you since forever," Mike whispered. He still didn't feel close enough to her. He wanted to be her second skin. Mike released her fingers, took her face into his hands and cradled it. He sucked on her cheek and savored its sweetness on his lips, a taste so pleasing to him that he finally capitulated. "You hear me? . . . Since . . . *forever!*"

Mike collapsed on top of her.

Sharice lay still for a couple of seconds, then reached up and rubbed the back of his head. "I know, Mike. I've always known."

Dexter lay next to Denise with an arm draped over her stomach. She breathed deeply.

"Now *that's* what I'm talking about," she said appreciatively. She patted him on the wrist.

Dexter smiled. "We all have our special gifts, Denise. In the kitchen, you wield a mighty frying pan, while I—"

"—sling a mean dick?"

Dexter looked at her with fake shock. "Why do you have to be so crass? I was gonna say, 'know my way around a vagina.' "

Denise turned to face him. "And I wonder how you got to be such an expert in that area?"

"How do you think? I paid attention in health class, of course."

They both laughed. Dexter started stroking Denise's breast.

"Are you gonna breast-feed?" he asked.

"I plan to. Why?"

"I was just thinking, me and Dexter the fourth are gonna have to come up with a schedule. His little ass ain't hogging these all to himself."

Denise's face turned serious. "Dexter the fourth?"

"Yeah." He took his eyes off her breasts and noticed the look on her face. "Right?"

"I don't like the name Dexter, for a child." She abruptly sat up and started putting her sweats on.

Not sure what was going on, Dexter sat up beside her. "Dexter Jonathan Holmes IV. I figured we could call him DJ for short."

"Did you, now?"

"Yeah, I thought you would choose the name if it's a girl, and I get to choose the name if it's a boy."

Denise put on her sweatshirt and looked at him with a look of utter incredulity. He knew what it meant. She was gonna name the child *regardless* of its gender. Dexter looked down at the carpet, feeling powerless.

Denise saw his forlorn look and placed her hand on his leg, wanting to console him. "Why don't we come up with a name that we both like?"

Dexter knew what that meant. A name that *she* liked. Besides, he wanted a namesake.

"How about Dexter as a middle name?" she asked.

Is she serious? Dexter wondered. What the fuck is up with the condescension? Trying to appease him like he was a third grader. He rudely brushed her hand off his leg.

Denise didn't take the dis kindly. "Humph," she said, rising to her feet. She had her face contorted, all ready to say something evil but caught herself. Instead, she took a deep breath.

"You hungry?"

"No." Dexter started putting his clothes back on. "I'm gonna head home."

Hurt spread across her face. "Dexter, I made this special for—"

Dexter saw the hurt but didn't care. "You eat it."

She turned and stalked toward the kitchen, turning back just before she reached it. "If I was you, I'd be worried about what your child's *last* name is gonna be."

* * *

Later that evening, when Mike came out of the bathroom, he noticed Dexter sitting in the living room in the dark. Mike knew something was on his mind.

"When did you get in?"

"About a half hour ago. Been waiting for your ass to get out the shower ever since. I hope you left me some hot water. Why do you gotta take such long showers?"

"Damn, Dex, I didn't know you were waiting," Mike sat on the arm of the sofa. "What's with you?"

Dexter tugged at the towel wrapped around his waist. "That fucking Denise."

"What did she do?"

"Mike, I know it's as much my doing as it is hers, but it's hard for me not to blame her." He looked at Mike. "I feel like she's fucking up my life. I mean, I planned out my life to go a certain way and then she comes along and now everything is—it's fucked up, that's what it is."

Mike sympathized with Dexter's plight to a degree. But he really thought that Dexter was discounting how much of a blessing a child was. "Dexter, we're at the age where we want to have children, anyway. Back when we were in college, we never thought that we would be thirty and still be childless."

"I know, I know, that's what I keep telling myself." Dexter shifted his weight angrily. "It might be the right time, but this is the *wrong* woman. We aren't on the same page with anything. She does things which I think are borderline retarded, and I'm sure she feels the same way about me. We are two incompatible people who because of circumstance have to deal with each other." He looked at Mike. "You know what she told me today?"

"What?" Mike asked, toweling his head.

"That if the baby is a boy, she wasn't gonna name him Dexter."

"That's important to you?"

"Important to me? Mike, you know how much I respect my father and grandfather. All my life I planned on naming my firstborn son Dexter Jonathan Holmes IV, and along comes this . . . this . . . fucking capricious girl throwing a wrench in my plans." Dexter picked up the washcloth off his lap and wrung it tightly. "*I don't like the name Dexter for a child,*" he mocked with contempt. "I'm talking about legacy, and she's talking about what she *likes*."

Mike tried to soothe him. "You still got time. Maybe she'll change her mind."

"I doubt it. She's . . . she's the wrong woman," Dexter reiterated. "Mike, you know me. I'm a white picket fence guy. I always thought that me and *my wife* would have children, Dexter IV and so on. Not some woman I can barely stand. I keep telling myself that maybe me and Denise can give it a go, but who am I kidding? I constantly find myself biting a hole in my tongue just so I don't curse her out."

"But there's no guarantee you're gonna find that white picket fence woman, either. And if you don't, then you'll still be blessed with a child."

Dexter knew Mike was making sense, but he wasn't of a mind to be placated. "I know, I know. It just won't be Dexter IV. I hope Denise and I have a daughter. Maybe I'll meet someone else who can give me a Dexter IV." He mulled this over for a second and then groaned. "But then, that'll be that half-sibling living in different houses shit I wanted to avoid in the first place."

Mike decided to use a different tack. "Dex, cheer up. Be a man and deal with it. 'Handle your business,' as Erika would say. You *un*made your bed, now lie in it. Stop feeling sorry for yourself and look at the bright side of things."

Dexter tried to scowl at him, but had to chuckle. "And just what is the bright side of things?"

Mike shrugged his shoulders. "At least you'll have a good-looking kid—if it doesn't take after you too much. Denise is *cute*."

"That she is," Dexter admitted.

Mike held up his hands and squeezed the air. "And she has the cutest little—"

"Watch it, asshole! That's my child's mother you're talking about!"

They both laughed. Mike walked into the kitchen for a glass of water.

"What are you doing here, anyway?" Dexter asked. "Shouldn't you be at Sharice's?"

"I was over there earlier," Mike replied from the kitchen.

"What happened? She kick you out again?"

Mike laughed. He came back out with his glass. "No, I left of my own volition this time."

Dexter sniffed his chest. "I still smell Denise on me," he said.

Mike hesitated before he spoke, but he needed someone to talk to. He sat down on the couch next to Dexter and put his water on the coffee table. "That's why I was in the shower so long."

"Ha-ha, I get it." Dexter said, standing up, "Denise's scent is on you, too."

"Naw, man," Mike said, "Sharice's."

Dexter sat back down with a thump. "Are you serious?" he asked.

"Yep."

"So tell me, man," Dexter's voice rose with excitement, "are all the stories true?"

Mike looked at him disdainfully. "How old are you?"

"Mike, please. Don't drop a bombshell like the fact that you *finally* fucked Sharice and then act like you don't want to divulge details."

"I didn't tell you so I could talk on her pussy, Dex."

"I know that. Talk about her booty, tongue and tits, too. I wanna know every detail."

Mike smiled at his friend's exuberance, but he was uneasy. He fidgeted with the belt to his bathrobe. "Man, I'm worried about the effect it's gonna have on me and Sharice's relationship."

"Why?" Dexter looked at him askance. "Oh, no, don't tell me your performance was *that* bad!"

Mike rolled his eyes. "I'm serious, Dex. It could get complicated. One, because of the years of friendship we've had, and second because of what she's trying to do as far as her faith."

"Oh, yeah," Dexter conceded. "I forgot about that. So, did she hit you with a load of guilt?"

Mike thought back to after they finished, when he was getting dressed. Sharice had looked like a flower that had just bloomed. She looked completely at ease with what had just occurred, lying there with her legs splayed and practically hugging herself. "No. As a matter of fact, she specifically said she didn't feel guilty. That she felt it was right."

"Then what are you worried about?" Dexter asked.

"Dex, you know better than to believe anything a woman says when she's in that state. Not while they're basking in the afterglow of 'dick-you-phoria.' "

"True." Dexter said grimly, thinking about Denise. "Is that why you're here?"

"Yeah. I would've loved to stay and cuddle, but I wanted to get out of there before she came down off her high."

They saw the headlights from a car pull into the driveway.

"Baby girl is home," Dexter said, standing up and looking through the window.

The other cause of sexual tension in my life, Mike thought. "I wonder what she's doing with her Saturday night." He hoped she had been out on a date.

There was a single knock at the door, and then Bunches walked in. She surveyed the scene. "Now, *this* is rather incriminating."

"Mike, did you hear anybody say, 'Come in'?" Dexter tightened the towel around his waist to make sure it wouldn't fall. "What if I was naked?"

Mike had a flash of Bunches nearly nude in front of him. He tightened the belt on his bathrobe to make sure nothing fell out.

"And? It's nothing I haven't seen before," she answered.

Mike swiveled his head at Dexter and Bunches. "Oh, really?"

"Yeah, I'm a medical student. I see naked male anatomy all the time."

"But not of my prodigious proportion," Dexter countered. "You might have been scared to death."

"Yeah, right. All I see is a dark room with two grown men—half naked. I can see why you wouldn't want anybody to come in. I'm interrupting y'all's flow."

"Chill with that, Bunches."

"Oh, the shame of it all," she continued. "What would Ibn say? Check that, I know what he would say; '*Batty boys, antimen,* it's a *disgracia.*' "

Mike and Dexter laughed.

Dexter headed for the bathroom, and Bunches growled. "Tsk, tsk, look at that body," she said. "What a waste. So tell me, Dexter, are you the pitcher or the catcher?"

Dexter mooned her as he walked into the bathroom.

"Well, there's my answer. You're the catcher." She laughed as she sat in a chair. She turned her attention to Mike.

Suddenly feeling uncomfortable, Mike quickly walked into the bedroom to get dressed. "What you do all day, Erika?" he called out.

Bunches had noticed Mike's hasty departure, but wasn't sure of the reason. Was he trying not to give her any ideas, or was he running from thoughts going through his head? "Tiana's drill team had a competition in Burlington."

"How'd they do?"

"They finished second, though they should've won. We were robbed by the judges." She kicked off her shoes. "What did you do?"

"Not much. By the way, Xavier got an eighty-eight on his last math test."

"All right!" Bunches exclaimed. "I got to give X-man a big hug the next time I see him."

"You'd better watch all that hugging. You know he has a crush on you."

"So? The boy should be commended for having good taste."

"So? Let me tell you something, Erika, you've never been a horny little boy. It's torture, believe me," Mike said. "And kids develop even faster nowadays. But don't listen to me, you just keep it up. Don't say nothing when you feel his little hard-on pressed up against your thigh."

Bunches laughed. "I wouldn't say anything. I'd realize that it's a natural biological function." She looked toward the doorway of Mike's bedroom. "Why? Would you be jealous?"

Mike momentarily froze, then continued putting on his T-shirt. "Jealous? Hell, no! I don't want his dick rubbing against *my* leg."

"Ha-ha."

Mike came back out with a bottle of lotion and a twenty-dollar bill. He handed her the money.

"What's this for?"

"Ibn asked me to go talk to Tiffany." Mike sat on the couch and turned on the TV. Then he started lotioning his hands.

Bunches jumped up and started doing a victory dance, stomping like she was a member of Tiana's drill team. She went over to Mike and waved the money in his face. "You can never lose betting on the frailty of the male mind."

"Yeah, yeah, just get out of the way."

"I'm in the money, I'm in the money . . ." she teased.

"You better leave me alone, Erika."

"Mr. Jackson." She kissed the bill. "I love you."

"You do realize that you're still blocking my view, right."

She looked at the ceiling dreamily. "Hmm, now what should I spend my newfound wealth on?"

"Why don't you buy something to get that crap off your face?"

She touched her cheek. "What crap?"

"This crap." Mike reached up and wiped a huge glob of lotion on her other cheek, smearing it across her chin.

"Uh!" She jumped on top of him and they rolled onto the floor. They struggled for a couple of seconds before Mike got the advantage and pinned her down.

"Let me go."

"I will, for twenty dollars."

She laughed. "You better get off me."

"Or what? You aren't exactly in a position to be threatening anybody."

"Oh, really? Dex-mmph!"

Mike muffled her mouth. "All right, all right. There's no need for that. Let's leave his big ass right in that shower. I'll drop the demand for twenty dollars if you agree not to yell for Dex. The last thing I need is his naked, wet ass jumping on me. Do we have a deal?"

She nodded. She had grown very still. *How about your naked wet ass jumping on me?* Mike took his hand off her mouth. He started stroking her hair tenderly, ending each motion by gently touching her cheek. Bunches felt a sweet tingle travel from the contact point on her scalp down to the base of her spine.

He stopped his stroking. "Why did you straighten your hair, Erika?"

"Because you liked it curly." She made a sneak attempt to get loose.

Mike pinned her back down. "Oh, really? You better lose that atti-tude. Have you forgotten who you're talking to?"

Their eyes met. Both read the other's gaze. It betrayed their true thoughts.

Bunches spoke first. "I'm well aware who I'm talking to. Who are you?"

"Just the man who knows your every weakness." He started tickling her, trying to return their interaction to one of innocence.

Bunches started shrieking and squirmed mightily. "Stop it! Stop, Michael!" she panted.

They heard a car pull up, but couldn't see who it was from their vantage point on the floor. Mike stopped. "You got a date?" he asked, still lying on her.

Bunches was still catching her breath. "And if I do?"

"Then it'll be my turn to call for Dex," he said.

From outside: *"You are armed."*

"That sounds like Charlie Goodtime's car alarm," Bunches said.

"He probably wants to discuss strategy before I go see Tiffany."

Mike finally got up. As Erika was let loose, she started kicking at him.

"Oh, we still have a problem here?" Mike grabbed her foot out of the air and started dragging her. He lightly bit her big toe before letting her foot go. Bunches hollered.

Ibn walked in without knocking. "What's going on?" he said to Mike. Ibn then noticed Bunches lying on the carpet in her completely disheveled state.

"Bunches, what are you doing down there?" Ibn asked. He then squinted at her to get a closer look. "And I ain't even gonna ask you what that is on your face."

Fifteen

Mike was glad that he had chosen this Sunday afternoon to go see Tiffany. He could tell by what had happened earlier that it wasn't gonna be comfortable between Sharice and him for a while. When he had gone to her place to pick her up for church, she asked him to sit down. Mike had immediately known by the expression on her face that she no longer felt okay with what had happened the evening before. He could also tell by the bags under her eyes that she hadn't had much sleep.

She wasn't able to look at Mike in the face, and then she started crying. This stung Mike. That she could feel so ashamed about making love to him. She told him that they couldn't do that anymore. Mike told her he understood.

Later, during the service, when the preacher made the call to the altar, Sharice stayed longer than anyone else. She prayed so resolutely that the veins bulged in her head. She also refused to take Communion, citing that she didn't feel worthy.

Afterward, on the ride back to her apartment, Sharice was disconsolate. She said very little to Mike, instead choosing to stare out the window. Normally the time that she was most bubbly and full of life was right after church. Mike was a little worried about her state of mind, but figured he was the last person that she probably wanted in her face. When he dropped her off, she asked Mike if they were still friends. He hugged her tightly and told her that nothing had changed.

It was a lie and they both knew it—because something was now irreversibly altered between them, and their friendship was in jeopardy. Mike's thoughts ran to Erika. He wasn't quite sure what was going on between them, but one thing was for certain. He couldn't allow the same thing to happen to them.

As he turned the corner into the cul-de-sac where Tiffany's parents' home was, he breathed a sigh of relief. Her Lexus was in the driveway.

"Hello, Mrs. Robinson. Is Tiffany here?"

After an uncomfortable amount of silence, while it looked like she was deciding what she wanted to do, she finally spoke. "Yeah," she said harshly and opened the screen door. She motioned for Mike to have a seat in the living room, then headed down the hall.

Damn, he thought as he settled onto the couch. What did Ibn say to her?

Mike rose when Tiffany walked into the room. She was wearing a flannel shirt, turtleneck, jeans, boots and a huge smile. "Hey, kid," she said to Mike.

"Hi, Tiff." He accepted a warm hug from her.

She drew back and looked him over. "Why are you so dressed up?"

"I went to church. What have you been doing, felling trees?"

"You might as well say that. I've been raking leaves. I wish you had come a couple of hours ago."

Mike snapped his fingers in despair. "Shucks. Me, too. Lord knows how much fun I have raking leaves."

"You want anything to drink, smart aleck?"

"No, thanks."

Tiffany's mother walked into the room, ostensibly searching for something, but really giving Mike the once-over, like he was there to rob her.

Tiffany saw it as well and grabbed Mike's hand. "Mom, we're going out on the porch."

"Wow," Mike said as he sat in one of the metallic chairs outside. "Did I wrong her in a past life?"

Tiffany sat down on the railing facing Mike. "She's not stupid Mike. She knows why you're here."

"I wish she would let me know, then," Mike said. "I just happened to be out for a nice, leisurely Sunday drive, and I found myself in the neighborhood. So I said to myself, 'Hey, Tiff lives around here! I should drop in for a spell.' "

Tiffany playfully cut her eyes at him. "Oh, so do your nice, leisurely Sunday drives usually take you through two states?"

"No. That's what made this one so remarkable. I figured that since it was destiny, I should definitely stop by."

They shared a laugh.

"Admit it, you were sent down here to handle me."

Mike smiled uneasily. "It's that obvious?"

"I'm just wondering what took you so long." Tiffany looked at Mike's car. "No Bunches this time, huh?"

Now, that would've made for an interesting trip, Mike thought. "No. I'm all by my lonesome."

"Me, too," Tiffany said wistfully.

Mike leaned forward in his seat. "Other than that, how you been?"

"Pretty good. I like my new job. Been seeing some of my old friends that I lost touch with since high school." She stared out onto the street. "Of course, most of them are now married with kids."

Mike tried to reassure her. "You got plenty of time for that."

"Yeah, but not enough that I can afford to be wasting it with the wrong man."

That caught him off guard. "Tiffany, you know Ibn loves you."

"I know he does. But I come second behind himself."

"Maybe, but, it's a *close* second."

Tiffany tried to smile, but it was more of a grimace.

"You have a job already?" he said quickly.

"Mike, for the past two months I've been coming down here interviewing. Ibn was too preoccupied with Ibn to notice. I resigned from my job in Mount Laurel last month. He probably still doesn't even know that. He has zero interest in me as a person, other than when I'm gonna hit him off, and that's just pathetic." Tiffany was getting riled just thinking about it.

This wasn't going the right way at all.

"I know Ibn isn't the most attentive person, but be fair, Tiff. He owns two stores—"

"I'm tired of being fair. When is he gonna be fair? I'm tired of being patient. I'm tired of waiting for Ibn to grow up and see what he has in front of him."

Good point, Mike thought. Tiffany was damn near the perfect girl. She was stunningly beautiful, smart, faithful, classy and above all, loved her some Ibn. Her only downside, as far as Mike could see, might be her taste for lavishness. But then again, first her father and then Ibn had spoiled her so much on that end, she really couldn't be blamed. Mike often wondered if the fancy cars, jewelry, and vacations to exotic spots were just means that Ibn used to control Tiffany.

"Mike," Tiffany stood up and stuffed her hands in her pockets. "Did Ibn tell you that I have proposed to him . . . twice?"

He leaned back in his seat, surprised. "No, Tiffany. He's told me that you had been dropping hints about marriage, but never that you had come right out and asked him."

She drooped her shoulders in resignation. "I never dreamed that I would ask a man to marry me. I can't imagine what my family would think of me if they knew that."

Mike was running out of options. "I heard that Ibn and your mother had words. Does that play a part in your reluctance to go back?"

Tiffany shook her head. "No. I don't pay that any mind. I know my mom has her bullshit with her, too." She looked over at Mike. She could see he was fumbling for words. "Finding out about my proposing to him has thrown you for a loop, hasn't it?"

"Yeah. I didn't know."

She scoffed. "I guess he should do a better job of prepping you."

"Right, before he sends me out to slaughter."

"Slaughter? Am I being that unpleasant?"

"Not you. But if looks could kill, your mother would have had me under the cemetery."

Tiffany allowed a faint chuckle and touched his head. "You're a true friend. I hope he appreciates you. It's a rather tough task, I would think, trying to point out to someone the positive aspects of Ibn Barrington."

Mike shifted his feet. "C'mon, now. It's not that hard, Tiff."

"It's not? Name them, then." She sat back on the railing.

He chewed his bottom lip. "Well, women seem to think he's very handsome."

"I know how good-looking he is, Mike. Problem is, so does he. Is that the best you can come up with, the physical?"

"No, that was the first thing that came to mind. . . ."

"I can believe it, the way he emphasizes it, with his shallow ass," Tiffany snarled.

"Secondly, he is generous."

"True, I'll give you that. He has done a lot for me over the years." She picked at a loose chip of paint. "I think that's one of the reasons why I have put up with him for so long—out of a sense of obligation."

"He's very funny, you have to admit," Mike said.

Tiffany smiled. "Yeah, but that's only because he's so unrefined, with his ignorant self," she said. "That's it, right?"

That about covered it, Mike thought. He stood up and put his hands into his pockets. "Afraid so. Unless you want me to add loyal, trustworthy, courteous, and kind."

Tiffany rolled her eyes. "Believe me, he's hardly a Boy Scout—wanna ask my mom how courteous he can be? Or loyal, for that matter."

"Sure he is. There's never been a time when one of his boys needed Ib where he didn't come through," Mike said.

"Oh, he's loyal in that respect. He's very strong in his allegiances. He's loyal to you guys, Bunches, his fraternity, his employees, his favorite restaurant, his tailor, and his favorite sports teams. But I seriously doubt if there's ever been a time when he was *loyal* to me."

Mike didn't like where this conversation was heading. He looked down and concentrated on Tiffany's boots.

"Unless I'm wrong." She came off the railing and stood right in front of him. "Mike, look me in the eye and tell me that Ibn doesn't sleep around on me."

She had never point-blank asked him that. Ibn's fidelity was the one topic never addressed when he and Tiffany spoke. Mike took a deep breath, preparing himself to lie. He lifted his eyes to meet hers. When he saw the torment on Tiffany's face, he couldn't bring himself to do it. Right now she needed him to be her friend, too. He looked back at the floor.

"The worst thing, Mike, is that I wished you could lie to me. You would have company, seeing as how I've been lying to myself for so long."

Sixteen

"So, how'd it go?"

Mike sat down on the sofa. Ibn sat in a chair facing him.

"Her mother sends her regards."

"Yeah, right." Ibn said. "So, how'd it go?"

Mike could tell that he was anxious. He had spent the entire drive back from Maryland trying to decide what he was going to tell Ibn. "She's not coming back, Ib. At least, not right now."

Mike saw the tension in Ibn's face. "What did she say?"

"She pretty much echoed the things she wrote in that letter. You don't pay attention to her—"

"What the hell is she talking about? I don't pay attention to her!" Ibn threw a short jab into the air in disgust and rose to his feet. "Every time I fucking drop a g into her bank account without her asking, I'm *paying attention* to her! Every time I pay her fucking outrageous bills without complaining, I'm *paying attention* to her! Every—"

"Do you wanna hear it or not?" Mike asked. "It isn't gonna do you any good to yell at me."

Ibn sat back down.

Mike continued. "I don't know why you think money is the answer to everything, like throwing money at a woman can make up for your deficiencies in other areas."

"Yeah, well, she never says no when I come out of my pocket, either, does she?"

"Ibn, you can't put a price tag on a woman's dignity. Each time you fuck around on Tiffany, it's blatant disrespect. All the jewelry in the world can't buy you a free pass for your infidelity."

"Maybe not. But let me ask you a question: Would she be with me if I was faithful but broke?"

"I don't know," Mike said, getting irritated with Ibn's refusal to see anything other than the monetary. He decided to shut his ass up. "But, to be honest, that's your problem. If you felt she was only with you because of what you could spend on her, then what does that say about you?"

Ibn was quiet while he processed that question. When he finally did speak, his voice was a lot quieter than before. "You're right. I know Tiffany loves me."

"I agree. So, will you get past what you do for her and start thinking about what you *don't* do for her, please?"

Mike accepted his silence as an invitation to proceed. "She also said you don't *listen*, and I can believe that. If somebody says something you don't wanna hear, you just shout them down. You even try to pull that shit with me, so I can imagine how hard you are on your woman."

"What does she want, Mike?" Ibn asked. "An engagement ring? She's still talking that marriage shit, ain't she?"

Mike couldn't believe this guy. "Ib, you know I love you, but you have to be the most self-centered asshole on the planet. Bar fucking none! Buy her an engagement ring—what's that gonna do? Placate her and buy you some time so you can resume fucking every stray skank you can, while you still have the good girl to come home to? I'm telling you, she's fed up. At this point, while you're wondering what she wants, you'd better start worrying whether or not she still wants *you*."

Mike walked into his living room and found Bunches lazing on the couch. She looked appetizing to Mike lying on her stomach like she was. Mike forced the image out of his mind by looking away.

"Hey."

"Hi." Bunches tried to appear casual, but she wondered if he could see in her face how happy she was to see him. She sat up.

"Where's Dex?" he asked, looking back at her now that it was safe.

"He went to get something to eat." Bunches extended her palms. "So, how'd it go?"

Mike sat down and started unbuttoning his shirt. He got about halfway down before he stopped, too agitated to continue. "You know, Erika, Ibn is a true asshole. This is the last day of my life I'm gonna waste on him. If it ain't what he wants to hear, then he doesn't wanna hear it."

"Didn't go well, huh?" Bunches' eyes involuntarily moved to his chest before she reined them in.

"I think she might be done with him this time."

"That bad, huh?"

"Yeah. I asked her could she afford to take that chance, you know, of finding someone better than Ibn. What if she doesn't?"

Bunches clucked her tongue. "Typical. Trying to play on a woman's fear of being lonely. Men think they are so indispensable, like even if a woman's miserable with her man, she's still better off than those sisters that don't have one."

"Well, I figure," Mike countered, "most women will stay with a man they know ain't about shit until they can replace him with a better man, justifying it in their minds with the belief that a sorry man is better than no man." He finished unbuttoning his shirt.

"Oh," Bunches folded her arms, "you really think so, huh?"

"That's been my experience."

"And your experience is so vast, right?" Bunches snapped.

"Of course. I've always been the man that ain't about shit who got replaced," Mike joked. "Remember those two sisters from Delaware me and Dexter were dating last year? Remember what they told us when we pissed them off?"

Bunches laughed. "I remember, *'Niggas like you and Dexter are a dime a dozen!'* " Bunches continued. "Wow, a dime a dozen—think about the magnitude of that statement. Individually, you two don't even have a street value of a penny!"

Mike chuckled at how much enjoyment she was deriving from the recollection. Her countenance had softened. She reached over and grabbed Mike's hand. "You worth much more than that to me," she said tenderly.

"Thanks, sweetheart." Mike brought her hand to his mouth and kissed it. He tried to be playful, but he enjoyed the taste of her skin, truth be told.

"If I hustled," she said blithely, "I'm sure I could get a nickel for the pair of you."

"Oh, so you wanna make with the jokes. Dexter isn't here to protect you this time."

Bunches menacingly waved a fist at him. "Son, you don't want me to put this heat on you."

Mike laughed. He stood up and completely slid his shirt off. "But you're right, it was a bullshit tactic to try to use on Tiffany," he admitted.

"Well, well, somebody's been working out," Bunches said.

"I been doing a little sumthin', sumthin'."

Bunches' eyes pored over his body. Her tongue was thinking about doing a little sumthin', sumthin'. She tried to play it cool. "You always had a good physique, but I don't ever remember seeing a six-pack."

"I've been hitting the gym pretty regularly." Mike started undoing his belt and walked into his room. "Either mine, or the one in Sharice's building."

"Oh." Bunches said, deflated. She imagined that Sharice had free rein to explore Mike's body, and she hated her for it. She quickly switched back to the topic at hand. "Well, I'm glad you at least recognize your approach as being wrong. So, what did Tiffany say to it, anyway?"

"She told me that she couldn't afford *not* to take that chance. The girl told me flat out that she was tired of wasting her time with the wrong man."

"Damn." It sounded like Tiffany wasn't playing this time, Bunches thought.

"And she wasn't even emotional about it, where you can say she was just saying it out of anger. She was calm and collected, like a person who had thought long and hard and was comfortable with the decision that she made." Mike shook his head. "She said she was tired of lying to herself."

"About what?"

"Ibn's cheating."

"Wow." Bunches said. This time was definitely different. "So, Tiff finally decided to throw off the shackles of denial and bring up the topic of Tommy One-nighter's systematic lechery."

"You *know* I wasn't expecting that." Mike walked back out wearing an Old Navy T-shirt and a pair of shorts.

Bunches drew her knees up to her chest and hugged them. "So, what did you say to that?" she asked.

Mike shrugged his shoulders. "What could I say, Erika? I'm tired of lying to her, too."

Bunches suppressed a smile. "So, how's Ibn taking it?"

Mike exhaled in disgust. "I just left that idiot's house. You wanna know the last thing he said to me?"

"I'm afraid to ask."

Mike spoke, doing a dead-on impersonation of Ibn: "*Fuck that silly-ass girl. She and her mother deserve each other. All I know is, she best start making them payments on that Lexus. Now if you'll excuse me, I gotta make a call. I want some company tonight. . . .* "

Ibn looked at the clock in the dashboard of his car. Midnight. Perfect timing.

It was a shame that none of his boys could appreciate rolling in style, Ibn thought as he pulled his big Benz up to the valet area of Club Timbuktu. A true shame that he had to go big pimpin' alone.

As a valet scrambled to his door and opened it, Ibn surveyed the scene. He saw that every eye was on him. The other clubgoers waiting in line to get in, the club bouncers, the valets, the other people pulling up in their cars—they all were craning their necks to get a better look at him. Especially the women. No problem, Ibn thought, he never disappointed.

He put one of his alligator shoes out onto the pavement and let everybody see him (and his long black fur coat) swing grandly out of his Benz. Ibn eyed many women giving their girlfriends "check that brotha out" nudges. He acted like he didn't notice, of course.

"Allow me to park your car, sir?" the valet asked.

"Naw, dawg," Ibn said. "Keep my shit out front." He slid a hundred-dollar bill in the young man's hand.

"Will do, sir, will do!"

After Ibn was moved to the front of the line and through the front door by one of the bouncers, he checked his coat in and took a seat at a small table near the dance floor. That accomplished two things. It allowed him to see, and to be seen. He ordered a glass of orange juice and a bottle of Dom from a waitress and scanned the room.

The place was packed. He saw clusters of sistahs that he put into one of two groups. Those scheming ones that were full of game, but they were "right for a night," and those good girls, who were going to run home and tell everybody about the scandalous shit they see here tonight.

Ibn sniffed the air. It smelled like pussy. There was definitely going to be some freaky shit happening in here tonight.

The waitress brought Ibn's order over. Ibn began sipping his orange juice as Miami bass pounded through the speakers.

While Ibn drank his juice, various women sauntered by his table in hopes that they would catch his eye and he would ask them to sit down for a drink. From redbones to chocolate sisters, from thin to chunky, from respectable to outrageous, from underage girls to too-damn-old-to-be-in-a-club women, they all tried to curry Ibn's favor on the sly, but none dared approach for fear of embarrassment. Who would dare? Ibn, whose model looks were intimidating and breathtaking enough on their own, was dressed to kill. He was wearing all black—a tight mock neck and slacks. He had on gator shoes and matching belt, and thousands of dollars in diamonds on his wrist, in his ears and around his neck.

Just then a sister caught Ibn's eye. She was wearing a flimsy, short rayon skirt and shaking her beautiful, thick ass on the dance floor in the middle of a semicircle. She was drawing a crowd of admirers.

When she went down into a three-point stance, Ibn looked closely. She wasn't wearing any panties. His mouth began to water. This was a sistah after his own heart. The only time that Ibn wore underwear was when he went to visit his mother or had to go to court. He got up to go over and make this woman's day.

As he was approaching, he was intercepted by a tug on his arm. "Hey, sexy," a voice said in his ear.

Ibn spun around. It was Tasha. She was a stripper who used to dance under the name Black Gold at the Suga Shack. She was a fine chocolate sister. Ungodly body.

Ibn allowed her to lead him over to the bar area of the club, where it was less noisy.

"Have they rebuilt the Suga Shack yet?" he asked

"No, not yet," Tasha said. "I wish they would. I miss that place."

"You?" Ibn said. "When I heard that the Suga Shack was on fire, I put a bucket of water in the back of the Benz. I just didn't make it in time."

Tasha laughed. "Ibn, you're so crazy."

Two fine-ass women came up to where Tasha and Ibn stood. He noticed two brothers hovering around them. Ibn could tell they weren't with them, but were definitely trying to *get* with them. The women were probably letting them hang around, in case nothing better came their way.

Tasha made the introductions. "Ibn, these are my girlfriends, Portia and Lynette."

"Hello, ladies," he said.

"Were you the brother who came in wearing that fur coat?" Portia asked.

Ibn knew full well she knew it was him. He saw Lynette's eyes gravitate to the jewelry on his body. He knew what these sisters were about. All three of them. He could see the stars in their eyes. They could just dispense with the formalities, go back to one of their cribs (because he *wasn't* taking these tricks back to his) and get to fucking.

Lynette looked at his fraternity ring. "Are you a Kappa?"

"No, I'm not." Ibn said. "I may be pretty and all, but don't let that fool you. I've been known to lick an ass or two when need be."

Lynette and Portia started tittering. Their would-be suitors shot Ibn a dirty look. He gave them one right back that said, Don't even try it. Unless you boys wanna be the niggas that get slapped up in the club tonight.

*   *   *

It was past midnight, but Bunches was still up when her phone rang. She reached onto her end table and picked it up. "Hello?"

"Hey, girl. You awake?"

Bunches smiled. "Hey, big sis, how are you doing? It's about time you called me, hooker!"

"Yeah, I've been busy. Sorting things out," Tiffany said. "I do like my new job."

"That's good. Is it in the same field? Child services?"

"Yeah it is. I'm coordinator of a foster care support program."

"Congratulations," Bunches said. She admired Tiffany for the work she did. It was through Tiffany that she and Mike had met Tiana and Xavier.

"So, what's new with you, tramp?"

"Nothing. With all this studying, my plate is full."

"No social life?"

"An occasional date, but nothing serious," Bunches replied. "I'm not looking for anyone right now."

"You're not looking for anyone because you already found him," Tiffany teased.

"Here we go." Bunches rolled her eyes. She thought of Mike and their interaction of late. How she had cautiously upped the ante with him, trying to get him to see her as a viable woman. "We aren't talking about me. I wasn't the one who jetted out of state."

Tiffany sighed. "I'm tired of Ibn's bullshit. It's time for me to move on."

"Yeah, that's all well and good. I want you to do what makes you happiest," Bunches said. "But what? You couldn't let a sistah know?"

There was a slight hesitation before Tiffany spoke. "I couldn't tell you. I know where your loyalties lie."

"What's that supposed to mean?"

"You know what I mean, Bunches," Tiffany said, her voice rising with anger. "How come you never told me about Ibn's infidelity?"

Bunches sat down on her couch. She had known this conversation was coming.

"Are you gonna try and tell me you didn't know?"

"No. I knew." Bunches answered quietly. "But I wasn't the only one that knew."

"I know. Mike told me when he came down here."

Bunches rose off the couch. "I'm not talking about Mike, either, Tiffany. *You* knew. You've always known and you chose to accept it. You didn't want anyone bringing it up to you, because then you would've been forced to deal with it. As long as no one mentioned it, you could pretend it wasn't happening."

Tiffany grew silent. She knew Bunches was telling the truth.

"You're right." Tiffany acceded. "I never flat out caught him red-handed, but my life ain't a court of law. I don't need irrefutable proof. I'm the judge, jury and executioner."

"Besides, a woman doesn't suspect without a good reason," Bunches added. "If a woman even has *suspicions*, you can bet ninety-nine times out of a hundred that her man is lower than snake shit."

"Yeah."

They both fell silent.

"So, what are you gonna do, Tiffany?"

"I'm gonna keep on keeping on."

"I mean, are you finished with him for real this time?" Bunches asked. She didn't think it would be right not to at least point out the other side of the argument. "There is good in Ibn, as you well know. You've put in a lot of years with him. It may be just a matter of showing a little more patience."

Tiffany let out a snort. "Do you even believe that nonsense?"

"I'm just playing devil's advocate," Bunches countered, "but, hell, stranger things have happened."

"Obviously, I've been thinking about him a lot, since I made the decision to leave him." Tiffany struggled to maintain control of her voice. "The thing is, Bunches, I gotta be able to look in the mirror every morning and like what I see. I can honestly say that I can do that now." Tiffany's voice cracked, and she began crying quietly.

There was a pause while Bunches waited patiently for Tiffany to compose herself.

"Because I *know* I deserve better than to be constantly disrespected and ignored and dismissed, and now I'm doing something about it. I'm reclaiming myself. Understand?"

Bunches sat back on the sofa. "Yes, I do."

"I want to have children someday," Tiffany continued. "How can I raise a daughter to accept nothing less than the best for herself when I'm not doing so? And what's the most important decision a woman can make if it ain't which man she chooses to build a future with? I will not have Ibn's children and subject myself or them to a man that disrespects and despises women. That's not the legacy I want to leave."

Bunches knew that this time Tiffany wasn't coming back. Her heart had hardened, not because of emotion but because of cold logic. And all the jewelry, fancy cars and shopping sprees in the world weren't going to soften it either.

Ibn opened his eyes. He had no idea where he was except on somebody's bedroom carpet. The only articles of clothing he was wearing were one sock and a condom still on his dick, which was stuck to his thigh.

Damn, what had happened? All right, now Ibn, get it together. Okay, he remembered leaving the club with three women, Tasha, Lynette and . . . what was her name? . . . Portia, that's it. They all hopped into his Benz. Okay, so this was Tasha's place. Cool. They had come back here and drank some Dom and some Alize. The women had even convinced Ibn to smoke a joint with them, something he never did.

Okay. He remembered the girls putting on a show for him. Freaky shit. A lot of lesbo shit. Ibn emptied his wallet throwing money at them. He remembered that when he ran out of cash, he started sliding credit cards through the crack of their asses. He started to laugh, but it was too painful to do so. His head was pounding something awful.

He heard noises coming from the living room. Ibn slowly got to his feet. He took off the condom and threw it in the wastebasket. He remembered fucking Tasha and Lynette, but didn't think he had fucked Portia, though she might have given him a blow job. He searched the room for his clothes and found them on a chair. He put on his mock neck; there was a big stain on it. Oh, yeah, he remembered that accident had occurred when he poured honey on Tasha's titties.

His wallet and jewelry were neatly lying on a dresser. He saw that all his jewelry was accounted for. He opened his wallet and saw that while all his cash was gone, all his credit cards had been neatly put back in his wallet. Ibn smiled and sighed. These hoes were good people.

Bunches was in Ibn's garage looking for his aluminum bat. She had borrowed the key to Ibn's house from Dexter because she knew he had a large collection of athletic equipment in his garage. She, Tiana, and a couple of other kids and the aides from the group home were going to the park to play some softball. She heard a car pull up.

It was probably Ibn. He could tell her where his balls were. She walked out of the garage, through the house and to the front door to meet him. She gasped at what she saw.

Ibn was staggering up his walkway clutching his fur coat. His eyes were so bloodshot she could see their red from a distance. His hair was a mess, as were his clothes. He had a big stain on his shirt that she didn't even want to guess as to its origin. She looked closely at him as he approached. He was even missing a sock.

"Ibn?"

Startled, he stopped dead in his tracks. Bunches realized that he hadn't even seen her standing there in his doorway.

"Hey, baby girl." Ibn tried to tuck in his shirt and fix himself up, but rapidly gave up, realizing it was of little use.

"Are you okay?"

Ibn nodded and proceeded up to where she was standing.

"What are you doing to yourself?" Bunches asked. "Why won't you admit you miss Tiffany?"

Clearly embarrassed, Ibn lowered his head and brushed past her into the house.

Colin swallowed hard. He was certain that he was sweating and felt the need to tug at his collar but fought the urge, thinking it would be too obvious. He was grateful when they reached the lobby and the doors opened.

They stepped off. Stephanie took his briefcase so that he could put on his overcoat. The intimacy of this struck him as odd, but he liked it. "So, if you're not sick, then why are you taking a half day?"

Colin hesitated as he finished putting on his coat. He remembered what Dexter had told him before about him not needing to be so candid about Stacy. "I have to take my mother to the doctor."

"Oh. Nothing serious, I hope." She handed his briefcase back to him.

"Thank you—no, it's just a checkup."

"Well, if you're going to go see your mother, you should look presentable." Stephanie tightened his tie and fixed the collar on his shirt. When she reached around his waist to adjust the belt of his coat, Colin protested.

"Stephanie—"

"I'm almost done," she said. She smoothed his lapels, letting her palms linger a little longer than necessary. "There you are." Stephanie smiled. "You look like a thousand bucks."

Colin returned her smile. "Thank you." Now he felt like a thousand bucks, too.

"So, how did we come out?"

"Fine. You're only short two items."

Mike had just completed auditing Terence's store. He and Terence sat down in the store's office.

"That's good. I don't think I have any thieves working here," Terence said. He was wearing a gray suit and a peach turtleneck. He took a sip of raspberry iced tea, eyeing Mike above the bottle. "There's a big show next month at Woody's on Locust Street."

"Yeah?" Mike asked, opening his briefcase.

"Yeah. A bunch of queens are coming down from New York to be in it. I'm gonna be in it, too."

"As who?" Mike asked while looking through his day planner.

Seventeen

While Colin was waiting for the elevator, Stephanie joined him. As usual, she looked great, Colin thought. He liked the way she dressed. She was wearing a brown wool skirt, with matching vest and a yellow blouse.

She saw that he was carrying his briefcase and overcoat. "So, where are you off to?"

"Home. I'm taking a half day."

Stephanie tried to mask her disappointment. "Why? Aren't you feeling well?"

"Well, actually, I do feel like the Indian food I ate last night is trying to make an encore appearance, but other than that I feel fine." Colin was really leaving to surprise Stacy with an afternoon visit.

The elevator came. They both stepped on.

"Up or down, Steph?" Colin asked.

"Boy, I'm going *dooown* . . ." Stephanie sang.

Colin laughed as he pressed the button for the lobby. "Okay, Ro Royce," he said, turning to face her.

". . . 'Cause you're not *aro-und*," she continued, looking h squarely in the eye.

Colin felt his cheeks flame. He turned away to look at the fl numbers over the elevator doors. "I didn't know you could sing. have a nice voice."

She lowered her head coyly. "There's a lot of nice things abou you don't know, Colin."

He knew that Terence occasionally performed in drag. "Somebody famous?"

"It's a secret." He waited until Mike looked up from his planner. "But I want you to come."

He had noticed the hope in Terence's voice. "Terence, you know you my boy and all, but—"

"C'mon Mike, you been promising me forever."

"I know, I know," Mike responded, laughing. "But, damn. Can't you think of another favor to ask that doesn't involve having me sitting up in a gay club?"

Terence held his cheeks in his palms and shook his head. "Mike, don't be so homophobic. Besides, most of the audience is straight. C'mon, I want you to see me perform. You've been promising to forever."

"I'm not being homophobic. I simply—"

"Then come see me perform." Terence said adamantly.

Mike smiled and relented. If Ibn could see him now. "Okay, when is it?"

"The Saturday after Christmas," Terence replied. "And bring Bunches if you're so worried about appearances."

"I'm not worried about appearances."

"Then maybe you're worried about a strapping young buck taking a liking to you," Terence teased, "and you liking it."

Mike laughed. "Yeah, that's got as much a chance as you landing into a piece of pussy and liking it."

Terence threw his hands up in horror and pretended he was gagging. "Don't say that word around me." He looked like he swallowed a lemon and his hands were around his neck. "Yecch! I don't trust anything that bleeds that much and doesn't die."

Mike ignored his histrionics. "I'll see if Erika wants to go."

His cell phone rang. It was Sharice. Terence stepped out to give him some privacy.

"Hi," Mike said, a little surprised since they hadn't been talking much lately.

"Hi."

He checked his watch. "Did you stay home today?"

"No, I'm calling from the school. I'm on a prep period."

Mike heard the door's chime, which signaled every time a customer walked into the store, go off. "So, how's your day going, Sharice?"

"Uneventful, which as any teacher will tell you, means 'good.' "

Mike didn't answer, still thinking about Terence's invite. He knew Erika would like to go. She thought Terence was great.

"I know it's late notice, but I was wondering if it was too late to accept your invitation to Thanksgiving dinner?" Sharice asked.

"Of course not."

"Are you sure? It's only a couple of days away."

"Sharice, my mom always makes just enough food to accommodate an extra thirty drop-dead gorgeous women. So if you have twenty-nine equally delightful friends you want to bring along . . ."

Sharice laughed.

"Of course not," Mike said reflexively. He felt an uneasiness, though, but it had nothing to do with the short notice and everything to do with the thought of Sharice and Bunches meeting each other. His two worlds colliding. Mike quickly decided he was making too much out of it and concentrated back on his conversation with Sharice.

Mike said his good-bye to her and put his phone away. The short conversation had lifted his spirits. He was glad that she had decided to accept his invitation to Thanksgiving. It had also been nice to hear Sharice's laugh. He hadn't heard it in a while. Mike asked Terence back into the office.

"Did you hire any seasonal help yet?" Mike took a folder out of his briefcase. It was full of selling strategies, sale promotions and store goals. "Black Friday is only a couple of days away."

"No. But I have a couple of interviews scheduled for tomorrow. One of the guys is cute."

Mike gave him a cutting look.

"I know, I know," Terence said. "I won't hire him just because he's cute."

Mike shifted in his seat but didn't change the look on his face.

"And if I do hire him, I wouldn't hit on one of my employees. You know me better than that."

"I know, Terence. Just remember, you got some guys that are so homophobic—real homophobics—they'll think every time you smile at them, you're hitting on them."

"Mike, I've been gay thirty-three years . . ."

"True, but unless you lied on your application when I first hired you, you've never been a manager before, in charge of your own staff. People are so litigious nowadays. Some would like nothing better than to sue their gay boss for sexual harassment. You like to kid a lot, and people like me, that know you, know when you're kidding—"

"Mike, you must think I'm an idiot." Terence rolled his eyes.

"Well, that notwithstanding—"

"You trying to teach me gay survival skills is about as silly as me trying to teach you black survival skills."

Mike aimed his index finger at Terence. "How many times I done told your ass about trying to compare gays to blacks?"

Terence gave him a "humph," and took a swig of tea.

"You can 'butch up' anytime it benefits you to do so." Mike rubbed his wrist with two fingers from his other hand. "This color doesn't afford me the same luxury. It doesn't come off."

"I'm not comparing—I've always been truthful with you. Some of my gay white acquaintances are the most virulent racists I know. Always getting on me for dating black men, calling me a 'ding queen.' I don't appreciate that shit."

Now it was Mike's turn to laugh. "I don't think I appreciate that too much, either. What the fuck is a 'ding'?"

"Some slur for black men that they have come up with." Terence answered. "You know can't nobody talk about you the way a fag can."

"Still," Mike shook his head, "a ding?"

"Best I can tell is, like when your clothes are dingy—you know, soiled or muddy. So a 'ding' would be . . ."

Mike threw up his hands. "I got it, I got it."

"So, anyway, what was my point?" Terence paused and stared at the ceiling while he waited for it to come back to him.

"You mean there was one?" Mike asked.

"Oh, yeah." Terence finally said. "I would never make my store an uncomfortable environment for my staff. I know it's a place of business."

"You don't mind busting Jeff's chops." Mike reminded.

"I ain't thinking about that closet queen." Terence flipped his wrist to emphasize his point. "*She's* confused, anyway."

Mike started emptying the contents of the folder. "Let's get to this stuff."

"But I will say this," Terence continued. "If two applicants are similarly qualified, I'm gonna always choose the better looking one to hire."

Mike sighed.

"Hey, I'm sorry," Terence said. "But you know I can't stand to be around no ugly people."

Colin had a spring in his step as he walked out of Compact Disc Universe. It was the third store he had been to and the first that had what he was looking for, the Guy CD with "Let's Chill" on it.

He had remembered that one night a couple of months back when he and Stacy had just finished making love. They were lying in bed cuddling, listening to the Quiet Storm on the radio. When "Let's Chill" came on, Stacy had started singing along with Aaron Hall and told Colin how much she loved the song. She said that when she was a freshman in college, she had played the Guy tape so much that it had snapped.

He had remembered that because, despite what Stacy said, he was romantic. And today was his day to prove it. Colin slid into his Honda and fastened his seat belt. He turned on the ignition but paused before he pulled off. He looked at the contents of the car and smiled. Lying across the backseat were a dozen pink roses that he had picked up from Flower World. Next to him in the front passenger seat was a bottle of Dom Perignon, candles, bath oils and the CD. He'd gone to the seafood store to pick up some shrimp, scallops and a couple of lobsters, so he could surprise Stacy with a meal of her favorite foods when she came in from work.

As Colin pulled into traffic, he thought about his friends and how they competed for titles. Since Mike knew the most about baseball, he laid claim to the title of "Mr. Baseball." Ibn's predictions about boxing were almost always dead-on accurate, so he was known as "Mr. Boxing." Dexter was "Mr. Basketball." Well, Colin thought, after tonight, Stacy is gonna want me to legally change my name to "Mr. Romance."

He pulled into the complex where he and Stacy lived. He was surprised to see the Mercedes there. Damn, he thought, she must have taken the day off. She was gonna ruin his surprise. He idled for a few moments while he pondered his next move.

He could go to Ibn's instead, get Stacy out of the house on some made-up errand and surprise her when she got back. Nah, he decided, too much hassle, and besides, he wanted to cook the food while it was fresh. Fuck it. He wouldn't be able to set up the condo the way he wanted, but at least he could spend the entire afternoon making love to Stacy instead of just the evening. Colin went to pull into his assigned parking spot, but he had to park in a visitor's spot because another car was occupying it. He hoped Stacy didn't have one of her girlfriends over.

Colin gathered all the items and got out. He looked at the strange car as he walked by. He didn't recognize it. It didn't belong to any of their neighbors. It was probably just somebody visiting a neighbor who didn't have the good sense to park where they were supposed to. Colin made his way up the stairs to the second floor. When he got to the door, he heard music playing; so loudly that he recognized the song, "Touch It," by Monifah. Stacy was probably exercising. Colin laid the roses along his arm carefully and shifted the bag with all the items in it to his left hand, so that he had a free hand to open the door. He put the key in and turned, fully prepared to make his lady's day.

Inside, the scene he saw caused his breath to leave his body. He began to tremble.

Stacy was lying on top of a man on the couch. She was naked except for her panties, which the man was tugging down her calves. The man saw Colin over Stacy's shoulder.

"Oh, shit!"

"Uhh," Stacy moaned. " 'Oh, shit' is right! I'm about to put it on you, baby!" she shouted over the music.

In his shock Colin dropped the bag. It tipped over, spilling most of its contents onto the carpet. The man flipped Stacy over so that she could see who'd come in. Colin saw the look of utter horror on her face. He also saw that her breasts were wet with slobber, which made him instantly nauseated.

The three of them were frozen for a couple of seconds. Colin was the first to move. He stepped over the candles and oils, laid the roses on the table and headed for the bedroom.

Once inside, he locked the door, sat on the bed and buried his face in his hands. His fingers were soon wet with his tears. Colin felt like the room was spinning as a million different emotions pierced him, each one ripping a little deeper. Anger at Stacy for disrespecting him. Revulsion at seeing his woman in another man's arms. Self-loathing for not being man enough to make her happy. Realization. For the events of today were slowly forcing him to come to terms with his worst fear. What he had always known, but exiled to a region of his mind where he didn't have to deal with it. And that was the knowledge that Stacy never had, or never would, love him as he loved her.

Colin heard the music stop and the front door close. He wiped his face, took his coat off and went to the closet. He pulled out a big duffel bag and started packing some clothes. It was time to move on.

The doorknob jiggled. "Colin," a timid voice said, "let me in."

He ignored her and continued his packing. He pulled out a couple of suits to get him through the week at work.

"We need to talk."

After a couple of more minutes of asking Colin to open the door and receiving no response, Stacy gave up and went back into the living room.

When Colin was done packing, he took a deep breath to compose himself. He was intent on not letting Stacy see him fall apart. It was bad enough that she would fuck a man in the house they shared, on the same couch they had spent endless nights entwined in each other's arms. He put his coat back on, slung the strap of the bag over his shoulder and picked up his suit bag. Get it together, he told himself as he checked his face in Stacy's vanity mirror. If anyone is gonna be bawling, it's her. Get through this with a shred of dignity. He opened the door and stepped out of the room.

Stacy was now dressed, wearing a pair of shorts and a T-shirt. She was standing near the patio door, with her hands jammed into her pockets, looking out onto the courtyard. She turned when she heard Colin enter the room. He noticed that her face was dry. When she saw that he had packed, her shoulders slumped.

"Colin, please understand, that was just me needing some attention."

He saw that the items he had bought had been picked up off the floor and set on the table. He looked over at Stacy. She dropped her head and dug her toe into the carpet. Colin continued to the front door. There he paused. "So tell me, Stacy," Colin motioned his head in the direction of the couch, "what you were just doing, was that romance, or was that just *fucking*?" He left before she could respond.

Colin got into his Honda and started backing out. He noticed that the car that had been in the other spot reserved for him and Stacy was now gone. The Benz then caught his eye. Stacy must have just had it washed because it was sparkling. Fuck this. Colin parked the Honda into the empty space and got out.

Colin took the duffel bag and loaded it into the Benz's trunk. He laid his suit bag across the backseat, got in and drove off.

"You didn't stab those motherfuckas up?"

Ibn was seething. His fists were balled in rage. He and Colin were sitting in his office. Ibn at his desk and Colin facing him. Actually, Colin was facing the floor because he couldn't bring himself to lift his head.

"No," Colin said quietly. He took off his glasses and rubbed the bridge of his nose.

"Why not? I would've bailed you out."

Colin shrugged his shoulders despondently.

"Never mind that," Ibn said. "There's still time. Tell me, do you know who the man was?"

"It was the salesman from the Mercedes dealership."

Ibn's mind raced. "The short, stocky one with the receding hairline?"

"Yeah."

"That midget motherfucker? Jesus Christ! The gall of him . . . and never mind that *bitch*! That fucking, trifling, skan'less ho-bitch! That's okay, I got something for their asses." Ibn picked up the phone.

Colin finally raised his head. "What are you doing?"

"I'm calling some niggas I know back home in Newark—Hakeem and Rashahn. They specialize in this type of shit."

Colin shook his head. "I don't want them Newark niggas down here."

Ibn frowned. "What, are you worried? They're very discreet. It won't get back to us."

Colin shook his head again, more emphatically this time.

Ibn sighed and hung up the phone. He looked at Colin, who had resumed staring at the floor. Though he loved Colin, he had no doubt that the brother was simply too soft. Ibn had noticed that when he called Stacy a bitch Colin had flinched. And never mind that Colin had left the condo without wrecking shop or, at the very least, breaking a rib or two, Ibn could forgive that. He knew it wasn't in Colin's nature to do so. But, damn, he didn't want any retribution at all? Ibn saw a tear escape Colin's eye and land on the carpet.

Ibn bet that Stacy's hoey ass wasn't anywhere crying, or even sorry, for that matter. Only thing she was upset about was getting caught.

"So, what's your next move?" Ibn asked.

Colin started speaking but kept his head down. "Well, you know, the condo belongs to Stacy . . ."

Yes, I do know, thought Ibn. He had been warning Colin for years how precarious it was for him to be staying in Stacy's spot, helping to pay the mortgage every month instead of living someplace where his name was on the deed.

". . . And I know all the spots we own have tenants now."

"Don't worry about that. You can stay with me for as long as you like, Colin," Ibn said.

Colin raised his head. "Thanks."

Ibn reached into his desk drawer and gave him his spare house key. Colin slid it into his pocket. He then put his glasses back on and slowly stood up, like he was in pain. "I'm gonna head over there now."

"You know the alarm code?" Ibn asked.

"Three-twelve-thirteen, Founder's Day for the frat, right?"

"Yeah."

"All right, man. Thanks. See you later."

"Yeah, see you at the crib. And cheer up, man. It's not the end of the world."

If anything, he should feel like he had just been emancipated, Ibn thought. He watched Colin shuffle out of the office like a broken-down old man. With his head drooped, his shoulders slumped and his back hunched—he looked like one giant, boneless sag. Ibn shook his head. What a *disgracia*. It was pathetic to see a man let any woman have that kind of control over him. And for a cunt like Stacy? That bordered on the criminal.

It was good that Colin was gonna be staying with him. Ibn wasn't gonna let his ass sit around all forlorn over Stacy, that's for damn sure.

Ibn stood up and went over to the coat rack. He was going to stop by the Voorhees store for an hour or two and then head home to keep Colin company. He probably needed someone to talk to. Though, Ibn figured, what he really needed was some new pussy.

As Ibn checked his appearance, he commended himself for being so tolerant. He had shown great restraint in not getting upset with him for not doing anything. One, for not beating that car salesman down. Second, for not wanting him to put that call in to Newark and most of all, for sitting there crying like some bitch-ass nigga when what he should have been doing was spitting fire at the audacity of that whore. No doubt about it, Colin was fortunate to have such an understanding friend like him. Though, Ibn admitted, it hadn't been easy.

Because what he had felt like doing to Colin was reenacting that scene from *The Godfather*. The one when Marlon Brando leapt from behind his desk and slapped up that singer who was boo-hooing like a woman in his office. Ibn sneered. Colin was his boy and all, but sometimes he swore that Colin could benefit from a backbone transplant. Ibn slid into his leather trench and checked himself in the wall mirror one last time. I mean, really. Be a man, goddammit. Be a *man*.

Eighteen

Mike and Sharice were silent as they drove to his parents' house in Pennsauken. Mike stole a glance at Sharice. She was looking out the window, drumming her nails along the door handle. They both were nervous, Mike figured. Sharice, at the prospect of meeting his family, and he, at the prospect of Sharice meeting Bunches.

Mike pulled up in front of the house. The driveway was full, so he parked in the street behind his brother's Sentra. "Well, here we are," he said. "My childhood abode."

"It's nice," Sharice said.

Mike looked past her out the window. The house was a rancher with blue vinyl siding that his father had just recently had put on. In the front window was a huge wreath. Christmas lights already framed the windows, and hanging from the eaves were those irritating fake icicles that everybody in the neighborhood started using a few winters back.

"Your folks are ready for Christmas," Sharice said.

"Those decorations are there all year long," Mike said. "My old man just waits for the holidays to roll back around," He added, kidding. "We look pretty stupid in July."

Sharice smiled.

"You ready?"

She nodded.

"Then, let's go meet the Lovetts," Mike said, opening his door.

They stepped into the living room, where his father, his Uncle Bill and his teenage cousin Kevin were watching a football game. Mike introduced Sharice to them. Everything was fine until she took off her coat so that Mike could hang it up and they first got a glimpse of her body; Mike could have sworn he saw an eyeball roll across the floor. They made their way to the kitchen.

"Mom, this is Sharice."

"Hello, Mrs. Lovett. It's a pleasure meeting you."

"Hi, Sharice," she answered, shaking hands.

"I see Uncle Bill and Kevin are here. Where's Aunt Janice and everybody else?"

Mrs. Lovett was subtly giving Sharice a once-over. "She went home to get me some vanilla extract. I ran out. Everybody else will be by later. Janice, your aunt Althea and Bunches were all over here last night helping me cook."

"You have a lovely home, Mrs. Lovett," Sharice said.

"Thank you. I'm glad somebody thinks so." Mrs. Lovett nodded her head in Mike's direction. "Obviously, it's not nice enough for others or they would visit more often. If it wasn't for Bunches, I wouldn't know whether certain other people even still lived in the area."

"Mom, please," Mike groaned. "Don't start."

A look of innocence enveloped her face. "I didn't name any names. You must have a guilty conscience." She winked at Sharice, who laughed.

Mike planted a kiss on his mother's cheek. "Where's Matthew?" he asked.

"I think he's in the den with Bunches."

"We're gonna go holler at them."

"Okay."

"It was nice meeting you, Mrs. Lovett."

"Mmm-hmm, nice meeting you, Sharice. I hope you're hungry."

Sharice gave her a playful look of caution. "Believe me, Mrs. Lovett, I can eat."

"She isn't lying, Mom. She eats like a bird—a pterodactyl. With her greedy self." Mike cracked himself up.

Sharice and Mrs. Lovett stared blankly at each other while they waited for him to stop laughing.

"A what?" Mrs. Lovett asked.

"A pterodactyl." He looked at each of their faces. "You know, those huge flying reptiles from the dinosaur age."

"No, I *don't* know." Mrs. Lovett picked up a wooden spoon and acted like she was gonna hit Mike. "What have I told you about making silly jokes that no one except you can understand?"

Mike ducked out of there before his mother could whack him. He led Sharice toward the den's double doors.

"You know, your mother is right," she said.

"What do you mean?" Mike asked.

"About your sense of humor."

"Are you calling me corny?"

Sharice laughed. "It's just that you do have a habit of referencing things that no one but you knows."

He opened the doors and Sharice entered first. Mike looked over his shoulder before he followed her in. His father, uncle and cousin were all giving him two thumbs-up on his choice of woman.

Matty and Bunches were lounging at polar ends of the long couch, watching a parade on TV. They were unable to see the door and were so engrossed in their conversation that they didn't hear Sharice and Mike enter. He held his index finger to his lips for Sharice to keep silent. One, he wanted to sneak up on his brother and pop him upside his head, as was his ritual. Second, he wanted to eavesdrop on the conversation.

". . . Just don't think that I've forgotten all those beatings you used to give me when we were kids," Matty said. "Taking advantage, just because you had five years and thirty pounds on a brother . . ."

Bunches looked utterly bored. "Your point, Matty?"

"My point is, now I have you by thirty pounds—at least. Look how big that sweater is on you. It looks like you're swimming in it."

"It's supposed to be worn big, silly boy."

"Please. I was with Mike when he bought you that sweater. It used to be form-fitting. Face it, Bunch, you're downright skinny, while I on the other hand . . ." Matty flexed his bicep. "Let's just say that a brother got his weight *up*."

"Oh, I see. I'm supposed to be impressed because you walked by a weight room or two. Brah, you can swell up all you want. Ain't nothing changed between us."

"You're crazy." He threw a pillow at her, and it barely missed his mark.

"Hey, hey, watch it now," she warned. "What are you majoring in at that school, Stupidity 101?" She balled up her hand into a fist. "Don't make me drop this straight right on you to *prove* that ain't nothing changed between us."

They both laughed, as did Mike. They sat up on the couch to look at the doorway. He and Sharice walked into the room.

"Sharice, this is my brother Matty." Mike acted like he was going to punch him in the arm. "I haven't disowned him yet, though I should, for his having the gall to pledge Sigma instead of my fraternity."

Matty stood up to greet Sharice, like any good Lovett son was taught to do when a lady entered the room. Mike noticed he had a little trouble making eye contact, as his line of sight got stuck temporarily in the vicinity of Sharice's chest.

"Hello, Matty." Sharice extended her hand.

Matty accepted it and finally raised his head to her face. "Nice meeting you."

"And the bantamweight over there is Erika, better known as Bunches."

"Hi, do you prefer Erika or Bunches?" Sharice asked.

"Bunches." She gave Sharice a taut smile.

Mike and Sharice sat down on a love seat. Matty sat back down on the couch, much more rigid than before. Bunches straightened up as well.

Mike saw that there was an empty pitcher of iced tea on the table. "Sharice, you want something to drink?"

"No, thank you."

"I could use a refill." Bunches held up her glass, tinkling the ice.

"Oh?" Mike said. "And have you forgotten where the kitchen is?"

Bunches sucked her teeth and set her glass back down. Not so much at Mike's comment, but because Sharice had chuckled at it.

"Erika and Matt, tell me if you think this is funny. If someone told you that a woman eats like a bird," Mike paused, ". . . a pterodactyl."

Matty sat there impassively. A smile tugged at the corners of Bunches' mouth.

"I guess you had to be there," Mike said.

"Believe me, that didn't help," Sharice replied.

"It might help if I knew what a pterodactyl was," said Matty.

Sharice looked at Mike smugly. "See?"

"A pterodactyl is a flying reptile that was around during the Mesozoic Era, when dinosaurs roamed the earth. Your brother's comment is marginally humorous because pterodactyls were huge," Bunches said.

Mike returned Sharice's smug look. "See? Some people do know what a pterodactyl is."

Bunches shot her a satisfied look.

"That's okay," Sharice said, "I don't need to know what a ptero-whatever is. Because I don't believe dinosaurs ever existed."

Matty stopped staring out of the corner of his eyes at Sharice's chest. "Huh?" he asked, turning his head fully.

"I don't believe in dinosaurs," she reiterated.

Here we go, thought Mike. He looked over at Bunches beseechingly, using his eyes to plead with her to let Sharice's comment pass. When he saw Bunches licking her chops, he knew it was no use. The dinner was gonna be a bumpy ride. Mike just leaned back and turned his attention to the TV.

"I don't understand," Bunches said. "It's not something you have to accept on faith. You can plainly see the evidence of their existence in museums."

Sharice flipped her wrist. "It's the work of man. They just found some old bones and arranged them any kind of way."

Bunches was fascinated. "Still, they had to find the bones. Where do you think these huge bones, that when put together form huge skeletons that happen to greatly resemble dinosaurs, come from?"

"I find no mention of dinosaurs in the *Bible*." Sharice said this in such a manner that it was supposed to end all debate on the matter. Like, though she didn't want to have to resort to it, Bunches had forced Sharice to use the big artillery.

"Nor will you find any mention of microwave ovens or computers, either, but they are quite real as well."

"True, but those are man-made items that were invented many years after the Bible was written," Sharice replied smoothly. "Tell me, why would God, with His infinite wisdom, create something like a dinosaur and have them roam the earth for a hundred million years?"

Bunches shrugged her shoulders. "You got me there, Sharice," she offered snidely. "I don't presume to speak for God, or know his reasoning."

"Exactly." Sharice said, leaning forward. "That's what we have the Bible for. It's His infallible word."

"But it was written by men," Bunches said. "How do you know that they didn't just find some old words and arrange them any kind of way?" She flipped her wrist like Sharice had earlier.

Matty stifled a laugh. Mike cringed.

"Because the Bible was written by men *inspired* by God," Sharice said smugly.

Bunches was about to say something back when she saw Mike's face. It was etched with discomfort. She decided to be quiet.

Sharice took her silence as an admission of defeat. When she was satisfied that Bunches had nothing more to say on the matter, she turned to Mike. "Can you show me where the lavatory is?"

"Sure, Sharice." He got up and led her through the den doors. "The second door on the right."

Mike closed the doors, thinking he should have some warning when Sharice was to return. He sat down and faced Bunches and his brother. Matty was stroking his chin and had a shit-eating grin on his face. Bunches was trying not to laugh.

"You know, it's ironic that she doesn't believe in the existence of dinosaurs. She has so much in common with them." Matty let that comment hang and took a sip of his iced tea.

"And what would that be, Matty?"

"Killer body and a walnut-sized brain." He and Bunches started laughing. Mike wanted to, too, but forced himself to hold it in. He sat down next to his brother and plunked him in his head.

"Yeah, but you aren't so concerned with her mental acuity, are you? When she comes back in here, you'd better stop staring at her chest. You act like you never seen a beautiful woman before."

Bunches stopped laughing.

Matty didn't. "What do you want from me? You gonna trot something like that in front of me and not expect me to stare? You caught me off guard. I don't expect to see any fine women in my mama's house."

"That's not true. What about Aunt Janice back in her hot pants days?" Mike said.

"Okay, you got me. That's one, but there ain't been any since then." They both laughed again.

Bunches got up and headed for the door. Mike noticed she looked pissed off.

"Erika, you *know* we think you're gorgeous—"

She threw open the doors and stormed out.

"Where are your other friends spending their holiday?" Mrs. Rogers asked.

"Mike and Bunches are at his parents' house. I think Dexter is at his girlfriend's parents' place," Colin said.

Mrs. Rogers noticed Ibn going to town on the food she had prepared and smiled. "How's your Cornish hen, Ibn?"

"It's delicious, Mrs. Rogers."

She smiled proudly. "I just felt it was silly to make a big turkey. Whenever I've made turkeys, I've been stuck with more leftover bird than I knew what to do with."

Colin looked at the spread in front of them. His mother might have spared them a turkey, but she still had gone way overboard with everything else. There was no way that three people could eat all this, though Ibn was giving it his best shot.

"Believe me, this is fine," Ibn said as he scooped yet another serving of macaroni and cheese on his plate.

Mrs. Rogers turned her attention to her son. "So, where is that girlfriend of yours?" she asked in an unpleasant tone.

Colin felt Ibn's eyes on him from across the table. "She couldn't make it, Mom." He jabbed at his stuffing.

Mrs. Rogers voice turned hopeful. "Why not? Did she go home to her parents?"

He was about to lie but was forestalled by Ibn's loud clearing of his throat.

"I don't know where she is, Mom." He hesitated before adding, "We broke up."

Mrs. Rogers put her fork down and loudly clapped her hands together. "Thank you, sweet Jesus! Lord knows, I've been praying on it. I was getting worried that you might actually marry that girl." She then saw the downcast look on her son's face and leaned over and patted his hand. "Colin, you can do much better than that girl. I don't know what you saw in her in the first place."

"Here, here, Mrs. Rogers," Ibn felt the need to add, raising his glass of ginger ale in the air.

"So why'd you break up with her?" Mrs. Rogers asked. "Did you catch her with another man?"

Colin once again felt Ibn's eyes on him. He regretted bringing Ibn with him. Colin had asked him to come so that he would have an excuse to leave—they were supposed to be going to Ibn's parents' house in South Orange for dessert—because he knew his mother would want to keep him there overnight. Colin also knew that once he told his mother about Stacy's infidelity, he would never be able to justify to her a good enough reason to get back with her.

But with Ibn bearing down on him, he felt trapped. How could he justify to Ibn and his other friends that in his mind, he hadn't completely ruled out the possibility of getting back with Stacy somewhere down the line?

"Yeah." he offered resignedly.

His mother's fork hit her plate with a loud clank. "I *knew* it," she said triumphantly. "I always *knew* that girl wasn't about anything."

Ibn again raised his glass in salute. "You and me both, Mrs. Rogers. You and me both."

Colin looked down at his plate. He tore off a piece of cornbread and jammed it in his mouth. His mother studied him for a moment, and decided not to say anything else to him on the matter. For now. Instead, she turned toward Ibn.

"So, how's that girlfriend of yours, Ibn? I forgot her name—that pretty, redbone girl."

Colin threw a smirk at Ibn. So there was some justice.

"Tiffany. She's fine, Mrs. Rogers . . ."

Colin cleared his throat.

". . . She's spending the holiday in Maryland with her family," Ibn finished.

Colin cleared his throat again, louder this time.

Mrs. Rogers turned back to him. "That sounds awful, Colin. Maybe you shouldn't go back out in this cold."

"Yeah, frat," Ibn added, his voice full of concern. "Maybe you should stay here tonight with your mother."

Later that evening, Colin and Ibn were getting ready to leave. "Thank you for the meal, Mrs. Rogers." Ibn leaned over and gave her a kiss on the cheek.

"You're welcome, darling. Don't forget your pie."

"I wasn't about to." Ibn walked over to the table and picked up the sweet potato pie that Mrs. Rogers had carefully wrapped in aluminum foil for him. He held it up to his nose, then stared at it lovingly. "I have big plans for you, my circular friend."

Colin and his mother laughed. "Here, Colin." She opened the closet and rummaged for a little while before she found a scarf that Colin could've sworn he had worn in fifth grade. "So that cough of yours doesn't get any worse."

"Thanks, Mom," Colin said, refusing to look at Ibn and give him the satisfaction of acknowledging the silly grin on his face.

"So, you're coming back next weekend, right?" Mrs. Rogers asked.

"Yeah," Colin said, putting on his coat.

She turned to Ibn and smiled. "Ever since Colin was a child we always make sure we get into the city at least one day to do some Christmas shopping—and stop by Rockefeller Center to see the tree." She turned up the collar on Colin's coat. "It's sort of a tradition."

"It sounds like a beautiful thing for a mother and son to share, Mrs. Rogers."

Colin eyed Ibn sourly. "Are you ready to go?"

"Y'all just make sure you drive carefully. There might be some ice on the roads."

"Will do, Mrs. Rogers."

"Colin, maybe you can see if Bunches can come up with you next weekend. I enjoyed her so much when you brought her last time."

Actually, that is a good idea, Colin thought. It would give his mother someone else to talk to. "I'll see if she's free, Mom. If there's one thing I know Bunches enjoys, it's shopping." He kissed his mother's cheek and followed Ibn through the foyer to the front door.

"She's such a sweet thing," Mrs. Rogers continued. A look of puzzlement came over her face. "How come you don't pursue her? She would be a great catch."

Ibn and Colin stopped dead in their tracks and looked at each other. They burst out laughing.

The bafflement etched on Mrs. Rogers face became more pronounced. "I don't understand. Did I say something funny?"

"Yes." Colin said, still snickering.

"What's wrong with her?" Mrs. Rogers asked. "She's a cute little thing."

"No doubt she is that, Mrs. Rogers," Ibn said. "It's just that Bunches is like our baby sister."

"Yeah, Mom. We've known her since she was a child," Colin finished.

"Humph, she ain't no blood relation to you," Mrs. Rogers said. "If you had any sense, you would snatch her up before somebody else does."

"That ain't gonna happen," Colin said.

"How do you know?"

"The ADS won't allow her to be snatched up. That girl is better protected than Chelsea Clinton."

"The AD—what?"

"The ADS, Mrs. Rogers." Ibn opened the door, stepped onto the porch and looked skyward. The nippy chill smacked against their faces. His voice took on an awestruck, deferential tone like he was referring to some mysterious cabal. He raised his arms slightly to give the appearance of veneration, but it instead looked like he was offering his sweet potato pie as a sacrifice to the heavens. "The mighty ADS never sleeps," he whispered reverentially.

*   *   *

Denise's face was set in a tight grimace. She raised her hands at Dexter. "Stop yelling at me!"

Dexter didn't drop his voice a single decibel. "So, tell me Denise, where the fuck did he get the idea, if not from you?"

"I just told him what you said, that you wanted a long-term commitment."

"I never said that," he snarled.

"Yes, you did."

"Trust me, I *never* said that!" Dexter answered as brutally as possible.

The vehemence of his denial ripped at Denise's core, but she was determined not to let him see how much his harshness was hurting her.

"What, my father isn't supposed to want his pregnant daughter to be married? You wouldn't want the same for your daughter?" She sat down and started taking off her boots. They were at Denise's apartment, after having Thanksgiving dinner with her folks.

"No. Hopefully my unmarried daughter wouldn't be pregnant in the first place. It's a little late for you to be playing Daddy's little girl, isn't it?"

Anger flashed across Denise's face. "Fuck you, Dexter, I didn't do this by myself."

"Yeah, but you're the only one of us walking around here pregnant."

Denise looked at Dexter like he was something vile that she had accidentally stepped in. He had been chewing her ass out since they had left her parents' house, and she had taken about all the shit from him she was prepared to take. She slowly finished pulling off her other boot and stood up. She puckered her lips and cooed at him. "What's the matter, Dexter? You upset because someone asked you to be a man and face up to your responsibilities?"

The sugary maliciousness in her voice pushed him over the edge. The venom that had been simmering in him for the past couple of months bubbled to the surface.

"I'll fucking tell you what's the matter with me—since you fucking asked. Since day one of this pregnancy your attitude has been shitty. For all the input I have in anything, you might as well had went to the sperm bank and been inseminated—oh, but you couldn't have done that, could you? Then who would've been the poor sap going around Bucks County with you looking at houses that he can't afford? Who would be the fool that has to keep the car he was about to get rid of because he has to buy his child's mother a new car so that she can get around safely? A child's mother, mind you, that thinks it's acceptable behavior to shake her ass at a club while she's pregnant. A child's mother that makes decisions like the name of the child without so much as a word of consideration from me. And when she's gonna quit her job without consulting me first, though it will be me ultimately footing the bills." Dexter fixed his coldest glare on her. "It seems like your work was done once you got pregnant."

Denise gritted her teeth. "What are you trying to say?"

Dexter turned his back on her and picked his car keys up off the table. "You figure it out. You got everything else figured out."

"Dexter, if you don't want to be a part of this baby's life, let me know now."

He whirled on her, pointing his finger. "No, don't even try to play that game with me. I can want the child without wanting *your* ass."

Denise gasped and buried her face in her hands. Dexter turned back around and headed for the door.

"Denise, get yourself a lawyer and I'll get me one. I want our communication to be strictly through our lawyers from here on in."

Dexter heard a thud as he reached for the doorknob. It was followed by a piercing guttural moan. He looked over his shoulder.

Denise was on her knees wailing. She took her fist and pounded it into the floor.

"You have no idea . . . what it's like . . . to be pregnant with a man's child . . . who you *know* does not love you."

Dexter stood there watching Denise's tears fall to the floor. She looked up at him through tear-soaked eyes. Her look was full of pleading desperation. She needed Dexter to tell her something, anything, to ease her grief.

Dexter started to say something, but nothing came out. He walked over, knelt down beside her and held her.

At first Denise resisted. After all, Dexter was the primary reason for her heartache. But as she continued sobbing, she leaned against Dexter, wetting his shoulder with her tears.

"I'm sorry, Denise," Dexter said as he smoothed her hair. "I promise you, everything will be all right."

Nineteen

Bunches and Tiana were out for a Sunday drive on the holiday week-end. Bunches didn't really have anything specific planned for them other than maybe grabbing a movie later.

"What are we doing today?" Tiana asked.

"I thought I'd let you choose," Bunches said as she wheeled her Celica onto the off-ramp at the Voorhees exit of the interstate. "But if you don't mind, I want to stop by Ibn's house first."

Bunches wanted to see Colin, who she knew was staying with Ibn. She had not spoken to him since the whole thing with Stacy's stank ass had gone down, and she wanted to see how he was doing.

When they came to a light, Bunches sneaked a peek at Tiana. She looked like she was gonna explode with excitement. Tiana prided herself on possessing a worldly sophistication far beyond that of other girls her age, so she was trying to play it cool. Even though she was wearing sunglasses, the same Liz Claiborne model that Bunches was wearing (both were gifts from Mike), Bunches could tell that her ten-year-old eyes were dancing underneath them. Bunches chuckled to herself as the light turned to green. The knowledge that they were going to see Ibn had sent Tiana into a state of rapture. I know exactly what you're feeling, little girl, Bunches thought. I've been there.

Ibn opened the door wearing sweats and a Homestead Grays T-shirt. The beam off Tiana's face nearly blinded him.

"Hi," Tiana and Bunches said simultaneously.

"This must be my lucky day!" he exclaimed. "How are you doing, baby girl?"

"Fine," Tiana and Bunches answered, once again in unison.

"Come in, it's cold out there."

Bunches took off her coat, removed Tiana's, and went with Ibn to the hallway closet to hang them up. When they walked into the living room, she saw Tiana giving herself a quick once-over. Calm down, sweetheart, you look beautiful, Bunches thought.

Though Tiana was far too appearance-conscious to let herself leave the house looking anything less than impeccable, if she had known she was going to see Ibn today, she most certainly would have worn her Sunday best.

Bunches and Ibn sat on the love seat, next to the chair that Tiana occupied.

"So, how have you been, Tiana?" Ibn asked.

"Fine," Tiana replied, cheesing from ear to ear.

"Bunches tells me that you are doing very well in school. Is that true?"

"Yes."

Ibn nodded approvingly. "That's good, Tiana. What do you wanna be when you grow up?"

You mean, besides Mrs. Ibn Barrington? Bunches thought.

"I wanna be a doctor, like Bunches."

"I'm not a doctor yet, T," Bunches reminded her.

"But she's gonna be come next year," Ibn said. He paused for a couple of seconds like he was mulling something over. "You know what, Tiana, I was just thinking about what you told me. I think you would make an excellent doctor, too. You and Bunches could open up your own practice together and cure all the sick people of the world."

Tiana's wide grin was proof that she loved the thought of that.

"Tiana, can I tell you something?"

She nodded her head up and down hungrily. "Yes."

"I once knew another young lady who was very smart, too, just like you. She was very pretty, too, just like you. She was very—in fact, you remind me of her a lot."

ked out his bottom lip. "What about me?"

 you holding up?"

 fine," Colin said, quickly putting a huge forkful of egg in

eyed him. "You sure?"

dded like he was annoyed by the line of questioning, and
he hot sauce on his omelet.

decided not to challenge his *que sera, sera* attitude even
as pretty sure it was bullshit.

ou ever need someone to talk to . . ."

, I'm *fine*." Colin got up abruptly and walked to the trash
 off the remanding food on his plate. He stood at the
is plate off longer than necessary, keeping his back to

nally turned around, he saw her staring at the tabletop,
ls of the Formica. "Besides," he said, taking the edge out
 I did need someone to talk to, I have Ibn's sympathetic
nderstanding, you know, in matters of the heart."

ked up at him like he had had a cup of stupid to drink.
 a nod of mock assurance.

 Colin walked back into the living room.

Colin said, taking a seat in the chair.

Tiana managed to get out, without losing her focus.
dministering an ass-whipping the likes of which had

n the arm of the chair Colin was sitting in and rested
shoulder.

er, watch the left hook!" Ibn begged. Really, he was
information she needed to knock him out.

up on it. Frazier left himself open. Holyfield threw the
and it was all she wrote.

Ibn pleaded.

no fight left in Smokin' Joe.

ches cheered Tiana's victory. Ibn immediately asked

"Who?"

Ibn pointed his eyes at Bunches without turning his head.

"Really?"

"What's the matter, T, you don't believe that I was once a little girl?" Bunches asked.

"With pigtails and braces, even," Ibn added. "You know, now that I think about it," he leaned over to whisper to Tiana, "I'm not sure she was as pretty as you. In fact, she was kinda funny looking."

Tiana started to crack up, and Bunches punched Ibn in the shoulder. He yelped like he was in agony.

"Where's Colin?" Bunches asked.

"In the kitchen," Ibn said. He looked over at Tiana while he rubbed his shoulder, his face twisted like he was really in pain for Tiana's amusement. He leaned away from Bunches toward Tiana again. "So, tell me," Ibn said out of the side of his mouth, "is she always this mean?"

Tiana looked over Ibn's head at Bunches, who gave her a "you'd better not" look.

"Yes," Tiana said.

Ibn sighed. "I feel for you, Tiana. I really do."

"Ohhh, I'm *mean* now, am I?" Bunches stood up like she was gonna leave. "Well, I know when I'm not wanted." She had taken only a few steps before Tiana ran over to her and placed a hand on her shoulder.

"I didn't mean it. I was only playing."

Bunches shrugged her hand off her shoulder and kept walking. "Yes, you did. Leave me alone, little girl."

"No, I didn't!" Tiana protested. She tried to block her path.

"Yes, you did," Bunches countered. She coldly sidestepped Tiana. "Or else, why would you say it?"

Tiana got back in front of her and tightly wrapped her arms around Bunches' waist. "I love you!"

Bunches, who had really gotten up for the purpose of talking to Colin in the kitchen, realized that Tiana was really upset. In fact, she was starting to cry. She was really worried about hurting Bunches' feelings, and her holding it against her. Bunches took her in her arms and hugged her. She could've kicked herself. She knew abandonment was something that she couldn't play with Tiana about.

"I know, sweetheart. I know you do," Bunches reassured her in a soothing voice. "You know I love you to death, too." She smoothed Tiana's hair with the palms of her hands. She brought Tiana back to the couch and sat next to her with her arms around her. Tiana leaned her body against Bunches.

Bunches and Ibn made eye contact. She could see that he was bewildered. She winked at him to let him know Tiana would be fine, and made a motion for Ibn to get her something to drink.

When Ibn left the room Bunches straightened Tiana up and grabbed a couple of tissues off the coffee table. "Wipe your face, Tiana."

The girl sat up and wiped her face. She sneaked a sheepish look toward where Ibn had been sitting and was relieved when she realized she and Bunches were alone. Which was why Bunches had sent Ibn out of the room. She knew Tiana would be embarrassed by losing her composure like that, especially in front of someone she had a huge crush on.

"T, I'll never leave you. You never have to worry about that, okay?" Bunches gave her a kiss on the cheek. "You know we're a team."

Tiana nodded, in between sniffles.

"I won't think you believe me until I see you smile. Which I want you to do, 'cause you know my word is bond, right? Right?" Bunches playfully elbowed her. "Right?"

Tiana laughed.

"That's my girl. So, do you wanna play some PlayStation?"

"Yes."

"I must be losing my hearing," Ibn said as he walked back in the living room and set glasses of orange juice in front of the two of them. He looked at Tiana skeptically. "I thought I heard somebody say they wanted to play some PlayStation."

She smiled shyly. "You did."

"So, I figure I better make an appointment with the ear doctor because I know everybody sitting here knows they can't beat me in no PlayStation, especially on my fifty-inch screen TV. People *know* better

---

than to challenge—" He stopped abru
lated, comic double-take that even Bu

"Excuse me, young lady, but did y
play me?"

"Yes."

"*Yes?*" Ibn mimicked like it was t
had ever heard. "What do you wann

"*Champions 2001,*" Tiana said
prospect.

A look of uncertainty came ov
fight with, Tiana?"

"Holyfield."

"Oooh," Ibn groaned, as if th
tugged at the neck of his T-shir
toothy grin. "Um, wouldn't yo
Lennox Lewis?"

"No!" Tiana insisted excited

"Um, okay," Ibn said, gettir
put my boy Smokin' Joe Frazie

"Kick his booty, Tiana," E
Tiana was fine now, and she
minute or two when Ibn let h
zier. "I'll be in the kitchen."

When she walked in, Co
the door. He was eating an
was the Sunday *Courier-Di*
behind him and tickled his

"Hey, sport," she said, §
down. She slid the chair
picked up a piece of his to

"What was Tiana upse

Bunches swallowed b
ter beating Ibn a couple

"That's good." Colin

"What about you?"

Colin p
"How ar
"Oh, I'm
his mouth.

Bunches
Colin no
sprinkled sor

Bunches
though she w

"Well, if y

"I told you
can to scrape
sink rinsing h
Bunches.

When he f
lost in the swi
of his voice, "i
ear. He's very u

Bunches loc
Colin gave her

Bunches and

"Hi, Tiana,"

"Hi, Colin."
Holyfield was a
never been seen

Bunches sat
her elbow on his

"C'mon, Fraz
giving Tiana the

Tiana picked
dreaded left hook

"Get up, Joe!"
But there was
Colin and Bur
for a rematch.

"Sure," Tiana said, menacingly raising a clenched fist and looking all the world like a miniature Bunches. "My Holyfield is a fighting champion. We don't duck nobody!"

The three adults doubled over in laughter. Bunches couldn't even bring herself to correct Tiana's double negative.

"All right, Tiana, you wanna start talking smack?" Ibn said. "Now I'm a have to put Ken Norton on you."

Tiana shrugged her shoulders indifferently. He would be just another victim for her "Real Deal."

"Okay, but first I need to excuse myself." She looked at Bunches proudly. She had remembered how a lady leaves a room to go to the bathroom.

Bunches returned her smile. "You remember where it is, right?"

"Yes." She looked at Colin and Ibn. "If you'll excuse me."

Colin and Ibn were shamed into standing up, not knowing what else to do. It wasn't often they encountered such a well-bred gentlewoman.

They chuckled after she was out of earshot.

"She's a trip," Ibn said, sitting back down.

"You know," Colin added. Bunches again leaned against his shoulder.

"You chaps act like you never came across a cultured lady before," she said in a snooty British accent.

"It's not too often. We're used to dealing with regular, run-of-the-mill, unspectacular women. You know, like . . . like . . ." Ibn looked over at Bunches.

"Brah," Bunches warned, "forget that video game. You about to get your ass whupped for real."

Ibn smiled. ". . . like Stacy."

As he picked up the controller and started practicing with Ken Norton, Bunches felt Colin's whole body go limp. He just stared blankly at the TV. Bunches shot daggers at Ibn over Colin's head, but Ibn either didn't notice the anger in her eyes, or chose to ignore it.

"Bunch," Colin said in a quiet voice, "my mom wants to know if you want to go shopping in New York with us Saturday. Do you have anything planned?"

"No, I don't. I would love to." Bunches couldn't remember offhand if she had anything to do Saturday, but even if she did, she was willing to cancel it for Colin.

"Why don't you tell her what else your mother said?" Ibn asked. He picked up the glass of orange juice he had brought out earlier for Bunches and took a sip.

Bunches could hear the mischief in Ibn's voice. She hated when he acted like such a bullying asshole.

Colin sighed, irritated. "What?"

"You know what I'm talking about," Ibn said. "About Bunch."

Colin hesitated, then looked up at her. "She just wanted to know why me and you never got together," he said quickly.

Ibn chortled like it was the funniest thing he had ever heard.

Bunches draped her arms around Colin's neck. "So, you never told your mom about us? I appreciate you wanting to keep it private, Colin, but it's not a big deal."

Colin and Bunches made prolonged eye contact. Ibn stopped laughing.

"I didn't want to disrespect you like that," Colin said.

"I know, but it was such a long time ago, it's no big deal." Bunches said.

"Y'all must think I'm stupid. I know that both of y'all are full of shit." Ibn interrupted, putting down his controller so he could take another sip.

"Oh, Ibn, cut the crap. Surely you must have wondered why Colin took me out so many times in college."

Ibn looked like a piece of pulp had lodged in his throat.

Tiana walked back into the room and sat down next to Ibn. She was eager to administer another thrashing. "You ready?" She asked, picking up the controller.

Ibn was still staring at Bunches and Colin. He then decided that they were just pulling his leg and picked the controller back up. "Yeah, sweetheart, I'm ready."

After a couple of more hotly contested bouts, with Tiana's Holyfield wreaking a path of destruction through the greatest heavyweights of all time, Ibn finally conceded defeat and handed the controller over to Colin.

He joined Bunches in the kitchen; she was sitting at the table reading the movie listings in the *Courier-Dispatch*.

"You spent Thanksgiving with Mike's family, right?" Ibn asked as he took down a bowl out of the cabinet. Bunches nodded. Ibn reached onto the refrigerator and took down a box of Frosted Flakes and started pouring it into the bowl. "So, did you meet Sharice?" he asked.

"Yep," Bunches said casually. She didn't want to reveal her dislike of Sharice to Ibn, thinking he might draw an inference as to why.

"So, what was that like?"

"What do you mean?" Bunches asked.

"How'd she look?"

"Huh?" Bunches looked up from the newspaper. Ibn was pouring milk into the bowl and keeping his back to her. "What?"

"You know, I mean, how was she dressed—what I mean is, did her scandalous ass embarrass Mike in front of his family?"

Bunches studied Ibn. He was eating the cereal, still keeping his back to her.

"Did you sleep with that girl, Ibn?"

"What?" He whirled around. "Bunches, please! What, because I ask you about her, it means I had to have slept with her?"

Bunches threw her hands up defensively. "Hey, sorry. My bad."

Ibn harrumphed, clearing his throat with a contemptuous snarl. "Everyone else has, though," he muttered. He sat at the table next to Bunches.

"Be that as it may, she was dressed modestly and conducted herself with the utmost respectability." In a pompous, pretentious way, Bunches added to herself.

"Oh, so you think she would make Mike a great wife, then, huh?" Ibn took in a spoonful of cereal in an attempt to conceal his smirk.

Bunches caught it, anyway, but decided to ignore it. "No, I'm not saying that." She looked at Ibn and lowered her voice. "If you say one word about this to Mike, I'm gonna throttle your West Indian ass."

Ibn laughed. "It stays here."

"Well, as a child I was always taught that Christians who are strong in their faith don't sing it, they bring it. Meaning they live it and show it with deeds, and don't have to constantly go around spouting off about it. They have an inner strength and peace that is so wonderful and infectious that people come up to them to ask them what they got and how they can get it as well."

"So Sharice was outreaching all over the place?" Ibn asked.

Bunches rolled her eyes. "Was she? Every chance she got, she found a way to inject God into the conversation. She spends a great deal of time expressing it, but I think it's more of an attempt to convince herself."

"Of course," Ibn said, sneering. "Like my grandma always said, 'Once a whore, *always* a whore.'"

Bunches looked at Ibn disgusted. "Did granny know that she was talking to a man who has had seen more rump than a butcher?"

Ibn pointed his spoon at her. "Double standard, baby girl. Double standard."

"Anyway, don't get me wrong, she's a pleasant enough girl," Bunches said, determined to sound impartial. "I'm just not sure if she's right for Michael."

"Well, I'm sure she ain't," Ibn said, wiping his mouth and putting down the bowl. "By the way, I want to know why you and Colin were fronting out there earlier." He emitted a mocking laugh. "Like y'all once had something going on between you."

Bunches' eyes fell to the floor. When they rose up and found Ibn again, there was a slyness attached to them. "What's it to you?" she asked.

"It's everything to me. You're my baby girl."

"Am I now?"

"'Now'?" he said, disbelieving. "Shoot, then, now, and forever will be, love."

She smiled at Ibn. Sometimes he could be so sweet, but she also remembered what an asshole he had been to Colin in the living room and wasn't done messing with him yet. "What is so hard to believe about that?" she asked, her voice tinged with mischief.

"Bunches, please." Ibn got up to put his bowl in the sink. "Like you and Colin are artful enough to keep that from us all for all these years."

He turned back around and faced her. "Well, maybe you are, but he isn't."

Bunches ran her palms along the tabletop and shrugged her shoulders. "Maybe Colin is a gentleman, understanding a young lady's need for privacy."

"Yeah," Ibn sneered, "and maybe you're full of doo-doo."

Twenty

Mike and Sharice were standing at the deli counter of the ShopRite, engaged in what they had mastered down to an art form: arguing over the most trivial things possible.

Sharice sighed with agitation. She shifted the strap of her purse from her right shoulder to her left. "Do you even know how much food that is?"

"No, Sharice, I don't know anything," Mike answered, "but, as usual, I'm sure you'll feel the need to enlighten me, of course."

She whirled on him. "What's that supposed to mean?"

He dug his hands into the pockets of his warm-up suit and focused on the many contours of the big dish of egg salad.

"Huh?"

Mike thought back to Thanksgiving at his parents' house. Sharice had felt the need to educate everybody in his family about the ways of the righteous—even going so far as to tell Bunches as they were leaving that she would pray for her. Sharice seemed to have the attitude that if you disagreed with her on any subject you were an abomination.

He drew a breath and exhaled. "Maybe I'm getting tired of everything needing the sanction and blessing of Sharice Watson. Why does everything always have to be your way, like you're Burger King or something?"

Sharice was momentarily taken aback by Mike's surliness. Then her response came back tinged with her own bend of nastiness. "Oh, I see. Because I point out the obvious to you, I'm bossy? Maybe I get *tired* of having to point out the obvious to you—like you're a child or something."

"So I'm a child now?" Mike asked.

"You're *childish*. And ridiculous as well. You just had a pile of turkey to eat."

"So? I like turkey."

"Mike, I am not ordering two pounds of sliced turkey. It's just gonna go to waste and turn slimy."

"No problem, I'll order it," Mike said.

". . . and stink up *my* refrigerator," Sharice added.

Mike turned his attention from the honey-roasted turkey in the deli case to Sharice's exasperated face. "Oh, so you're pulling rank, are you?" He threw his hands up defensively. "Don't worry, Ms. Boss Lady, I know whose refrigerator it is—whose condo it is. I'se knows my place."

Sharice's face contorted even more. "You are *so* ridiculous."

The young man at the counter called out for ticket number twenty-eight. The ticket Sharice held in her hands.

"One pound."

"*Two* pounds."

Sharice and Mike conducted an impromptu stare-down, neither side blinking for a good ten, fifteen seconds. Finally, Sharice sighed heavily. The deli man took this as an admission of defeat and began slicing two pounds.

As they were driving home in silence, Mike decided to turn on the radio to 99.8. A rap song came pulsating through the speakers for a good five seconds before Sharice hit the OFF button.

"You know I don't listen to that noise."

Mike groaned. Oh, yeah, he had forgotten Ms. Sanctified no longer listened to worldly music. He pulled up to a stoplight and looked over at her. With her smug, self-righteous ass. When he was with her, they only listened to music that she deemed acceptable. Only watched television shows that she found tasteful. Only went to places that she found agreeable.

And apparently he could forget about making love to her again. On the rare occasions that she let him touch her at all, she was the only one allowed to instigate it. She looked at him like he stole something if he touched her without her sanction.

He knew Sharice was trying to do the right thing, turning her life around for the better and all, and he was trying to be supportive. He really was. But it did bother him that he wasn't permitted to make love to her, especially in light of all those men who had done so in the past. Men who hadn't given a damn about her. He tried not to think about that. However, it was a constant struggle for him. The part of him that wanted to do right by Sharice versus the part of him that just wanted to *do* Sharice.

But his issues with her went beyond just their lack of intimacy. What he was especially tired of was getting everything shoved down his throat. Being preached and lectured to. Who was she to constantly force her will on him? He was sick of it. He turned the radio back on as the light turned green.

"If I can listen to your gospel nonstop, you can listen to this."

Sharice gave him a death stare. "You can't even compare that to this garbage."

"Why can't I?" Mike asked. "If he was saying 'King of Kings' instead of 'Bling Bling,' your head would be bobbing."

"Because—just listen to it—it's talking about disrespecting women, getting high, drinking, while the music I play—"

"—Is good for me, right? And you know what's best for me, right? You know what's best for everyone, right? You got the direct pipeline to God."

"No, I don't," Sharice said, "but I know where the blueprint is. My Bible!"

"Oh? And where does it say, 'Thou shall not play Cash Money Records'? Leviticus?" Mike asked as he pulled up in front of her condo.

"If you're gonna blaspheme, you can take yourself home! That's nothing but the Enemy speaking in you!"

"No, it's not the enemy, Sharice, it's Lil' Wayne and Juvenile." Mike started rapping to the song, "*Bling, Bling, what, Bling, Bling, what—*"

"Shut up!" Sharice grabbed the bag of groceries and got out of the car. "And take your *juvenile* self out of my face!" She slammed the door.

Mike watched her as she stormed up the steps to her balcony. She was pissed off. He knew it would be a while before she calmed down. The hell he cared. He put the car into reverse and began to pull out.

Guess she was right. She shouldn't have gotten so much turkey. It was only gonna turn slimy.

Dexter was lying in bed, staring at a spider working his way along the wall. He could hear the faint sounds of the TV in the living room. Mike was watching the Monday Night Football game between the Rams and the Packers. Dexter had watched the first half, but then decided to turn in, too consumed by his thoughts to enjoy the game anyway.

As usual, his thoughts were of Denise.

He had spent the entire weekend with her. They had talked and each had vowed to be more understanding and receptive to the other's thoughts, feelings and ideas. Mostly, they had agreed to cooperate with each other. They both understood that something larger than themselves was at stake.

His phone rang. He looked over at the caller-ID and saw Denise's name. Speak of the devil. "Hello?" he answered.

"Dexter," said a shaky voice on the other end.

Dexter propped himself on an elbow. "What's the matter?"

Denise breathed heavily. She was having trouble keeping her composure but finally managed to steady her voice. "Marla's taking me to Saint Joseph's. Will you meet me there?"

On the way over to the hospital, Dexter's mind was swirling with varying emotions. He had heard the ache in her voice. He was genuinely worried about her well-being, he hoped that Denise wasn't in any kind of pain, or heaven forbid, serious danger. He knew his worry was real because any anger he felt toward Denise had been rendered irrelevant.

Dexter thought about his seed growing inside her belly. His child, and his callous attitude toward it from the second he had found out she was pregnant. He had thought of it as a cancerous growth that he wished he could excise.

He had mistreated his child already. He had been an absentee dad, withholding the nourishing love of a father. No, he had done far worse. He had prayed for its demise.

Now that the moment was at hand, his feelings couldn't be more contrary. He wanted his child to live. Dexter starting praying.

He walked into the emergency waiting room, where Marla met him. Dexter could see that she had been crying.

"Is she all right?" Dexter asked.

Marla nodded. "But she's lost the baby."

Dexter's heart fell into his stomach. "Where is she?"

Marla led him onto the elevator and up to the third-floor waiting room. She sat down heavily in a cloth brown chair and crossed her ankles. Dexter remained standing.

"What happened?"

Marla concentrated on a spot on the rug and grimly shook her head. "She was in pain this morning . . . and evidently . . ." She stopped short and shrugged her shoulders.

Dexter felt his knees wobble. For months he had thought fatherhood was inevitable. In an instant, it was gone.

He sat down next to Marla and looked down the corridor. "So what's going on now?"

"She's having a D and E done," Marla said.

"A what?"

"A dilatation and evacuation," Marla replied. She hesitated, but anticipating Dexter's next question then added, "That's when they clean out the remains."

Dexter leaned back in his chair and closed his eyes.

They sat motionless for almost two hours. The only time Dexter moved was when he stepped into the lounge to use his cell phone.

He felt the need to talk to one of his friends. When he was unable to reach Mike, he made the mistake of calling Ibn. When he heard the news, he mistook what he was feeling, thinking that Dexter was calling him to express relief or even happiness. Dexter couldn't hold it against him too much, however. If he couldn't quite grasp what he was feeling, how could Ibn be expected to?

A nurse came into the waiting area.

"Are you Dexter and Marla?"

They both nodded.

"Denise would like to see you now."

Dexter looked at Marla, then back at the nurse, who upon closer inspection of her name tag wasn't a nurse at all but a volunteer. "Who did she ask for?"

The volunteer seemed confused by his question. "She asked for a Dexter or Marla."

Marla had understood the purpose of Dexter's question, and she stood up. "Dexter, I have to get home to my children. Will you make sure Denise gets home?"

Dexter stood up. "Of course. Thank you, Marla."

She gave him a strained smile. "Tell Denise I'll call her later."

"Okay." Dexter picked up her coat and helped her put it on.

"Thank you." Marla picked up her purse, adjusted the strap and left. Dexter's eyes followed her out the door. Maybe he had her pegged wrong.

"Sir, are you ready?" the volunteer asked.

Dexter picked up his coat and readied himself. "Yes."

He followed her down the hallway to the last door on the right. She stayed in the hallway while he walked into the examination room. Denise was wearing a hospital gown, sitting on a bed with her feet not quite reaching the floor. Dr. Harris was talking to her quietly.

When Denise saw it was Dexter, she turned away, choosing to look at a far wall instead of his face. Dr. Harris faced him instead.

"You can take her home now." He looked back at Denise. "I'll give you some privacy."

After he left, Dexter and Denise were left alone in uncomfortable silence. Neither knew what to say. Just as neither knew exactly what the baby meant to their relationship, they had no idea what the loss of the baby portended either. Any urgency they had felt to deal positively with the other was gone. Their need to work together to build something lasting was gone.

"Are you okay?" Dexter asked. Though he didn't know what else to say, he immediately felt stupid for asking that.

Denise barely nodded. Her eyes remained vacant, directed away from him. She gripped the edge of the bed tightly as if she were in danger of falling.

Dexter uncomfortably shifted his coat from one arm to another. "Marla had to go. I'm taking you home, okay?" He waited for a reaction, but there was none. He saw Denise's clothes on a far chair. "I'll leave to give you some privacy."

Dexter opened the door and had one foot in the hallway when Denise, in a voice barely above a whisper, finally spoke:

"It was a boy."

Dexter closed the door behind him, leaned against the wall and cried.

Twenty-one

"No, we haven't ordered yet. . . . Yeah, I'll see you in a little while. Okay, bye." Mike folded his cell phone up.

"Erika is stopping by," Mike said.

Ibn nodded to acknowledge that he heard him but was more attentive to the sight of Colin walking down the aisle to where they were sitting.

"Erika is joining us, Colin," Mike said.

"Yeah?" Colin said as he settled back into the booth and set his cell phone on the table. Ibn looked at it and then up at him.

"Where'd you go?" Ibn asked suspiciously.

"To the bathroom."

Ibn's eyes narrowed. "I just took a piss break. I didn't see you in there."

Mike looked up from his menu at Ibn, wondering what he was thinking.

Colin shifted nervously but quickly caught himself, opting to get indignant instead. "Damn, Ib. I didn't know I had to answer to you. I went to get something from my car, too. Damn!"

Ibn noticed Mike's eyes on him. "Mike, do you know this nigga has yet to go out clubbing with me?"

"I went to Club Egypt with you," Colin protested.

"Oh, yeah," Ibn said sarcastically. "Let me amend that, he went out *once* with me."

Mike shrugged his shoulders. "Maybe it's not his scene."

"Ain't that the truth," Colin agreed.

"I don't even wanna hear that bullshit," Ibn replied with irritation. "Look, Colin, your girl and my girl are no longer in the picture. I always say, the best way to forget a bitch, is with a bitch. Multiple bitches, if you can." He became exasperated. "Hell, man, you just *gotta* go where the hoes go."

"Like those two you brought back to the crib last weekend?" Colin asked.

"Exactly!" Ibn agreed. "Nikki and Tammy—good peoples, if ever there was any. I brought one back for you and what did your ass do? Went to sleep!" Ibn looked at Mike for help. "Not to bed, mind you, but to sleep—alone! Jesus Christ!" Ibn shook his head in disgust at the memory. "How many cats do you know will hand deliver a skank to his boy like that? That's some brotherhood for your ass right there!"

"I don't know why I bothered," Colin said. "I didn't get any sleep." He also looked over at Mike. "There were noises coming from the garage all night."

This was a new one, even for Ibn.

"The garage?"

"What are y'all ordering?" Ibn asked, all of a sudden extremely interested in the menu.

"Yeah, the garage," Colin repeated.

"I think I'm gonna have the chicken cheesesteak. . . ." Ibn said.

"What type of noises?" Mike asked.

"A lot of squealing, hollering, grunting . . . and the sound of machinery."

Colin and Mike both looked at Ibn, whose eyes were buried in the menu. He was trying to contain a grin.

"Good Lord, man," Mike mouthed in amazement.

"What?" Ibn finally looked up, his eyes full of innocence.

"What, nothing."

"Hey, now," Ibn protested, "I will not confirm your slanderous insinuations."

"It's only slander if it didn't happen. Do you deny it?"

"I will neither confirm nor deny. But what I will say is, and I get emotional when I think of this, so bear with me." Ibn hesitated, took a sip of water and bit his trembling lower lip before he continued. "I think there is nothing, and I mean *nothing*, in this world as tragic as letting a good trollop go to waste."

"You are so silly," Mike said, shaking his head.

"I'm right, and you know it." Ibn smirked. "But hey, Dex tells me you're knocking Sharice's ass out of the ol' ballpark."

Leave it to Dexter to run his mouth. "Uh-uhn, we only made love once."

Ibn looked at him wide-eyed. "What?"

At first Mike regretted admitting his lack of a sex life with Sharice, regardless of the reason. He knew, in Ibn's eyes, it certainly didn't help his cause. But, strangely enough, he didn't care. He was coming to the realization that his relationship with Sharice wasn't worth defending.

Ibn searched the room for their waitress. "I have to get Lorraine to move my seat away from you two clowns. I can't be seen sitting in the non-fucking section."

Mike ignored him. "Erika's here."

Bunches saw that she had Mike's eye and smiled as she approached the table. She was wearing her black wool pea coat and navy blue wool slacks.

"Hi, all," she said as she slid into the booth next to Mike. She set her purse on the seat near the aisle.

"Hey, Bunch," Colin said.

"Hey, cutie," Ibn said.

Mike helped Bunches out of her coat and laid it on top of his, Ibn's and Colin's in the adjoining booth.

"Dex was just coming in as I was leaving, Bunches said. "He told me to tell y'all he couldn't make it." She tugged at the sleeves of her three-quarter-length white cotton shirt. "So, I decided to join you guys in his place."

Bunches' and Mike's hands brushed underneath the table. She playfully grabbed his index finger and gave it a squeeze. He hastily pulled it back.

"Did he say why?" Ibn asked indignantly, like he was owed an explanation.

"No." Bunches said, looking at Mike's menu. "I got the impression he didn't want to be bothered."

Ibn shrugged. "I don't know about that cat lately. He's been acting strange. All quiet and shit." He threw a thumb in Colin's direction. "One nigga acting silly over a woman around here is enough."

"Man, be quiet," Colin said.

"What do you expect, Ib?" Mike asked. "He and Denise just had a miscarriage."

"That's what I'm sayin'," Ibn said, slapping his hand against the table for emphasis. "The nigga should be celebrating."

Colin and Mike looked at each other, partially disbelieving what they had heard—partially considering the source. Bunches just glared at him.

Ibn noticed the group's reaction. "Yo, y'all need to look at the bigger picture."

"From across this booth, all I see is the nigger picture," Bunches said.

Ibn wasn't the least bit repentant. "Fuck it, I'm just being real. I think Denise trapped him. Besides, wasn't the nigga praying for a miscarriage, anyway?"

That was true, Mike thought. But he, too, had noticed that Dexter hadn't been himself since the miscarriage. He thought that maybe Dexter had had a change of heart regarding fatherhood and now felt ashamed that he had prayed for his offspring's death.

Lorraine came over to take their orders. Colin and Ibn ordered fried chicken platters while Bunches and Mike ordered the catfish.

From the jukebox in the bar area, the song "You Make Me Feel Mighty Real" drifted to where they were sitting.

"Heyyy," Bunches said, bobbing her head.

"Who played this?" Ibn wondered aloud.

Mike liked this song, though not nearly as much as Terence, who had to be the biggest Sylvester fan going. Speaking of which.

"Erika," Mike said, "you wanna go with me to see Terence perform?"

"When is it?"

"The Saturday after Christmas."

Bunches thought about it, mentally picturing the scribblings on the calendar hanging in her kitchen. "Yeah, I'm free."

"Perform?" Colin asked. "What does he do?"

"A top-notch Bette Midler and a hellified Teena Marie, from what I hear," Mike said, causing him and Bunches to laugh.

He could tell by the blank expressions on Colin's and Ibn's faces that they didn't have a clue what he was talking about. Slowly, a hint of recognition started to form on Ibn's face.

"Jesus Christ, he's a drag queen?"

Mike shrugged his shoulders. "He's an entertainer who works in illusion."

"The only 'illusion' is that that fat cherub was born with a dick instead of a pussy," Ibn snarled. "I can't believe y'all going to see that nonsense—men parading around wanting to be women."

Bunches, who had turned the ignoring of Ibn's rantings into an art form, rummaged through her purse.

"Why wouldn't I?" Mike asked. "Terence has done a lot for me. He's been a model employee who has made me look good to the higher-ups on more than one occasion. What? I shouldn't support him because you don't approve of his lifestyle?"

"Oh, so you're Mr. Forward Thinker now?" Ibn jeered. "Do you approve of his lifestyle?"

"He's my friend, regardless," Mike said. "I don't approve of everything your ass does, either."

"Hear, hear," Colin agreed, raising his glass of water. "Ibn, you have embarrassed me more times than I care to remember."

"Ain't that the truth," Bunches said, applying lip balm.

"And as a matter of record, I don't think gay men who perform in drag necessarily want to be women, Ib. I'm sure they make good use of their dicks. If you don't believe me, I'm sure Terence would be more than happy to prove that fact to you."

Colin and Bunches chuckled.

"Watch that shit, Mike. It ain't funny."

"But why do they dress like women, then?" Colin asked.

"Well, I'm no authority, but from what Terence tells me, it is a way to pay homage to women they admire. And like I said before, the idea is that the illusion should be as uncanny as possible."

"Why don't they dress as men entertainers, then?" Colin asked.

"Because they're fagboys, that's why!" Ibn snorted.

"Where is the illusion in men dressing like men?" Mike replied. Turning to Ibn, he added, "Why are you so intolerant?"

"I'm not, really," Ibn said. "Hell, my thinking is that life is hard, so as long as you're not hurting anybody, a person should get pleasure anyway they can."

Mike had to admit that really was the way Ibn conducted his life. One gigantic, unyielding pleasure hunt.

Ibn continued, "So if a man finds it pleasurable to have some nigga's balls in his face—"

Bunches cut him off. "So, what you're saying is, regardless of ancillary circumstances, like race, gender, age, prior relationship, et cetera, that if a person isn't hurting anybody or breaking any laws—and the other person is willing—they should pursue their opportunity at happiness. Right?"

"That's exactly what I'm saying," Ibn said, "just not as eloquently as you."

Bunches smiled. "I'm so glad you feel that way."

Colin and Ibn were too preoccupied with the food that Lorraine was setting in front of them to notice the suggestive tone in Bunches' voice, but Mike had caught it. It was hard for him not to. Bunches had grabbed his hand when she said it.

Twenty-two

Stephanie stopped by Dexter's cubicle. "Why the long face?" she said as she poked her head in.

Dexter fidgeted with some items on his desk. He had just tried to call Denise again and had received no answer. He was sure she was screening her calls and avoiding him. Several weeks had passed since he had seen her. They had spoken just once, last week, and the conversation had been curt. She gave him the impression that she didn't want to be bothered. He was starting to come to the belief that Denise had decided that moving on would be easier if she just cut him off totally.

"I've had a setback recently that I was thinking about."

"Oh," Stephanie said. "Is there anything I can do to help?"

Dexter raised his head and looked at her. She seemed to really mean it. Stephanie was a genuinely sweet person. "Thanks, no. I'll snap out of it. It certainly doesn't solve anything to dwell."

"Wish your buddy had your perspective," Stephanie said, nodding her head in the direction of Colin's cubicle. "He's been down and out for a while lately, like he lost his best friend."

More like his worst enemy, Dexter thought. "He'll be fine, believe me."

"Are you sure? He's been moping like this for a while now."

Dexter saw the look of concern on Stephanie's face as she peered in the direction of Colin's desk. He could tell she was dying to ask him what was wrong. It suddenly occurred to him that he had been so preoccupied with his own worries that he was letting a golden opportunity slip away.

"Well, actually, Steph, he and his girlfriend broke up."

"No, really?"

Dexter studied her face. She was trying to contain her glee. He could tell that was the reason she had been hoping to hear.

"Yep. They're kaput."

Stephanie had become quiet. Her mind was working overtime. She was definitely hatching something. After a minute or so, she said, "You know, Dexter, I almost forgot to tell you what I came over here for. I'm having a little get-together Saturday at my apartment."

"Yeah?" Dexter rested his chin in his folded hands and pretended to act like he didn't know where this was going.

"Yeah. Nothing fancy, you know, just some good food, some good conversation."

"Should I bring someone?"

Stephanie shrugged. "If you'd like. Maybe you can bring your girlfriend—Denise, right? When is her due date?"

He decided not to tell Stephanie about Denise's miscarriage. It was okay to tell Colin's business, but not his. "Not for a while," he replied. "Thanks, I might just do that."

She smiled. "All right, then."

Dexter returned her smile, and Stephanie started to walk away. He guessed it would take her a good four steps before she turned back around.

"Oh, Dexter," Stephanie said, spinning on one of her pumps, "I just had an idea."

Damn, Dex thought, three steps. Off by one.

"What's that?"

"I think I'm gonna invite Colin, too. Maybe it would cheer him up."

"That's a good idea!" Dexter said, slapping his palm against his forehead with mock enthusiasm. "I never would have thought of that! You're such a thoughtful person."

Stephanie tried to smirk but laughed instead.

*   *   *

Ibn was on his way to his store when his cellular rang. "Hello?"

"Hi."

Ibn nearly drove off the road.

"Hold on," he managed to say.

He decided to pull over before he killed someone and turned into the parking lot of a 7-Eleven. The lot was full, so Ibn wheeled his Benz into a handicapped space. An old man coming out of the store glared at him for doing so, but Ibn ignored him.

"Tiffany?"

"Yep. You got it on the first try, huh?"

Ibn's heart was racing. "It was easy. You're the only woman who has my number."

Tiffany emitted a snarl-laugh. "Oh, I've got your number, all right."

Ibn caught sight of himself in his rearview mirror. His face was full of hope and expectation. Calm your ass down. "So how have you been, Tiff?"

"Fine. Just working."

Ibn was listening intently to Tiffany's voice to see if he could discern loneliness, regret or even desperation, but it didn't reveal anything. "How's the car holding up?"

"No problems."

Ibn took a deep breath. There was a lot he wanted to say, but he wanted to feel her out first.

"It's good to hear your voice."

"Likewise," Tiffany replied. "How about us seeing each other as well?"

"Yeah, we should do that," Ibn agreed, his wariness diminishing. "Do you want me to come down there?"

"No, I'm coming up there Friday night. How about you get us a suite at Inn of the Dove?"

Aww, shit. Ibn grinned. He gave a momentary thought to playing hard to get. Playing it cool. After all, Tiffany had jetted on him in October, and it was now December. How did she know her ass hadn't already been replaced? And who was she to come up here after months of separation demanding dick? Was she worthy?

But he couldn't have if he wanted to. First of all, he had yet to be with another woman who could work him out sexually like Tiffany could. Second, he missed her something ridiculous.

"Yeah, I'll do that," Ibn said with an air of forced nonchalance. "Only thing is, I can't be there until later, like around ten-thirty."

"Okay," Ibn replied, still keeping up his pretense of indifference. "I'll leave a key for you at the front desk."

Tiffany paused. "So, it's a date then, huh?"

"Yep," Ibn replied. "It'll be nice."

"Oh, I guarantee it's gonna be nice," Tiffany purred, "and tight, too."

He felt a rustling in his pants.

When Ibn pulled into his driveway that evening, he was still on cloud nine. He was glad to see Colin's car there. He was dying to share with somebody the news that Tiffany was back.

He picked up the trash cans at the end of the driveway—doing a quick soft-shoe along the asphalt—and put them in their proper position in the garage. After first stopping to wipe a speck of dirt off his Benz's hood, he went through the garage door, which led into the pantry.

Once inside, Ibn made his way toward the kitchen. When he entered, he saw Colin quickly folding his phone. He was a little jumpy, and Ibn got the impression that he had startled him by coming in through the garage.

"Why are you using your cell phone in the house?" Ibn asked.

"Oh, I—I was talking long-distance to my mother," Colin said, walking over to the refrigerator. "I didn't want to put it on your bill." He pulled out a Snapple peach iced tea and turned around. "What's up with you?"

Ibn beamed. "I'll tell you what's up with me." He hesitated to savor the taste of his words, rolling them around on his tongue before he let them pour out. "Tiffany called today."

Colin stopped in midgulp. "Uh-uhn!"

"Hell, yeah," Ibn said triumphantly. "Think about it, like she really had a choice in the matter. She can't replace the mighty Ibn Barrington! Not in this lifetime, Jack!"

Colin wasn't so sure. Like everyone else, he had thought Tiffany was really done with him this time. "What did she say?"

Ibn shrugged. "That she can't live without my dick."

"What?" Colin laughed. "She did not."

"In so many words, that's exactly what she said." Ibn sat down at the table. "She wants me to set up a rendezvous at our spot for Friday night."

"Damn," Colin said, taking a seat across the table from him, "that's amazing."

Ibn scoffed. "No, it isn't, frat. You just gotta know how to handle women." He leaned back in the chair and smiled. He was really starting to feel his oats. "Let me explain something to you. Tiffany expected me to kiss her caramel behind, go down there boo-hooing and making a general ass out of myself when she left."

"You think so?" Colin said, taking a sip. "I don't know, Ib. I think she was really through this time."

"Oh, please," Ibn jeered. "You giving her too much credit. That girl hasn't had an independent thought in her life." He shook his head. "Tiffany 'through' with me, imagine that. The only thing she knows about being through is when she spreads her legs and I run through her."

"Okay," Colin said, not convinced.

"Oh, you still disbelieving, huh? You should be taking notes," Ibn said, rising from the table. "What this was, was a power struggle. An attempted coup for the reins of our relationship." Ibn opened his refrigerator and grabbed a plum. "Then the cold reality of life without Ibn hit her ass." He leaned against the counter and took a bite. "She lost, so now she has to come back to me, on my terms. It's called waiting a girl out."

"Congratulations. You're the man." Colin also rose from the table. He put his cellular into his pocket. "I'm going to the store. You want anything?"

"Nah. I'm gonna need some more fruit for my skank-out with Tiffany, but I'll pick it up later in the week."

"Uh-oh, you breaking out the fruit?" Colin asked. "Does she know what she's in for?"

"No, but she probably has a good idea, though. Why do you think her ass is coming back?"

They both chuckled.

"But do me a favor, don't tell Bunches, Mike or Dex about this yet. I wanna see the look of surprise on their faces when all of a sudden Tiffany is back like nothing happened."

"No problem, I won't say anything to them." Colin added on his way out, "Just don't make her eat too much crow."

"Frat," Ibn said, "there's only one caveat to the 'waiting a girl out' theory."

Colin turned around holding the kitchen door open. "What's that?"

"You have to make sure it's a girl worth waiting for. Not some skank that wasn't worth your time in the first place."

Colin let go the door, leaving it swinging. Ibn didn't hear another sound until he heard the front door slam.

Oh, well, Ibn shrugged as he took another bite of his plum. Jack Nicholson was right. Some niggas can't handle the truth.

Mike looked over at Bunches and smiled. "What do you want for Christmas, Erika?"

She gave him a look of annoyance. "Michael Lovett, Christmas is next week. If you haven't thought enough of me to do your shopping yet, then don't bother."

Mike laughed at her. Her ass was spoiled beyond redemption. "Calm down, I've already done your shopping." He reached over to where her hand sat on the gear shift and stroked it lightly with his thumb.

There was a beat in which the only sound was the quiet humming of the car.

"What did you buy me?" he asked.

"I can't say."

"Don't want to ruin the surprise, huh?"

"No, it's not that. It's just that I really can't say." She laughed. "I haven't gone shopping for you yet."

Mike muttered. "You ain't sh—"

"Hey, watch it, sport. Or you'll be walking home—in the rain, no less—because it's supposed to storm tonight."

Mike laughed.

"So, have you spoken to Tiffany lately?" Bunches asked.

She was driving back home from Camden, where they had just attended a meeting for their mentoring program. They and other mentors got together once every six weeks to exchange ideas and experiences concerning the children.

"No." Mike looked over at her. "Have you?"

Bunches turned onto the exit for 676. "Yeah. But not in a while."

"So, where is her head at?"

"Not thinking about Ibn, that's for damn sure."

"Really?"

"Yep. I think she came to the opinion that Ibn's bad outweighs his good."

"Wow."

Bunches shot him a look. "Why is that so hard for you to believe? You didn't think it was bound to happen sooner or later?"

Mike pulled down the visor to look in the lighted mirror. He was in need of a shave. "Honestly?"

"No. Lie to me, Michael."

He closed the visor. "Well, I was beginning to have my doubts that Tiffany was ever gonna break clean from Ibn."

Bunches shook her head. "That's a failing of yours, Michael."

"What, that I look at the evidence?"

"No, that you want to relegate women into a certain position." She took her eyes off the road and glanced at Mike's face in the darkness. "Remember something: What we are at any given point is not all that we're destined to be."

"All I know is that Tiffany has left Ibn many times before only to come back. Only a fool would not take a person's past actions into account when guessing as to what they might do in the future."

"Oh, so what you're saying is that a person's past dictates the future?" Bunches asked.

"Yep," Mike replied confidently. "I find this to be true especially in women, who are creatures of habit far more often than men are."

"Hmm, okay." She turned on her CD player. Maxwell's voice started to serenade them.

Mike saw the quizzical look on Bunches' face and turned the volume down. "What?"

"Oh, I was just wondering"—Bunches signaled and moved into the fast lane—"if you honestly feel that the past dictates the future, especially with women, then what are you doing with Sharice?"

Mike searched for an answer but didn't have one. He turned the volume back up and looked out the window. Truth be known, he had been asking himself the same question lately. They had spoken only sparingly in the last couple of weeks and hadn't seen each other since their blowup in the car.

Mike didn't really care and he doubted that Sharice did either. They weren't the same people they had been in college. And as far as a romantic relationship, it was obvious that the chemistry wasn't there. So, why had he been so intent on forcing it?

No, if he was honest with himself, he did know the answer to why he had been with Sharice lately. He hadn't wanted to admit it, but for him Sharice had simply been a diversion so that he wouldn't act on his true feelings. For a while now Sharice's purpose had been to keep him preoccupied so he wouldn't think about the person he really wanted to be with.

The person sitting next to him.

"Well, it doesn't matter. Sharice and I decided to cool it," Mike said, continuing to look out the window. "It was misguided on my part, anyway."

"Why?" Bunches asked as she pulled into the driveway. Mike's Altima sat out front, but Dexter's car was gone. The house was shrouded in darkness because Dexter hadn't turned on the porch light before he left. A smattering of raindrops softly pelted the windshield.

Bunches turned off the ignition, unfastened her seat belt and looked over at him. Mike couldn't meet her gaze.

"Why?" she repeated.

"You know why."

Mike heard her take a deep breath. When she spoke again, her voice was full of yearning. "I need you to tell me."

Mike swallowed hard. He knew she needed to hear it and she deserved to hear it, but it wasn't an easy thing for him to do. Because
what he was about to say was going to change the course of their relationship forever. Was going to change everything about them forever. He wouldn't be able to joke his way out of it. But he needed to say
it. Better than that, he wanted to say it. The time for being cute was
over. He turned and faced her.

"Because I'm in love with you, Erika."

Bunches gasped, took his face in her hands and brought his lips to
meet hers.

As Mike responded, exploring the suppleness of her lips, the soft,
gentle probing of her tongue, he knew what he had always supposed
was in fact true. She did taste as perfect as he had always envisioned.

Bunches pulled away so that she could see him. Tears welled at the
bottom of her eyes. Mike slid his hands down her forearms and held her
hands.

"Shame on you for making me wait so long, Michael Lovett."

He tenderly stroked her hands with his. "You're right, Erika. Shame
on me, indeed."

As they kissed again, Mike heard a roll of thunder. There was no
doubt about it, he thought, a storm was definitely brewing.

Twenty-three

Dexter was vexed, and the cause of his irritation was the person on the other end of the phone. "What do you mean, you're not going?" he asked again.

"I'm not up to it," Colin replied.

"Frat," Dexter hesitated, but then decided that he'd better say it, "I think Stephanie put the whole thing together with you in mind."

"Oh, that's supposed to make me more comfortable?"

"It would make me!" Dexter replied emphatically. "Stephanie is cute, she's funny, she's smart—"

"Then you date her, Dex."

"Nigga, I would! But she doesn't want me, she wants you. Unfortunately for her, I might add."

"Whatever."

Dexter was seething. Here Colin had a golden opportunity with a good as gold sister, and he wanted to act a fool? A man who had endured so much abuse from Stacy was going to blow a chance with a quality woman? He tried again to reason with him.

"Look, Colin, Stephanie is a sweet person, a true friend. She's seen you down in the dumps at work, and she just wants to cheer you up. I forgot that I have to go to my cousin's wedding in New York on Saturday, so I can't go." Dexter exhaled deeply, for emphasis. "C'mon, Colin, Stephanie will feel bad if neither of us show."

"Sorry, but I can't make it. I got something else to do."

"Wait a second," Dexter said, his voice rising. "Which one is it? You're not up to it, or you got something else to do?"

"Both."

"Both! What the hell is that supposed to mean?"

"It means just what I said, both." Colin answered in a calm voice. "And stop yelling at me."

"Colin, what do you have to do?"

"Even if it's just jiggling my balls, it's my business. I'm grown, Dexter. I don't have to explain myself to anybody."

The "I'm grown" speech? Dexter was finished with this cat.

"All right, fine, man, I'll talk to you later."

After Dexter hung up, he was in a boil. Something had to be done about Colin. An intervention was definitely in order. He decided to call Ibn.

"Colin, I told you. I wasn't having my needs met."

He and Stacy were just finishing another of their clandestine meetings, the only kind of encounters they'd had since Colin moved out. They had just eaten dinner at Cafe Melange—Stacy's treat—and they were now parked at Rancocas Park in a spot usually reserved for lovers. He knew she had not chosen this spot by accident.

"What wasn't I doing to meet your needs? Huh?"

Stacy winced. The glow from the streetlight softened her features, made her seem more harmless and sympathetic. "It's hard to put a finger on exactly. I guess, I didn't feel you noticed me anymore. My self-esteem was sinking."

"And that car salesman was better equipped to lift your spirits than me?" Colin asked angrily.

"Look, I know I went about it the wrong way. I was just vulnerable." She placed her hand on Colin's arm and looked at him earnestly. "I want you to know that man meant nothing to me."

"But now he means something to me, Stacy, because he put his hands on something I hold sacred," he said, his voice rising. "And you let him."

She shrugged. "It wasn't the right thing to do. I know that now."

"You got that right," he muttered.

"But good could come out of it."

Colin looked at her in disbelief. Had he just heard that right? "What good could possibly come out of it, Stacy? My mother, who already distrusts and dislikes you for no apparent justification, now has a reason. My friends, whose relationship with you was strained at best—"

Stacy exploded. "There you go again! Who the hell told you to tell your mother, then, huh? And do you think I give a good goddamn what your friends think? Huh? I don't know why you do! Do they think about you when they decide who they're gonna be with? No! They don't live for you, so why do you live for them?"

"It's not about me living for them." Colin answered coolly. "If that was the case, I wouldn't have been with you in the first place, never mind for as long as I was."

Stacy rolled her eyes. He had a point there.

"However, I would be a fool not to consider their opinions. These are people who care about my well-being." He gave Stacy a hard stare. "None of them have ever betrayed me."

Stacy softened her approach. "But since they never liked me, can you honestly say they are gonna give you an unbiased opinion?"

He shrugged.

"Colin, this time apart can be a positive thing for us. It's like I said—and I want you to listen to me, honey—if it's something that makes me value more what me and you have, then ultimately it can be a good thing."

Colin's face contorted. "That's some convoluted logic, Stacy. What, you can't see the value in me unless you're riding another man?"

"Colin." Stacy took a deep breath and put her hand on his forearm. "I have told you that it wasn't the right thing to do. I know that."

He stared ahead out the windshield. It was fogging up because of all their talking. He wasn't sure if Stacy truly knew how much she had hurt him. No, she couldn't, or she wouldn't have done it in the first place. Not if she had an ounce of feeling for him.

He looked out his window. He was starting to choke up. He had promised himself he wasn't gonna cry in front of Stacy. One, because of the weakness it showed. Second, he'd noticed that since this whole thing had gone down, Stacy hadn't shed one tear. What did he look like bawling his eyes out, when her ducts were as dry as the Sahara?

Stacy seemed to sense his weakness and gripped his hand tightly. "Look, honey, I know I haven't made things easy for you, but I hope you will give me another chance."

Colin turned to face her. She moved her hand to his knee.

"Don't throw away all these years because of one error of judgment on my part." She felt confident enough to lean over and give him a peck on the lips. He didn't resist. This was the first kiss they had shared since the incident.

Stacy leaned back and suppressed a smile. Colin could tell she was debating whether she should go for the kill and try to fuck him tonight. He also wasn't sure what he would do if she did try.

"So, we getting together tomorrow night, right?" she asked. She took out a handkerchief and wiped off the rearview mirror.

"Yeah." She must be going for the home run then, Colin decided.

Stacy started the car and put on the defroster. "All right, so I'll pick you up at Ibn's at about six-thirty, okay."

"No, no," Colin insisted, "let's meet somewhere like we've been doing."

"But I can just swing by Ibn's on the way from work," Stacy contended. "Why take two cars?"

"No, I don't mind, really."

Stacy looked at Colin and smirked. "Would you stop pretending that you aren't keeping me a secret from your buddies?"

Colin played dumb. "What?"

"Come off it," Stacy needled wickedly. "The secret meeting spots, the strictly cell phone calling, the way you have to cancel sometimes at the last second—"

"Can you blame me?" Colin asked. "Do you think I wanna hear their mouths? Especially Ibn's?"

"Where do you tell them you've been when they question you?" Stacy asked.

"They usually don't. The only one that does is Ibn." Colin took off his glasses to clean them. "I usually tell him I was doing something with Corey or Andre, at one of their games or something."

Colin noticed Stacy shaking her head in disapproval.

"Like I said before, 'Can you blame me?'"

Stacy pondered that for a moment before responding. "No, I can't. But what I will say is this." She put the car into reverse and slowly backed out. "Ultimately, you gotta do what makes you happy. If your friends can't understand that, can you really say that they're your friends?" She put the car into drive and wheeled off.

Before Colin could answer, Stacy dropped one more thought.

"Colin, anybody that truly cares for you will want to see you happy, unconditionally. Not just on their terms."

Colin put his glasses back on and looked over at her in the darkness. Sometimes, he swore that Stacy had missed her true calling, horticulture. For nobody could plant seeds of doubt and nurture them like she could.

Tiffany drove to the last bungalow in the complex and pulled into the parking space next to Ibn's Land Cruiser. Before she cut off the engine, she turned on the interior light and looked into the rearview mirror. She studied her hair. It looked good. She had just had it done, though she didn't know why, because it was about to become a sweaty mess. She checked her makeup, applied some more lipstick—Ibn's favorite, Maybelline Plum Crazy. She breathed deeply and looked at the clock—10:47. She grabbed her purse and quickly made her way toward the cottage.

She opened the front door with the key left for her at the front desk. She stepped inside to the foyer to escape the cold December night. The foyer offered a toasty respite from the chill. She turned and locked the door behind her.

"Ibn, I'm here."

There was no response. She took off her coat and hung it in the hall closet next to Ibn's. She paused momentarily to look at the two matching leather trenches. Ibn had bought them last winter.

"Ibn," she again called out, making her way along the marble floor to the large open room at the end of the hallway.

She stepped through the entrance onto the plush carpet and

scanned the room for Ibn. He was nowhere to be found, at least not in the flesh, but there was abundant evidence of his presence.

A fire was crackling in the huge marble fireplace. Tiffany dropped her purse on the sofa and the key on the coffee table. She walked over to the flickering flames to warm herself further. Her only light beside the flame was the foyer light.

While unzipping her boots, she saw a dizzying array of colors on top of the huge mahogany table in the dining area. She walked over for a closer inspection.

A colossal bouquet of roses awaited her. There had to be at least four dozen of them, and they were multihued—peach, red, purple and cream. On the other end of the table was a gleaming silver platter of fruit. Two kinds of grapes, cherries, strawberries, and peach and melon slices were all situated lovingly on the tray. In between the flowers and the fruit was a bottle of Dom Perignon chilling in a tub of ice and two long-stem champagne glasses. Ibn could teach Martha Stewart a thing or two, thought Tiffany, for this table looked like a work of art. She admired its symmetry. The colors of the flowers matched the colors of the fruit platter, and knowing Ibn the way she did, she knew it wasn't by accident.

Due to this foreknowledge of Ibn, she pushed the flowers aside. Sure enough, hidden beneath them were three black jewelry boxes.

She opened the largest one first. It was a white gold V-shaped necklace with a diamond pendant. Tiffany took off her cream turtleneck, laid it across the back of the chair and put on the necklace.

Next was the smallest box, which she guessed correctly contained matching diamond earrings. She put them into her bare ears. In fact, she had come to this rendezvous with her whole body completely devoid of jewelry, because she knew Ibn, and how he thought, and how he *thought* she thought.

She opened the last box. It was a diamond-encrusted bracelet. She draped it around her wrist, then turned in the direction of the fire so the flames made the diamonds glisten. Not bad, she thought. She hadn't expected a bracelet.

Her body was now craving two things. The feel of Ibn's skin and the taste of the fruit. She walked over to the bar area and opened the little refrigerator behind it. Inside was the solitary can of whipped cream she was looking for. She took it and sprayed some cream on a couple of strawberries, which she quickly polished off. Her appetite was whetted further, but the food could wait. She was ready to taste her some Ibn.

Before she left the open area, she climbed the three steps to toss the container of whipped cream onto the mammoth raised four-poster bed set off by itself on one side of the room. She then walked past the Jacuzzi, back down the steps and opened the door to the bathroom.

No sign of Ibn in the shower. She then went over and checked the small steam room. It, too, was empty.

Now her craving was really getting strong. She turned and looked in the mirror over the marble sink. The look on her face nearly startled her. She was horny as all hell.

She slid off her bra and massaged her breasts slowly, running her fingertips along her nipples. She unfastened her jeans and slid them off, draping them on a towel rack. She rolled off each of her knee-highs and hung them and her bra on a hook on the back of the door. She gave a thought to taking off her thong, but decided against it. She wanted to leave something for Ibn to do.

She opened the other bathroom door, which led down another hallway. She flipped on the light. This corridor was tiled and there were mirrors on either side of it. Tiffany caught a glimpse of herself as she walked. The diamonds were shimmering on her body.

Tiffany opened the door at the end of the hallway, to the heated pool area. There she finally found what she was looking for.

Ibn came up from underneath the water to find Tiffany standing along the edge of the pool.

"Hi, stranger," she said as Ibn caught his breath.

"Hi, Tiff," Ibn swam to the edge nearest him. He was at the opposite side of the small pool. He stretched his arms along the ledge and faced Tiffany. "You look good."

Tiffany's eyes pored over Ibn. She didn't bother returning his compliment because he already knew how handsome he was. Maybe it was due to their time apart, but he looked absolutely flawless. Hair perfect as usual—it looked like it had been cut just that afternoon. Nails freshly manicured. And the rivulets of water streaking along his skin were doing a glorious job of accentuating his muscled body. Tiffany shook her head in appreciation. Ibn dry was joy enough, but Ibn wet was downright enchanting.

Further adding to his appearance was that he was sparkling. He had on a matching set of jewelry to the one Tiffany had, just bigger versions. Diamond studs in each ear, a diamond bracelet on his right arm and a diamond necklace draped around his neck.

"I don't even have to ask if you're naked, do I?" Tiffany asked.

"Why don't you come in and find out?" he replied.

"Don't have to." Tiffany shrugged. "I already know you are."

"Then why don't you come get wet, anyway?" Ibn asked.

"Don't have to," Tiffany replied sweetly. "I'm already wet." She turned on her heel and left the pool area.

As Ibn's eyes followed Tiffany's ass, he felt his manhood surge underneath the water. It was good she was ready, because he wasn't interested in a whole lot of getting-reacquainted small talk either. He climbed out of pool and reached for his towel.

When Ibn found Tiffany again, she was standing by the foot of the bed with her back to him. "I need you, Ibn."

Ibn came up behind her and spun her around. He cupped her face in his hands and studied her. There was a vacancy in her eyes. He chalked it up to the lack of him in her life. He didn't want to make her eat crow; he only wanted to eradicate that empty look. He kissed her lips softly, then probed her mouth with his warm tongue.

"I missed you too, baby." He slid his arms around her waist and held her tightly. He lifted one hand in between her shoulder blades and pressed Tiffany even closer. Ibn's heart was filled with so much joy at holding her again that he felt like he was going to burst.

Tiffany began kissing his neck, running her tongue along his necklace. Ibn spun her back around and returned the favor. He wrapped her waist tightly with his left hand and fondled her breasts with his right. Her intensified breathing and racing pulse coincided with the throbbing penis that pressed against her backside.

"I need you, Ibn," Tiffany panted.

Ibn clutched her breasts with both hands as he hungrily nibbled at her shoulders. Tiffany ran her fingers through his curly hair. Ibn began licking down her spine, gingerly guiding his hands down along her heaving rib cage.

When he got to the small of her back, he knelt down and slid her thong down her legs so Tiffany could step out of it. Seizing the opportunity, he slipped his thick fingers in between her thighs and started exploring her wetness.

Tiffany sighed deeply and spread her legs wider. She leaned forward onto the bed, running her palms along the bedsheet.

When Ibn took his hand from in between her legs, Tiffany propped herself up on her elbows and peered over her shoulder. Ibn returned her look while he slowly licked his fingers. "You taste so sweet, baby."

Tiffany fell onto the bed and closed her eyes. She felt Ibn's hands along her hips, guiding her farther up on the bed and then around her thighs, spreading her legs even farther apart. The next thing she felt was Ibn's practiced tongue exploring her pussy. She groaned appreciatively and clutched the bedsheet.

"I've been craving your taste, your scent, all day, Tiffany," Ibn said, while he greedily sucked her.

He moved his hands to her inner thighs and bit her lightly on the behind before he went back to his ravenous slurping, sucking on her clit just the way he knew she liked.

"Yes, Ibn, right there! Don't stop, Ibn!" Tiffany panted.

Her body started to tremble. Ibn continued licking her hot spot until her whole body quivered uncontrollably, when he finally backed off, leaving Tiffany to writhe on the bed unencumbered. He knew she didn't like being touched when she was having an orgasm. She rolled over and continued convulsing, finally ending up in a fetal position, while Ibn waited.

Tiffany opened her eyes and smiled at him. "Come here." She patted the bed next to her.

As Ibn stood up, he saw her eyes travel to his erection. It was his turn, but he wasn't quite through with her yet. "Hold on."

Ibn walked over to the table and got the big plate of fruit. When Tiffany saw it, she got excited. "Let me get in the middle of the platter." She scooted to the center of the bed and spread her legs. He placed the platter of fruit in between her legs and sat down on the bed.

Ibn took a piece of melon and brushed it across Tiffany's lips before putting in her mouth. He then licked the excess juice from her lips. He next took a stalk of grapes and slowly rubbed it across her breasts, lightly touching her nipples, before he lowered them into her mouth.

Ibn spotted the whipped cream on the far edge of the bed. He grabbed the container and urged Tiffany onto her back.

He sprayed some on a strawberry and teased Tiffany by holding it just out of reach of her mouth. Eager to play, she fixed a seductive gaze on him and licked off the cream with her tongue.

Ibn moved the platter off to the side and sat on his knees between Tiffany's legs. He shook the can up and grabbed Tiffany's calf, holding her leg up in the air with his left hand.

Starting at her foot, he began spraying a long stream of whipped cream. He went past her ankle, down her calf, along her thigh and right along the outer folds of her pussy, making an oval, then filling in the middle.

"I'm about to have me a Tiffany split."

Tiffany reached over onto the platter and put a cherry in the middle of the cream. She looked at him and smiled. "With a cherry on top, babe?" she asked.

Ibn felt like crying tears of joy. *Damn*, he had missed this girl. "With a cherry on top." He went back to her foot and began to eat.

As Ibn swallowed the cherry, he again waited for Tiffany to finish trembling. As she moaned, he congratulated himself on his generosity. How many brothers would sit there with a hard-on while they pleased their women with their mouths not once, but twice? But, he had to admit, it was also self-serving, for a couple of reasons. One, he wanted Tiffany to *know* what she had been missing. Second, hell, he was a freak. He simply lived for the taste of Tiffany's pussy.

Ibn figured he would allow her some time to recover. Then it was gonna be his turn. He got up to get himself a glass of champagne.

"Uh-uh, get back here," she snapped.

Ibn smiled. So, it was gonna be one of *those* nights. It wasn't often that Tiffany's drive was equal to his.

He got back on the bed and lay on his back. Tiffany sat astride him and began licking his torso, tracing her tongue along his neck and chest, playfully biting his nipples. She teased him by gyrating up and down, letting the tip of his penis touch her opening, but not letting it in.

Ibn closed his eyes and groaned. When he opened them, Tiffany was looking at him. "You feel so good, Tiff."

She tenderly stroked his face with her hand. "Yeah?"

"Yeah, you have no idea how good."

She smiled. "I'll be back."

She shimmied her way down his body. She grabbed his penis in her hand and started licking the underside of it, slowly dragging her tongue from sac to tip before taking it fully in her mouth.

Ibn's body jerked at the sensation. He reached down and stroked her hair. "That's beautiful, baby."

Tiffany's head bobbed up and down while Ibn's fingers played in her hair. She didn't try to bring him to completion, though, because she wanted him inside her.

Tiffany rose, stood above him, feet on either side of his body.

"Give me your hands."

Ibn complied. She locked her fingers into his, palm to palm.

Tiffany crouched down and lowered herself onto his erection.

She started bouncing, using Ibn's hands to balance herself. Ibn moaned gratefully.

"Tiffany, you don't know how much I missed you."

"I can feel it."

She released his fingers and stood up. She put her knees around his waist and slipped him back inside her.

Ibn placed his hands on Tiffany's hips. Her gyrations were taking him back to a place he had almost forgotten. He closed his eyes. He now remembered how marvelous she felt. How good a person she was. How good she treated him.

She cooed something, but he was too consumed in his thoughts to hear it. He opened his eyes and looked at her. She looked so sexy, with her hair bouncing in her face like it was. To be honest, the women he cheated with couldn't hold a candle to her. Really, what did he need them for?

He rolled Tiffany onto her back, staying inside her while doing so. Sweat beaded on his forehead as he rhythmically rotated his hips, punctuating each revolution with a long, slow thrust. Then he quickened the pace.

"Oh, Ibn, don't stop, don't stop!" Tiffany pleaded.

Her eyes rolled to the back of her head. She was in a frenzy, which excited him. He felt his ejaculation coming.

Sensing it, Tiffany reached down and grabbed his butt. She clenched it as he began to climax.

"Kiss me!" Ibn pleaded.

Tiffany obliged, whirling a tongue into his mouth. Ibn finished surging and collapsed on top of her. After a while, he lifted himself onto a palm and brushed her hair out of her face. "Baby, I *missed* you."

Ibn rolled over and reached for Tiffany. She wasn't there. He quickly propped himself up onto his elbows and frantically searched the room. He heard a noise and looked in the direction of the bathroom. Ibn saw the light emanating under the door. He relaxed and laughed. He had been worried that maybe it was all just a dream.

Ibn glanced at the big red numbers of the digital clock. It was 7:02.

He lay back down, clasped his hands behind his head and took a deep breath. Life was good. His girl was back, and because of their time apart, she now knew what a good thing she had. Hell, if for no other reason than the dick he was able to put on her. Last night her drive had been so amazing that even he almost had trouble keeping up with her. *Almost,* he smiled, congratulating himself. After their encounter on the bed, they had made love on the carpet and in the Jacuzzi.

What she had come to, Ibn figured, is the realization that life with him was a whole helluva lot more appealing than being by herself. She hadn't said that—they had been too tired to talk about it last night and had gone straight to sleep—but Ibn knew. He knew when he saw the emptiness in her eyes when he first cradled her face.

However, he also remembered what Colin had told him about not rubbing Tiffany's nose in it, so he wanted to be tactful.

Besides, he had learned something, too, in their time apart. The women he was skanking it up with really weren't worth the time he was taking from Tiffany. How many times had he cheated on her just in the past year? Shit, too many to count. No doubt, he was definitely gonna scale back.

Ibn looked over at the bathroom door. He decided to make it easy on her and save her the trouble of asking.

"You know, Tiffany, you should take the truck back to Maryland with you. It'll make it easier for you to move your things back up here." Ibn waited for a response, but there was none. She was probably too choked up to answer him. Ibn smiled and stretched out on the bed. He decided to throw her another bone.

"Colin has been staying with me for a little while, but I was thinking that as soon as he gets settled into his own spot, we should redecorate the house. You know, the way you always wanted to."

There, that should do it. Ibn smiled. He was being magnanimous beyond belief.

The bathroom door opened. Ibn readied himself. He was expecting Tiffany to run over and jump her naked ass on top of him, overcome by his beneficence.

She stepped out. "Did you say something?"

He looked over at her. Not only was she unemotional, she was fully dressed.

"I said . . . um, where are you going?" Ibn asked.

"Home." Tiffany walked over to the couch and picked up her purse.

"What's your hurry?" Ibn sat up in the bed.

"I got some things to do."

His eyes followed her as she made her way over to the table where the jewelry cases lay. She picked them up and put them in her purse.

"So, are you gonna take the truck?" Ibn asked.

"For what?" She began lotioning her hands with a small bottle she kept in her purse.

"To get your things, for when you move back up here."

Tiffany looked at Ibn like he had said something demented. She slowly put the bottle back in her purse and closed it. She stared at the flowers, then chuckled to herself.

Ibn was riled. He didn't appreciate the look she had given him, and he damn sure hadn't remembered saying anything remotely funny. He climbed out of the bed.

"Look, Ibn." Tiffany tried to pick up the flowers but they were too cumbersome, so she set them back on the table. She didn't look at him, out of fear—fear that she would laugh in his face. "I'm not moving back in with you." She made her way to the foyer.

"What?" Ibn said in utter disbelief. He stalked behind her, with his dick swinging out in the open. "What do you mean, you're not moving back in?"

"Just what I said." She hung her purse by its strap on the doorknob and opened the closet. As she was putting on her trench, she turned to face him. "What gave you the impression I was moving back in with you?"

"What gave me the impres—?" Ibn threw his hands up, agitated. "What was all this, Tiffany?"

She looked at him, then around the foyer, to the ceiling, the floor, his dick and back at his face again, totally bewildered. "All of what?" she asked in a soothing voice like she was talking to a child. A child with special needs.

"This! Last night!" Ibn yelled. "You know good and well what I'm talking about!"

"Oh, last night," Tiffany said, her voice even more sedate than before. She picked her purse off the doorknob and put the strap around her shoulder. She turned and faced Ibn, who was standing there naked, demanding an explanation.

"Last night was not about reconciliation, Ibn. It was about me needing some attention."

His mouth fell open. He was numb. He stared at the floor, not having a clue about what to say.

Tiffany turned and opened the door. The cold air spilled into the foyer, but Ibn was oblivious to it, too confounded to notice.

She paused in the doorway and faced him again.

He looked up hopefully, trying desperately to find something familiar in Tiffany's eyes.

All he found was the same emptiness they had held last night, and they were now focused solely on his penis.

"I'll call you," she said, and closed the door behind her.

Twenty-four

Saturday morning, Dexter walked down the hallway to Denise's apartment. He had been on his way to get on the turnpike to head to New York when she called asking to see him. Dexter didn't mind delaying his trip, because he wanted to see Denise.

Just as he was getting ready to knock on her door, it came open. A slender, dark-skinned man walked out, brushing shoulders with Dexter as he walked by. He didn't even acknowledge Dexter as he continued to the stairwell and down the steps.

Denise, sitting on the couch, saw Dexter standing in the hallway. Slightly embarrassed, she stood up and walked over to the door. "Come in."

Dexter walked in. He thought about giving Denise a kiss, but decided against it because he didn't know how it would be received.

"What's my man so upset about?" he asked, taking off his coat and laying it across the back of an armchair.

She shook her head to indicate either nothing, or none of his business, Dexter couldn't be sure. She went back to the couch and sat down.

Dexter remembered meeting him once before. "What was his name again?"

"Kwame," Denise said, watching for his reaction.

"Oh, yeah, that's right." Dexter sat on the couch beside her. He noticed Denise's rapt expression. "How you been?"

She nodded to indicate she was doing okay. Dexter noticed the way her eyes were searching him, hoping he would reveal something in his countenance or his body language. But he couldn't help being secretive, because he had no idea what was on Denise's mind.

What was on his mind, however, was why Kwame had been there so early in the morning. Had he just shown up unexpectedly or had he spent the night there? And if his visit hadn't been unexpected, why would Denise call him when she already had another man over? Denise was fully dressed—wearing jeans, oversize black and red plaid shirt with a long john shirt underneath and thick cotton socks—but that didn't mean anything. She could've put that on after she called Dexter.

"Would you like anything to drink?" she asked.

"No, thanks."

Denise folded and unfolded her hands and looked down at her lap, then back up at Dexter. "First of all, let me apologize for being so short with you the last couple of weeks."

"That's all right," Dexter replied. Hell, it was understandable. He was sure that she harbored some resentment toward him over her pregnancy, feeling that he should've been more supportive.

She shifted her weight so that she could look Dexter squarely in the eye. "I also want you to know that I did not try to trap you."

Dexter nodded to let her know that he heard her, but his jaw tightened. He simply didn't believe her.

Despite his attempts to hide his doubt, Denise picked up on it. She decided right then to just cut to the chase. She ran her palms along her thighs. "Dexter, you know I care about you. However, I'm at the point in my life where I'm gonna need certain things from a man to be happy."

Dexter looked down and shifted his Lugz boots along the beige carpet. He knew what was coming.

"Kwame is prepared to give me those things . . ."

Dexter's back stiffened. He hadn't expected this. Denise was throwing down the gauntlet.

". . . and he's been after me a long time." Denise continued. "So, unless you're prepared to give me some kind of commitment, then . . ." Her voice trailed off.

Dexter looked up at her. He couldn't give her what she was asking for. He simply didn't feel enough for her. And he had serious doubts whether Denise truly felt enough for him in return. What he did know was that she *didn't* feel enough for Kwame, or she would've been with him by now.

It was almost like she was giving Dexter the right of first refusal. Maybe because he was a more viable option than Kwame. Or maybe because the miscarriage was such an ordeal for her that she wanted something positive to come out of it.

Whatever her reasoning was, it didn't matter. He knew she wanted something he was unwilling to give. It wouldn't be fair to her to get her to take part in some wishful-thinking, "I can't give you that right now but maybe one day" drama. That was a role Dexter was unwilling to play, anyway. Furthermore, the implicit threat in her ultimatum rubbed him the wrong way.

He stood up and walked over to the chair. Denise's eyes followed him expectantly. When he picked up his coat and began putting it on, her eyes fell to the floor.

Dexter opened the door and looked over his shoulder. "I wish you and Kwame the best of luck." He then closed the door and left.

Colin came down the stairs and walked into the kitchen. He saw Ibn standing at the sink, peering stoically out onto the backyard. Colin opened the refrigerator door and grabbed an apple. He took a bite and noticed Ibn still hadn't moved. He had been like that all evening, un-usually subdued, like he was in mourning.

What was also peculiar is that he hadn't offered any information on how the night before had gone, choosing instead to stay inside his bed-room until late afternoon.

"So, how did last night go?" Colin asked.

Ibn turned around, seemingly startled that Colin was in the room. "Huh, what?"

"Damn, you really were lost in your thoughts. I asked you how last night went."

Ibn smiled tightly, preparing to tell Colin some bullshit, but couldn't bring himself to do it. He needed to unburden his soul. He made his way over to the table and took a seat. "Not too well, frat."

Colin could tell Ibn wanted to talk. Something was really troubling him. He glanced at the clock on the microwave. He didn't have a lot of time to spare before he was supposed to meet Stacy, but she was just gonna have to wait. He took a seat at the table. "What happened?"

Ibn rested his chin in his hands. "That's what I'm still trying to figure out. One minute I'm feeling as good as a person can possibly feel. The next minute I'm . . . like, what the fuck just happened here?"

"Tiffany showed up, right?"

Ibn looked up at him. "You know, I don't even know."

Colin gave him a look of bewilderment.

Ibn looked down at the table. "I was with a girl that looked like Tiffany . . . smelled like Tiffany, even fucked like Tiffany, but I'm still not sure who that was I was with last night."

"What do you mean, Ib?"

He looked up at Colin and took a deep breath. It wasn't an easy thing for him, being in this weak state in front of anybody, especially over a woman. But he was reeling, so he decided to tell Colin everything.

"Well, me and Tiffany had a wonderful night—a great session of sex," Ibn began. "Some of the best we've ever had."

"I bet," Colin interrupted. "Inn of the Dove, roses, jewelry, the ever deadly fruit platter. You went all out."

"Yeah," Ibn sighed.

"So, how long did it take for you to get her into bed?" Colin asked. "Y'all had a whole lot of catching up to do. What was her agenda? Did she want some assurances or set any conditions on you before she gave you any?" Colin looked at him askance. "Did you have to cough up any tears, nigga?"

Ibn stared at Colin. At the time he hadn't realized how peculiar it was that Tiffany hadn't wanted to talk. That she had been so eager to bed him.

"No, she didn't give me a hard time at all." Ibn said pensively. "All she said was that she needed me."

"Wow," Colin said. "That's it? She really must have been jonesing for you. You're the man."

Ibn continued, "Yeah. Well, anyway, after we finished fucking all over the bungalow, we went right to sleep."

"Really? Right to sleep after all this time apart?" Colin asked. "Y'all still didn't talk?"

Ibn grimaced. "Naw, we were too tired. But I figured, you know, we would talk in the morning."

"Okay," Colin said expectantly. He realized that Ibn's despondency wasn't fading. In fact, it was the very opposite. The longer he talked, the more morose he got.

"This morning when I woke up, she was already dressed. So, I asked her when she was moving back in."

Colin nodded his head compassionately. "Oh, let me guess. She told you she wasn't moving back with you until you married her, huh?" He smirked. "So, she just wanted to give you a little taste of what you've been missing, huh?"

Ibn closed his eyes and shook his head. This guy wasn't making it any easier. Hell, he wished it was just Tiffany begging him to get married again. He'd give anything to go back to those days again. But he had come to the realization that the emptiness in Tiffany's eyes last night wasn't loneliness for him: it was detachment *from* him. That's what he had thinking about all day, what had been searing his heart. Her eyes. He now knew what he meant to her—something familiar, but still flimsy and meaningless. She was with him in body only. He seriously doubted if he was ever again gonna be offered anything else of hers. Soul, mind, much less her hand in marriage.

Ibn remembered the last part of his anatomy Tiffany's eyes had focused on. As if to say, that was where his worth to her now lay. His mission, if he chose to accept it, was to be her occasional stiff one when she was horny. That's it. And that was only until she found someone permanent. Someone worthy of her all.

Ibn opened his eyes. "No, she doesn't want to get married, Colin." He took a deep breath. "She told me that I was just a fuck."

Well, go ahead, Tiffany, with your bad self, Colin thought. He set his apple on the table.

Ibn bit his thumbnail. "That she just needed some attention."

Colin exhaled loudly, which irritated Ibn slightly. "So, what are you gonna do?" he asked.

Ibn shrugged, feigning indifference. "If she just wants to fuck from here on in, I'm cool with that. That's all she was ever really good for anyway. She'll just be another one of my many occasional pieces of pussy." He leaned back in the chair, gathering steam. "Ya know, this is a good thing, it lets me off the hook for doing anything for her, anymore. Hell, Tiffany lacks depth, she lacks . . . substance. That's why I never wanted to marry her ass."

"Yeah, right," Colin said. "You're just trying to convince yourself into believing that nonsense."

Ibn was riled. Even if he was just trying to rally himself with some bullshit, who was Colin to point it out? "Nah, I'm serious." He glared at Colin. "You see, some of us do know when to leave a bitch alone and move on."

Colin got up from the table and threw the apple core in the trash, then turned around and faced Ibn. "So, in the span of five minutes you've gone from being Mr. Pitiful to thinking it is a good thing that Tiffany's gone? You moved on already? Yeah, right, Ibn."

"Maybe, maybe not," Ibn countered, "but I tell you one thing. I won't be sitting around here moping over some unworthwhile bitch, too paralyzed by fear to move on. That's a play you've perfected."

"Tell me, how did this get to be about me?" Colin threw his arms out. "Huh?"

" 'Cause I'm making it about you!" Ibn said, rising from the table.

"Why? Because it's too painful for your ass to do a little introspection? To realize that Tiffany treated you the same way that you have treated so many women?" Colin smirked. "Hell, no! Ibn Barrington can't do that! He can't look too deep within, can he? Because he might then have to address his own self-hatred . . . his own self-destructive tendencies . . . and why he fucked up the best thing that ever happened to him!"

Ibn glanced at the toaster, giving a thought to how good it would feel to bash it over Colin's head.

"Oh, you wanna play pop psychiatrist with me? Your ass?" Ibn looked around the room like he couldn't believe it, like he must have just stepped into Oz or something to hear anything that fantastically preposterous. "Who has issues of self-hatred? Nigga, I love myself! You're the one who refuses to give decent women a chance because you're pining over a cunt, skank ho-bitch who treats you like shii-ot. You think that was the first time Stacy cheated on you? Hell, that was just the first time you caught her trifling ass." Ibn snarled. "And you know the sad thing about that is, you *know* it!"

"Fuck you!" Colin turned and stormed through the kitchen door.

"Naw, Colin, but that's what Stacy's been doing to you for years," Ibn called out after him.

Bunches was sitting on her couch flipping through her old photo album. It was full of pictures of her and her brother. It also contained numerous shots of Colin, Dexter, Ibn and Mike in their college days. Each picture told its own story. She laughed at the bald heads of the fellas when they were on line and smiled at the exuberance on their faces once they went over. Then she reached the page containing her favorite photo, the one where Trevor, sporting an early nineties box fade, had his arms draped around her. Rather than looking at the camera, Trevor was looking at her, and in his eyes was the most tender, devoted look imaginable.

Warm tears streamed down her cheeks. When she lost her brother, her grief was such that she was sure that her insides were decaying and that she would eventually die of an internal rot. Trevor had been her life, her instrument through which she saw the world. She ran her fingertips along her brother's adoring face. She missed being that precious to someone.

Bunches heard someone coming up the stairs and wiped her face. There was a soft knock at the door. She turned the lamp off so that she was in darkness, still working to compose herself. "Come in," she said quietly.

The door swung open. It was so dark that Bunches couldn't make out the silhouette, but she didn't need to. She intuitively knew who it was.

"Hey, sport," she said as genially as she could muster.

"Why are you sitting in the dark?" Mike asked.

"Just thinking."

Mike stepped into the apartment, using the dim light coming from the streetlamp outside to navigate his way over to where Bunches was sitting. "Are you okay?" he asked.

"Yeah, I'm fine."

Mike knew her too well to accept that. He could hear the melancholy in her voice. Mike turned on the lamp and noticed the photo album open on her lap. He sat down next to her.

"You do know that Trevor is somewhere smiling his ass off right about now. All he used to talk about was his brilliant, straight A, child prodigy baby sister. Got so a brother wanted to tell him to shut up. Bunches this, and Bunches that—"

"He wasn't that bad," she protested.

"What? I remember one time, sophomore year, when I having trouble with this math course, Trevor had the nerve to tell me that you were available to tutor me—for a fee, of course. 'Cause you know the businessman in him was always scheming."

"So? We all need a helping hand sometime."

"Maybe, but not from a ninth-grader. Do you know how embarrassing that would've been for me?"

"Yeah, I guess that would've been kinda rough," she agreed.

"Almost as rough as failing the course, which I did."

"You *dummy*."

They both chuckled.

Mike put his arm around her shoulder. Bunches put the photo album onto the coffee table and leaned into him. She rubbed her face along his neck, smelling his cologne.

"Where's Dexter?" she asked.

Mike hesitated before he answered, because he knew why she was asking.

"He's staying with some relatives in Queens. He had a wedding to go to. He'll be back tomorrow night."

Bunches moved onto his lap and softly kissed his neck. There was no tentativeness or hesitation in her action, which helped put Mike at ease. In fact, he was surprised at how natural Bunches felt in his arms. How right.

"So, do you have anything planned for tonight?" she asked, rubbing her cheek along his chin.

"Yes." Mike closed his eyes so he could concentrate on the softness of her skin. "And no."

Bunches stopped her canoodling and looked at him. "Huh?"

Mike opened his eyes. "I plan on being with you, Erika. But it's going to be for a whole lot longer than just tonight."

They kissed softly.

They looked into each other's eyes, each having the same thought. How right that kiss had felt. How much they meant to each other. How supremely confident they felt putting their fate in the other's hands.

Bunches then smiled and stroked his cheek. Mike scooped her up in his arms and carried her into the bedroom.

Mike looked down at Bunches. She was strewn across his body, sound asleep, resting her head on his bare chest. He gently rolled her onto her back and began kissing her neck. It woke her up. She loosely wrapped her arms around his back.

"Michael, no, you're gonna wear me out," she said in a soft, drowsy voice.

"This has been too long in coming, Erika." Mike kissed her chin. "We gotta make up for a lot of lost time."

"Yeah," Bunches agreed, "but we ain't gotta make up for it all in one night."

They shared a chuckle. Mike stopped kissing and started playing with her spiral curls. She was wearing her hair the way Mike liked it. It was for him, he was certain, because he knew Bunches didn't like the style on her nearly as much. But it was almost as if she knew that she and Mike were destined to make love that night, and that he was going to want to run his fingers through her curls.

"You're right, baby, but let me say one thing before you go back to sleep." Mike hesitated to get his thoughts together. He felt the emotion rise in his throat. Bunches saw it, too, and lovingly stroked his forearm.

"Erika, from this night on, I never want another night to pass for you where you close your eyes not knowing that you are loved more than any man can possibly love a woman." Mike took a breath. "And when you wake up, I want you to do so with the knowledge that you are the single most adored lady on this planet. Because . . . even now, I feel like my heart is gonna burst." Bunches started crying and Mike, despite swallowing hard, couldn't check the tears from flowing down his cheek. "You've encompassed so many things in my life for so long, and now that you're my lover—and I'm allowing myself to love you—I know this is where I need to be."

Mike wrapped his arms around her back and held her tightly. "Erika, we belong with each other, because we belong *to* each other. I've always been yours, just as you've always been mine. Thank you for giving me an opportunity to be happy. Truly happy. I love you."

"I love you, too, Michael." Bunches clutched him tightly. "I love you, too." She wrapped her legs around his waist and decided that sleep could wait. She wanted Mike inside her again.

"What's the matter with you?" Stacy asked.

She and Colin were in the Burlington Mall, which was open late for Christmas. Stacy was taking advantage of every extended minute as she shopped for shoes.

Colin tried to will the scowl off his face, but it was too ingrained. "Nothing." He looked over at her, and decided to be honest. "It's Ibn. He can be the world's biggest asshole."

Stacy twisted her mouth. "You just finding that out?" She stopped and looked in the window of Nine West, contemplating whether she wanted to go in there or not.

"No, I already knew, but . . . well, just because things didn't go well between him and Tiffany last night, he feels he can unload on me." Colin jammed his hands into his jacket pockets.

Stacy's ears perked up with the mention of Tiffany's name, but she didn't want to appear too eager for information. She kept on studying the display case. "Yeah?" she said nonchalantly. "So, Tiffany is back in the picture?"

"Hardly." Colin snarled. "That's what pissed him off so much. He set up this romantic date for them at the Inn of the Dove, spent all this money expecting a reconciliation, and all he got for his efforts was dissed."

Stacy looked at him. "No! You lying."

Colin gave her the "All right then, don't believe me" look. Which of course, only served to reinforce that he was telling the truth.

"What happened?" Stacy asked. "Tiffany didn't show up?"

"Worse," Colin said. "She did."

Colin saw that Stacy needed further explanation.

"She slept with him, then while he was talking about how he wanted her back—no doubt, prattling on like an idiot—she told him in no uncertain terms that all he was to her was a fuck."

"What?" Stacy gasped.

Colin snickered, nodding his head up and down. "And to think, he was deciding how much crow he was gonna make *her* eat."

Stacy started laughing so heartily that she had to sit down on a bench. "The master playa getting played. I love it!" she said, enjoying herself immensely, "I can just see the expression on his face"—she shook her head, grinning happily—"all dumbfounded and shit."

"Yeah, me, too." Colin agreed. He eyed Stacy with dislike. She sure was deriving a lot of enjoyment from Ibn's woes.

Stacy sputtered a few more giggles. "So, how did you become involved?"

Colin hesitated, but then decided he wanted to tell her. "Well," he said, looking down and kicking at a gum wrapper, "he started taking swipes at our relationship."

"Humph." Stacy stood back up and took a piece of bubble gum out of her purse. "He's so juvenile."

Colin lifted his head before he spoke again and took a deep breath. "He seems to think that you cheated before, but just hadn't got caught."

Stacy's mouth fell open, revealing her partially chewed gum, but she didn't emit a sound. She sat back down on the bench and chewed slowly, trying her best to appear casual, which annoyed Colin. He could always tell when Stacy was being secretive. She wasn't nearly the actress she thought she was.

Stacy blew a bubble and gazed at the window full of shoes. She was pretending that she didn't notice how intently Colin was looking at her, trying to gather herself until she was ready to respond. "I hope you don't believe him, do you?" she finally said, with an edge to her voice.

Colin shrugged. "What did you call him earlier, the Master Playa? Who's a better authority than him on the subject of infidelity?"

"Well, he's wrong this time," Stacy insisted. "It was just the one time, Colin, honest." She stood up and drew close to him and placed her hand on his chest. "You do believe me, don't you?"

Colin turned from her, subtly removing her hand. "I don't know what I believe." He started to walk away.

"Where are you going?" she asked.

"I'm not sure." He stepped onto a nearby escalator. "I'll talk to you later."

"But—"

"I'll talk to you later," Colin said more forcefully than before. Stacy watched as he made his way down, got off on the first floor and disappeared without so much as a glance back up at her.

She seethed. The mall had been the most public place that Colin had agreed to meet her since their breakup. What had been a very promising evening had turned into a setback. All because of Ibn's ass. Stacy couldn't understand why Colin couldn't see that Ibn wasn't about shit. It was clear as day that he was nothing but a smooth-talking, sorry-ass bastard. Even someone as blind as Colin should be able to see that. She sat back down on the bench, deep in thought. A smile slowly started to form on her face.

Maybe Colin just needed someone to clean his glasses for him.

Twenty-five

Ibn was sitting in the office of his Voorhees store, going over yesterday's receipts. Karl, a college student he employed, was in the office with him, sipping coffee and reading the Sunday paper.

Ibn was thinking about his argument with Colin. He shouldn't have been so harsh with him. He knew how sensitive Colin was.

Really, he couldn't ask for a better friend. He loved all his friends; Dexter was his running buddy, Mike, his conscience and Bunches was the closest thing he would ever have to a pure love. But Colin was his confidant. Granted, they were polar opposites, but Ibn always felt an extra affinity for Colin, that he had to look out for him.

Colin had gotten in late last night and had left out again early that morning, so Ibn hadn't had a chance to talk to him and apologize.

There was a loud banging at the front door.

"What the hell?" Ibn asked, aggravated. "Somebody trying to break my glass?"

"Maybe it's Miguel," Karl offered. He rose from his chair.

"Naw, Miguel has a key," Ibn said. "Damn, can't people read? The sign says we open at one o'clock."

While Karl went out on the sales floor to deal with the source of the banging, Ibn put yesterday's take back into the safe.

"Who is it?" he called out.

"It's three women," Karl yelled back. "One of them is your friend, um, Mike's girlfriend."

Ibn figured he was talking about Bunches. Ibn had noticed lately that a lot of people made the mistake of thinking that Bunches and Mike were a couple. But what he was more interested in was the other two women with her. A couple of Bunches' med school buddies here to pretty up his day, perhaps? Ibn quickly checked his appearance in the mirror.

"Let them in," he said, sitting back behind his desk to look more impressive.

Karl unlocked the door, "Good mor—"

The three women, who were dressed in their Sunday finery, brushed past Karl, making a beeline for Ibn's office.

Ibn looked up from his paperwork to coincide with their arrival at his office door and smiled. "You trying to break my—" He stopped short, and the smile fell off his face.

Karl had evidently gotten Mike's and Colin's names mixed up, because Stacy was standing in front of him, with two other women. One he knew, her name was Debbie. The other one he didn't know by name, but he had seen her around.

Stacy didn't bother with an introduction. "Let me tell you something, muthafucka!" She leaned on Ibn's desk and stabbed the air in front of him with her index finger. "You need to stay your ass out of my business! Your trifling ass? As much fucking around that you have done, you got the nerve to judge me?" She scrunched up her face for emphasis, making herself even uglier in Ibn's eyes. He recoiled.

Stacy shifted her weight and switched hands. "Me and Colin are gonna be together, regardless, and there ain't a damn thing you can do about it. You, Mike, Dexter or that little bitch princess of y'all's! Not a *damn* thing!" she said, swaying her head side to side for emphasis.

Ibn looked over Stacy's shoulder. Karl was standing in the doorway. He then looked at Stacy's two friends, standing on either side of her, nodding their heads rhythmically like they were her backup singers or something.

This shit was almost comical, Ibn thought. *Almost.* He turned his attention back to Stacy, who evidently wasn't done yet.

"Furthermore, your shit ain't in order! So, how the hell can you say anything about me and Colin's business? . . ."

Ibn slowly tuned her out, like in movies when the picture gets fuzzy right before a dream sequence. This shit was almost surreal. Stacy's next comment, though, snapped him back into reality.

"That's why Tiffany left your ass looking stupid in that hotel room." She laughed harshly. "You went all out, didn't you, dummy? Inn of the Dove? More like *End of the Love*, 'cause all you were to her was some triflin' dick."

Ibn glared at her. She was catching her breath and bobbing her head, giving Ibn the "that's right, I said it" look. He also noticed that his assistant manager Miguel had just arrived and was standing next to Karl in the office doorway, wondering what the hell was going on.

"As many women as you done cheated—"

Ibn had had enough. He sprang to his feet, sending his chair crashing against the wall. "Bitch! *You* got caught with *your* titties out! You fuckin' ho-bitch! You can run that shit on Colin, but not on me. I know what a bottom-feeding skank you truly are! I can't even call you a hooker. I'd be doing an injustice to prostitutes the world over. My mother wouldn't even let a scandalous whore like you onto her porch. You ugly piece of shit!"

Stacy was reeling, and Debbie tried to come to her rescue.

"Who the hell do you—?"

"Slut? You talking?" Ibn cut her off and turned toward her. "Are you still sucking niggas' dicks in the parking lots of clubs? What about at house parties? You give that up yet? Inquiring minds wanna know."

Debbie's mouth fell open. How did he know?

"Picture your dick-sucking ass sitting in somebody's church! Probably licking the deacon's balls in the last pew. Whore!"

Ibn turned toward the other woman to see if she had something to say. She looked sheepishly at Stacy, then toward the carpet. She hadn't signed on for all this.

"Furthermore, cunt," Ibn continued riffing at Stacy, "all any *decent* woman wants is a man that has a job, halfway decent credit and who'll be a good provider. You had all that, *and* a man who loved you to death and you still couldn't keep that stank snatch of yours under wraps!"

Stacy tried to recover from Ibn's barrage. "Colin still loves—"

Ibn cut her off again. "For a good deal on a car your legs fly open? Damn, bitch, what will you do for a new freezer? For a new set of tires?

What, ho? Tell me!" Ibn climbed onto his desk and grabbed his dick. "I'll give you a good deal on a cellular." Ibn grabbed his member and jabbed it in Stacy's direction. "Now come on and suck on this big black dick!"

"Eh!" Stacy and her friends took a step back in shock.

"What?" Ibn feigned surprise. "I'm not your type?" He motioned to his employees, "Well, Karl or Miguel can hook you up, too."

Stacy had had enough. She knew Ibn was crude, but this was too much. She turned toward the door.

Karl and Miguel had grabbed their groins on Ibn's cue.

"I got a sweet deal for you on some pagers," Karl said.

"*Puta*," Miguel said, grabbing his crotch area, "maybe you'd prefer my big brown one instead. *Mama bicho!*"

Stacy screamed. In tears, she brushed past Debbie, leading the stampede toward the emergency door.

"What, you don't suck dick on Sundays, Stacy?" Ibn asked. "Don't worry, me and the boys will be here tomorrow, with our nuts hanging. 'Cause somebody's suckin!"

The alarm went off as the emergency exit door flung open. Stacy and her friends spilled out into the alleyway. Ibn leapt off the desk after them.

Seeing him appear in the door, Stacy lost her footing and fell against the Dumpster.

"How appropriate," Ibn said. "I do feel like I'm taking out the trash."

She righted herself with Debbie's help. Her other friend was already thirty feet down the alley.

Ibn shut the door, muffling the cries of "Bastard!" He turned to his employees, who were laughing their asses off.

Ibn thought about what he had just done. He knew he had gone overboard, but fuck it, he'd just have to deal with any potential lawsuit.

"That felt good," Miguel said. "I *hate* that girl. She's always coming in here, throwing your name around, Ibn. Treats us like her goddamn peons."

"Well, you don't have to worry about that anymore," Ibn said.

Karl was leaning against the wall. "Imagine, a girl having a no-dick-sucking-on-Sunday policy," he snorted, then resumed his laughing.

Ibn picked up his chair and set it upright. He was too steamed to enjoy replaying the scene that had just unfolded.

Miguel and Karl, still giggling, went out onto the sales floor to prepare for the store's opening, leaving Ibn alone in the office.

Ibn sat down in his chair, his mind racing. He realized what he had to do. He was going back home. But first he picked up the phone.

"What's up, Dex? . . . Do you remember that girl you were telling me about? . . . Yeah, her . . . Let me have her phone number."

Colin turned the key and stepped into Ibn's house. When he entered the living room, he saw Ibn sitting in a chair, watching TV. He also saw his two suitcases parked by the door. His belts, books, job manuals, shaving kit and all his other personal belongings that wouldn't fit into his luggage was sitting in a neat pile on the couch. Across the pile lay his two garment bags. Shoes and sneakers were in front of the couch on the floor. He looked over at Ibn. "What's this?"

Ibn flicked the remote. "It's what it looks like," he replied casually, not even giving Colin the courtesy of eye contact.

Colin was stunned. Just because they had exchanged some angry words, Ibn was putting him out? He had never known him to be so petty. "Oh, so now you want me out?"

Ibn nodded, but still didn't look at him. "Yep. You gotta go."

Colin stared at him, waiting for him to add something, like a reason why, but Ibn apparently didn't feel the need to. Well, Colin knew one thing, he wasn't gonna try to change his mind.

He shrugged and picked up both suitcases. "Hey, it's your house."

"That it is," Ibn agreed.

Colin began carrying his things outside. As he went back and forth to the living room and his car, he and Ibn didn't speak or even acknowledge the other's presence.

On his final trip, Colin picked up his two remaining pairs of shoes and his shaving kit. He peered over at Ibn, who was still impassive. "Let me just say this to you." Colin said, shifting the items in his arms.

Ibn flicked the remote again.

"You are a fraud, Ib. With all your talk about brotherhood and loyalty, you have shown that you don't really know the meaning of those words."

At that, Ibn sprang up from his seat and faced Colin. "Lemme tell you something. Don't come in my face talking no bullshit about no brotherhood, loyalty, friendship or anything else, Colin." He squeezed the remote. "Not when your fucking bitch girlfriend comes in my face today repeating verbatim what I told you in confidence yesterday."

Colin was floored. And his expression showed it.

"What the fuck is that dumb look for?" Ibn asked, irritated. "You just did what you always do—show what a idiot you are for Stacy. So, she did what she always does, which is play you for a fool." Ibn sneered. "She knew she was betraying you by telling me, so why do you think she told me, huh? I'll tell you why. So she can let me know how much power she truly wields over you! How you jump through her hoops. To let me know where your allegiance lay, that you will betray me to run off and tell her something. To cause a riff between us so she can isolate you from your boys. Why? Because unlike you, we know she ain't about shit."

Ibn shook his head in disgust before continuing, "And you're dumb enough to let her do it. So, go move back in with her, because it's obvious that's where you belong. Congratulations, nigga," Ibn mocked, complete with applause, "you don't have to sneak around anymore. Like the bitch told me today, y'all gonna be together regardless."

Colin stood there frozen, trying to absorb all that Ibn had just told him.

"Go on," Ibn motioned with his arm for Colin to leave. "Beat it. Believe me, Stacy's expecting you on her doorstep any minute."

Colin was doing three things simultaneously: driving, dialing and collecting his thoughts. He was driving his packed Benz, thinking about where he was gonna lay his head for the time being, as well as a long-term solution. He tried to reach Dexter and Mike on their cellulars and at home and got their voice mail. He then tried Bunches' and got hers as well. He left messages with all of them to call him.

He was angry at Ibn, but even madder at himself. He knew he had been wrong for telling Stacy Ibn's business. Hell, Ibn didn't even want Mike and Dex to know about what went down with him and Tiffany, much less Stacy.

His phone rang. Colin figured it was Mike, Dex or Bunches returning his call.

"Hello."

"Hi, Colin."

Colin searched his memory for the owner of the voice. It sounded familiar.

"Stephanie?"

"Yep. You recognized my voice, huh? Good. How are you?" she asked.

Not too well, Steph. Colin was deciding how much he was going to confide in her, but first he had a more pertinent question. "How did you get this number?"

"Dexter gave it to me." She paused. "You don't mind, do you?"

"No, not at all," Colin replied. And truth be told, he didn't. It felt good to hear a voice independent of Ibn's, Stacy's or the one rattling around in his head.

"What's up?"

" 'What's up' is that I'm mad at you for not coming to my little soiree last night," Stephanie said.

Colin wished he had. This whole thing with Ibn wouldn't have gone down if he had been at Stephanie's place, which is where he probably should have been, instead of with Stacy at the mall.

"I'm sorry, Stephanie." Colin pulled into the parking lot of a Pathmark. He wanted to talk to her without having to deal with driving, and besides, he really didn't know where he was driving to anyway. "I'll make it up to you."

"You can," she replied, "by coming over here now."

Her reference to the present snapped Colin's thoughts back to his current dilemma.

"Now is not a good time, Stephanie."

"Uh-uh, buddy," she answered. "Now is the *best* time. I have all these leftovers from last night."

Colin chuckled, but he still wasn't sure. He was gonna need to find a place to live. All the places he co-owned with his frat brothers were rented out. Crashing at Bunches' or at Dex and Mike's was just a temporary solution. Besides, did he really want to put them in the middle of his falling-out with Ibn? So, he really needed his own place. Which meant he had to take time off from work next week to go looking for one. He was thinking about going back to Stacy's for a little while. Not for the reasons Ibn suggested, he told himself, but just until he found something permanent. It would only be temporary. Hell, it was the least she could do seeing how her actions had precipitated this whole problem.

"I don't think I'd be very good company tonight, Steph."

"Why don't you let me be the judge of that?" she responded. "Believe me, I'll tell you to scram if you start working my nerves."

Colin smiled and then, to his own surprise, he heard himself say, "Okay." Next thing he knew, he was taking down Stephanie's address. He hadn't known she lived in Center City, only a couple of blocks from their workplace.

He hung up and looked in the rearview mirror. The tautness in his face that had been present a couple of minutes ago had passed. Stephanie couldn't have had better timing.

As Dexter walked into the house, he took note of who was home. Mike's car was absent while Bunches' Celica was parked out front. He laid his overnight bag on the couch and noticed that Mike's cell phone was lying there.

Dexter picked it up, turned it off and took it to his room, where he buried it inside his closet. He then walked back through the living room, outside and up the steps to Bunches' apartment.

He thought about what he wanted to say to her for a couple of seconds, then knocked on her door. After a minute of knocking and receiving no response, he took out his key ring and used the spare to let himself in.

Bunches is probably out with Mike, Dexter thought as he went into her living room.

Dexter noticed her photo album sitting on the coffee table. He went over and sat down on the couch to take a look at it. He laughed heartily as he saw some of the old pictures of Mike, Trevor, Colin, Ibn and himself, especially those taken while they were pledging. He smiled at a photo of Bunches and Trevor. Dexter then remembered his reason for being in the apartment and put the book back on the table. He got up and searched the living room. Not finding what he was looking for, he headed toward Bunches' bedroom.

Once inside, he spied what he wanted and smiled. Bunches' cell phone was on her dresser. He walked over and picked it up. Good.

As he turned to leave, he heard a crinkling sound under his foot. He looked down.

It was a condom wrapper.

Dexter looked at the wastebasket next to the dresser and found further evidence of shenanigans.

Jesus Christ, Dexter thought as he headed back out of the apartment. He knew Bunches was grown and all, but damn. What? He couldn't go away for one day? Time he turns his back some nigga is up in here?

And where was Mike while all this was going on? Dexter wondered. Mike just let some cat waltz in here and dip his stick?

Dexter locked the door and headed down the steps. He went outside. Again he noticed that Mike's car was missing and that Bunches' was parked out front. Yeah, they were probably somewhere together.

As Dexter put his hand onto the doorknob to go inside, he froze. And it had nothing to do with the fact that he was outside in December without a coat on.

He stood there in the frigid afternoon air, unable to move. He was being held captive by a notion so stupefying that it paralyzed him.

Dexter finally mustered the strength to put it aside long enough for him to escape possible frostbite. He walked into the house and headed for his bedroom. He turned Bunches' phone off and put it inside his closet next to Mike's. Dexter closed the closet door and sat on his bed.

The crazy thought from before refused to leave him. Dexter decided he'd better do something to slay it before it set up permanent residence in his head.

He stepped into Mike's room and went over to his dresser. He hesitated before opening it. He didn't want to open it. He didn't want to believe it was *necessary* to open it. After all this was Mike he was talking about.

But he did. So he did.

Inside Mike's sock drawer, Dexter found the same brand of condoms that he had seen in Bunches' room. Trojan Shared Sensation. Ribbed for her pleasure.

Dexter closed the drawer and gripped the edge of the bureau tightly. He glared into the mirror sitting over it and bared his teeth.

Maybe Mike was the nigga doing the dipping.

If so, breaking his ribs will be my pleasure, Dexter thought.

That night Dexter was watching the Sixers do battle against the Lakers when he heard a single knock on the door. "Come i—"

Bunches was inside before he could get it out.

"Why do you even bother knocking?" he asked.

"Why don't you lock your door?"

"Because I know, as sure as my next shit, your ass is coming by."

"Shut up." Bunches said, popping him on the head before sitting on the sofa next to him. "You know you live to see my pretty face."

Dexter gave her a playful smirk at that. Earlier when she and Mike had returned from seeing a movie (so they said), he had decided not to confront them. Not yet. His evidence was only circumstantial so far. But he was going to be on alert from here on in and watch Mike's ass like a hawk.

Mike had gone back out to visit Xavier. Before he left, he hadn't acted any differently around Dexter, hadn't acted guilty of any misconduct. But, hell, he might just be a great actor.

"Oh." She yawned. "So when was the last time you spoke to Denise?"

Dexter noticed the yawn. So she was tired? "Yesterday." He looked at her. "You didn't get any sleep last night?"

Bunches looked at him slightly startled. "Huh?"

"Why are you yawning?" Dexter asked innocently.

"Oh." She relaxed. "No, it isn't an indication of lack of sleep." She cut her eyes at him. "Or the quality of the company I'm in."

Smart ass, Dexter thought. I bet your little hot ass is pretty excited in Mike's company, aren't you?

He decided to change the subject. "Kobe Bryant is single-handedly beating our boys."

"I'd wish he'd single-handedly beat his hair with a comb," Bunches said. "What's with the uncombed, nappy 'fro look?"

"I don't know," Dexter replied.

Bryant swooped in from the baseline for a thunderous dunk.

"Damn!" Dexter had to stand up for that one. "I told you! He's killing 'em!"

"Did Michael say when he was coming back?" Bunches asked.

Since he was up, he decided to go get something to drink. "Do I look like that nigga's daddy?"

"No, and it's fortunate for Michael and any offspring he might have one day that you don't, but that's not what I asked you."

"Ha-ha," Dexter replied snidely from the kitchen. "I don't know."

The game went to a commercial. Bunches changed the channel to BET.

He decided to fuck with her some more. "You love you some Mike, don't you?"

"Of course, I love all of my boys," she replied. "By the way, have you seen my cell phone? I can't find it."

Dexter came out of the kitchen armed with a glass of root beer and a chicken leg. "No, did you leave it here?"

"A man that'll clean my kitchen?" Stephanie smiled. "Where have you been all my life?"

Colin smiled back. "It's the least I can do. That chicken was on the money."

"Thank you. I made it for someone special."

Colin felt himself blushing. He remembered what Dexter had said about him being the impetus for Stephanie's dinner party.

Stephanie stood leaning in the entrance to the kitchen grinning, making Colin more and more self-conscious.

"What?" he asked.

She folded her arms and shifted her weight. "I don't know. Something about seeing you elbow deep in sudsy dishwater, wearing my apron . . . it just looks *so* right."

"Yeah, okay," Colin laughed. He was having a good time with Stephanie. They had gone to the George Theater earlier to see *Love and Basketball*. On the way, she had noticed all his stuff in the backseat of his car and asked him why it was there. Colin began to open up to her, cautiously at first, giving her bits and pieces. But Stephanie had such a soothing, caring manner that by the time they were finished eating dinner back at her apartment, Colin had opened up to her completely.

Stephanie didn't judge him. She didn't tell him what he should do or shouldn't do. All she did was listen. Colin appreciated that. It was what he needed right now.

After he was done in the kitchen, he and Stephanie went to the living room to watch the Sixers game on TV.

"That Kobe Bryant is something else? Isn't he?"

"Yeah, he sure is."

As Colin was watching the replay of Bryant posterizing three Sixers, he felt Stephanie's eyes on him.

"So, what are you doing for tonight?" she asked.

Good question, Colin thought. He had forgotten about his homeless predicament. His phone had been turned off since he was in the theater, so maybe Bunches, Mike or Dexter had gotten home. He could crash with one of them. Or maybe he could grab a hotel room in the city.

He got up and opened Stephanie's closet. He grabbed his phone from his coat pocket and checked his messages. There were none from Dexter, Mike or Bunches, but repeat messages from Stacy. He started playing them.

—"Hi, Colin. I, um, was expecting you to—wondering what you were doing, give me a call at home. Bye."—

As Colin played the next one, he felt Stephanie's eyes on him.

—"Hi, it's me again. I'm sure you probably heard some nonsense from Ibn by now. Let me say, it's not true, but that . . . it doesn't matter anyway. So what if you told me something about him he feels you shouldn't have? So, the fuck what? He had no problem telling people all our business. That's why I went there today and told him off. So he could see how it felt . . . You don't need him anyway, he's not really your friend. . . . Call me."—

Colin momentarily took the phone away from his ear to digest that last message. Then he put the phone to his ear and pressed the button for the next message to play. At the same moment Stephanie spoke.

"Colin," she said.

—"Colin,"—Stacy's voice spoke at the same time.

"Yeah?"

"You're welcome to stay with me."

—"You're welcome to stay with me."—

Colin folded up his phone, and Stacy, and put them in his pocket. He looked over at Stephanie. "Are you sure?" he asked.

"Why not?" Stephanie patted a cushion on her couch. "This sofa lets out into a fairly comfortable bed." She smiled. "I think you know I enjoy your company, Colin."

He returned her smile. He enjoyed hers as well. Something he hadn't let himself do before. "It'll just be very temporary, I assure you."

Stephanie shrugged. "You keep doing my housework for me, and you can stay as long as you like."

Later that night, Ibn explained to Mike and Bunches what had transpired with Colin and the reasoning behind his and Dexter's actions. At the same time Dexter was studying both of them, to see if they did anything revealing.

"What I don't understand is, what gives you guys the right to make that decision for Colin?" Mike asked.

"Here we go . . ." Ibn muttered.

"Agreed," Bunches added. "This is his life, not some rotisserie fantasy baseball league. Ken Griffey on the Yanks, Sammy Sosa on the Dodgers, Colin Rogers in Philly with Stephanie."

"The touchy-feely police bringing down their chastisement again," Ibn said. "Ya know, you two are a trip. What, y'all never heard of tough love? First of all, I'm offended that you would think that we would do something drastic like this without putting a lot of thought into it. Me and Dex love Colin just as much as you two. Plus, you two don't even know Stephanie—"

"And neither do you." Mike interrupted.

"Yeah, but I know *Stacy*, don't I? And so do you. Everybody here knows what a garbage human being she is—that Colin has no business being with her. Name one healthy aspect of that relationship for Colin. She cheats on him, she lies to him, she juices him financially, she treats him like a fucking child, rebuking him and shit. She's mentally abusive—she's got him believing that he can't find anyone better than her." Ibn spread his arms out. "Tell me, Mike, how can Stephanie be *worse?*"

Dexter put in, "As the only person here that does know Stephanie, let me assure both of you that she is a terrific lady. Sweet as syrup, and loves Colin to death. I think she really admires Colin's qualities, and I know she'll value him and treat him great if Colin will just give her a chance."

"Which he never would have done if he was with Stacy," Ibn added. "Let's be real. We all know that Colin has been sneaking around, still seeing Stacy. Hell, she even barged into my office this morning and told me so. The only reason he hadn't gone back to her yet was that he didn't want to look bad in our eyes. But, trust me, he would have eventually gone back with her and fallen into the same routine."

"This here was an intervention, plain and simple," Dexter said. "Same as you would do for a loved one strung out on heroin, or an alcoholic. Colin doesn't have the courage to quit Stacy, so we're attempting to force-feed him something better."

Bunches and Mike looked at each other. They both sighed in resignation. While they might not totally approve of Ibn and Dexter's methods, their contempt for Stacy was such that they could see they were doing it for the right reasons.

"If Colin knows I orchestrated his being at Stephanie's house, he won't give her a chance," Ibn said. "All I ask is that you don't tell him what my true motivation for kicking him out was."

"Then why did you feel the need to tell us?" Mike asked.

"Hey, I know y'all are gonna be talking to Colin, though I know he isn't gonna have too much to say to me for a while. I didn't want you guys to think I was an asshole that just put my boy out in the street for no good reason."

"Speaking of that, I'm sure Colin is gonna be calling me. What am I supposed to say if he asks me to stay with me? No?" Bunches asked.

"That's up to you," Ibn said. "Hopefully, it won't come to that. When I spoke to Stephanie earlier, I got the feeling that once Colin is in her place, he isn't gonna want to leave."

Dexter reached into his back pocket. "Here's your cell phone, Bunches." He had already put Mike's in his room.

"So, you did have it." She snatched the phone from him.

"I didn't want Colin to be able to reach you," Dexter said. "It would have been easier for him to turn to you than going to Stephanie."

Later that evening, Dexter and Ibn were in the living room watching *Sportscenter* while Bunches and Mike were in the kitchen washing dishes.

"You know we have to tell them sooner or later," Bunches said.

Mike stopped drying. "I vote for later."

They shared a chuckle, but it was a tense one. Neither of them, especially Mike, was looking forward to telling their friends about their new relationship.

"Well, I think Dex is already suspicious," Bunches said.

Mike looked toward the living room. Dexter and Ibn were entranced by the basketball highlights. "Why do you say that?"

Bunches took a Brillo pad and began scrubbing a frying pan. "Don't tell me you haven't noticed how strange he's been acting since he got back."

"Yeah, but I figured that was because of the whole Colin thing," Mike said. He hadn't been too concerned about Dexter coming across anything incriminating, because they had made love upstairs in Bunches' apartment.

Just then Mike stopped short and looked at Bunches. "Where did he get your cell phone from?"

Bunches stopped scrubbing and tried to think. She turned to Mike. "I don't know if I had left it in my place or down here."

Mike looked back toward the living room. This time he found Dexter staring back at him. When their eyes first met, Dexter's look was so icy that Mike felt a chill run down his spine. Mike gave him a head nod. "What y'all watching?" he called out.

You, nigga. Dexter wanted to say.

"The highlights," Ibn said. "Oh, Jesus Christ! Kobe dropped a triple-double on the Sixers." He started to make supplication to the TV. "We're not worthy! We're not worthy!"

Dexter and Mike exchanged uneasy laughs at Ibn's effusiveness. Mike then turned back to Bunches. "I think it's safe to say that the phone was in your apartment."

"Why do you say that?" Bunches asked, handing him the pan.

" 'Cause this cat is looking at me like I stole his last chicken wing."

Twenty-six

Colin and Stephanie stumbled into her apartment, full of laughter. Colin had just told her some ridiculous joke, which Stephanie was enjoying immensely, mostly because he had butchered the punch line. She threw off her coat and toppled facedown onto the couch.

Colin slouched into a chair and looked at her. He had stayed on Stephanie's couch the whole week. It had been enjoyable, more so than he could have possibly imagined. They had walked to and from work together, and alternated cooking dinner when they got home. They had similar interests: Italian food, politics, theater, ice skating in the winter, roller blading in the summer, and both shared a secret passion for Sidney Poitier movies.

While her face was buried in the sofa cushion, Colin stared at her butt. It was snugly wrapped in her blue jeans and was poking in the air quite nicely.

The only impediment to his feeling at complete ease around Stephanie was his growing physical attraction to her. He always felt awkward and unsure when trying to express his feelings to a woman. Awkward and unsure? he thought. Hell, who was he kidding? He was *terrified* of the prospect of stepping to a woman like that, which is probably why he stayed with Stacy so long.

And speaking of Stacy, he had been avoiding her all week. He had spoken to her just once, later that night he got kicked out of Ibn's. It had been late, while he was lying on Stephanie's couch, when he had called Stacy and told her that he wanted nothing more to do with her.

However, he could tell that Stacy didn't believe him. She had even told him that it was "just his anger talking" and that it would pass. When the conversation ended that night, as far as Stacy was concerned, the matter was still unresolved.

Since then she had left numerous messages on his cell phone and at his job. He knew he at least owed her the courtesy of talking to her again, even if only to tell her more emphatically where to go. It was just a matter of time before Stacy showed up at his job for a face-to-face, anyway, but he didn't want to talk to her. Not out of fear, he told himself, but because they really had nothing more to talk about.

Yet a small part of him wondered if his reluctance to talk to Stacy again was a way of hedging his bets. If he didn't speak to her, then he couldn't make the final break. He could always get back with her down the road and just say his avoidance of her was a cooling-off period. That she was right, his anger had passed.

But he knew Ibn (another person he had absolutely *nothing* to say to, by the way) was right about one thing. Stacy was no good for him. Colin knew it, hell, he had known it for years, but he had never been strong enough to break off the relationship.

Colin emerged from his thoughts to find Stephanie gazing at him. His face turned warm. He was certain that she had caught him looking at her butt. He had been careful all week not to let her catch him ogling her, something he had found himself doing with increasing frequency.

Stephanie silently got up and walked to her bedroom door. Colin remained sitting in the chair, frozen with trepidation.

"Colin," the voice came from the bedroom, "I don't want you sleeping on my couch anymore."

Colin closed his eyes and sighed. He couldn't blame her. Why would she want a man around her leering and smacking? Any woman would be uneasy in such a situation.

"I understand, Stephanie." He rose from his chair. "Listen, I want to thank you for putting me up for the week." He reached into his coat pocket and took out his checkbook. He wanted to write a check for her as a way of showing his appreciation for her time and trouble, as well as for the expenses he had accrued.

"No, I don't think you understand. The reason I don't want you sleeping on my couch anymore . . ." Stephanie repeated.

Colin looked toward the bedroom entrance. She was standing in the doorway wearing a barely-there negligee. Colin's jaw dropped and his penis lifted. He wasn't even pretending he wasn't staring now.

". . . is because I want you in my bed," she finished, lowering her eyes seductively, giving Colin a come-hither look.

Colin gulped, dropped his checkbook and hithered.

Bunches and Mike had come to Woody's to see the drag show. They were seated at a prime table next to a small runway that extended from the stage. Mike was nursing a beer and Bunches was already working on her second strawberry daiquiri. They had been among the first to arrive, mainly due to her insistence on getting there early. Terence was going on first, and she wanted to make sure they didn't miss him.

Mike scanned the room. The small cocktail tables with black tablecloths were covered with silver glitter—in fact, silver was all over the place. Silver lamé was hanging along the tops of the walls, running along the front of the stage, and around various fixtures in the room. Two large disco balls dominated the center of the ceiling. On the walls throughout the room were large framed pictures of various women. Mike looked at each one. Barbra Streisand, Judy Garland, Diana Ross, Marlene Dietrich, amongst other prominent women.

Bunches leaned over and kissed Mike softly on the lips. "Thank you again for my Christmas presents."

Mike smiled. He took her hand and kissed it. "You're welcome." Bunches was wearing two of them, a gold bracelet and a wool sweater.

"You made out like a bandit this year, didn't you? I think Ibn spent his Tiffany budget on you."

Bunches grinned. "Hey, I wanna make Ib happy. He likes doing for me."

"How big of you, you're a saint," Mike said, rolling his eyes. "Anyway, thank you for mine, especially that George Foreman griller. I'm really gonna make good use of that."

Bunches smiled mischievously. "I'm counting on you to."

Mike laughed. "Erika, you're the only person I know that only gives out gifts that can benefit you."

Her eyes opened wide. She was the picture of pure innocence. "Michael, I'm sure I don't know what you're talking about."

"Oh, you don't?" Mike said. "What about one of your gifts for Dexter? A two-year subscription to *Essence* magazine?"

"Hey, he needs to get in touch with his feminine side."

"Yeah, well, Ib's hard on women. So, how come he didn't get one?"

Bunches laughed. "Because he doesn't live in the same house as me."

Reminded of something, Mike took out his cell phone and began dialing. "I'm gonna see what Colin's up to."

"Hey frat, what's up with you? . . . Me and Erika are in the city. . . . Yeah, okay—bye." Mike slowly set the phone on the table and rubbed his chin.

"You sure didn't talk long," Bunches said.

Mike leaned back in his chair, staring at the phone pensively.

"So, what's the latest?" she asked.

Mike then looked at Bunches. "If I'm not mistaken—and I really don't think I am—I just interrupted Colin in the middle of coitus."

Bunches' mouth fell open. Excitedly she said, "No! You serious?"

Mike nodded. "He told me, 'It's not a good time,' and I heard a female voice and the sound of kissing—like she was kissing on him while he was trying to talk."

Bunches closed her eyes and winced. "Please tell me it wasn't Stacy."

Mike smiled. "I don't think it was!"

They raised their glasses in the air and toasted what they hoped was the end of Stacy's reign of terror over their friend.

"So, do you think Colin will ever forgive Ibn?" Bunches asked, taking a sip of her drink. "I had lunch with him yesterday, and he still seemed pretty steamed."

Mike shrugged. "I don't know. Colin can be pretty obstinate when he wants to be. Hell, look how long he stayed with Stacy. I figure, if he really hits it off with this new girl, he might end up thanking Ibn."

The tables around them were rapidly filling up. Taking the table adjacent to theirs were three lesbians. They made a point of speaking to

Bunches when they sat down. One, an African American named Terry with a short natural cut, was particularly friendly. When she went to the bar, she asked Bunches if she could bring her anything back. Bunches thanked her but declined.

After she left, Mike smiled. "What's that silly grin for?" Bunches asked, sipping her drink.

"Nothing, it's just the way the sistah's eyes lingered on you, it's obvious that she's in love."

Bunches rolled her eyes. "Maybe she's just being friendly, Michael."

"Uh-uh, she's way beyond friendly, Erika." Mike sniffed the air. "I smell *amore*, sweet *amore*."

"What's the matter," Bunches asked, looking at him over her straw, "you jealous?"

Mike pretended to ignore her question, but, if he was completely honest with himself, he had to admit he was a little jealous.

"I gotta go to the bathroom," he said, rising from the table. "Answer my cell for me. Colin said he was gonna call me back."

"Okay. I suggest you don't loiter in the men's room," Bunches told him. "Somebody might get the wrong idea about your intentions and think you're in there for something else, sailor." She sniffed the air. "I smell *amore*."

Mike peered down at her and laughed. "Oh, a George Michael–type scenario."

"Hey," Bunches warned, "many a romance has blossomed over a urinal."

"So?" Mike joked. "Would *you* be jealous if I met someone special?" He began to walk away.

"Yes," Bunches said softly after Mike was out of earshot.

"Where you been?" Dexter said as he walked in. "I've been calling you all day."

Ibn had been brooding all day and didn't want to be bothered. He had received unsettling news that morning. It had come in the form of an envelope with no return address. When he opened it, there was a picture from the *Baltimore Sun*'s society page enclosed.

It was a picture taken at some fancy charity black-tie affair. The caption underneath stated that one of the smiling couples in the picture was Ms. Tiffany Robinson and her *beau*, State Senator Harold Hawkins III.

Ibn had also found a piece of paper in the envelope. In red ink it read, THERE IT IS, YOU WEST INDIAN ASSHOLE!!!

It had Tiffany's bitch mother's imprint all over it.

He decided not to tell Dexter about it.

"Sorry, I've been out." Ibn said as he walked Dexter into his living room. "So, what's up, frat?" They sat down on the leather couch.

Dexter had called earlier and told Ibn he needed to talk. He was definitely ready to bring someone else in. He had been sitting on this information for a week while watching Bunches and Mike like a hawk. While he hadn't procured any more incriminating evidence, nothing had occurred to ease his suspicions, either. Hell, they were out together in Philly right now.

Dexter took a deep breath. "I think something is going on with Mike and Bunches."

Ibn absorbed the statement, then relaxed his body and chuckled. "Dex, you're crazy."

"I am, ain't I?" Dexter said. "Well, let me tell you what I know. Lately, weird shit have been happening with those two. Like, I pull up in front of the house, and they're just sitting in her car in the driveway with the glass all foggy."

Ibn shrugged. "They're just talking, Dex."

Dexter continued. "And, she gets out of the shower and calls down for some lotion. Why this nigga go up there and don't come back? What is he doing while she's up there naked putting on lotion?"

"He could've been in the living room talking to her," Ibn said, still not convinced.

"Okay," Dexter said. "Last Saturday when I was gone to my cousin's wedding, did you stop by my place?"

Ibn thought about it. No, he hadn't. That was the day after his rendezvous with Tiffany. He had moped around the house all day. "No, I didn't," he said.

"Well, that Sunday I went upstairs to get Bunches' cell phone so Colin couldn't reach her, remember?"

"Right, right," Ibn said, distractedly brushing some lint off his slacks.

Dexter paused. "How come I found condom wrappers in her room?"

Ibn bolted upright. "What?"

Dexter held up his hand to let him know he wasn't finished. "The *exact* same brand Mike has in his drawer—and yes, before you ask, there were a couple missing from his box."

Ibn slumped back onto the couch. His mind was racing, trying to assimilate what Dexter had just told him with relative information already stored in it. Like the fact that Tiffany had always told him that Bunches had a thing for Mike—Ibn had always made light of her notion. And that everybody, like his employees, always mistook Mike and Bunches for a couple.

But most important, he remembered that conversation at Sam's a few weeks back when Mike had told him Sharice wasn't in the picture anymore. It had been awfully easy for Mike to let her go. Why, because he knew he had someone else? Well, for one, he wasn't fucking her. But if he wasn't fucking her, then who was he fucking? Aww, shit.

Ibn raised up like a shot. "Dex, don't even tell me that dirty bastard is fucking Bunches!"

"All right, Bunch, tell him to call me back when he gets out of the can." Colin laid his phone on the nightstand next to Stephanie. He sat on the bed, leaned over and kissed her on the cheek. "Has anyone ever told you what a beautiful woman you are?" He traced his index finger along her lips.

"Yeah, but I've been waiting for *you* to notice."

"Sorry for taking so long. Forgive me for being blind."

"You're forgiven." Stephanie reached over and picked up his glasses. She put them on and yelped, immediately taking them back off again. "With these thick-ass things, I'm surprised you saw me at all."

Colin took them from her, put them on and kissed her again, this time on the lips. Getting up, he walked into the bathroom and looked in the mirror. It's a new day, Colin Rogers, a new day. And you're a new man. He smiled. For the first time in longer than he could remember, he was completely at ease with what he saw in the mirror.

He decided to brush his teeth. While he had a mouth full of tooth-paste, his phone rang. Mike, no doubt. "Steph, get that for me?"

"All right." Stephanie reached over and picked up the phone, "Hello."

Colin brushed quickly and rinsed his mouth out. He couldn't wait to tell Mike about Stephanie. As he turned the faucet off and wiped his face, he could hear her voice increasing in volume:

"What? . . . Once again, who are you? . . . What! What's that you called me? . . . Bitch? . . . Look, heifer, I don't know you, but let me tell your hard-luck ass something. . . ."

Well, it definitely wasn't Mike. Colin walked over and gently took the phone from an increasingly agitated Stephanie.

"Look, Stacy . . ."

"Who is that *bitch*? And why is she answering your phone?"

"The lady who answered the phone is someone I hope to make my lady, and you won't disrespect her," Colin answered smoothly, looking at Stephanie while doing so.

Her face softened. She liked the sound of that. She lay back down and smiled at Colin.

"What the fuck do you mean, 'your lady'? Huh, nigga! I'm your woman!"

"You're a part of my past," Colin said. "But as I told you before, it's over. I have a chance at happiness with a good woman, and I'm not gonna blow it for someone I know isn't right for me."

"What are you talking about, Colin? You gonna throw six years away on someone you just met?"

"No, that would be more your MO, Stacy," Colin said. "Or, were you and the car dealer a long-term thing?"

"I told you that was nothing!"

Colin laughed. "You're probably right. He's probably just one of many. A mere drop in the bucket."

"What?" Stacy stammered. This new, self-assured Colin was throw-ing her for a loop. When did he get balls? "I—I don't believe you said that . . . that's that nigga Ibn speaking, not you!"

"Actually, Stacy, it is me. In the last week I've realized that I've already thrown six years of my life away—wasted them on you." Colin shifted the phone. "But I refuse to squander another day. You won't get any more of my time." He looked at Stephanie, who was patiently waiting for him to finish. "As a matter of fact, you're keeping me now . . ."

"Fuck you, Colin! Fuck you and the whore that had you!" Stacy yelled.

Speaking of his mother, Colin thought, he was gonna set her straight, too, next time she called. "You already have, Stacy, you already have."

"You know what, Colin? Fuck your sorry ass. If your dick wasn't so little, I wouldn't have had to go nowhere else."

He smiled at Stephanie. "Well, Stacy, fortunately for me, I got a woman now who likes my dick just fine."

Colin hung up the phone and crawled back into his woman's bed. Stephanie embraced him and kissed him softly on the neck. Colin took a deep breath, not one of resignation like usual, but one of contentment. Though he wasn't totally sure where they were headed or how long it would last, he had no doubt that it was a whole lot better than where he had been.

Mike returned to the table just as the emcee was taking the stage.

"What took you so long? I told you Terence is going on first," Bunches said. "I was beginning to think you made a love connection."

"I put some more change in the meter," Mike said. He slid into his seat and held Bunches' hand, then leaned over and gave her a long, slow kiss.

"Yum," she said after she opened her eyes.

Mike looked over to see if Terry had seen it. She hadn't.

"Colin called."

"Did he? I'll call him back later." Mike turned to look at the stage.

The emcee was a short, squat man dressed entirely in black. "Ladies and gentlemen, I would like to tell you about a celebrity we have in our midst, right here tonight. A member of our nation's esteemed First Family, no less!" He hesitated to let the impact of that statement settle in. He then showily put the back of his hand up to his forehead, like he was in pain. "But, alas!" he cried, "she has been shunned, scorned, turned away for her beliefs . . . her lifestyle, why, she has been branded the pink sheep of the family!"

The crowd laughed. Mike had to give it to this guy, he was very theatrical.

"But will she compromise herself for social acceptance! Oh, no, not this proud, talented lady. She remains unfettered, unbowed—well unbowed, that is, unless a really cute guy insists. Then she bows down real quick, honey, let me tell you!"

Bunches laughed heartily. "The slut!"

Mike laughed, too, mostly at Bunches. He couldn't believe how loud she was. He was gonna have to limit her alcohol intake from here on in.

"But I digress," the emcee continued. "So without further ado, may I present to you the ultraglamorous, ultratragic, ultrahypnotic sensation that is . . . Rose Bush!"

The emcee quickly exited stage left while the crowd applauded. The room went black, except for a solitary spotlight focused on the center of the stage.

"I'm telling you, I'm not going," began playing. The spotlight moved slightly to the left and captured the enigmatic presence of Rose Bush. She'd had her back to the audience but turned around right in time. She begin mimicking Jennifer Holiday's booming voice.

"Oh, *girl!*" Bunches said when Rose turned around.

"Shhh, Erika," Mike somehow managed to say. But really, he was more than a little taken aback himself. The transformation was definitely complete. Terence, for all intents and purposes, no longer existed. There was only "Rose" in his place.

She was wearing a stunning beaded, long-sleeved pink evening dress. It fit her snugly in the hips and flared out at the bottom with a fishtail train. It had a high collar, and the beads around it were larger, giving it an appearance of a choker. The waist was cinched tightly, no doubt with the help of a girdle, giving her a shapely hourglass figure, albeit a rather large hourglass. Mike didn't even want to guess what she was using for breasts. Rose had on a layered strawberry-blond wig. It cascaded past her shoulders to the small of her back. Her makeup was flawless, right down to the subtle hint of blush along her cheeks.

When Rose started to walk, stalking the stage in step with the music and making it her own, she revealed her matching satin pumps.

"I told you Terence would do a sistah's song," Bunches whispered triumphantly. "Rose is a lady with soul."

Mike chuckled. "That up there on that stage is *no* lady."

Bunches and Mike then settled down, mesmerized by the stately bearing of Rose Bush. In fact, she had the entire audience entranced. Rose had all the mannerisms of an *uber*-diva. She put her hands on her hips and shifted her weight to the beat of the music. She rolled her neck to emphasize the lyrics and strode spiritedly to accentuate a build in the music.

"Uh-oh, here comes the big finish!" Bunches said.

Rose Bush started to work herself into a frenzy as the song reached its crescendo. She had the crowd eating out of her hand. She kicked of her pumps, accidentally sending one flying toward the audience.

"Heads up!" Mike yelled.

Terry, sitting at the neighboring table, didn't move fast enough. The shoe hit her in the arm and landed on the table, spilling her drink.

"Motherfu—goddamit!" she yelled. Pissed off and in pain, Terry picked up the shoe and, with her one good arm, winged it back at Rose Bush, barely missing her queenly head.

"Now this here is entertainment!" Bunches said, roaring.

Twenty-seven

"Hey, fellas." Mike settled into the booth next to Dexter and across from Ibn. He laid his coat in the adjacent booth. "You guys order yet?"

"I just ordered some mozzarella sticks," Ibn said, as he scanned the room. "I don't know where Lorraine is with them," he said, irritated.

"I didn't even know they sold mozzarella sticks here," Mike said, taking off his coat.

"Neither did Lorraine," Dexter said.

"Well, it's shouldn't be on the menu, then," Ibn said stubbornly. "I told Lorraine's lazy self to go find me some." He was nervous about Colin's coming, Mike could tell.

Though it had only been three weeks, Colin and Stephanie were going strong. Mike had never seen him so happy. Colin's only beef was that he hadn't left Stacy's ass sooner.

Stephanie had also helped patch things up between Ibn and Colin. She told Colin of her conversation with Ibn on the phone three weeks ago. How she had promised Ibn that she was gonna be the best thing on this planet for Colin.

Ibn, Dexter, Mike and Colin were all meeting for a late lunch today at Sam's in Camden. It was gonna be the first time that Ibn and Colin had met since their falling-out.

Lorraine brought Ibn's mozzarella sticks to the table.

"It's about time, Lorraine, What? Did you have to go to Italy and make them by hand?" Ibn asked.

"Naw, I just had to go across the alley and dig them out of the pizza place's garbage can. I had to go clear to the bottom before I got a complete set."

Ibn looked down at his mozzarella sticks skeptically.

"Do you wanna order now, Mike, or are you gonna wait for your partner to get here?" Lorraine asked.

"I'll wait for Colin, Lorraine. I'll just take a Coke."

Before she left, Lorraine smiled sweetly at Ibn. "Enjoy!"

Dexter and Mike laughed. Then Dexter looked up.

"Look at the spring in this cat's step," Dexter said, laughing. "He's in love!"

Colin made his way over to the table. He was grinning from ear to ear. Ibn stood up and met him in the aisle. They gripped each other up and then embraced. No words needed to be spoken between the two to know what the other one felt.

"Hey, break it up, you two. This ain't that kind of joint," Lorraine said from across the room.

Colin and Ibn slid onto the bench on the other side of the booth. Colin opened the newspaper he'd brought to the sports section. "Not only am I in love, I just had a long talk with my mother."

"And you're smiling?" Dexter asked.

"Yep. Because I set Mrs. Rogers straight on what will and what will no longer be tolerated from her." He smiled, obviously proud of himself. "I was tough yet fair. I simply told her of the ground rules that she would now have to adhere to. Number one is respecting me and my lady."

"Congratulations, Colin," Mike said.

"Yeah, man," Dexter added.

"Yeah, kudos, Colin," Ibn said. "But you didn't piss her off too much, did you?"

Colin shook his head. "I was tough yet fair," he repeated.

"Good," Ibn said, sounding relieved. " 'Cause that lady makes a mean sweet potato pie."

Everybody chuckled.

Ibn then looked at Dexter. He was ready to resume the conversation they were having before Mike and Colin joined them. "So, what were you telling me about these women again?"

Dexter straightened up. "Yeah, the other week when I was at my cousin's wedding, I met some fine sistahs and they jumped on my gills immediately."

Ibn laughed. "You know how women get at weddings, all husband hungry and shit."

"Right," Dexter continued. "Well, I told them I had some boys back home who I'd bring up with me next time I saw them. They got excited."

"Yeah?" Ibn asked. "And you say these bitches are fine?"

Dexter nodded. "And receptive. There's three in all. Daphne, Belinda and Dawn, they share a town house together. They insist that the three of us stay at their place when we visit."

Mike looked at him. Three?

Ibn was practically salivating. "You know I'm down! We'll wine 'em, dine 'em, maybe catch a show, then . . ." Ibn smiled salaciously, "back to the crib." He looked at Colin. "Well, I know your in-love ass ain't interested."

"You got that right." Colin smiled smugly. He folded up the sports section and took out the movie listings to see if there was anything playing Stephanie might be interested in.

"So"—Ibn turned to Mike—"I guess that leaves you, playa."

Mike gave him a tight smile.

"We're leaving Saturday morning, Mike," Dexter said. "I wanna spend all day with these sistahs—"

"So that we're *old* friends by nighttime," Ibn finished.

"Ya know!" Ibn and Dexter laughed and gave each other a pound across the table. Colin laughed, too.

Mike wasn't laughing. Nor had he given them an answer. A fact that Ibn and Dexter were keenly aware of.

"So what's up, Mike?" Dexter asked.

Mike picked up his menu and started looking through it. "I'm not gonna be able to make it."

"Awww," Ibn said in disgust. "Come on, Mike. We need you."

Mike scrambled. "I promised to spend Saturday with Xavier."

"But you can reschedule that," Dexter countered. "Look, I was saving this as a surprise, but I showed the girls a picture of all of us that I have in my wallet. Belinda—the finest one—wants to get with you."

"What?" Ibn said, shocked. His head swiveled back and forth between Mike and Dexter. "She chose Mike over me?"

"Yep."

"I know your ass better go now," Ibn said.

Mike grimaced, pretending that he wished that he could. "I'm sorry, boys. You're gonna have to find somebody else."

"Mike, what's it gonna look like if we go up there with someone else?" Ibn said. "They're expecting the man in the picture."

"Mike." Dexter nudged him in the arm and looked him squarely in the eye. "Please, do this for me."

Colin, surprised at the earnest tone in Dexter's voice, looked up from his reading.

Mike returned Dexter's look with one just as definite. "I'm not gonna be able to do it."

Neither wavered from their stare-down. There was an uneasy silence at the table, which was broken by Ibn.

"Well, Dex, it looks like it's just me and you, then."

Dexter turned to Ibn. His mood lightened. "Yeah, I guess we're gonna have to handle things as a duo."

"Hell, me and you are equivalent to five or six normal men anyway," Ibn said.

"True, indeed. True, indeed." Dexter nodded in agreement.

Mike looked at his watch. "You know what, I gotta go." He slid out of the booth and stood up.

"What? You're not gonna eat anything?" Ibn asked.

"I just remembered something I had to do." Mike put on his coat. "I gotta check on something at Terence's store. I wanna get there before closing time." He looked at each of them. "I'll get with you guys later."

"All right, Mike," Colin said.

"I'll see you back at the house," Dexter added.

Mike patted his coat pocket to make sure his keys were in there, then turned and left.

Dexter's eyes followed him out. "That motherfucker," he muttered. He looked at Ibn. "You see that shit?"

Ibn nodded. "Right now he's probably gone off to tell his partner in crime that there is a change in the itinerary for this weekend."

"Oh, there's definitely gonna be a change in their itinerary," Dexter said emphatically.

Colin was beyond puzzled. "What's going on?"

Dexter and Ibn looked at each other and nodded. They decided to clue Colin to the covert happenings of Mike and Bunches, and what they had in store for them.

Twenty-eight

Mike and Bunches were driving back home. They were returning from Mike's parents' house, where they had just told Mr. and Mrs. Lovett of their new relationship. His mother had been thrilled, as Mike figured she would be. She loved Bunches to death. Mike's father had been happy, too, though Mike sensed he wanted to ask what had become of the big booty girl he had met at Thanksgiving.

Mike pulled into the driveway and turned the car off. He reached for Bunches' hand. She smiled back at him, thinking the same thing he was. How nice it was going to be to make love at home instead of a hotel. They hadn't been able to since their first night together.

Dexter and Ibn had left that morning for their trip to New York. Mike had called Colin barely an hour ago, and Colin had told him he planned to rent a movie and spend a quiet evening home with Stephanie.

So, he and Bunches knew they wouldn't be disturbed.

She leaned over and kissed him. "Let's go, lover."

Mike ran his thumb along her lips. "Your place or mine?"

She parted her lips and sucked his thumb. "Mine."

Once upstairs, Bunches finally opened the door to her apartment. It took some doing because Mike was pulling, grinding and groping her. The place was pitch-black. Mike shut the door with his foot, while his hands relieved Bunches of her coat. She then helped him out of his. In the darkness, he kissed her along the back of her neck and started unbuttoning her blouse.

"You're not wasting any time, are you?"

Mike licked the back of her ear. "Do you want me to slow down?"

"Hell, no," Bunches said, moving his hands under her blouse. "Ravage me."

Mike unzipped his pants so that she could feel his erect penis along her backside. He held her hips and pressed it against her ass as they walked to the bedroom.

"Now, what are you gonna do with that?" she asked as she stood bracing herself in the doorjamb.

"I'm gonna slide and ride, gorgeous."

"Well, then, I guess you'll need this," a voice said.

Bunches shrieked. Mike pulled her out of the doorway and stepped in front of her.

Light from a lamp illuminated the room.

Dexter, who was leaning against the dresser, angrily flung a condom at Mike. Ibn and Colin were sitting on the bed glaring at him. There were looks of pure hate in their eyes.

"What's going on, frat?" Ibn said coldly. His eyes worked his way down Mike's body to where his penis was sticking out of his pants.

As Mike tucked it in and zipped up, he searched each of his friends' faces. It looked for all the world like he had a severe ass-whipping coming his way. His heart, while still pounding, was starting to recover from the shock they had given him.

He took a deep breath. He had known this day was coming, just not so soon.

"What?" Dexter asked. "The cat got your fucking tongue? What's going on here?"

Bunches had pulled her blouse back down and collected herself. She stepped around Mike and into the room. "Who the fuck are y'all to be asking questions?" she asked. "As far as I'm concerned, he's the only one that has a right to be here. What the fuck are you three doing in my place—in my bedroom? Spying on me?"

Not only did Dexter, Ibn and Colin ignore Bunches, they looked right through her. In their fury they only saw Mike.

"Huh? Y'all couldn't step to me like men and ask me?" Bunches angrily asked. Again she received no response.

Mike looked right back at each of them, squarely in the face.

Colin noticed his defiance. "You sure don't seem repentant," he said.

"I've got no reason to be," Mike replied.

"Oh, you don't think so?" Dexter straightened up. Mike thought he was stepping to him and instinctively balled his fist before he even realized what he was doing.

Dexter noticed Mike's reaction. Before he could decide what he wanted to do about it, Ibn stood up in their path.

"Let's take this downstairs," he said.

"Y'all ain't takin shit downstairs except yourselves!" Bunches replied, pushing Ibn in the chest. By this point she was too through with being ignored.

Colin stood up. The men formed a half circle around Mike.

Oh, Mike thought, so his friends were going to give him the bum's rush down the stairs. His only choice was whether he wanted to go down the easy way or the hard way.

He shrugged. "All right." He turned and walked out of the room. Bunches got in the doorway between him and the other men, impeding their path.

"Bunches, move," Colin said.

She shook her head emphatically.

"Move." Dexter repeated.

She stubbornly folded her arms across her chest and shook her head again. Tears started to well in her eyes. When she began to speak, a torrent of tears streamed down her face. "You wanna beat him up?" she asked, her chest heaving. "If he did something wrong, ain't I guilty, too?"

The three of them were silent.

She faced Ibn. "Isn't it always the woman's fault? Isn't that what you always say?"

He grimaced. "Look, Bunches, all we want to do is talk to him."

"Erika, please," Mike said gently. "Let them pass."

Bunches hesitated as she searched Ibn's, Colin's and Dexter's eyes for understanding. When she didn't find it, she stepped aside.

Downstairs, Colin closed the front door behind him. Dexter sat on the arm of the sofa, Ibn in a chair and Mike stood against the far wall, facing them.

"You cut your trip short, fellas?" Mike asked sardonically.

"Something like that," Dexter replied.

"Mike," Colin asked as he walked into the living room, "how could you do this to Bunches?"

"And Trevor," Ibn added.

"Do what?" Mike asked. "Fall in love with her?"

Dexter rose with a great deal of agitation. "Oh, so now you're telling us you're in love with Bunches? Since when?"

"Dex, I don't know." Mike thought about it. "To be honest, I'm hard-pressed to remember because I've loved her for so long."

"Speaking of that, how long has this been going on?" Colin asked.

"That's what I'd like to know," Dexter said. "Right under my fucking nose."

Mike knew that Dexter felt lied to, even more so than Ibn or Colin, because he lived with them. He felt that Mike and Bunches had been sneaking around behind his back.

"Not long. We just started last month," Mike said quietly. He paused for a moment while he chose his words. "I know it makes me look bad for not coming to y'all and telling the truth about me and Bunches. Or better yet, telling you guys about what my intentions beforehand. I knew how difficult it was gonna be, but I know I should have. I shouldn't have been so cowardly."

"Not only that, pardner, it makes you look guilty," Ibn said suspiciously. "Maybe you didn't want us to know because you know you're not coming correct. Maybe all you're doing is taking advantage of her having a thing for you."

"Now, that's some bullshit," Mike replied. "When have y'all ever known me to have the mind-set of using a woman? Fucking her just because I can?"

He waited for a challenge from one of them. When it didn't come, he continued.

"Now, if I was to start running games on sistahs like that, do you really think I would start with Erika?" Mike looked at the ceiling. "Jesus, don't y'all know that's my heart up there?"

"Yeah, she's all of our hearts, but you're the only one sleeping with her," Dexter said.

"I'm also the only one in love with her," Mike responded. "And I'm tired of denying myself the woman I want to be with." His voice took on a desperate bent when he spoke again. "I've been doing a silly dance with Erika for years, where I get jealous if she sees someone else, she gets jealous if I see someone else—I'm tired of it. We're both tired of it."

As if on cue, they heard Bunches coming down the steps.

"I'm still the same man that has known y'all for twelve years," Mike continued. "I haven't changed."

Bunches came through the door and into the living room. She had composed herself by this point. She stood next to Mike and faced the others. In a steady, controlled voice, she said, "I just want you people to understand something, while you're down here discussing my fate like I'm a nonentity. I'm a grown woman. I have the same needs, desires, hopes, fears and wants as any other grown woman on this planet."

Ibn, Dexter and Colin looked at each other and groaned. Not the "I'm grown" speech. "We all know that, Bunch—"

She cut Ibn off. "And as such—a *grown-ass woman*—I will decide who is worthy of my affection, my time and my body. I love you, I love you and I love you," she said, pointing at each member of the trio, "and I believe that each of you love me." She clasped Mike's hand and gripped it tightly. "I'm in love with this man. Now, if you love me as you say you do and as I believe you do, you will want me to be happy."

Bunches let Mike's hand go and stepped toward the others. "You've been a part of my life forever. You've done more for me than any person has a right to hope for or expect. I'm grateful to you, and I love you for it."

"We know, Bunch," Dexter said quietly.

She raised her index finger. "Then please, know this as well. I'm gonna be with Michael." She eyed all of them but focused on Ibn, since he was closest to her. "Did you hear me? I'm gonna be with Michael."

Twenty-nine

Mike stared at the ceiling. He wondered if Bunches had gotten any sleep. As far as the hot topic of last night, nothing had been decided. Well, as far as Bunches was concerned, the point was moot because she was determined that she and Mike were going to be together, regardless of what anybody else said. Mike believed her and he loved her for feeling that way, but he also knew there was a hint of fear behind her steely resolve.

If the fellas never came around to accepting her and Mike's relationship and severed ties, Mike knew it would be extremely hard on her. She would be losing three of the dearest people to her on the planet.

He would, too, of course. But as he lay in the bed, he had realized an uncompromising, irrefutable truth. Nothing mattered as much to him as being with Bunches.

Mike prayed that all they needed was some time. He and Bunches knew that even in the best-case scenario, there was going to be an adjustment period for their friends.

They decided not to press the issue last night. Bunches had slept upstairs in her place, the four men downstairs. Not feeling like driving home, Ibn and Colin were asleep in the living room. Everybody had been exhausted from being up half the night talking.

Mike got out of bed and walked to the window. He opened his blinds and had to look away as the bright sunlight pierced his room.

Yet he noticed that something was amiss. He squinted and peered through the window again. Bunches' car was missing.

He sat down on his bed and tried to think if she had told him of anything she had to do today. No, he couldn't think of anything. Mike walked over to his dresser to pick up his cell phone. He wanted to call her to make sure she was okay.

Before he dialed, his eyes traveled to the *Women of the Ivory Coast* wall calendar hanging next to his dresser.

He noticed the date. He put the phone down. He knew where she was.

Mike walked up the small asphalt lane that led toward Bunches. Bundled against the cold, she was facing away from Mike, kneeling in front of a headstone, clearing away debris. She took the freshly cut wreath of flowers she had brought with her and planted it at the corner of the headstone. Then she stood up.

"Hi, Michael," she said without turning around.

Mike heard her voice crack. He walked up to her and put his arm around her shoulder. "How did you know it was me?"

"I knew you wouldn't forget Trevor's birthday."

Mike looked at the inscription on the marker.

TREVOR LAMONT TRUITT
JANUARY 14, 1971–AUGUST 8, 1994
IN GOD'S HANDS

"I can't believe it's been seven years," Mike said quietly.

Bunches breathed deeply. When she exhaled, Mike saw her breath rise as a frosty gust. He removed his hand from around her shoulder and gently turned her to face him. He clasped both her gloved hands and held them tenderly.

She smiled at him and they embraced.

"Tough night, huh?" she asked as they separated.

Mike nodded. "But we knew it was coming."

Bunches searched his eyes. "Did it change anything?"

Mike nodded again. "Yeah, I thought I was gonna be holding you last night, not dreaming of holding you. But other than that, no."

She smiled and squeezed his forearms through his coat.

"Erika, nothing will ever come between us."

Bunches unzipped his bomber jacket and wrapped her arms around his back. While squeezing him tightly, she felt a pressing along her pelvis.

"Unnhh," Bunches snorted.

"Well, nothing except that," Mike said.

They parted and laughed. Bunches nodded in the direction of the headstone.

"You oughta be ashamed, being in that state in front of my brother."

"He understands, believe me," Mike responded. "He already knows how crazy I am for you."

They embraced again.

"Break it up, you two."

They turned in the direction of the voice. Ibn, Colin and Dexter were coming down the lane.

"Did you tell them you were coming here?" Bunches asked as they separated.

"No," Mike said. "They were still sleeping when I left."

They waited for the threesome to join them.

"Hi, boys," Bunches said.

"Oh, we're not 'you people' anymore?" Ibn asked.

She smiled wryly. "That's still to be determined. I was just being pleasant."

"How did you know where we were?" Mike asked.

"What," Ibn responded, "you think you're the only one mindful enough to remember Trevor's birthday?"

"Actually, I remembered it," Colin said, shivering in his parka. "This clown thought y'all had eloped."

"Hey, stranger things have happened," Ibn said.

After their quiet chuckle died down, Mike spoke: "No, we haven't eloped." He looked over at Bunches and held her hand. "Though I have to tell you, I do have every intention of spending my life with this lady."

"But you don't have to run, Mike," Dexter said. He paused, then added. "We want to be there, and I want to be your best man."

Mike grinned. The words were like sweet music. Despite the chill, he suddenly felt warm.

Bunches released Mike and stepped forward. All of them were smiling. She hugged Dexter tightly.

"I love you." She reached for Colin. "I love all of you." Bunches started crying. She looked at the entire group. "How'd I get so lucky?"

"Good question," Ibn said as he and Mike gripped each other. "But a better question is why this fool here thinks he would be the best man."

"What?" Dexter asked.

"*What?*" Ibn mocked. He adjusted the collars on his trench coat. "I'm the clear choice. I give new meaning to the term 'best man.' "

"Please," Colin said. "You'll be too busy talking to the bridesmaids to do your job. I, on the other hand, am the right choice."

"How about you guys let Mike and I have a relationship first before you marry us?" Bunches admonished.

Mike really didn't mind their talk. He was too in love to care. "How about I just let Matty be the best man?"

The three of them all looked at him aghast.

"But, Mike," Dexter cried, "he's a Sigma!"

"Y'all ready to go?" Colin asked. "I'm freezing."

"Yeah, let's go to a diner," Dexter said.

"Wait a second." Mike turned back to Trevor's grave and knelt down. He traced his fingers along the inscribed name.

"Trev, I promised you that I would take care of your sister. I believe I've kept that promise to you. We all have." Mike motioned to his friends. "I believe I speak for the rest of your line brothers when I say that it hasn't been a task or a duty, but rather an honor and a pleasure. We felt privileged to do so, and blessed to have her in our lives."

Colin leaned over and gave Bunches a kiss on the cheek. Tears returned to her eyes.

"However, I feel I'm especially blessed, because something has moved your sister's heart to where she loves me in the fashion that I love her." Mike smiled. "Was that you that did that, frat? Somehow, I know you had a hand in it."

Ibn chuckled softly. "I wouldn't put it past him. That was one hands-on nigga."

Dexter nudged him to be quiet.

"You see," Mike continued, "I know she's a gift to me. A gift I unwrap every time I lay eyes upon her and a blessing I can look forward to enjoying for the rest of my life. Mike kissed his hand and placed it on the headstone. "Remember to thank God for me."

As they walked down the path, Bunches slid her arms inside Dexter's and Mike's.

Dexter shook his head.

"What's the matter?" Bunches asked.

"I'm just trying to figure out how this nigga got past the ADS."

Ibn laughed. "I'm glad he did. I was worried he would hook up with Sharice."

Colin looked at Ibn like he was crazy. Why would he bring up Sharice now? "We know, we know. You didn't like her," Colin said.

"More than that, it would've been awkward." Ibn hesitated. "I slept with her in college."

The entire group stopped in disbelief.

"I asked you!" Colin said.

"So did I," Dexter added.

Bunches just shook her head. She remembered asking him as well. "You are a true piece of work."

"Hey," Ibn said, shrugging his shoulders. "I figured if she wasn't gonna say anything, I certainly wasn't going to."

Mike thought it was funny and burst out laughing. There was a time when he might have given a damn. But that day had long passed.

The rest of the group realized it *was* funny and joined in. They resumed walking.

"Well, I'm glad you hooked up with Mike," Ibn said.

"By the way, what happened since last night to change y'all's minds?" she asked.

"This morning when I woke up, something occurred to me, that I then shared with the fellas," Dexter said.

"Yeah, brah had an *epiphany*." Ibn added.

Mike laughed at Ibn's choice of words. "What was it, Dex?"

"Well, you know how overprotective we are of Bunches."

"To say the least," she agreed.

Dexter continued. "We came to the realization that, who better than Mike to be with our Bunches?"

Bunches smiled and squeezed Mike's arm. "Because he's such a good person, right?"

"No," Dexter replied. "Because if he acts a fool, we know where to find that nigga."

Bunches and Mike started laughing. Mike then noticed his friends' faces were impassive.

Ibn spoke. "Um, Mike, we ain't playing."